DEATH BELOW

The tower stairs narrowed the higher they went, old stones, rounded at the edges from deterioration of both time and man. At the top, the glow of the torches were bright, and below light still burned across the cavern. Just beneath them the horde stood beating upon the gate, but they were not so wild, and several of them were drifting away from the stronghold, their eyes set upon the tunnel leading into the cavern.

"Where are they going?" Astrid asked.

Lennox shook his head and shrugged.

Boom! Another explosion echoed throughout the cavern, this one twice as loud as the first, accompanied by a wave of warm light that burst forth from the tunnel before disappearing in an instant. The ghoulish horde stopped instantly, their bodies turning like a single mass of bones and flesh to face the cavern tunnels.

A third blast flared, this time shaking the tower slightly before a wave of fire streamed through the tunnels like dragon flames.

The
FLEETING
PRINCE

JACOB MARC SCHAFER

THE AGE OF WATCHERS, BOOK 1

Bold Venture Press edition September 2020
ISBN: 9798683794132

Available in electronic book edition.

All persons, places and events are fictitious, and any resemblance
to any actual persons, places or events is purely coincidental.

Printed and bound in the United States.

Published by Bold Venture Press
www.boldventurepress.com

THE FLEETING PRINCE

RETURN

IN the Age of Foundation there was nothing … nothing but the void of infinite darkness. But the voice of the Creator fluttered against the face of the void saying, "Let there be light;" and light was. And with it came illumination, exposing an abyss of cold and distant land below.

The Everlasting Serpents, now revealed by the great light, coiled in anger. The Eternal Giants, now uncovered, appeared from the forests. And humankind, now empowered by the light, emerged from the mountains. With the strength of gods, they waged war, Serpents, Giants, and man. Mountains crumbled, great forests were leveled; and many fell into the seas until finally the Giants were no more.

Then from the heavens, they descended, the Watchers sent to guide mankind. Batraal, the first of the Black Flame. The Sorcerer of Armaros, with the knowledge of enchantments. Azazel, the Lord of War. And Shem, who held the knowledge of all names.

With the Watchers there to lead man, the tides of war turned against the Serpents. Azazel taught man the ways of war; and with the fire of Batraal mankind burned their flesh. The enchanted armor of Armoros kept them safe from poison. And Shem revealed the Serpents' names, separating the chasm and casting them into the depths.

With the Serpents abolished, the voice of the Creator called out to the Watchers saying, "Return;" but they did not. Worshiped as gods, they stayed, placing themselves above the cities of man and ruling as tetrarchs. The Age of Man deferred, thus began the Age of Watchers.

(from *A History of Beginnings.*
Author unknown, *The Age of Watchers*)

7

1

MEN of bones stalked across the hallway, never once turning their heads towards the cell, never once looking inside. They couldn't if they wanted, stuck almost in a dream. Their armor was heavy, but it didn't show. Large, circular shields of iron were carried with ease. Thick chainmail covered their heads and chests, falling down below their waists. In their hands were simple straight swords, the steel old and chipped. They paced endlessly, never stopping, never taking a break. Their slow steps rattled their chainmail. The tip of their swords dragged limply on the stone floor behind them. Their minds gone; they were shadows of themselves.

Lennox sat inside the cell with his back leaning against the wall. How long had he been imprisoned? He could not remember. His eyes were closed, and he listened to the steps of the guards. He was beginning to forget what they looked like. Not the charred and empty faces they wore now, their true faces. What they were before they had become hollow.

"What were your names again? I'm beginning to forget." Lennox spoke the words aloud, but to no effect. The hollowed men continued their empty walk. "Golliff, right?" he asked, watching as one of the men strode across his cell. "I don't remember your brother's name, but then, he never spoke. At least not to me."

Large torches hung on the walls lined the hall in each direction. Great, thick spirals of iron held the flames, casting warm light into the air.

"We could have helped each other... it would have been mutually beneficial, I think. But alas — " The roof shook. He tilted his head back; it was hard to look up in his armor, but he managed. He kept his gaze on the wooden beams above and waited. The roof shook a second time, and then a third, then a fourth.

"Hmm … " He looked back towards the iron bars and watched. Not long now, he thought.

The roof shook a fifth time, and a sixth, and then he stopped counting. He was waiting for the caretakers. He wouldn't have to wait long, not with the beast rampaging so markedly. They would come soon, too much to repair if they waited long. The Undead Cathedral was large and had been built tall and strong, but time had passed, and the stones were old and weary, and with the bishop dead, most of the caretakers had left. But not all.

Lennox smiled underneath his helm and waited. He could wait, though he was tired of his cell. It was a primal place, dark and damp with a hole cut into the stone floor that acted as a latrine. He had never once used it, but the unbroken stench still lingered in the air, his constant companion. He could endure it. He had endured so much already.

A bench of rotten wood acted as a bed, but it was even more uncomfortable than the floor. At least the floor was even, and he had grown accustomed to sleeping in his armor. How long since he had taken it off? He could not remember. To take it off meant death.

The room grew cold. Lennox watched the torches on the wall begin to dwindle down until only the smallest flames remained. The men of bones continued their march, when around the corner, two other men approached. Cloaked in black with their faces hidden, they moved like ghosts, almost floating across the hallway. The cowls were pinned forward, hiding their smooth, white skin from the light of the flames, but not from Lennox. They walked in a single file, each of them turning to look inside the cell as they passed.

"I see you," Lennox said as he peered inside their eyes, past their enchantments, into the deepest part of what they were. They continued to move past his cell when Lennox spoke aloud. Words in a language he should not have known. The caretakers faltered, pausing momentarily. Lennox smiled beneath his helm. But a moment later they continued, and his smile vanished. "Pity." He shook his head. "I felt so sure this time." He watched them reach the end of the hallway and begin to ascend the stairs when suddenly he called out to them, "Weren't there three of you last time?"

But they were already gone, the hallway abandoned except for the hollow guards.

A great pounding shook the cathedral from above then and continued for some time before gradually growing quiet. The wooden beams above ached as they bent back and forth with the sway of the great stones they supported. One of the beams could endure no longer and split down the middle, tossing up a puff of dust that lingered in the air for the briefest of moments before drifting down and finally settling onto Lennox. He hardly seemed to notice. The great pounding ceased, and all had been still for some time before once again the flames diminished. Lennox watched his breath pour out of his helm and disappear into the frozen air. With each inhale the air grew colder, and the flames a little bit darker.

Not a sound could be heard as the caretakers descended the stairway, not so much as a whisper. They kept their eyes forward this time as they passed, no longer interested with the man in the cage. Lennox said nothing; he was done for the time being. He had failed again, but no matter, he would triumph in the end. It was the only certainty he knew.

With the caretakers gone, peace returned to the Undead Cathedral. The burning torches grew brighter casting their light into Lennox's cell. The outline of shadowed bars fell upon him quivering gently. The men of bones continued their march, and he watched them for some time until finally he closed his eyes, not to sleep, he no longer slept, but to dream a living dream and to help time pass. He had been in here so long, how much longer must he wait? It was irrelevant, eventually all ages must come to an end.

***

An unfamiliar sound boomed throughout the stone archways of the cathedral. Lennox opened his eyes, lifting his sights up first to the wooden beams above and then back down towards the guards. If they had heard the disturbance, they showed no signs of it. All was quiet for some time, and Lennox was beginning to doubt what he had heard when a loud and shrill scream echoed in the distance. It was not the cry of an undead, little or nothing at all left their mouths once they had become hollowed, this was a man with blood and soul intact.

The distant sounds of a skirmish would begin and end with large gaps of silence between them. Lennox was unsure how many guards still remained in the Undead Cathedral. How many men would this mystery knight have to fight through? What was his constitution? How strong was his will? Was he here to ring the bell atop the tower? With each scuffle the sounds of battle and clashing swords drew nearer, but it had drawn near in the past only to fall short like so many times before. Lennox would not be taken in; he remained a statue. With his back against the wall and his eyes forward, he would wait for the knight's arrival.

Salvation was close; it would not be long now.

Finally, the knight appeared. Lennox could hear him before he could see him; the familiar sound of a suit of armor was known to him. The heavy steps of a man of war were unmistakable to those who knew how to listen. The men of bones were pulled out of their dream. They both stopped just outside of Lennox's cell and stood with their shields raised and their swords held high, watching as the knight approached. A small part of what they once were returned, just enough for them to do their job, enough to kill any intruder who walked unwelcome inside the Undead Cathedral.

At last the knight stepped into view. A beast of a man, over six feet tall in height, his armor charred black from head to toe. He wielded a large kite shield in one arm, and a one-handed warhammer in the other. Engraved into the iron and sprouting up from the bottom of the shield was the image of an archtree. He was a sight to all who laid eyes on him, and even Lennox was surprised.

The guards moved towards him with reckless speed, swinging their swords down upon the intruder. The black knight blocked their attacks with ease, turning his shield sideways so that he could not be flanked. Slowly he pushed forward. Occasionally they struck at him, but each time he simply blocked the attack and took another step through the hall until finally he was just outside Lennox's cell. The black knight glanced upwards, and seeing that the roof had risen, rushed forward, swinging his shield to the side, and casting Golliff to the ground. He lifted his great warhammer and brought it down on the second guard who was attempting to raise his shield. The hammer hit the shield like thunder and sent it crashing down. The knight brought his hammer up for a second strike, and this time the hammer found its mark, crushing the guard's skull beneath its heavy iron. He fell limply to the ground just as Golliff rose.

They faced each other for a moment, the black knight and hollow ghoul. Lennox watched, a quiet spectator.

Golliff shifted backwards before lunging towards the knight. Lennox didn't think the undead could move so quickly. The black knight side-stepped and brought up his shield deflecting the sword at an angle before charging into Golliff and pinning him against the iron bars of the cell. In one smooth gesture the knight quickly let go of his warhammer and drew a dagger from his side. He brought the blade up to Golliff's face and leaned forward. A moment later Golliff went limp.

The black knight stepped backwards, removing his blade from the hollow's skull. Golliff fell to the ground with a crash, his round buckler rolling loudly on the stone floors before coming to a halt.

"Well done... you handle yourself beautifully," Lennox said. He was standing now, and moved up close to the iron bars. Had he wished he could have reached through and touched the black knight, had he wished.

The black knight shifted his gaze up towards Lennox and examined him for a moment. "Oh? Still human, are you?" He wiped off his dagger and return it to its sheath. Then he took a step back and picked up his warhammer and leaned it against the wall before looking once more at Lennox. His eyes took in the golden knight standing inside his prison. "Why is there a cell inside a cathedral?"

Lennox folded his arms. "Well... there certainly is a reason, but not one that I know. It was already here when I arrived."

The black knight stood silent for a moment and then turned and took up his warhammer and began moving towards the stairs.

"Sir, I would not go to the roof alone if I were you. A giant gargoyle guards the tower, and I have yet to see anyone return alive."

The black knight turned. "A gargoyle?"

Lennox nodded.

"He guards the bell tower?"

"Yes."

The black knight moved back towards Lennox and stopped just outside the bars. "Tell me about the creature."

"Please, I have duties that cannot be left undone. Release me and I will tell you all I know, and fight with you against the creature."

"Are you here to ring the Bell of Calling?"

" … Of course, but that honor will be yours; if you free me from this cell than I will be in your debt. My sword will be yours and I will help you fight against the creature."

The strange knight considered Lennox's words for a moment and then turned to leave. "You're lying."

"Sir! My blade will be yours. I give you my word. If you leave me here than I am sure to die … and dying men's lips seldom lie."

"Farewell, golden knight."

Heavy iron footsteps disappeared down the hallway as warm light flickered against the charred black armor of ash; slowly the giant knight disappeared up the stairwell. Yet another lamb rushes to slaughter, Lennox thought. He turned and walked back towards the wall of his cell and sat down, leaving one of his legs bent to lean against. The hollow guards lay dead in the hallway, truly dead now, and no longer moving. Golliff's twisted and broken face lay in plain sight. "Another wasted opportunity," Lennox said aloud, shaking his head. He had time.

His vision was narrow inside his helm, but he wore a mail coif instead of a steel collared gorget, which let him turn his head freely. He tilted his head back and looked up towards the wooden beams, carrying his gaze past the wood towards the stone roof above. There was a crescent arced window cut out of the stone high above that would have let in light had there been any to let in. Endless darkness lay just outside the crescent moon, but he gazed up at the window none the less, until finally the roof began to shake. It was different than before, a true fight, not just a hungry beast. He was hoping for a show and was not disappointed despite his limited view.

Streams of fire flew past the crescent window lighting up the night and illuminating the beast, only for a moment, but still the great gargoyle was revealed. The beast appeared just as Lennox had remembered him, and then the flames were gone, and with them the beast. The roof continued to shake as the fight went on. The black knight seemed to be doing better than Lennox thought he would, but eventually the flames stopped and soon after a quiet calm returned to the Undead Cathedral. The stones were once again silent, the shaking had ceased. The caretakers would come again; it was rare to see them so soon after their last visit.

***

Golliff's twisted head lay staring at Lennox. Dark, empty sockets where eyes should have been haunted him, endlessly gawking, as though it were all one big joke. Lennox had seen dark souls staring back at him before; he could bear the eyes of some undead soldier. Still, it was unpleasant if he thought about it. He considered turning the head away but ended up leaving it as it was.

In the quiet calm of his cell he could hear a latch begin to open, and the heavy footsteps of a fully clad knight descending the stairwell. The black iron knight returns at last, Lennox thought. It's bad luck I didn't catch your name.

The black knight's movements were not what they had once been, they were dull and sluggish; the movements of a dead man made up only of bones. His armor was still intact, but was cracked all along the chest piece and dented inward. Lennox watched the knight move and speculated how he might have died. Crushed to death I suppose, he thought. The traditional smell of burnt flesh was absent, why is that? He had seen the flames. It was something to ponder so he didn't mind, anything to help pass the time.

He watched the black knight slowly stalk through the stone hallway, meticulously making his was around Goliff and his dead brother. He was much louder than the brothers had been but the change was welcome. Soon the flesh would rot and the smell would be unpleasant, but that would pass quickly. Overall, it would be a nice adjustment; he had enjoyed his conversation with the black knight much more than with the brothers. He let his head fall back against the wall and watched the endless march of the black knight. The caretakers would come soon, too soon for him to try another incantation, but as always, their coming was welcome.

***

They arrived even sooner than he thought. Distant and hushed footsteps echoed down the hallway but a strange thought quickly occurred to him. Lennox let out a breath but saw nothing. The air was warm. The torches on the walls burned bright, and he remembered that the caretakers made no noise when they moved. He looked at the dead corpses of Goliff and his brother. They had not been moved. The black knight continued his march up and down the hallway, undisturbed by the noise. How long had he closed his eyes? It was hard to gauge time now that it no longer mattered.

Lennox sat up. He looked at the wooden beams and then past them to the crescent window and then down to the black knight. The distant footsteps were not so distant anymore, they were close, just around the corner, and then he appeared. Lennox's eyes grew narrow inside his helm as he took in the stranger, dressed more like a thief than a knight, he wielded a dark-blue short bow and was gliding down the hallway, the bow drawn back and arrow nocked. He moved quietly toward the black knight who remained oblivious to the stranger's presence.

The black knight turned and the stranger released the arrow. It flew fast and true, catching the knight in the opened Y-shaped slit of his barbute helmet. The knight faltered for a moment before falling to his knees. In a flash of silver, the stranger drew his scimitar and brought it down across the black knight's neck, sweeping it from one shoulder blade to the other. The iron helm flew against the wall as the headless body crashed loudly against the floor.

The stranger quickly turned back and dropped to one knee, listening quietly to the murmurs of the cathedral. Soon, the last echoes of the black knight died and a quiet calm fell upon the stones. The torches burned softly, and inside his cell Lennox remained unmoved, still settled with his back against the wall. He could as well have been a corpse. The stranger was different than the others before him, no enchantments, or none that he could see, yet there was an element of sorcery about the man, something that he could not place; that alone made him wonder.

The stranger rose. He sheathed his scimitar as he made his way back to his bow and picked it up off the ground where he had let it fall. He spun it around in his hands checking for cracks and then pulled on the string to test the tension. Satisfied, he walked back over to the black knight and took the arrow out of his eye and cleaned it off before returning it to his quiver.

When he had finished, he made his way back in front of Lennox's cell and took a seat opposite him and leaned back against the wall so that he mirrored the prisoner. He rested his bow against his knee and looked up. "I was told about you … perhaps I was too hopeful. As you are now, I don't see how you could help me."

Well this is strange, Lennox thought. He leaned forward slightly, his armor shining gold in the torchlight. "Oh? I certainly see how it might appear that way. I suppose it comes down to what you mean by helping you? If you can take me at my word, I promise you I'm rather capable. I'm sure I can assist you in whichever pursuit you might ask of me… I'm actually, quite curious how you know me at all. But that can wait. If your here to ring the bell then I must warn you that there is a dangerous beast that guards the tower. If you release me from this cell, I will swear my sword to you and help you fight the beast."

"I'm not here to ring the bell, and I don't need help against the gargoyle. I already know I will have its head."

"The wonders never cease with you stranger, you know so much, yet I know not even your name."

"I am Shiva of Cataron, Captain of the Guard and First Warden to Oracle Sayola Sune. And you are Knight Lennox of Marshiel."

Lennox leaned back and ran his hand against his knee. "I have not heard that name in a long time. I was called that once, Knight Lennox of Marshiel, it was so long ago. How is my city? How is Marshiel?"

"It is a silent city," Shiva answered, he said the words slowly. "Full of monsters and magic. Only treasure hunters and mad men go there in search of the Four."

"I see … I'm sorry to hear that. I appreciate your candor, Sir Shiva."

"Just Shiva," he replied. "My mistress would have a word with you. I have come to take you to her."

"In Cataron?"

Shiva nodded.

Lennox looked up at the crescent window and the darkness that lay past it. He sat motionless in the seclusion of his cell looking out at Shiva. The hard, stone floor beneath him was comforting; he had grown accustomed to it, the darkness of his ancient home. His prison did not bother him, but the unease he felt as he gazed out at Shiva upset him. The man was more than he appeared to be.

"Very well, if you release me, I will accompany you and speak with your mistress."

"She will ask a service of you; you must swear that you will see it through. That is the price of your freedom."

"What is it she would have me do?"

"If I knew that I would tell you. I know not what my mistress sees, but I believe whatever she may ask of you will take you back to Marshiel."

"Ahh, what wonderful luck. I wish to return to my home. I have work I must get back to there, it is quite important, to me at least. I have left it alone far too long now. Yes, far too long."

Shiva pushed himself up off the ground and slung his bow upon his shoulder. Lennox watched him closely, his eyes hidden behind the slit of his helm. There was something troubling about the warden that he could not place. He watched as the strange man stepped close to the cell and slung back his leather hood. After seeing Shiva fight, he had pictured him as young, but he was not. At least, he could not put any age to him. At first he was struck by how old the man looked, but the longer he looked the more he realized it was a weariness that he carried. There was a distrust about his large, dark eyes, a hint of knowing that no man could be trusted. For a moment Lennox thought those eyes could see through him, see him as the man he was beneath his armor. This is a very dangerous man, he found himself thinking, and rightfully so.

Lennox rose and stepped close to the bars so that Shiva was but several feet away. He found himself looking up at the man, a head taller than him at least, one hand resting on the hilt of his sword. His cloths were a dark grayish black that faded into shadow, and black leather boots that were silent and mute. His hair was long and black, pushed back from his face so that it rested at his shoulders. That face was weathered but youthful, except for the eyes.

"I would have you swear your service to my mistress," Shiva said.

Lennox nodded. "I swear it."

"I would have you swear an unbreakable oath," he said.

Lennox was surprised when he saw the man reach through the bars and open his hand revealing a red copper ring that grew wide at the top and was engraved minutely with indecipherable script. He was stunned to find that he could not read the lettering. A frightening magic pulsed forth from the copper band. "This is old magic," he said, his eyes locked on the ring. "Where did you come by such a thing?"

"Ah, you have keen eyes to notice so quickly! My mistress gave this to me. It will bind you to your word. If you were to abandon your duty, well… the world is not big enough to hide you from me…"

"This ring's twin," Lennox whispered. "Your mistress wears it?"

Shiva nodded. "She made them, the pair, and bound them to each other as brother and sister."

"More like master and slave," Lennox growled. "This is dangerous magic."

"Only if you break your oath."

"What is it she wishes me to do?"

"I have told you already, I do not know. But I will be with you; and two others as well."

"To Marshiel?"

"In the end, yes. But I cannot say when. You are the second of three I was sent to gather. The first is waiting for us outside of this mountain, and the third resides in the Wizards Guild near Solaire."

Lennox reached his hand towards Shiva's and left it hovering just above the ring. How long had he been imprisoned? An eternity. He could continue waiting. Another knight would come, eventually, one who would free him with fewer demands. It was a great debt before him, and the weight of the ring was heavy. Could he bare it? He was not one to go against his word. I'm simply trading one prison for another, he thought.

He picked up the ring and looked up towards Shiva. "My work has waited a long time. I suppose it can wait a little bit more," he said and slipped off his glove before placing the ring onto the ring finger of his left hand. He quickly replaced his glove. "Now, I would be very grateful to you if you could free me from this cell. If you make your way up the stairs just down the hallway you'll come to the attic. There should be a wooden case hanging on the inside wall. The key should be there."

Shiva smiled, and Lennox questioned if he had just made the wrong decision in taking the ring. He could feel it burning him where he stood;

its magic calling out to its master. It was then that he saw a similar ring resting on the middle finger of Shiva's hand. Curious, he thought. He watched as Shiva stepped away, his eyes still taking in the golden knight, weighing him upon the scales of his mind. There was no telling how well he had measured. The stranger turned and made his way along the hallway, placing his hood back upon his head as he reached the stairwell and ascended.

***

Lennox looked down at the engraving of his ring, the etchings of letters and symbols that he could not identify was alarming. A new form of lettering possibly? But it looked familiar. He twisted the ring on his finger and attempted to pull it off; it remained firmly in place. He smiled, that would have been too easy. Dropping his hands, he looked out his cell towards the stairwell, where was Shiva? More than enough time had passed for him to have found the key and returned.

The roof began to shake.

"No!" Lennox shouted as he looked up to the crescent moon window. "No! No! No! That imbecile! Why? What are you doing!"

The stones creaked and groaned as blasts of fire flashed across the window, an endless stream of flame. Left, then right, the fire roared; and right, then left, dogged Shiva. Lennox could catch only glimpses through the window, his angle was horrible and the fight quickly drifted further and further from the crescent frame. The cathedral shook as it always did when the beast raged war, an endless pounding as the massive creature flew into the air before pouncing down upon its prey. Lennox had seen it before, and he watched it now in his mind.

Again, the fighting lasted longer than he imagined it would, but soon the flames were sparse and the pounding on the roof began to diminish until the stillness of the stones returned. That fool, Lennox thought, as rage began to take him. He grabbed at the iron bars and screamed into the silence… and that is when he heard it. Overtaking his calls of anguish came a piercing shriek; a long, drawn-out call of death. It was nothing close to human, more beast than man; it was something else, a demon.

Lennox's hands ran down the rough iron bars, the cold texture was lost upon his thick gloves. He stepped along the bars until he reached the far corner wall of his cell, hoping for a glimpse of something, anything, through the crescent window. Lennox's heart raced. He was not afraid, far from it; a rapturous hope filled his heart. It seemed as though he had been standing a long while when, at last, he heard the feint sound of footsteps descending down the stairwell. Lennox wished Shiva would hasten his return, as it was; there was nothing for him to do but wait.

When at last Shiva appeared, he was moving rather slowly, and was favoring his right leg. Still, his movements had a certain grace to them, a poise lost to men who dawn full suits of armor such as himself. Lennox found himself watching the mysterious stranger in a daze, the limping figure moving towards the door of the cell, his hand gripping a large circular ring with an excess of keys dangling and clinking together with each step.

He stopped just outside the door opposite Lennox. "Which one is it?" he said, lifting the large ring up for Lennox to see.

"Ahh, well, let me look." He reached his hand out and took the ring from Shiva, pushing the keys aside one by one until he had reached the end. He held the ring up and passed it back to Shiva. "I couldn't say. I guess you'll have to try them all."

An irritated scowl flashed across Shiva's face; it was gone a moment later as he quietly went about trying each of the keys on the cell door. One by one he tried them all until at last the key turned inside the lock and the door swung open.

"You'd better be worth all of this," Shiva said, staring at Lennox through the open door.

"I imagine we'll find out soon enough… the both of us." And with that Lennox stepped outside of his cell and closed the door behind him.

2

LENNOX stood outside with his hand still resting on the door. He looked inside. Three stone walls, a bed of rotten wood. The room reeked of stale death. It had been all he knew for so long. How much had changed, he thought, more than he dared imagine. Irrelevant, he would resume his work where he had left off. He rolled the oathkeeper ring around his finger. He had time. He could feel Shiva's eyes on his back, ever watchful … not much escapes that one, Lennox was sure of that.

He turned his back to the prison. Shiva was leaning against the wall, his hand resting gently on the hilt of his sword, his hood pushed back showing his face.

"How is your leg?" Lennox asked.

Shiva watched him closely.

"I only asked 'cause it seemed like you were favoring it a little. Once I retrieve my things, I believe I can help you, at least a little bit. I'm no mage, but I know a few minor healing spells."

Without answering him Shiva turned and began making his way towards the stairwell that led up to the attic. Lennox followed, making note that Shiva was indeed favoring his right leg, but mostly pleased to be free of the cell. He knew he would get out eventually, there was no uncertainty about that, but still, it had been trying and unpleasant, more so than he had imagined. The undead guards had offered little solace. To be utterly alone is an awful thing.

They reached the stairwell and ascended. The stairs were narrow and led to a single square room lit by torches with a ladder that led to the roof in the corner, and a wooden hatch that was unlocked and open. Large barrels lined the walls, dark, rotten wood that looked dull in the light. Weapons filled each barrel to the brim, some of them so full the swords and daggers and axes had overflowed and were scattered on the ground in large piles. The oldest of the iron blades had rusted away to nothing long ago, leaving behind red stains on the old stones where they had once rested. An eternity has come and gone, Lennox thought. For a moment he wondered just how long he had been imprisoned. It scarcely mattered.

He walked over to one of the closer barrels and picked up a small short sword that had been resting on top of the pile. Lennox remembered them all, each and every blade, and the knights who carried them, many of them became his own personal guard, like the black knight and the brothers before him. So many, yet they all fell to the gargoyle.

Lennox turned. Shiva was stepping from barrel to barrel looking inside. "What are you looking for?" he asked.

Shiva either ignored the question or was too preoccupied to hear it, Lennox assumed the first. He stood watching as Shiva began pulling out weapons and tossing them to the floor. Not all of them were old and shattered, some of the steel was well made, castle forged with jewels glittering in the hilt and blade. Shiva tossed them to the ground, the red rubies scattering across the stone floor like sparks of fire.

"I need an axe. A large one, heavy, and with a sharp blade," Shiva said.

"Oh? Well I can help you with that." Without waiting for a reply Lennox turned and looked furtively out across the room at the different barrels. He walked slowly across the room until he found what he was looking for. He stepped up close to one of the barrels and tipped it over spilling out the contents, blades and swords alike. "Here," he said, and knelt down before pulling out a huge double-bladed battle-axe, a cruel weapon, heavy and sharp on both edges.

"Why, look at you. That will service me nicely." Shiva moved towards Lennox who handed him the axe happily.

"You have a fine blade," Lennox said. "What do you need this for?"

"The beasts head," Shiva answered. He handled the axe with ease, a heavy war-blade that Lennox could scarcely lift.

He watched Shiva move towards the ladder and begin his assent. The man was an everlasting mystery to him. He followed up the ladder and emerged upon the rooftop of the Undead Cathedral. It was just as he remembered it to be. The large, slanted roof was long and wide; entire sections of the wooden shingles still burned red from where the gargoyle's fire had landed. Some of the wood still glowed fiery and black like coals. On the other side of the roof stood the bell tower, its entrance a small doorway one must cross the roof to reach. Lining the tower were spiraling torches like the ones inside the cathedral, but larger, much larger, their fire was the only light the cathedral would ever see. Their warm flames were bright, their reach long, even from here Lennox could see them illuminating the walls of the mountain which surrounded them, he could not quite see the roof of the cave, but the light crawled up the cold stone walls to an incredible height.

He stepped off the stone ledge onto the roof, his eyes landing upon the beast that lay slain by the bell tower, resting on its side almost as though it were sleeping. Shiva was already moving towards the beast, the mighty axe in hand. He was moving slow, limping slightly as he walked. Lennox followed.

"Do you plan on cutting him up into pieces?" Lennox asked. The beast was larger than he remembered. Nine feet tall at least, with broad shoulders, broader than any two men put together, a towering giant. The gargoyles spear lay fallen beside it. A black piece of iron, long and sharp, the longest spear he had ever seen.

"No," Shiva answered. "I only want its head."

"Naturally … You should have let me fight the beast with you, perhaps then you would have avoided that injury to your leg."

"And have you shared in the hunt, hah!" Shiva was looking at him with a wildness in his eyes. It left just as quickly as it had come, but it had not escaped Lennox's notice.

He watched the hunter move towards the gargoyle's head and then step to the side, carefully lining up the blade of the axe. He took off the beast's head with a single sure stroke. Blood sprayed out across the rooftop, red as wine, shining brightly in the torchlight. Lennox watched it seep into the cracks; the wooden shingles drank it eagerly and dyed the dark wood black.

A hint of a smile touched Shiva's mouth as he dropped the war-axe and walked towards the severed head. He picked it up by of the horns and displayed it to Lennox as his prize. "The lone hunter scores the best treasure," He said.

Lennox nodded. "I must ask. What treasure is a gargoyle's head to you?"

"Oh, don't worry now. I will show you when we return to Cataron. Why spoil a surprise?"

Shiva knelt down and produced a large black sack and placed his treasure inside. He slung the sack over his shoulder and turned to face Lennox. "I appreciate your patience. My work here is done and we are free to leave now. Perhaps you should retrieve a blade from the armory before we depart."

"Thank you, yes. Though there is one more task I must do before we leave." Lennox was already moving towards the tower as he spoke.

"…hm…" Shiva followed after, content with his treasure, and curious as to what business the golden knight could have in the bell tower. He felt foolish a moment later when they begin to climb the stairs towards the top. "You wish to ring the Bell of Calling? My mistress says it's a fool's errand."

"I am growing more and more curious about your Lady Sune," Lennox replied. "She knows much. I have never heard of such a powerful seer." Lennox waited for Shiva to reply, but after a moment of silence he continued. "She's correct. It is a fool's errand… for anyone but me."

"How so?" Shiva asked, but this time it was Lennox's turn to stay quiet.

The Bell of Calling hung at the top of the tower mounted upon a headstock cast of iron and fixed upon two stone pillars to bear the weight. The bell itself was cast of silver and gold, as well as some copper and tin. Writing was engraved from top to bottom around its circumference.

"What does it say?" asked Shiva.

"It's a record," Lennox answered.

Shiva stepped up close to the bell and rans his fingers across the imprinted script. "It looks old."

"It is old," Lennox replied. "It very well might be the oldest bell ever made. It once sat atop the Third Temple of Rahlar, during the Age of Foundation. Some say the Four Lords crafted it themselves, and that it rang loud signaling the victory of the Lords when the final Serpent was slain... at least, that's what some say." Lennox was circling the bell, looking for the rope and switch. He found the lever fastened to the stone floor opposite the staircase. The switch was cast of the same gold and silver as the bell, the same copper and tin. It was almost as tall as Lennox, coming just up to his chest. "It's not true though."

Shiva watched as Lennox grabbed at the lever and tugged.

"Huh..." Lennox stopped and took a knee and looked down at the base of the lever. "It's rusted through." He placed his hands back on the lever and set his foot against the wall and pushed. After a moment there was a clear and audible click, and the lever released. Lennox pulled it back and stepped away.

The web of ropes that hung above the bell began to move, and any slack in the lines grew taut before at last the great bell turned. It reached the height of its arc and dropped, swinging wide. The internal clapper at last found the hollow cup of the bell and released, it was perfect; the large bell struck note on E, its hum tone a near octave below. All else rang true, the minor third, fifth octave, and major third sang beautifully, its sound untainted by the passage of time. The tower was heavy with noise. Shiva stood with hands clapped across his ears to guard them from the sound, but Lennox stood with his head tilted back and his eyes up among the ropes and pulleys of the tower. He smiled underneath his helm; his eyes gleaming. He had not been free until this moment, not truly. All concerns that the tower may have fallen to disrepair were washed away, baptized by the clean song of the bell.

The last chime echoed out as the swinging arc diminished and the bell finally came to rest. Shiva dropped his hands. He was looking at the bell but shifted his eyes towards Lennox and waited. The golden knight remained where he stood looking up into nothing. Shiva opened his mouth to speak but nothing came. He closed his mouth and moved towards one of the windows and looked out. The tower was high, higher than he thought. He could see the headless remains of the gargoyle below, its lifeless body still as sin.

"Right then," Shiva said. "You've done it. You've rang the bell… what happens next?'

Lennox turned to face him, his eyes still gazing upwards. "Well, we make a fire."

"Where, here?"

"No. Beside the cathedral, up close to the water." Lennox answered. He was making towards the stairs and Shiva followed after.

"Why a fire?" Shiva asked as they descended.

"I've rang the Bell of Calling. Now we must light the signal. The shore along the ruins runs a great distance, a fire is required."

"The legend speaks of ringing the bell; I've heard nothing of lightning a signal."

"Well, it seems like what you've heard is incomplete then. I promise a fire is necessary, very necessary; and a large one at that, a very large one. I would set the cathedral ablaze if it were not made of stone. As it is, the wooden pews in the main hall should suffice. They were still there when you arrive, were they?"

"They were."

"Good."

They descended, passing by the cold remains of the gargoyle. Lennox took one final look. He cared little for the beast, his one-time captor. Cold eyes looked away; he was glad to see the guard dog dead. They moved back across the cathedral's roof; the stench of blood filled the air like rot. Lennox was happy to be leaving when the crescent window he had peered up at for so long caught his eye. Surely it would not matter if he delayed their departure for a just a moment longer? Just enough for him to peek down at his cell, he was curious what it would look like from above.

"What now?" Shiva asked as Lennox moved towards the window.

Lennox held up his hand. "Just a moment, please," he replied.

The crescent window only came up to his knees now that he stood beside it. He knelt down and placed his hand on the stone and peered inside. He saw his cell dimly lit by torchlight, empty. It looked bigger from the outside. It had not felt big at all, not while on the other side of the iron gate. Silence filled the cell and hallway below… and then brooding shadows appeared, moving quickly across the bars followed swiftly by their masters. Lennox's heart wavered. The caretakers glanced inside the empty cell and turned away in a flurry, their milk-white faces hidden in shadows, their eyes searching. Lennox backed away just as they gazed up at the crescent moon.

Had they seen him? Lennox couldn't be sure.

He dared not move; the roof was old and creaked with every step. Shiva stood watching him, somewhat curious by his actions. Lennox was happy for the man's silence when realization struck. He glanced up to the bell and then back to Shiva. "Guard the hatch! More sentries have come!" he yelled as he ran back towards the gargoyle.

Shiva released the gargoyle's head and moved to the side of the hatch and crouched low ready to strike at any head that might pop out from below. He glanced up and saw Lennox retrieving the war-axe that lay next to the beast. He wanted to call out to the golden knight but resisted, least he betray his position.

Lennox was running back across the roof with the axe in hand but slowed as he drew closer; his eyes narrowed, and his chest rose and fell in labored gasps, winded from the sprint. He thought they would have appeared by now. He met Shiva's eyes but said nothing. He broke into a crouch and once again moved towards the crescent window. Hesitantly, he peeked down; both the cell and hallway lay calm and empty. He shuffled across the roof and hopped onto the stone ledge opposite Shiva.

"How many?"

"Two," Lennox answered.

"Two is not very many." Shiva's tense figure grew calm as he shifted backwards. "You frightened me a little. Something in the way you moved. These men are all hollow, easy enough to fell as long as you're careful." He whispered the words.

"No. These are no mere guards; they are the caretakers… sorcerers, strong ones."

A look of disgust touched Shiva's face. "Pyromancy?"

Lennox shook his head.

"Curses! I'd prefer fire casters over true sorcery," Shiva growled.

"I think they retreated back into the cathedral," Lennox said. He lifted his axe and after a moment gathered up his courage and slowly stepped forward. He looked down the wooden staircase into the storage room and let out a long, silent breath. "It's empty," he said, and began his descent.

Once down, he placed his axe on the stone floor and leaned it against one of the barrels. He moved along looking inside each of the wooden casks for a weapon more to his liking. Shiva followed closely, carting the gargoyles' head on his back as he kept his eyes on the stairwell. His right hand rested softly on the pommel of his blade.

Lennox continued his search, pulling out a large double handed great sword. He swung it once through the air testing its balance, and then he recalled the black knight lying dead beside his cell. He placed the sword back inside the barrel he retrieved it from and shuffled along the wall until his eyes saw what he was looking for. The ball-and-chain flail hung on an iron spike hammered deep into the wall. It was one among many but Lennox could see the ruins etched into the wooden haft, a common spell but reliable, put there to ensure the weapons strength. The metal ball and its iron chain would rust long before the wooden handle ever did.

He swung the ball in a rough arc above his head and then let it fall to the side. It moved well; he was pleased. Lennox hung the flail on his belt and moved towards a table in the corner, a pile of daggers and small blade rested atop the stand, it was the only stack that didn't look as though it would fall over at the slightest touch.

"There are some good blades here, if you are in need of a dagger," Lennox said, half looking over his shoulder towards Shiva. The quiet servant remained where he stood.

After a little more looking Lennox settled on a pair of matching daggers; well balanced and thin. He tossed one in the air and watched it spin and tumble before catching it cleanly and returning it to its sheath. A rack of bows caught his eye for a moment, but he quickly turned away, he had never been great with a bow, and he failed to see any crossbows. He would stick with the daggers.

"If you're about finished, Knight Lennox, how about we depart from this cursed cathedral? I feel its charms are few indeed, with you free and the beast slain."

"As you wish, Shiva. I've no more desire to stay here any longer than I must. I've been here quite long enough already. But I find leaving might not be as easy as you think… and, well, only jesters and fools run off before they're armed."

Shiva drummed the pommel of his sword with his fingers, weighing, considering. He turned towards the stairs, moving as softly as a shadow-cat, his dark cloak waving behind him like a twin specter. Even with his bow wrapped around him and the gargoyle's head slumped over his shoulder, the man moved like a predator, with eyes ever watchful. He favored his leg a little less, Lennox noticed curiously.

They stepped down the stairwell into a familiar hallway. It was strange, not being locked inside. Lennox felt as though he were dreaming. He hadn't dreamed in so long, not truly, but he remembered.

They walked along cautiously, Shiva in front. "This won't do," Shiva said. "Guard the hallway for a moment."

Lennox nodded and watched as the warden set down the gargoyle's head. He walked past Shiva and moved towards where the black knight lay slain, the dead knight's black kite shield rested beside him. Lennox picked it up and gripped the leather handle tightly in his fist. It was light, lighter than it should have been. The black shield smelled like ash, and the archtree design ran all along the back of the shield as well as the front. He looked at the ruins etched along the inside and smiled; at least he would be safe against fire. It wouldn't help much against the caretakers, but there were other beasts who wielded flame; and they would be out soon enough.

Shiva had tied the sack around him like a shoulder sash so that the gargoyle's head now hung on his back leaving his arms free. He had his bow in one hand and an arrow nocked in the other, ready to draw. His eyes met Lennox's. He moved forward with a slight nod, once again taking his place in the front. Lennox was happy for it; he had seen the man move. He had seen him slay the gargoyle; well… he had heard him. Shiva could no doubt handle the caretakers by himself, but Lennox's was happy to help. He smiled at the thought of swinging his flail into the pale milk faces of the men. It was less than they deserved. The two escapees moved down the hallway and turned the corner, Lennox's cell at last behind him.

Spiraling torches lined the walls, illuminating a narrow hallway with small living quarters packed close opposite the torches, their wooden doors rotting or already fallen from their posts. Each room sported a wooden bed similar to the one in Lennox's cell, each bed just as foul and decrepit as his own. More than a few of the rooms held corpses, truly dead men, they had not moved in a long time. The rooms smelled of earth and dust.

Shiva moved cautiously down the gloomy hallway, glancing warily inside each of the doorways. He would not be caught by surprise. They passed the final room and moved down a spiraling staircase across a second hallway packed with even more rooms than the first. There the hallway turned and the pathway sloped downward in a long half-arc, and ended in medium sized room that rested behind the main amphitheater. The once decorated room now stood in ruin. Large, torn tapestries hung black and charred; half burned down from a fire long ago. The ground was covered in dirty puddles and scattered pages of decaying books.

Lennox remembered what it had once looked like, long ago. It made him sad to see such a beautiful room reduced to such a state, though, nothing lasts forever, he thought. The whole cathedral had been beautiful once, a shining beacon that stood above a now flooded city.

The light was dim in the room, only a single torch burned, but Lennox's eyes were accustomed to the blackness of the cathedral. He hopped over one of the larger puddles and stepped up to the door. His hand found the heavy ring set in the middle and wavered … hesitantly, he pulled at it. For a moment, the door resisted. Then it released, and slowly began to swing inward with a groan so loud Lennox was certain its echo could be heard all throughout the cathedral. He opened the door just enough for Shiva to peek through, and see out into the auditorium.

"Hmm… it's no good. The angel is wrong, I can't see anything."

Lennox pulled on the door once more, this time it swung easily. Unlike the dim room in which they stood; the main auditorium was a mass of burning light. Familiar spiral torches lined the pillars and walls, and three chandeliers ran across the roof; each one twinkling in the light of a thousand candles. The chandeliers were decorated with all kinds of rubies and sapphires, each gem glowing exquisitely in the light, as though the stones themselves were set ablaze.

"Well, I won't lie. I'm worried a trap lies ahead. But, well …" Lennox felt the oathkeeper ring on his finger. "We have our obligations."

Shiva nodded, and stepped forward.

They moved down the center walkway, gazing down the aisles one by one; their eyes dancing across the auditorium. The trap was sprung just as they reached the center; the large chandelier fell without noise, not a single sound, five hundred pounds of iron and fire crashing down in utter silence. If Lennox had not already been looking up it would have crushed them in the beat of a heart, but Lennox had been looking up. He rushed towards Shiva, tackling him to the ground as the chandelier fell behind them.

All sound was lost, stolen by sorcery, and then the caretakers were upon them. Lennox was just rising to his feet when a white orb flew past his head, glowing hot white like lightening. Lennox ducked down as a second orb flew past him and smashed into the broken chandelier tossing up shattered iron and burning candles into the air. He took cover behind one of the pews and ducked low. Shiva was across from him, one aisle over with his head bent down.

He was trying to get a better look, lifting his gaze to no avail. Each attempt only brought forth a new orb. He looked towards Lennox, signaling for him to run.

Lennox understood, grimacing beneath his helm. Curses, he thought. Curse this whole damned cathedral! It should have been built a prison! Very well, he pushed himself up to one knee and nodded; a moment later he was sprinting across the amphitheater, moving towards the stone pillars.

White orbs flew at him two at a time, flashing like lightening and crashing into the pews behind him. The wooden benches cracked and splintered in the cold silence, casting up wooden shards high into the air. He reached the pillar and looked back towards Shiva. The hunter was kneeling with his bow drawn back. He seemed to be waiting for something. Another white orb struck the pillar close to Lennox's head and the golden knight quickly looked away. When he turned back Shiva had let fly his arrow, and the white orbs stopped.

Suddenly the noises of the cathedral returned. "Are you well?" Lennox called out.

Shiva didn't answer. He had already nocked his bow with another arrow and was pulling back on the string. He was aiming the bow just above Lennox's head when he let the arrow fly. Lennox's feet slipped out from beneath him as he ducked down, out of the path of the arrow. He landed on his back, and like that, his shield was thrown clear. When he turned his head to look for it he saw the second caretaker on the ground beside him, an arrow sticking out of one of his arms. The man showed no sign of pain and eyed Lennox with a cool gaze. The caretakers hand went for a dagger at his side but Lennox was already swinging his flail in a high arc. The spiked ball found its mark, and blood gushed forth beneath its dark iron. The caretaker's foot jerked, and then his hand, but nothing else. He lay motionless from then on.

Lennox let his head fall back.

He was lying in a small pool of water with blood slowly seeping in, turning the liquid a smoky red. Lennox didn't move. He didn't care. His chest rose and fell as he looked up at the ceiling towards one of the chandlers. He could hear Shiva's footsteps as he walked through the scattered puddles. Lennox couldn't see him, but he knew Shiva was searching the fallen caretaker; claiming his loot, Lennox thought, or treasure… whatever he wished to call it. It was all the same to Lennox.

He pushed himself up so that he was leaning back on his hands and listened as Shiva made his way across the cathedral. "You move well … very quick… I've never seen someone move so spryly in armor before." The tone of the words seemed to pose a question.

Lennox grinned inside his helm. "Thank you, sincerely. That's high praise coming from someone who moves like a shadow-cat."

Shiva laughed, though Lennox couldn't guess why. He took the handle of his flail and pulled the spiked ball free. The caretakers face was caved in like a crater and blood had pooled at the bottom, covering some of the grotesque and beaten flesh. Lennox looked away. He stood up and searched the surrounding for his shield. He found it two aisles over and wondered how it had been thrown so far. To cross swords is a queer and dangerous dance, Lennox thought, anything may occur. He was safe in his armor, but it was incomplete, he would be vulnerable until he retrieved the rest of his belongings. He shook away the thought.

"Shall we carry on?" Shiva asked.

Lennox looked towards the warden. He was wet from the puddle and tasted fresh blood in his mouth. He wanted to take off his helm and breath in fresh air … but no, he was still so week. He was confident he could cast a decent glamor, but Shiva had penetrating eyes that saw much. Would he see through it? Would he care? As it was, Lennox didn't even raise his visor.

He nodded and moved across the auditorium towards Shiva and together they continued towards the main entrance. Lennox observed that Shiva was no longer favoring his right leg. What a specimen, Lennox thought, as he took in the bear sized man. He thumbed at his oathkeeper ring, rolling it on his finger beneath his glove. Shiva had one as well; it was identical to his own.

The warden wore other rings on his left hand, four in total, Lennox counted. The oathkeeper ring, and three others. Only the gods knew what enchantments were upon them … but no, even they didn't know, Lennox was certain of that.

At last they stood before the heavy stone doors of the Undead Cathedral's entrance. Lennox hardly knew what to think. He glanced back towards the caretakers, his eyes landing on the one he had killed, and then moving to the other, watching them, making certain they were truly dead. He would have to check thoroughly, after he had set the fire. They would not rise quickly. The one he had killed would not rise at all, now with the wound he had inflected, but the other … he was not so certain.

Shiva placed his hand upon the stone and pushed. The door opened quietly. Shiva stepped out but Lennox paused at the foot of the door and looked out into the darkness beyond. He could see a trail of torches that hung upon the side of the cave's wall and traveled up into the distance before turning black completely. The first steps home are often the hardest, he thought, and stepped outside, away from the cathedral and into the surrounding darkness.

3

LENNOX stood at the shore of the black lake gazing out across the void. The spiraling torches of the cathedral burned behind him, accompanied by a towering bonfire, ten feet tall, fueled by the wooden pews of the Undead Cathedral. The fire burned hot and the flames were heavy, yet the light barely touched the water's edge. Its radiant glow absorbed by the surrounding darkness.

A silvery mist streamed forth from the black lake. The haze came up to Lennox's knees and clung to his armor in large liquid clumps that gathered and spilled down to the earth and gathered again. He stood there for some time, not speaking, looking out across the water, the smallest of waves lapping up against the sloping stone floor. Not far from the edge, peeking out from the black water stood the tops of three high towers. Lennox tried to remember what the buildings had once been. He couldn't recall. A small sadness fell upon him as he thought about the drowned city.

"This is a queer land," Shiva said. He sat on the steps outside the cathedral, bow in hand, as he looked out past Lennox towards the towers. "Even the wildest stories say nothing about towers in the black lake, or of gargoyles."

"Oh? You seemed to have known of the gargoyle, if I recall."

"I had mistress Sune to guide me."

"How fortunate for you, to have such a perceptive oracle for your mistress." The words came out sharper than Lennox had intended. Who knows how long he would have had to wait before another knight may have come and released him, ten years? Fifty? A hundred? He couldn't even begin to guess. Azazel knew how long he had been imprisoned, Azazel ... and perhaps a few loyal subjects. He remembered the day of his imprisonment; it burned hot in his memories. Parts of it had faded; small details ... but mostly he remembered.

***

The floodgates had been closed and he stood atop the cathedral looking down into the city of a thousand fires watching the water rise. One by one the rising water quenched the burning fire pits of the great city, flames that had burned endlessly for hundreds of years sputtered into nothing at the touch of the cold water, casting up small puffs of steam before disappearing forever. Still the water rose, reaching next the great torchlights that hung along the city's tall stone buildings.

In the streets men fought and died in battle ... or fled. The women ran with their children in their arms and babies at their breast. The men moved beside them, carrying what little they could from their homes, food mostly, but for others it was gold and silver and jewels. They moved along the pathway that ran below the cathedral and along the mountainside. A few of the city's fire pits and torches still burned, and their light filled the cavern city; but as the water rose the light faded and chaos grew.

Lennox's eyes followed the beast as it descended, translucent wings untrained and spread wide, charging through the air like a bull. A blue knight rode atop the creature, his dark cloak blowing in the wind. The gargoyle hissed, and the blue knight leapt clear, landing on the roof of the cathedral like a blow from a hammer. A moment later the beast stood beside him.

"I looked for you... at the Tower of the Gods," Lennox said to him.

"I was not there," the blue knight answered as he rose, "or father and Lord Shem would yet live, and you would burn in sheol."

"I went to the red shrine looking for sister, and found the remains of Lord Batraal and Lord Armoris ... but you were nowhere to be seen."

"Sir Gillian had fled. I followed after, but he was gone. Woe to him had I found him." He unsheathed his bastard sword from his back and held it with both hands. The blade was pale white, and shined like glass.

"Look no further," Lennox said, pointing down to the flooded city. "He is there, dead and gone, slain by Ricon Stone, just before the floodgates were closed and the water ascended."

"Sir Ricon was a brave man, good and true. He will be remembered with songs, his deeds recorded." The blue knight moved towards Lennox. "I've come for the Lord's tomes."

"Buried… below the city; beneath the water, along with Sir Gillian and my effects."

The blue knight continued forward; a sad smile touched his lips. "A traitor, I would have him die a thousand times."

"No," Lennox said with grief in his voice. "This age was already dying… crumbling and wasting away, so that something new may be born."

The blue knight would hear no more. He dashed forward as the gargoyle leapt into the air. Lennox cursed the cheap steel blade he held in his hand and the rotten wooden heater shield he'd found in the cathedral. Without his weapons and rings, he'd have little chance. Curse me, he thought, and charged towards the blue knight. They came together in a rush of steel and blood, the shadow of the gargoyle hovering above.

"Finish it," the words rung in his mind, distant words from a fallen queen. "Lennox … end it!"

***

"Lennox …" the name echoed from the dark.

The golden knight turned, stirring as though woken from a dream. He blinked inside his helm, his eyes ever hidden, gazing out through the bare slit of his visor. "What is it?" he asked.

"The water stirs." Shiva was on his feet, eyes narrow and cautious. Lennox turned back to the lake.

Small dark wrinkles fell and broke on the sloped shore growing in size as a cool subterranean chill swept in from the lake and pushed back the mist, revealing the wet stone earth below. Scattered puddles bathed in the torchlight of the cathedral, fire flickering in the cool still mirrors of their surface. As the mist that hung over the lake continued to dissipate, scattered ripples could be seen popping up along the surface, great circular rings that began small then swept out wide and stirred the water into large crashing waves two or three feet tall that beat at the shore where Lennox stood. The golden knight moved back, closer to the cathedral, and kept watch.

"I knew you had some magic," Shiva started, "but what folly have you called down upon us? I would have you speak of your sorcery." There was a tone buried in the voice that hinted of fear.

"Hmm… you surprise me, Shiva. I thought you could see more. This is no sorcery of mine. I am at a fraction of my strength, and even then, I was always one for enchantments. I'm like you, I dislike arcane magic." Lennox glanced back, his eyes lingering on Shiva's face, searching the man for something true, something hidden deep inside the shadows of his hood.

Slowly, the great stirring began to subside and peace returned to the surface of the lake. A stillness hovered above the water, and a great calm filled the mountain city. Shiva held his bow low, an arrow nocked and ready to draw. He looked out across the surface with searching eyes, and for a long time neither moved nor made a sound. His heart pounded inside his chest, he knew something was queer, but what? At last it donned on him … since when had there been four towers?

Shiva moved noiselessly down the steps of the cathedral. "The second tower on the right," he whispered.

"I know," Lennox answered.

Together they stood and watched as the tower drew forth, wading through the darkness like a pillar of smoke and ash; but as the column drew closer the cathedral's light pealed back the darkness and transformed the black and grey stones into scales, and turned the tower's hollow windows into yellow eyes that burned like golden moons with slits running through them. Shiva took a half-step back and went to draw his bow but stopped short. Lennox endured, remaining where he stood, his gaze piercing across the water into the eyes of the everlasting serpent.

The beast stopped short of the shore, its head swaying high above the two men as it looked down upon them. There was something human about its face, Shiva thought, especially the nose, but the skin around the mouth was red and scarred, as though it had been cut off. The serpent sat motionless in the shallow waters of the shore; but behind it, the creature's tale pushed back and forth along the surface, and every so often the serpent's gold liquid eyes would shift to Shiva before returning just as quickly to Lennox.

At last the serpent spoke. "No one has rung that bell... not for a very long while. I count two, but truthfully, I thought there would be more. No matter, I will not be dismayed. I am Faid, the last of my kind, and friend to man. You have called and I have come, as I was bid. Shall I elucidate your fate, that you may face the trials that await you?" The serpents forked tongue flickered out. "Reveal yourselves to me. I would look into the eyes of those who called me, and know thy names."

Shiva stepped forward, swinging his bow about his shoulder and pushing back his hood. He looked up at the mighty serpent and went down to one knee. Leaning forward, he pressed the knuckles of his right hand against the stone floor while his left hand rested on the end of his sword hilt. But he did not bow his head. He kept his eyes on Faid. "Undying one," he began, "I am Shiva of Cataron, Captain of the Guard and First Warden to Oracle Sayola Sune. It is an honor to speak with one who witnessed the creation of all, the most sacred of days."

"I am only an old serpent... but if you wish, step forward, and we shall speak."

Shiva moved; his leather boots splashed gently in the shallow water of the shore. Once he reached Lennox he stopped and returned to one knee.

The serpent's tongue flickered. "Ooh, you smell of old magic. Strong wards." For a moment, Faid seemed puzzled. "Did you ring the bell?"

Shiva shook his head.

"No ... of course not. You are strong, to be sure, with a will of iron. You will break before you bend, but your will is not your own. You have the scent of a servant, and your fortune is not mine to tell." The serpent paused for a moment, and then said. "But if you like, I may give you a word. As to whether you will like it, I cannot say."

"I would hear it," Shiva answered at once.

"Very well, servant. What drives you? It is not a question for me, it is for you. This life is beautiful, bright, and glorious. It bewitches you to the point of obsession; yet you are a pawn in the game... but a pawn can kill the king just the same. Some serve themselves; others serve kings and queens, and still others the gods. So, I ask you again, what is it that drives you? You'll need to know, if you wish to endure."

If the words had meant anything to Shiva he didn't show it. His face was a stone mask. He remained quiet for a moment, wondering if perhaps Faid had more to say. He didn't, and at last Shiva spoke. "Thank you, undying one," he said. "I shall think upon your words, for they are sure to be wise counsel."

The serpents tongue flickered out, and a hint of pleasure shimmered in his cold yellow eyes. He nodded his head slightly and turned his eyes upon Lennox. "Thy name … "

The golden knight stood with his arms folded looking at Shiva who remained kneeling. He stood casually, as though he were watching a play, and the great show amused him. After a moment he unfolded his arms and turned to face the serpent. "Has it been so long," he said, as he reached up to remove his helm, "have I grown so weak … that I am a stranger to those who would know me?"

Shiva's eyes widened as the golden knight lowered his helm. The taint of the undead had made its mark. The decayed flesh that wrapped around his skull was a pale blue, as though he had been drowned. What little hair remained clung thin and clumpy to the patchy flesh, and large chunks of bone poked through where skin had rotted away.

"Transient being … I see only a cursed man, and one without much time remaining." The serpent spoke in a rich, deep voice that held the knowledge of ten thousand years. He dipped his head low and kept his eyes on Sir Lennox. "You are brave, I see it clearly. But are you wise? I cannot say. You fascinate me, to be sure. There is something familiar about you, a glint in your eyes, an index of sins… you lost everything, and seek to take back the taint. You heard whispers that I might break the cures. Well, that's not true at all. So then, how am I to guide you?"

Lennox looked down for a moment shaking his head. "I thought for sure you would know me, but I thought wrong. Tis a terrible pity really, just how far have I fallen." Lennox lifted his head. "I am not cursed, at least, not how you believe. I did not breathe in the taint." Lennox's eyes flickered to Shiva. "My vessel has decayed, but what is done can be undone, and you will help me as you promised you would."

The serpent's eyes regarded the golden knight carefully, considering the words that had been said. After a long moment the serpent spoke. "I do not know your face, Sir Knight, perhaps your name?"

What good is a name, Lennox thought, he does not recognize me. He thinks I'm some half-crazed hollow. "Sir Lennox of Marshiel," he said at last.

The serpents tongue flickered out. It flickered a second time, and then a third. Then he spoke. "Yes… very good. I knew a Lennox of Marshiel once, long ago. He was a prince. Are you a prince?"

I've suffered this foolishness long enough, Lennox thought. He turned his head and saw Shiva staring back at him with cold and curious eyes. "Well, it hardly matters who I say I am. You are bid to aid those who ring the bell. I have rung it, and I am in need of your assistance."

Faid bowed low. "What would you have me do?"

"I seek the Lord's tomes. Below the lake in an unmarked grave sealed by magic they wait, as well as my effects. Only you can break the seal, and only when bid by one who rang the bell. I know you swore yourself to Sir Gillian … I have come to see you true to your word.

The serpents tongue flickered. Behind the beast, a great stirring within the water began once more as quickly as the serpent's tail emerged and crept along the black water. The end of the tail was long and thin, coiled in on itself in many layers… but, ever so slowly, the coil began to unwind as it reached the shore. "Take this, it is a gift freely given," said Faid.

Lennox looked down as the tail and saw imbedded into one of the scales a ring of pure silver. He picked up the ring and held it in his palm. The band was a perfect replica of Faid. Shaped like a serpent, the silver snake wrapped itself around in a circle with its tail curving away, and placed upon the head were two yellow sapphires for eyes. He could feel the magic woven into the silver as he could with all rings of power. But what power do you hold, he thought. He could place the ring on his finger and find out, but that was not always the wisest choice. "A sweet gift, indeed. What is its purpose?" he asked.

"It is a ring of great illusion, forged for a wizard long ago. It will hide your curse from the eyes of men, but, like all enchantments, it can be broken by a strong spell. And it will only bewitch the eyes. Your flesh will still be as ice to any who touch you."

Lennox had already taken off his glove, and reached out to take the

gift. He slid the ring onto his middle finger and the effect was instanta-
neous. The skin along his hand looked warm with blood as color returned
to his flesh. A descent spell, he thought, but incomplete. A true enchantment would have brought warmth back to the skin as well, though that
would be a powerful ring indeed. He turned and saw Shiva staring at him
from the corner of his eyes. The big man was standing now and even had
a small amount of surprise breaking through his icy features.

Lennox chuckled. "Well, I suppose I have seen better days. It is a gift
gratefully accepted."

When he turned back to face Faid the serpent's eyes gleamed in recognition, and the ancient snake bowed his head low, almost to the water's
surface before raising it again. "My prince," he began; his tone rich and
unsettling, "you look as though you have been born anew. Please …
forgive my ignorance. Truly, I thought you dead long ago. I needed to
see who you really were, not the hollow that you appeared to be." Though
the words were pleasing, the serpent's eyes remained lifeless and cold.

Faid the Unfaithful, that was your name once, Lennox remembered.
Blood and ash, how do you know when a serpent lies? He grunted and
smiled up at the creature. Faid was still bound to his word; the serpent
would serve when commanded. "The tomes, and my belongings," he
repeated.

Faid's tongue flickered out. "It seems … " he paused; his voice
uncertain. "Young prince, fate is cruel. You seek the Lord's tomes and
ask me to play my part, and I will, truly, but much time has passed and
your journey has only just begun. A hydra lives among the tombs; an
abomination shaped from my kind by the Darkmoon Alchemist … another
failed experiment. Whether the beast escaped or was sent is unclear, but
the fact remains. While he guards the crypts I cannot approach, least he
should destroy me. And with me gone all hope of recovering the tomes
vanishes."

"What are you telling me then?" Lennox asked. "That you are craven?
That you would forswear your vow!"

Faid's reaction was minimal, which didn't much surprise Lennox.
The serpent looked vaguely puzzled at first, then slightly amused. He
gave a faint, thin smile and quietly rose high up into the air. "I swore to
undue the spell placed upon the grave … not battle a hydra. Young prince.

I am a key, not a sword." The serpent's tongue flickered. "Has your hope shattered? Have you amalgamated yourself with the crestfallen of this world? You were mighty once; can you be mighty again?"

"You're asking me to slay a monster," Lennox replied.

"I seek nothing from you. I offer you instruction and make known the way. Fate has forged your path; it is your yoke to bear." Again the water stirred as Faid's long coiling tail withdrew from the shore and melted into the blackwater of the lake. The mighty serpent stared down at Lennox, tall and strong as a stone tower. Slowly, he began to slip back into shadow. "Raise the floodgates. Drain the city. Kill the beast. Then I will fulfill my vow." The low mist returned slowly, its silver gleam seeping back along the water's edge as Faid drifted further and further away, his long neck dipping down into the darkness until the creature looked only like one shadow among thousands. His last words were heard echoing across the stillness of the lake. "Fleeting prince … may we meet again." Then, the serpent was gone.

Shiva remained on the shore looking out across the void, but Lennox turned and left without a word, his face empty. All light was gone from his eyes.

***

Shiva found Lennox inside the Undead Cathedral sitting in one of the few pews that remained. His helmet was off and Shiva could see his long hair falling dark across his golden armor. The big man stood at the doorway and took in the ruined hall. Shattered crystals and bent steal littered the floor where the chandeliers had fallen; otherwise, the hall was empty. The bodies of the two caretakers had been thrown in with the pews to help fuel the fire, they had burned hot and bright, but went to ash quickly, and now nothing remained of the fire outside but the red embers of an extinguished flame.

Shiva took another step forward, his feet resting in the shallow water of a large puddle. He could feel the water beginning to seep through the soft leather stiches. "Sir Lennox," he called out. He let the words echo and die before he continued. "You have just now been freed; it is too early to descend into misery."

What drives you …

Lennox remembered Faid's words to Shiva. He wanted to know as well. He sat with his eyes closed as he rolled the oathkeeper ring round his finger. Shiva had one as well, he had seen it. He cursed Faid the Unfaithful, and wished him burn in sheol. The Lord's tome could wait, but without his belongings he was weak and vulnerable. He might even die, well … not die, but go hollow, or close to it, even without the taint. He looked down at his helm and reached out and took it up and examined it. He ran his fingers across the small dents and scratches that littered the right side, and along the runes that were etched beneath the bottom of the visor, so small one could hardly see them at all. A part of him wanted to smile. Despite its age and heavy use, the armor was still strong, the enchantments flowed through the gold, his enchantments, the strongest a man could ever cast. He must never take it off … never.

He placed the helm on his head as he rose and began making his way towards Shiva. The warden watched him pass and followed him outside. Lennox picked up his flail and shield from where he had left them. He hung the ball and chain on his hip and swung the black knight's kite shield across his back and turned to Shiva.

He nodded.

Shiva nodded back, and they left, making their way towards the only path there was to follow, a long and windy road leading up alongside the mountain's wall lined by a thousand torches.

***

When they had passed by several hundred flames Lennox peered over his shoulder towards the Undead Cathedral. He was high above the church now, and it looked small next to the black lake and surrounding darkness. Its large torches burned bright, illuminating the stone structure, but nothing else. It was as though the cathedral hung inertly in a pitch of black.

Lennox turned away. "You mentioned some companions."

Shiva didn't respond right away, and after a long silence Lennox thought maybe he had not been heard. He was about to speak again when Shiva answered. "I did." Again, there was a moment of silence as Shiva thought about what he might or might not say. In the end he must have decided there was no need to keep anything back "The girl waits for us outside the mouth of the mountain with the mounts. The beasts refused to enter, even when led by foot. Though… her wolves did not seem afraid."

Wolves? Lennox wanted to know more but kept silent. He would see her soon enough. "And the other? I believe you mentioned he resides near Solaire."

"Just so. Another prince, like you." Shiva laughed. "The king of Solaire has a mighty appetite. Prince Oscar is his ninth child, and fifth in the line of succession. Mistress Sune says he will soon pass the mage trials and be granted his wizards robes, despite his young age."

"You make him sound as if he were a child."

Shiva turned to face Lennox. "Hmm … he is five and ten, almost a man grown."

This time it was Lennox who laughed. They were all children to him: the young wizard prince, the girl waiting outside, the oracle and her warden. Only children, Lennox thought. And children can be stubborn. "What if this boy decides he doesn't want to join us?"

Shiva turned back and continued along the trail, his right side lit up by fire, his left hidden in shadow. "He will not have a choice."

"Ohh really?

Shiva shrugged. "Did you? Mistress Sune has seen it."

"Ahh… Mistress Sune has seen it," Lennox echoed.

After that they did not speak, they moved along the pathway and Lennox's golden armor clamored and clinked while the Warden's cloak draped him in a stillness and silence that can only be brought on by magic. It was the silence that caught Lennox's notice. Even when he watched the big man's footsteps, he heard nothing, not even the silent scuff of soft leather on smooth stone.

The man is enveloped in magic and enchantments. I must not take my eyes off of him even for a moment, Lennox thought. Not even a second.

4

THE sun was beginning to get low as the evening glow spread across the floor, lighting the mouth of the mountain passage. The entrance had been divine once, large ivory pillars so shiny one might have thought they were cut from pearls, and so wide that six wagons pulled by elephants could have passed by one another and not have come close to touching. A honeycomb of tunnels had run along the ceiling of the tunnel, filled with murder holes and arrow slits, and cut from the stone in the shape of stars and crescent moons that twinkled by firelight at night. The sleepless stars they had been called, both lovely and lethal.

All of it was gone now, reduced to rubble. The shortcomings of rock and stone made visible to mankind, to be seen by anyone who knew what it was they saw. Lennox knew. It made him sad. He had played in the honeycomb tunnels as a child; the memory came to him from far away. He didn't even know he remembered it, until it was there with him.

He made his way around fallen boulders and large chunks of stone that stood twice as tall as he did and littered the pathway. Most of the stones lay shattered, but a few still held some of their original shape. He climbed up the arc of a crescent moon for a better view and saw a stone cut like a twinkling star with a large crack straight down the center up ahead by about thirty paces. Shiva was there, walking through the fallen star towards the light of the sun. I've fallen behind, Lennox thought, before leaping down.

When he reached the cracked star the Warden was gone, but the mouth of the cave was in sight and the golden knight continued forward. He could feel a cool draft blowing across the stones and cursed softly. Just once he would like to feel warm, it had been so long, but they were high in the mountains he knew. True warmth wouldn't come yet … but soon. He would endure, he would always endure, not like this twisted ruin.

The mouth of the cave had been glorious, now it was merely a small passageway cut into the side of the stony mountain, hardly enough for a horse to pass through let alone a wagon. It was no surprise Shiva could not get the horses to walk through this, thought Lennox, as he shuffled through the pathway. He wasn't so sure he would get through without scuffing his armor, but he did.

***

The icy wind came in gusts, howling along the mountainside and whipping Shiva's cloak back like a banner, its grayish black cloth a dark blur against the white drifting snow. In the distance the clouds were storm black, but above they were thin with wisps of white against blue. Lennox searched the sky for the sun. It had been so long since he had seen it, since he had felt its warmth. He began to laugh when he saw it dip below the mountains far away, it final rays burning the sky red and orange, the colors of fire … but he did not feel its heat. He leaned back against the stone mountain and watched the colors swirl and burn above him. He smiled inside his helm. I am free, he thought, now I can get back to work.

He wasn't sure how long he stood there, but the colors were gone from the sky and night ruled the air when he spotted Shiva walking towards him, a black ghost surrounded by white. He was rapped tight in his cloak to guard himself against the harsh bite of the wind. With a quiet command for Lennox to follow, Shiva led off along the mountain.

Lennox looked out warily at the trees as they passed, looming now in the night with their tall peeks and thick needles. Shadows seemed to take shape and move and then fade away before finally taking shape once more. A cycle of illusions made worse by the howling wind. Occasionally, dark wings could be seen flapping between the branches.

This forest has tasted the taint, Lennox thought as he watched thin tendrils of silver-gray fog drifting low across the base of the trees, following them. More than a taste. "How much further to this girl companion of ours?" Lennox murmured.

"Not far," Shiva answered. "Astrid told me there was a small grotto just south of the mountain's entrance. It's warm and dry, and she said the wind doesn't reach it. She'll be waiting for us there." Shiva pointed back along the ridge. "We've passed two small peaks. Just one more now."

Uncertain, Lennox's eyes watched the forests edge. The fingers of the gray mist had splintered and grown fat as the mist oozed out along the tree line not more than knee high off the ground. A faint, silvery light accompanied the fog and grew brighter as the mist collected. Yet the fog clung closely to the tree line, extending only a foot or two out into the clearing between the trees and the mountainside.

He broke off from the mountain trail and walked slowly toward the fog. The misty tendrils were as thick as arms now and swayed back and forth aimlessly. He stopped well short of the tree line and studied them as they hovered softly in the air.

"What are they?" Shiva asked from behind.

"Something very dark," Lennox replied. "It is the taint, the curse of the undead taken shape. Unseeing, unthinking, it leaches through water and burrows through earth seeking hosts to attach itself to. If you breathe it in you will be corrupted and the curse will be upon you."

"Can we burn it away?"

Lennox's laugh was bitter and short. "The taint is vast, Warden, the entire lake is corrupt and I'm sure the surrounding lands as well, still, it can only spread so far from its source. Once we're clear of the mountain we'll be safe enough. In the meantime … if you happen to fall or trip … it be best if you held your breath."

"Hah! Don't worry now," Shiva answered, he was smiling as he spoke. "I can't remember when last I've faltered."

"Ohh … Well, perhaps I was mistaken in my concerns."

"Showing concern for a friend is never a mistake."

Is that what we are, Lennox wondered. He nodded to the big man and made his way back to the trail.

Shiva was staring at the fog, his eyes unfeeling and cold. When Lennox reached the path he turned, and together they continued their march into the wind.

The third peak was not far now but the wind blew harsher with each step. Shiva's cloak was caught and ripped from his grasp. He threw the dark wool to his side in a tangled rage. He murmured something in an angry tone and wished his coat were thicker that it might not catch the wind so easily. Trying to keep his cloak around him was near impossible. He had just gotten a handful of the cloth when a strong gust grabbed at his cloak once more, ripping it from his shoulders. The garment would have blown away completely had the warden not had quick hands.

Lennox watched through the small slit in his helm with amusement in his eyes and a smile tugging on the corners of his mouth.

He passed the Warden, leaving the big man alone in his struggles as he marched the last few paces alone towards the peak. The cold was everywhere. It hung on the mountain and blew in from across the forest cutting through his armor like a heavy blade, but the girl had spoken true. Not far from the small peak was the grotto, hidden just behind the next pass. The side of the mountain burned red like a kiln, beckoning for him to come.

Ahh … hello there, Lennox thought. He turned and called out to Shiva. "We've made it!" He had to yell to be heard over the howling wind. "I can see the fires glow! Not long now!"

Somehow, Shiva had managed to reattach his cloak despite the wind and was trudging along the trail towards Lennox. The snowfall was heavy. Large white flakes as big as silver coins swirled about them, and would soon hinder their vision if the weather continued to worsen.

Now it was Lennox who led them. With the grotto in sight there was only one way to go. Shiva followed behind, ever grasping at his cloak. From time to time Lennox would throw a watchful look back as they walked, but the weather had turned bad quickly, and soon they found themselves in the heart of a storm. It would not do to get separated so close to refuge, Lennox would not have it, as weak as he was, he needed the warden. The world was dangerous, and had changed much, Lennox knew. It would not do to face it alone.

He glanced back once more and called out to Shiva. Silence answered … silence and snow. His heart raced and he took a step into the blinding white of the storm and called out for the warden once more.

"I'm here," a voice answered. It sounded far away but a moment later Shiva appeared, huddled in his cloak. He shook off the snow and lifted his eyes upward. "How far?'

"I couldn't say," Lennox answered shaking his head. "I can't see the fire anymore."

"If we follow the mountain, we'll come across it soon enough. We'd have to be blind to miss it."

"We are blind," was all the Golden Knight replied. Then he turned and continued on, with Shiva safely visible behind.

They heard the deep howls of wolves behind them before they had gone half a league, and later more howls from the forest to their right. Shiva grunted but said nothing, leaving Lennox alone in his fears. At least we have the mountain on one side, he thought. It would be hard to fight if they got surrounded on all sides by a pack. The small comfort left him when his mind wandered to shadow-cats. He realized the beasts could be stalking them from above and he would never know it. He pushed the thought aside.

Again, the wolves took up the call. "Blood and ash," Lennox cursed, and picked up his pace.

Doubt of ever reaching the grotto was rising quickly in his mind when at last he saw the orange glow of the stone walls and cried out. "We're here, yes! We're here!" He turned just as Shiva moved up beside him. The big man said nothing and together they took the final steps out of the storm and into the burning warmth of the grotto.

***

They found the cavern empty.

No, not empty, Lennox observed, only the girl and her wolves were missing. Otherwise, everything was how it should be; better, truthfully. He took off his helm as Shiva grabbed a few logs of wood from a small pile by the horses and fed them to the flame. He took a few more and tossed them in as well before removing his cloak and taking a seat.

"This cave looks well kept," Lennox said in a surprised tone. The fire pit wasn't much, but there was a descent supply of wood and a small fence built from crudely cut beams in the back that served as a stable for the horses. He set his helm down and drew a breath, letting the warm air fill his lungs; now that they were inside, the cold left him quickly. He wouldn't have died, not from the cold alone … what made his heart race was the taint, and the monsters it bred. They would not be as strong as the gargoyle or the hydra in the lake, but they would be dark creatures still.

"Mountain clans hold these lands," Shiva started. He had pushed back his hood and his black hair hung wild across his shoulders. Methodically, he began to strip off his small mail vest, leathers, and sweat-soaked woolens, all of which were either black or dark gray, even the small vest of mail, which burned a dull black in the flames. He sat staring out the cave into the storm. "They're always warring with each other, but they're smart enough not to destroy a cave like this. In winter, this shelter in the rocks can mean life or death for their raiders; and what belongs to the Moon Brothers today might be claimed by the Flint Crows tomorrow."

"Hmm, the Moon Brothers and Flint Crows you say … How many other clans live in these parts?"

"Dozens," Shiva told him. He had moved a few more logs closer to the fire and was draping his cloak over them to catch the fire's heat. "Though, not so many as there once were. They have been driven out. Mistress Sune says there are queer things growing in these mountains … dark things."

"The taint," Lennox said. "Darkness breeds darkness."

Shiva nodded. "The cursed." He looked as though he wanted to say more, but it took time before the words left his mouth. "The gargoyle at the bell tower, and the hydra below the water. These creatures, there are others like them. Men believe they are creatures of the deep, beasts cursed by the taint, like the hollow men. But the Serpent mentioned another, my mistress has heard his name whispered in the twilight hours as well … the Darkmoon Alchemist."

Lennox stood staring back at Shiva, regarding him curiously. The words held a question in them and were spoken in a sullen tone, but the Warden's eyes gleamed. This one is mad, Lennox thought. His eyes flickered to the black cloth that held the gargoyle's head. He seeks dangerous prey and takes their head for his prize, but for what? Proof, he supposed. Lennox felt the oathkeeper ring tighten softly around his finger like a noose. The man is a servant … and now so am I.

"It is a name best left in whispers," the golden knight answered quietly. Perhaps he thought Shiva would let it end there.

"She says he is the father of all the greater beasts … their maker. The great serpent called them failures, but they do not seem like failures to me."

"These are questions best left alone." Outside the wind howled and the night grew darker, the air colder.

"Mistress Sune wishes to know more of this alchemist and his creations."

"All she needs do is ask and I will tell her what I can. But she is not here, and I will speak of it no more tonight."

Shiva shrugged and turned to his pack and began shuffling aside, his casual indifference both confused and vexed Lennox. He'll get his answers sooner or later, the knight understood. He's in no hurry.

A moment later Shiva pulled out two large strips of salted beef and a small loaf of stale bread. He returned to his pack and pulled out a small block of hard cheese to round off the meal. He held out the block of cheese to Lennox but the knight shook his head no.

"Do you even eat food?" he asked.

"No," Lennox answered.

Shiva nodded and produced a small dagger from his belt and began to cut the cheese into small slices that he placed on the bread and ate together. Afterward he checked his cloak and was pleased to find it dry. "Do you sleep?" he asked turning to face Lennox.

Lennox shook his head.

Shiva eyed him sharply. Then he laughed, a quick short laugh of amusement that came bursting out his mouth. He shook his head as the laugh turned into a smile. "Well ... we need not draw lots for the watch then. The night is yours, and you have sharp eyes too! I might just sleep well tonight." He had rolled his cloak into a ball and set it under his head as he lay out before the fire, happy for its warmth. "Keep watch for the girl. I suspect she'll make her return sooner or later."

The girl ... he had not forgotten about the girl. "I thought perhaps she may have left us," Lennox replied.

"Ha! We all serve Mistress Sune, Sir Knight, the girl most of all. She'll return, and you need not fear her wolves. She has them well trained." He turned his head to the fire. "She's half wolf herself that one, a pure-blood from the northern clans across the Slinder Sea ... not like these vagabonds that fill these cursed mountains."

"Does Kay still stand?" Lennox asked; eager to hear of the outside world.

"So the norther folk say," Shiva replied. "But the girl says the ice is spreading quickly and that half the city has been consumed by the cold and left abandoned. In another hundred years the entire city will be lost, in a thousand more the land as well."

"And what of the other Jewel Cities?"

The Wardens eyes perked up. He gazed across the fire with renewed curiosity, as though Lennox had just whispered some great secret. "Just how long where you imprisoned?"

After a lengthy span of silence Lennox answered. "A long time."

Shiva smiled.

He's a bit more cheerful now that we're out of that cursed mountain, Lennox observed. But then who wouldn't be.

"Mistress Sune told me about you, Sir Knight. Were you there when the taint fell upon Marshiel?"

"I suspected it would come," Lennox said gloomily. "But I was never there to see it." He was looking at the fire but his eyes were in the past. Shiva's words drew him back.

"Doom fell upon the city quickly once the taint appeared. A great judgment sent down by the Four. There are many tales of that day, many stories and legends, all grim … and only fragments are known, even to my mistress. But they all start with the taint. Some say it appeared suddenly, others that it crept in slowly, seeping up from out of the sewers like a morning fog.

"My mistress believes it happened slowly. First it was the beggars and orphan boys who lived in the sewers … little by little they disappeared, and the streets were cleaner than they had ever been. Others say it was the sewer castellans; they went into the depths of the city and never returned. No one truly knows. The disappearances continued and a calm fear fell across the city, even the king was no longer seen atop the white plateau.

"The young prince sent the Grey Cloaks down the dark tunnels and the next day the cursed men appeared in full, swelling up from the sewers like rats. Madness swept through the streets then, and the city fell to chaos. Many fled. Others stayed and fought just to fall and rise again cursed … either way, one day the city was alive and well, and the next it lay soiled and in ruins, where no man dared enter." Shiva fell quiet and a stillness filled the room, beside them the fire cracked softly against the stone walls.

"And … what followed after that?" asked Lennox.

Shiva looked across the flames and held his hands up in mystery. "The city collapsed into a great silence. No one came or went for a long time until the Black Iron King called forth the knights of Bedivere and raised an army in the hopes of purging the silent city. More is known of that catastrophe, but in the end the king failed, dying brilliantly in battle. Even now the knights of Bedivere don black iron suits and carry large kite shields with the king's crest engraved across the iron in honor of the fallen king. I slew one of their ranks in the undead cathedral, and even now you carry his shield."

The heavy shield stood leaning against the wall just behind Lennox. The iron was a dull black, and reflected little of the light that came forth from the fire leaving it dark and bleak against the damp stones of the cave. Even then, the engraving of the archtree stood out along the shield, its branches billowing out a thousand different ways along the top. "It is a strong and true shield," Lennox said. "I felt safe with it before me."

Shiva nodded.

Lennox continued. "And the other cities?"

"Solaire still stands, as well as Bedivere and Cataron. But cities are like rivers, they bend and change shape with time. I have stood before the guild halls of Solaire … old buildings made of strong stone, but I imagine they will not appear as you remember them. And the woods that were once said to surround the iron city are no more, cut down and used to fuel the iron mills … you'll find Cataron closest to how it once was. It is a city of sand and water; its people move but the city endures.

"As for Ector and Safier across the western waters … I cannot say. Their great ships stopped coming the day Marshiel fell. If Marshiel has become the silent city, then Andor has become the silent land. The common folk wouldn't even recognize the names of those ancient cities. No one goes west of the Rhon Sea, except to rummage through the silent city for treasure, or mad men who seek the Four to end the long silence."

Lennox rose to his feet. The horses had begun to whine and he wanted to see them up close. "A curse sent down by the Four," he said.

"Too true." Shiva answered with a smile. He lifted his gaze and watched the golden knight as he moved across the cave. "There are some oats in the satchel by the wood. If you're bored you could feed them." Lennox picked up the satchel and took out a handful of oats and offered them to the horses. Shiva dropped his head back down to his rolled-up cloak. "Keep watch for the girl."

"She is called Astrid, yes?" Lennox's asked.

"That was the name she gave me, though Mistress Sune says she has another." Shiva closed his eyes. "Storms pass quickly in these mountains, Sir Knight. The watch is yours. I expect we shall see the sun rising by the morrow."

Shortly after the warden was asleep. His chest rose and fell in silent waves. *Even in his sleep Shiva is as quiet as a phantom's shadow,* Lennox mused. *The man is an enigma. An assassin perhaps?* He would think on it. The Serpent's words burned in him like hot iron. *Just a pawn in their game … but a pawn can kill the king just the same.*

***

The storm had raged for ten days now, and every so often Lennox would let out a mocking laugh, mumbling something about storms passing quickly. At first, he had been upset at the storm; wishing to set his eyes upon the warm sun after so long a time only to be greeted by cold winds and white snow. But his anger had subsided quickly. He was a patient man. He had learned patience … been taught it well. He had learned to endure and persist, and it was as much a part of him as his own beating heart.

Sometimes the winds would soften and the snow would cease and the orange glow of the sun could be made out behind the gray and black clouds. But it was a false sky, and as quickly as the light came it would disappear.

All of the joy the big man may have shown upon leaving the Undead Cathedral had been stolen away by the cold. They talked little, and more than once Lennox caught the warden staring him down with his cold dark eyes, calculating eyes … hunter's eyes. He had known the type; he had seen them on an uncle once, long ago, so very long ago. But the Serpent's words … the creature said the warden smelled like a servant. It must be the ring. He played with his own oathkeeper ring, twisting it around his finger. I'm a servant too now, a slave in truth. Perhaps he should have denied the warden. Someone would have come, some hedge knight, some sellsword or treasure hunter. He had seen them come before, though he had failed to secure his release. Too late. He shook his head; he would think of it no more. He would pay the oracle's price and be done with her.

Not a night went by without the endless cry of howling wolves, large packs of roaming beasts. The storm meant little to them it seemed. Though they never got too close to the grotto.

The wolves' howls brought forth thoughts of Astrid. Her absence had not gone unnoticed, but if it bothered the warden, he kept it to himself. It seemed an inconvenience to him more than anything else, like he was waiting for her return so that they might finally depart.

The big man mostly kept to himself, honing his large scimitar with a wet stone from his pack, or checking the tension of his bow. Sometimes he would pull out the gargoyle's head and look it over with a small smile that touched the corners of his mouth and gleamed in his eyes. Hmm … I wonder how many prizes this man has taken? Lennox pondered the thought as he watched Shiva. For a moment he meant to ask, but in the end, he held his tongue and left the warden to his treasure.

He spent much of his time with the horses, just watching them. He enjoyed the creatures, but they seemed wary of the knight. Perhaps it was the way he smelled? He couldn't tell. The horses would stretch their necks past the gate to snatch the oats from his hand, but their trust ended there. They would shy away from his hand if he went to stroke their neck, and their distrust remained as strong for the knight on the tenth day, as it had the first.

He had hoped feeding them would put to rest their fears. It had not. Still … he was happy for the creatures.

Of the four white stallions, one stood out among the rest. He may not have liked Lennox, but he did not seem afraid of the Knight. He would take the oats freely and then leave as carelessly as he had come. Lennox found himself smiling as he watched the big horse. "Hmm… which is it?" He said the words aloud. "Do you not know fear? Or perhaps it's only the oats."

The horse looked away.

Lennox smiled. That one's smarter than he seems, he was certain of it. "Go on then, keep pretending you didn't hear me. We both know the truth." The trials will come soon enough.

He left the horses and returned to the fire, sitting on the ground with his back against the wall as he had been in his cell. It was a good fire, and he often found himself sitting alone beside the flames while the rest of the cave slept, letting the warmth spread throughout his armor and protect him from the cold chills that sometimes leapt through the stones.

He enjoyed the silence and closed his eyes as if to sleep. Though he did not sleep, did not dream, only recalled a past that he could not change.

It was a world of shadows, the past, half remembered in the corners of his mind. Details would turn to smoke if he didn't concentrate, or become black shadows lost completely in the far reaches in his mind. But the most precious memories, the ones that mattered were never far. He had etched them along the inside of his armor … in-between runes of magic and other enchantments where he could reach them at will.

Other memories he had locked away in his rings or etched onto the back of his great war shield that lay below the lake with the Lord's Tomes. They were important too, each and every memory a piece of lost knowledge waiting for him to reclaim.

But the memories that mattered never left him; they haunted him every time he closed his eyes.

***

"Finish it," the queen said as the blood pooled around her. "Lennox … end it!"

He looked at her through his narrow visor. The queen … his queen, draped in red from head to toe. The dead were everywhere, palace guards, struck down by the golden knight, pierced by his lightening spear. The tip of the blade dripped with blood and crackled blue with magic.

"Finish it!" she was screaming. "End it!" The words were a high shrill. She was holding onto the great Lord Shem, her red eyes a blaze of fire …

***

The soft crack of a burning log stole him away. He lifted his drooping head and inside his golden armor his chest tightened as he took in a short breath and held it.

Two wolves stalked across the cave, their eyes sharp and lips peeled back to show their large white fangs. They were silence wrapped in fur and moved slowly towards the fire. The larger of the two had smoke grey fur with yellow-gold eyes, the smaller was jet black and looked half a shadow, its eyes a pale green.

With as little movement as he could manage Lennox nudged at the warden with his foot. "Shiva," he whispered. "Wake up!" He kicked at the big man once more, this time striking at the back of the head.

Lennox saw the warden's head rise slightly. A moment later he spoke. "What happened to your sharp eyes, knight?"

The words had a sleepy tone to them, and Lennox wasn't sure if the big man was making some small jape, somehow, he didn't think so. Not with the wolves creeping closer and closer to the fire, their black shadows monsters on the wall behind them.

Shiva set his head back down onto his cloak. "Right then, she's finally back. Go and see if she needs any help."

Astrid … the girl has returned. Lennox eyed the wolves once more. They were watching him, the both of them, he was a stranger to them and his smell was queer, but the warden was there, and the fire was warm. They were not frightened of the knight, but when they reached the fire to lay down they had kept their heads up, and it wasn't until Lennox had reached the mouth of the cave that the smaller of the two finally closed its pale green eyes and nuzzled in close against the thick fur of the big grey wolf.

Outside the wind had ceased. It was one of the rare moments in the storm where the sun managed to break up the clouds and send its light streaming down across the woods below, but not far away Lennox could see the storm raging brutally.

An abnormal storm, Lennox thought.

He stepped out of the mouth of the cave and saw the girl standing beside a small sled with a large deer slung across the wood, its long body hung over the edges on both sides nearly touching the snow. She was on one knee with a short knife in her hand cutting at the rope. She looked big wrapped up in leathers and cloak, and was draped in a thick wolf skin pelt; but when she stood Lennox saw just how tall she was.

Not much shorter than myself, he thought as he made his way towards her. She turned and saw the golden knight approaching when their eyes met. The hood of her soft gray cloak shaded her face, but her blue eyes watched him cautiously. She looked calm, clutching her knife firmly.

"Hmm … hello, might I take you to be Lady Astrid?" Lennox asked.

She nodded slightly and looked him up and down, "The prisoner." It was not a question. She gestured towards the dead deer, "Grab the other side."

As Lennox stepped around the sled a great howl went up from the woods as a hundred wolves bellowed as one. The golden knight stopped and scanned the woods through his helm but the light was fading as the clouds above curled black. Astrid finished cutting the last rope and went to grab the deer. "Prisoner," she said again, loudly.

Lennox turned. "My lady, please … call me Lennox."

But Astrid was already reaching down, and Lennox moved quickly to assist her. He would be spending some time in the company of both the warden and this girl, best not to start off strained if it could be avoided.

They carried the deer inside and set it down beside the fire to thaw. Much of the carcass was frozen solid, hard as ice, with an inch of snow resting atop the body. Lennox brushed off the loose snow as Astrid went back for her sled. She left it at the mouth of the cave, and once back beside the flame, removed her large pelt, placing it on the same pile of logs Shiva had once used. Then she took off her cloak and dark brown leathers and set them by the pelt.

She was in only her wool undergarments now, they looked wet too but she kept them on. Lennox was grateful for that.

Well … she's hardly a girl at all. Lennox smiled as warm a smile as he could manage. Her hair was a light blonde, so fair it was almost white. It streamed, unconfined, in flowing waves down her back, despite having just been hidden behind a wet cloak. Her wolves stirred briefly before moving sleepily alongside their master as she took a seat beside the flames. They rested one on each side, before finally closing their eyes and falling back to sleep. The woman sat stroking the grey wolfs head as he laid it on her lap. "So, Shiva said you were a prisoner … "

Lennox wasn't sure if Astrid was making a statement or asking him a question. " … of sorts."

"What did you do?" Her voice was warm and surprisingly deep, but she did not smile, and her eyes were ice.

After a moment of thought Lennox answered. "It's difficult to say. I did a great many things, my lady, but no single one was why I ended up in that cell. It was a culmination, really."

"Did you steal?"

"I did."

"Did you murder?"

Again, Lennox kept silent for a moment as he considered the question. " … Is it murder if the men were armed?"

This time it was Astrid who paused, she eyed him uncertainly. "Was it a fair fight?"

"Never, when I am the foe." Lennox looked at her coldly. "But the men I killed had sword and shield in hand … and they could have run or yielded. I have never struck down a man who bent the knee."

Astrid's hand stroked the grey wolf's neck, her fingers running through the thick fur. "Yes, of course … I would not be presumptuous; I have only just met you."

Oh my, Lennox mused, what an audacious woman. It's almost insulting. She has not stopped judging me since the moment she laid eyes on me.

He grinned. "Well, let's not hold back our true thoughts. I have only just met you and I am certain that you are an unpleasant sort. And to you, I believe I am no more than a common thief … and perhaps a murderer." Astrid's face remained a dead pool, devoid of all emotion. Lennox continued. "But we are both servants of the Lady Sune." He had taken off his glove and was holding up his hand for her to see the ring.

"Our futures are murky, my lady, we need not be too friendly… but we do share common ground."

"Well spoken," she answered, irritated by the knight's bluntness. "What is it you propose then?"

"A partnership. We need not be friends, but we will be traveling together, and I would much prefer an amicable atmosphere over an air of mistrust and suspicion."

"Do you find it difficult for people to trust you?"

Lennox frowned. "You think me a common thief and murderer … I am not."

"Hmph, you sound like a knight. Very well. I see no reason to disagree with you. How might we seal this partnership?"

"With secrets," Lennox offered casually.

Astrid studied him warily. "What do you mean?"

He gave her a crooked smile. "Secrets, my lady. I mean exactly that. We need not be friends, but if we know something about one another … something we don't want shared, well, then we might begin to trust each other. A shaky trust, true, but a trust none the less."

"I suppose you wish me to speak first?"

"My lady, I wish nothing of the sort. I will go first, and you may determine the severity of my secret and choose your own accordingly … or share nothing at all if you like. At least then you will hold a secret over me, and I would be most grateful if you kept it safely locked inside your mind."

Shiva stirred by the fire. The two grew quiet and watched as he shifted his cape beneath his head and laid it back down gently.

"Shall we get started?" Lennox asked.

Astrid nodded her head slightly, but it was enough. He slipped off the silver ring that Faid had given him and watched her blue eyes grow wide. She inhaled a quick breath, then, a moment later; her face was calm again.

"It's not the taint," he said dully.

Astrid said nothing, her eyes fastened to his decrepit face.

The silver ring sat in his open palm. He leaned forward to examine it under the firelight. "But the mark is similar, and it's not something I want known." The red flames flickered across the smooth silver, its yellow sapphires burning orange. It was a wicked looking ring Lennox knew. He slipped it back on and looked towards Astrid. "The ring offers me a small disguise, but my touch is still cold … my skin rotten and failing."

"You say it is not the taint. Why are you a corpse then?"

"A good question," Lennox said, "but I've told you one secret already. I don't need to tell you a second."

The lady nodded. "Of course, another time perhaps?"

"Perhaps."

"Very well. I suppose you want a secret of my own."

"Just one, and only if you wish to tell it."

"A secret of equal, severity … as you put it."

Lennox shrugged.

Astrid glanced at the warden. "What has he told you?"

"Only that you are a pureblood of the north, and that Astrid is not your true name."

"My true name." She replied. "Sad, isn't it? When one must hide themselves under falsities."

"What are you hiding from?"

"That's not the secret I wish to tell you. You showed me what you truly are, I will tell you who I really am. My name is Lyanna of Kay, the bastard daughter of King Kaster of the northern lands."

In a golden flash Lennox was kneeling before the fire and taking Astrid's hand into his own. His swiftness startled the lady, and a moment later he kissed her ring. The same oathkeeper ring he bore on his left hand.

"My lady, your father is a king. Then you are a princess. I'm sorry for my crude words earlier."

Surprised, she let her hand linger in his own. "I am a bastard's daughter. Many say I am no true princess."

"Kings and queens, princes and princesses … you are what you make yourself to be, my lady." And with that he let go the lady's hand, turned, and went back to his seat. Another log cracked and crumbled, tossing the flames high and casting a burning light across his golden armor. He smiled, and for just a moment, hidden beneath the illusion of his ring, Lennox of Marshiel looked as true a knight that Astrid had ever seen.

5

I T had been ages since Lennox had last ridden a horse, but the stallion he now sat was well trained and the motions returned quickly. They had been five days traveling, but at some point, the mountain paths had turned into no more than game trails, easily lost beneath mountain snows. Still. Astrid knew the ways, and they rarely got lost or had to double back.

The storm had passed but the skies were gray. Most of the time the sun remained hidden from view, but sometimes at mid-day its rays would pierce through the clouds, lighting up the mountain range and surrounding woods. It was nice. Lennox would always stop then and let the warm rays knock back some of the cold that crept in through his armor.

"Speed is of great concern here in these woods," Shiva said as he passed by atop his horse. "We cannot stop every time the sun appears. We have spent too long in these lands as it is."

True to his words, he moved on quickly, pushing his horse to a trot. Lennox picked up his reins and turned his horse when Astrid rode up beside him.

" … I would not name him a patient man."

Lennox watched the warden as he rode off before them. "Oh? I'm not so sure of that. I believe he knows how to wait, when waiting is needed. Just as I believe he knows how to move, when moving is called for. That storm kept us trapped for some time."

Astrid laughed contemptuously. "He wishes to return to his women."

"The Lady Sune?" Lennox said. "He is bound to her as we are bound.

He wears the oathkeeper ring."

"Yes, he wears the ring … but he is not like us." Astrid turned her head, her cold eyes shone beneath her gray hood. "I've watched you, Sir Knight, seen you staring into the fires as you fiddle with your ring. We are her slaves. He serves willingly. I think he loves her."

Lennox remembered the serpent's words. The scent of a servant … that is what Faid had said.

"Humh, he is a wild man," Lennox answered. "He lives to hunt and kill. He is calm enough now, but his eyes." Lennox shook his head. "He has no room in him to love a woman."

"Think what you will. Either way he is unlike us. It would be wise to remember that."

"I will, thank you." He smiled beneath his helm, his tone suddenly cheerful. "See? This trust of ours is already producing rewards. Tell me. Do you know much of our fourth companion, Prince Oscar?"

"The boy prince." She spoke with distain, her mouth tight with disapproval; but Lennox saw a flicker in her eyes, something soft.

Well … that's odd, he thought, and continued on. "The boy is five and ten, I am told. Closer to a man than a boy at that age I would think."

"Not in the north," was all she said.

They were falling behind so Astrid gave her steed the reins and kicked into a slow gallop, Lennox followed after. They gained on Shiva quickly and soon were at his side before falling back into a trot.

They had been riding down narrow paths and thick forests for two days, and Lennox was relieved to see they were finally approaching a proper pathway. It was not the paved marble streets of Marshiel, nor the tightly packed bricks of Bedivere … not even the cobblestone roads of Solaire. The path was nothing of the sort; barely wide enough for a wagon. The dirt was a mix of mud and snow, but the trees were somewhat cut back, and it ran straight enough.

"I should think we'll make better time now," Lennox offered as he led his stallion around a newly fallen pine thick with brush. He jumped the cracked stump and emerged onto the road.

"No," Astrid answered. "It will only grow more dangerous now. At least until we clear the woods."

Lennox gave Astrid an inquiring look. "We're well below the drowned city now, well away from the taint."

It was Shiva who answered. "It's not the taint we're thinking of. Further south the merchant road is well traveled and kept safe by the guilds. This path is used by the mountain clans, but not often. There is not enough commerce for the guilds to keep patrols and clean out the thieves. Many believe that retched band of filches keep their stronghold here among these woods."

"It's not just the thieves," Astrid commented. "We're clear of the taint, true, but the cursed wander this entire forest none the less, thousands of them, hollows that stumble down from the drowned city. Some of them are as old as the cursed forest, their shields still bearing the hammer of the mountain city. Their armor is strong and well enchanted with old magic. It is greatly prized among the clans."

"There rarely are more than two or three together," Shiva said. "They are nothing to fear if you have good eyes." He shot Lennox a flat look. "Easily avoided."

Astried nodded. "I agree, but they are too dangerous to be ignored altogether."

Lennox looked out through his helm. The mountain trails had led them south and then east, cutting through narrow pathways in the stones before finally setting them on the eastern bank of the mountain range. There they had broken away from the high trails and began their descent. After that it had been two more days of slow travel before finally emerging in the heart of the woods. But something had felt wrong for some time now, ever since their descent.

It's still so cold, he thought. This shouldn't be.

The snows had stopped falling, leaving behind towering columns of white that swayed as the wind blew across the tops of the pines. He lifted up his visor, confused at what he saw.

"We should be well below the snowline now. How much further to warmer lands?" He turned just in time to see an uneasy glance pass between Astrid and Shiva. "Well ... that does not bode well. Tell me quickly and have it done with."

"This forest has been frozen ever since the drowned city first fell more than a thousand years ago," Astrid answered.

"A remnant of the tainted waters above," Shiva added sourly. "Not enough to corrupt life, but a cold mark none the less. We will not be warm until we're east of the woods. By then we will be close to Solaire."

With a sigh Lennox turned his steed so that he sat facing the warden. For the first time since his release he felt tired. He felt dirty too, and wanted a bath. He wanted to be clean and warm, but no … he would not remove his armor. He would not even think it. He would endure, he would always endure.

Even so, with his visor up, it was clear Lennox was agitated. "If this road is as cold and as dangerous as you say … why do we not just travel around it? Why not follow the mountain trails north and take a boat across the sea to Solaire?"

Shiva shook his head and muttered some curse under his breath before answering. "There are no more towns along the mountain coasts. When Barra fell, the coastal towns had no one to ferry. And when the cursed began to wander down from the mountains the people either moved to Solaire, or sailed to the northern lands."

Lennox turned away, frustrated with the world around him. "And south?" he asked. "Why not travel south around the forest?"

Shiva shook his head. "It would take us weeks out of the way."

"Weeks?" Lennox scoffed. He looked up at the cold gray sky and then back as Shiva. "I have been locked away for a millennia … why must I risk thieves and the undead? Young Oscar can wait, what are a few more weeks but a breath of time to me?"

"You swore an oath to serve."

"Aye, I swore an oath to serve … to serve your oracle, your Lady Sune. And I will. But she's in Cataron. So, it seems to me that I'm heading the wrong way."

Shiva shifted noiselessly in his saddle, his hand resting gently on the pommel of his scimitar. "I was told to move quickly … and that I was not to return until I had retrieved all three of the lady's retainers."

"Retainers." Lennox repeated the word and let it hang in the cold air. He eyed Shiva crossly, suddenly angry. "Carful warden, I thought you were wiser than this."

The warning meant nothing to Shiva. He sat like a statue; his face cold … his eyes beginning to shine.

An uneasiness grew in Lennox's gut, churning his stomach; but a line had to be drawn, and sooner rather than later. If it came to a fight could he win? The knight was unsure. He needs me, Lennox knew. He will not fight to kill.

"Hmph, are you two so foolish as to come to blows here and now, deep in the forest with no camp set and the sun beginning to fade?" Astrid pressed her horse between the two men. Pushing back her hood, her eyes furrowed with displeasure. "We don't have time for this nonsense!" She looked to Lennox. "This is not a fight worth your time."

The knight looked curious.

"We're halfway through the woods already; its two days back to the mountain, or two days east to the clearing. What difference does it make now?"

None, Lennox realized. He tilted his head slowly; keeping his eyes locked on the warden before holding up his hands in a playful manner. "You're right," he said in a casual tone. He flashed both Shiva and Astrid a quizzical grin. "I apologize for being … difficult. I've been alone a rather long time."

Shiva was quiet for a moment, and then nodded stiffly. The glimmer in his eyes dwindled, but his hand remained atop his sword.

Lennox eyed the blade once more, wondering.

Astrid took up her reins hoping it was settled. "Once we're clear of the path we'll set up camp." She had already turned her mount and was leading the horse down a small slope that ran along the road.

Lennox followed behind; all tension seemingly washed away as he carefully led his horse along the narrow tread Astrid had created in the snow. The trees were thick with white, but the ground remained more or less traversable, with the snow only ankle high off the ground.

It wasn't until Lennox's back was turned and he was half way down the slope that Shiva finally removed his hand from his blade. He watched the knight with a cold expression, his face a mask of tranquility. At last he followed after, bringing up the rear.

***

A half span from the road they found Astrid's two wolves sitting in a small clearing of tall pines, their branches so thick and intertwined that the ground beneath was all but dry, with only small patches of snow encroaching along the edges. The two beasts seemed to have been waiting for their master and the black one's tale shook with joy upon seeing her. Astrid seemed pleased as well, and dismounted quickly as the two rose to meet her.

It was a fine moment and Lennox watched intently, she looked softer than the first day he had met her. If only the same could be said about the warden.

"I had not seen them for days," he said. "I thought perhaps they had left us."

"These two," Astrid said with a laugh. "I think not. They have barely left our sight since we entered the forest."

Lennox seemed troubled by the words.

The women only smiled. "Don't worry; I doubt the warden knew as well."

Shiva made no attempt to argue as he dismounted from his steed and tied him to a tree.

Astrid knelt down, running her hands through the black fur of the young wolf. "This is their home, Sir Knight. The woods and trees and snow, this is where they were born. They know it better than we ever will."

"Hmm … are there any packs we should be worried about?"

Astrid shook her head. She looked as though she might say more but kept it to herself.

"I'll brush the horses down," Lennox offered. "You two should rest."

Neither of them argued. They shared a meager meal of bread and cheese, and finished off the rest of Astrid's deer before curling up beside the smallest fire the knight had ever seen. Hardly more than a pile of embers, but it was better than nothing he supposed.

The cold was different for him. It was a discomfort, but it couldn't kill him. It could hardly slow him down for that matter. Still … as night fell, he found himself sitting before the embers, one leg crossed beneath him as he leaned against the other. The dying flames burning against his golden armor.

He had taken off his helm and set it beside the flames and watched as it glowed warm in the firelight. Shiva was fast asleep, a silent specter beneath his black cloak. If Lennox had not seen the smallest rising and falling of the man's chest, he would have sworn the warden dead.

Astrid had taken longer. She had spent some time sitting beside the fire with her wolves, running her hands along their necks and feeding them treats from her sack; but soon enough she lay sleeping before the flame, a wolf nuzzled up beside her on either side.

Night carried on in a perfect stillness and Lennox enjoyed the silence. He was used to silence. He knew it well, and he liked it. But he knew its dangers, he had drunk them deeply. There were stretches in his cell where he had had no guard, and was left alone with himself. In some of the longer stretches, being alone had nearly driven him mad. Man is too splintered to be anything but bad company with himself ... but another knight would always come and fall to the beast above and return to him hollow, his new guardsman. Lennox remembered their faces, all of them, if not their names. He saw them sometimes when he closed his eyes. He saw them now. They had been his salvation. He had been left alone for so long, but to be left alone is not always to be forsaken. The Creator had seen him ... seen and provided. It was a comforting thought, and it made him smile.

Sitting beside the fire, Lennox watched as Marrok lifted his head and gazed out into the woods. The wolfs ears perked up as he looked out among the trees and drifting snow. Lennox turned towards the woods but all he could hear was the soft crackling of the flame.

"Hmph ... did you hear something?" he asked looking towards the beast.

A moment later Zev lifted her head as well and stared out alongside her brother.

"Blood and ash," Lennox muttered as he reached for his helm and placed it on his head. He took up his kite shield and turned to face the trees where the wolves were looking. He stood there for a long time ... him and the wolves, ever watchful. On impulse he took a step forward, his hand tightening on the grip of his shield.

A flicker of motion caught his eye and he froze where he stood, his shield half raised in defense. The light from the fire barely reached the closest trees, beyond that, shadows filled the air. He scowled beneath his helm, utterly aware now of just how vulnerable they were.

Curse the light, he thought as he eyed the flame. A fool's error!

The movement came again, this time the black shadow stood out clear against the darkness, but only for a moment before vanishing once more. Strangely, Lennox found his throat grow dry as he waited in the stillness. He was uneasy, his breath steaming out from the slit in his helm.

Marrok had risen up and was now standing beside the golden knight, his large ears perked up to listen. Zev had stayed where she was, but her eyes still searched the surrounding woods. They did not seem scared; not as far as Lennox could tell … more like they were unsure, curious even.

At last Marrok made his way to the edge of their camp just along the tree line where the firelight ended and true darkness began. The large wolf stopped then and turned back to Lennox. He looked as though he wanted the knight to follow him.

This was a dangerous place; Lennox knew that now. The trees before him bathed their great heads in the waves of the surrounding darkness while their roots where planted deep in gloom, and all around, firelight flickered against the rich brown of the decayed leaves and fallen pine-cones.

How far has the taint spread its misery? There was a time when he knew this world … but no more.

I am ready, he thought.

He turned towards Zev and said, "Keep watch," then followed Marrok away from the camp and into the woods.

The knight moved slowly at first, every step carefully placed so as not to trip on some unseen root. The wolf moved much quicker, but always stayed near, his shape never lost upon the knight.

Slowly, step by step, the campfire began to fade, its shy glimmer lost behind the trees, and as the distance grew his eyes began to adjust to the darkness. Every so often the trees would open up to a cloudless sky. The stars burned bright and the moon most of all, but the woods were thick, and the branches would return, reaching out to quickly block what little light the moon and stars offered.

A silent breeze flowed through the woods, a cold draft that chilled the bone; and with no fire to cut the cold the knight found himself shaking if he stood still for too long.

Even after his eyes had adjusted it was difficult to see. Many of the trees were heavy with snow and Lennox had to crouch low and trudge through thick slush to follow after Marrok. The wolf seamed to cover twice as much ground as the knight, his gray fur folding into the shadows to scout what lay before them, or dropping behind to sniff at some missed scent. It was all the knight could do but follow, moving slowly when the beast moved, pausing when the beast paused ... his eyes always searching set deep within his helm.

After what seemed like hours, Lennox finally had to stop. Marrok disappeared and reappeared in the distance, and when it was clear that the knight was not going to follow the wolf drew close.

"No more," the knight said aloud, as though the wolf could understand. "We've gone further than I would have liked as is."

The wolf patted even closer then, his large paws leaving behind a small trail in the snow. He looked up at the knight, his gold eyes shimmering, and then bent low as if to nod.

Lennox stood silent for a moment; then nodded back.

The trip back seemed to take twice as long. As before, Marrok would scout ahead, disappearing and reappearing like the stars and moon above.

The wind stiffened as the long night stretched forth. Lennox was beginning to grow restless having seen no sign of camp; but Marrok kept on, keeping the knight barely in view. He cursed under his breath with every step, and was beginning to doubt the beast's intelligence when he suddenly emerged into a clearing and saw the wolf far off, standing at the base of a large archtree.

Marrok turned briefly, glancing at the knight before turning once more to the tree.

"Well ... you certainly found something here, didn't you?"

The ground was thick with humus, its dark soil swallowing the sound of Lennox's steps as he made his way across. There was a deep scent of moist earth and decay, and the trees that grew were few and scattered, old sentinels, and mighty oaks. And at the center of them all a massive archtree ... twice as tall as the tallest pine, its branches wide and thick, twisting together up into the sky and weaving a dense canopy overhead.

It was an old grove set in the heart of the forest. Strange, that none of the pines had spread throughout the soil. Lennox frowned as he tilted his head back to take in the massive archtree.

The tree's bark was bitter black, its leaves a shimmering white, hidden now by the snow. They had once ruled all the world, their branches stretching from coast to coast, but no more, not for a long time now. The last remnants of an age long past. It made him sad ... his shoulders fell as he let out a sigh.

The tree only grew in size as he approached; nearly nine meters in diameter as best he could tell, with large boulders set all around it. The clearing was a quiet place; peaceful, the very air seemed warmer as it swirled around the knight.

Beside the trunk of the archtree surrounded by ancient stones, all noise seemed to disappear. "There is magic here," Lennox found himself saying aloud.

Marrok turned once more, looking at the knight briefly before turning back to the tree.

Then Lennox saw it, an emblem carved deep into the bark of the tree, two crescent moons perched against a full moon set in black.

His eyes widened as he took a step back, away from the tree; then he stiffened defiantly. "Is this what you wanted to show me?" he said looking at the wolf. Marrok bent his head low once more. Lennox understood. He nodded back. "Were leaving," he said, and turned his back to the tree.

He saw them instantly, two men walking like ghosts across the clearing. They made no sound, but took no effort to hide themselves either as they moved, weapons drawn, towards Lennox and the wolf.

Both men were clad in full armor that shined red like dirty brass, their helms shaped like beasts of the field. The taller of the two stood near eight feet tall and wielded a giant hammer. He was fat too, unimaginably fat. The shorter man was more Lennox's height, and held a curved scimitar in his right hand, much like the one Shiva wielded, and in his left was a short rapier.

"Halt!" Lennox called out. "And lower thy weapons!"

The men moved forward, untouched by Lennox's words.

"Alas," he muttered. "How easily things go wrong." He tightened his grip along his kite shield and strode quickly to meet them. He didn't want to get trapped with his back against the archtree. To his great relief he saw Marrok striding beside him as he moved out from the base of the tree.

"I said halt!" Lennox tried once more.

Again, the men ignored his call.

"Fine then, so be it!"

He moved first, darting towards the fat one, hoping to get close quickly; but the hammer swung wide and fast, faster than he imagined it could be swung. He backed off quickly, barely managing to dodge the blow. The short one came after him then, cutting downward with his scimitar. Lennox took the blow with his shield and jerked back, just in time to avoid a piercing strike from the rapier. Lennox circled to his left, hoping desperately to keep from being surrounded. The short knight followed after, slashing with his scimitar, but Lennox danced away, dodging each blow as they came.

It was difficult fighting a man when you could not see his face, it made them harder to read, and was half the reason Lennox wore a helm himself. The short knight was quick, slashing and thrusting one blow after another, trying for Sir Lennox's legs but falling short. Lennox dodged them all, or blocked the blows he could not avoid.

At last he managed to put some distance between them, and took a moment to really look at his opponents, only for a moment, that's all he had. The short knight's helm was forged in the shape of a jackal, Lennox thought it fitting. The jackal was his main foe it seemed; the big knight only swung his hammer when Lennox went on the offensive.

Marrok hovered close to the fighters, his fur bristling and teeth bared. The wolf was crouched low, trying desperately to lunge at his foes and sink his claws into their flesh, but every time he drew close the fat one would swing his long hammer, pushing the beast back.

Lennox continued left, side stepping across the soft soil, placing each foot carefully on the uneven ground. The two knights watched him with indifferent eyes, the jackal and the glutton. Something about how they moved reminded Lennox of the hollows back at the cathedral.

That cannot be, he thought. They work too well together, each of them moving to protect the other. He clenched his teeth inside his helm. "Blood and ash!" he yelled. They're too smart to be hollows!

Beside him Marrok growled deep and low before barking loudly.

Lennox was strong and his armor light … but without his rings he would tire soon enough. He had to separate them by some means, but how? He eyed the jackal and pressed forward, swinging his flail at the small knight. This time the jackal stood his ground, catching Lennox's flail with his sword before thrusting once more with his rapier. Lennox let go his flail and danced back, narrowly avoiding the blow.

The jackal hesitated for a moment, surprised maybe that Lennox had evaded him. He turned to face the golden knight as Lennox drew his dagger.

Still moving left, Lennox circled the two men. Marrok moved opposite the golden knight, circling towards the glutton, hoping to separate them, if only a little bit. The giant man eyed the beast but kept his focus on Lennox.

Clever wolf, Lennox thought; still circling, always moving. He made one more attempt at speaking to his foes. "Your names, Sirs? I would know the names of my foes."

"Heh heh heh." The gluttons laugh was long and deep, his whole body shaking. There was no other reply.

Certainly not hollows, Lennox knew at once. He had never heard the undead laugh.

The jackal was matching Lennox's stride step for step when suddenly Lennox stopped and instead pushed backwards. The jackal lunged, slashing down with his scimitar. Lennox took the blow on his shield and ducked low, sidestepping between the jackal and the glutton just as Marrok lunged for the giant man's feet. The glutton grunted as he swung his heavy hammer down. Marrok jumped back, escaping the blow with ease. The glutton turned back, swinging his hammer in a wide arc towards the golden knight.

Lennox knew the blow was coming; he threw his dagger at the jackal's face before diving to the ground. The jackal struck at the dagger with his scimitar, tossing it to the floor just as the glutton's hammer took him from the side. The small knight managed to raise his arm in defense just as the hammer struck, crushing the thin lobstered metal that protected his elbow in a loud crunch before beating into his side and sending him flying to the ground in a twist of metal and bones.

The glutton pressed forward, showing no remorse for his fallen comrade. He raised his hammer up for another strike … and then Marrok was on him, bearing him down. He twisted around and kicked at the wolf before losing his balance and falling to the ground with a shout.

Lennox took up the jackal's fallen rapier and ran forward, falling to one knee as he grabbed at the glutton's helm and pushed it to the side revealing a small unprotected spot of flesh. He drove the rapier forward, leaning into the sword with all his weight until the blade was half-way into the glutton's chest. The giant man shuddered and lay still.

Lennox fell away, silent except for his labored breathing. He looked over towards the jackal, but the knight lay unmoving, his body broken near in half.

Marrok stood beside the glutton's corpse, teeth bared, waiting to see if the man would rise. When enough time had passed, he left the glutton and moved to the smaller man and began sniffing at the body. Lennox was about to call out to him when the wolf bent down and tore into the jackal's throat. That put to rest any thoughts that the man was still alive.

"Well fought," Lennox said as Marrok padded his way across the soil to where the golden knight rested. He took off his golden helm and placed it to his side before turning to the wolf. Marrok flinched slightly as Lennox reached out and laid his hand atop his head. "Thank you … sincerely. If I can, I will repay you for this."

The wolf looked back at Lennox, and the knight was sure he understood.

Lennox smiled.

He patted Marrok warmly along his neck and took one more look at the jackal and the glutton before picking himself up off the ground. He slung his shield across his back and tucked his helm under his arm, moving then towards his flail that lay half buried in the hummus.

He picked it up and turned towards Marrok. "Right then," he said. "Let's head back. It will be morning soon."

The wolf's ears perked up and he was off, bounding into the snowy woods, away from the archtree and back into the frigid forest. With a sigh Lennox shifted his shield atop his back and followed after.

6

BOTH Shiva and Astrid were awake when Lennox returned to where they had set camp. The clouds were clear for the first time in days and the sun was just cresting in the sky, its golden rays flooding through the frozen trees. Nothing moved as he peered out through the woods. The morning was cold and peaceful.

It was strange to Lennox how different the woods looked during the day. The gloom seemed to be lifted away with the morning light, but some of the magic was gone as well. He frowned slightly beneath his helm.

Shiva watched him emerge from the brush, his hand resting atop his hilt; his face stark, his eyes grim. Astrid seemed less interested. She was gathering the saddles and placing them upon the horses. The stallions watched her with sleepy surprise. She spoke to them quietly and made soothing noises as she tightened the girth straps and loaded what little remained of their supplies. They accepted the extra weight with little fuss.

"Well … " Lennox began. "I hope the two of you managed to get some rest. I had a rather unpleasant night myself."

"I find it difficult to rest when the man on watch proves himself lacking." Shiva's tone seeped with disapproval. "Letting the wolves sneak up on you in the cave I can forgive … but abandoning us altogether? We would have been easy prey had ghouls or thieves fallen on us."

"Oh? I'm not so sure about that. Zev was here when I left, and she's ten times the guard any one of us could be." The warden gave Lennox a hard look but said nothing, and behind him Lennox saw Astrid glance

81

towards him with a pleased expression. "That aside," he continued. "Why do you think I left in the first place, huh?"

The warden shifted coldly but remained silent.

"A situation has developed."

An unpleasant expression darted across Shiva's face. It was gone as quickly as it came, leaving him outwardly calm, though his displeasure was clear. "What is this situation?"

"I'll show you."

***

Before they set out Shiva went over the campsite inch by inch to make sure there was no sign that anyone had ever been there. He righted any overturned rocks and quieted the fire, making sure to spread out the remaining ashes. He did it all quickly, taking only a few minutes, but they did not leave until he was satisfied and the ground looked untouched.

Marrok lead then, taking them through small trails of snow and slush, weaving his way through a maze of trees and thick brush until at last they caught a glimpse of the towering archtree in the distance. During the night the sky was black, hiding the mighty tree as it stretched its branches out into the air, but in the light of day the tree could be seen a mile out. Marrok quickly disappeared then, and they were left to weave the rest of the way themselves.

By the time they reached the clearing gray clouds ruled the sky. The last rays of sunlight dwindled into nothing and a cold breeze began to blow through the trees.

A pity, Lennox thought. He was tired of being cold.

In the daylight he could see it all. The clearing was a perfect circle with the towering archtree standing square in the center. The smell of earth and decay was heavy, and the dark humus stood out in stark contrast to the white snow of the surrounding woods. There were a few trees interspersed throughout the clearing, but beside that it was open land.

"Where is the snow?" Shiva asked aloud.

Lennox gestured to the archtree. "There is magic in the tree … it keeps the land warm and the soil alive with life."

"What is this place?" Astrid asked speaking up.

"A garden," Lennox answered.

"This does not look like any garden I've seen."

"I'm not surprised. This land was crafted by the giants before the war destroyed them. With no one left to cultivate the land, they quickly disappeared … except for a very few. It is said Armaros himself set the wards, protecting the archtrees and preserving the legacy of the giants." He smiled sadly inside his helm as he looked once more upon the massive tree. "This might very well be the last living garden of the giants … and now it's been tainted." He said the last words quietly to himself as he kicked his horse forward. The others quickly followed after.

The bodies of the two men Lennox had slain lay sprawled out across the earth, their forms settling into the soil where they rested. The jackal was on his side, half broken, wrapped in twisted and warped metal; the glutton on his back, the rapier sticking up from the side of his neck. They were as Lennox had left them.

"Why, look at you!" Shiva said as they drew near. "Hunting alone in the middle of the night. I can't say I approve … though, I would have done the same." He was smiling as he spoke, the joy of the hunt clear by his expression. He pushed ahead, eager to reach the fallen knights. "The fat one must be three meters tall," he called back.

Lennox turned towards Astrid.

The women's eyes were fierce, her face displeased with what she saw.

"You are familiar with these men?" he asked.

"Perhaps," was all she said.

They continued forward towards Shiva who had already dismounted for a closer look, tying off his stallion to a nearby oak. They followed suit, dismounting from their rides before tying them off together. Even in her mute state, Astrid's eyes searched all around them, staring out across the clearing as if there was something to see except the same cold forest they'd been traveling through day after day. If she did see anything, it evaded Lennox.

He eyed the two men cautiously as he approached, raising his visor for a better look. Their armor looked faded to him somehow. In the heart of night as they fought, their rust red armor almost seemed to glow, as though the men themselves had been wrapped in embers. Now it looked pale and dead, as lifeless as the men it once protected.

"Sir knight," Shiva called out, still smiling, waving for Lennox to come to him. "You'll want to see this."

A deep knot began to form in Lennox's stomach. He mistrusted Shiva's smile.

"Just here." Shiva said pointing. He was on one knee cradling the jackal's helm in his hand and twisting the head so that the sigil could be seen clearly. "These are his servants ... the Darkmoon Alchemist. This is his sigil, yes?"

The crest was etched into the back of the jackal's helm, a perfect match to the marking set in the archtree. Lennox inhaled quickly, surprised at his own foolishness. He turned and strode towards the glutton, bending down to examine the fat man's helm. He found nothing. Unsatisfied, he grabbed at the rapier pushing it forward with all his might, hoping to turn the glutton's head. When nothing happened, he called out to Shiva for help. With the two of them together they managed to turn the body enough for Lennox to grab the helmet and lift it clear of the hummus. He turned the head sideways before letting go. The heavy helm hit the earth with a thud, and the Darkmoon's sigil showed clearly on the glutton's forehead.

He stepped away, looking once more at the jackal's twisted body with furrowed eyes. He was breathing deeply, and was angry. He had suspected, but to see the Darkmoon's sigil so blatantly imbedded on the archtree and in the knight's armor ... it was troubling.

He retrieved the rapier from the glutton's head, tugging at it several times before it finally came loose. Both Astrid and Shiva watched him with curious eyes but kept quiet. With the rapier in hand he made his way to the archtree, pausing only a moment before plunging the swords tip into the etching on the tree. Piercing the black moon with the blade as he called out old words from an ancient tongue. "Emundationem Lucem!"

The world went white as light spilled fourth from the pierced tree, a striking blast, as bright as the sun but without the heat ... momentarily blinding all who gazed upon it. Large clusters of smoke followed, billowing out in clumps of dark death. They engulfed Lennox, blocking him from sight as he clutched at the rapier and screamed out another spell.

The building chaos only grew, until, all at once, the light retreated and the earth grew silent.

For a time, no one moved, and a resting stillness fell upon the woods. "Sir Knight!" Astrid called out, taking a step.

"Wait," Shiva said taking her by the wrist "Don't go into the smoke." She hesitated, looking back into the thick cloud of black. She went to move forward. "Stop it I said. He just broke a curse, a powerful one. That smoke could kill you if you breathe it in, or worse."

With great hesitation, she relented.

The warden released his grip and together they waited, watching as the smoke hovered about the archtree like a morning mist, until, at last, it began to dissipate, and the smallest glimpses of Lennox's golden armor could be seen twinkling through the smoke. He was kneeling with his head bent low, his armor rising and falling in slow rolling breaths. Astrid watched nervously, when, to her great surprise, Lennox rose. She could see it was difficult for him, his hunched shoulders and heavy head seemed to way him down until finally he took off his helm and let it fall to the ground as he emerged from the thinning smoke.

It was Shiva who met him first, taking his arm and resting it along his shoulders as he helped the knight away from the archtree towards one of the smaller oaks. "No need to go quick, Sir knight" he said before helping Lennox to the ground and leaning him against the trunk of the tree.

Lennox sat there for some time, sitting in a somber and crestfallen daze, his face troubled. He shook his head, his long hair dripping with sweat. The cold returned quickly, but he didn't mind. He drew in on himself, saying nothing.

His companions waited as well, watching the golden knight ... waiting for him to come back. For once Shiva looked concerned, and after a time the warden knelt beside the knight and took him by the chin, turning his head gently. Shiva's mouth tightened, but when he spoke, all he said was, "Can you ride?"

Some sort of understanding returned to Lennox then. His eyes rolled to Astrid and then back to the warden before nodding yes.

Shiva seemed pleased, and nodded back. "You poor fool ... Ha!" He patted Lennox on the shoulder and rose. "Astrid, we need to leave. Gather his helm, I'll retrieve the horses."

The black smoke and ash that surrounded the archtree was all but gone. Astrid moved quickly just the same, snatching the golden helm from the dark soil and returning to Lennox. He looked worn down, pale with sweat, but his eyes were present and bright. She knelt beside him, placing the helm in his lap.

He chuckled, "Thank you." He held the helm in his hands, gazing down into the empty visor. "I don't remember losing it."

"You were having trouble breathing … after taking in so much of that foul smoke."

He nodded as though he already knew. "Yes, well. It was a foolish work, but it needed to be done."

"I don't understand. Why risk yourself breaking the curse … and who is this, Darkmoon Alchemist, Shiva keeps speaking of?"

Lennox blinked in surprise. She had recognized the two knights, he was certain of that, yet she knew nothing of the Darkmoon Alchemist. What is her part in this?

"Those men," he said gesturing to the dead knights. "You know them. Don't deny it."

"I can't be sure," She answered.

"You can, and you are. Now tell me."

"I can't!" She said. "You assume too much. I have never seen those men."

"As you say, my lady, but you know them none the less, yes?" He watched her eyes closely, watched as doubt crept in.

"I told you," she started, her words softer this time. "I don't know, but … their armor … their masks." She shook her head, her eyes stern. "I cannot say. My father would not approve."

"My lady. You have obligations to fulfill, as do I, else I would not have put on this oathkeeper ring. But there is no reason we can't help each other in these tasks, even if only a little. Tell me what you know of these men, and I will do the same."

Astrid paused, her eyes shifting towards Shiva for a brief moment. "Very well, but later. The warden knows too much already. I wish to keep this from him. Consider it another secret between allies."

Lennox chuckled deep in his throat, a tired laugh. "Of course, my lady, nothing would please me more. When the moment presents itself, we shall speak on the matter."

Satisfied, Astrid gave a curt nod just as Shiva appeared atop his stallion leading the horses towards the small oak. "It's time," he called out. "It would be unwise for us to delay any longer."

"Of course," Lennox said with a nod, sounding as if he had found a second wind. He placed his helm atop his head and held out his hand. "My lady, if you may?"

She took his arm and helped him to his feet. His body shook as he rose, but once on his feet he seemed steady enough.

"Are you sure you can ride?" Shiva asked. He eyed the knight warily. Lennox lifted his visor. His eyes were strong. The warden nodded and threw over a pair of reins, watching as they quickly mounted. "Right then, off we go. Be sure not to fall behind."

He wheeled his horse about as Astrid and Shiva followed wordlessly after.

***

Shiva led the way, clad in a shadowed cloak atop a black steed; the big man was almost invisible in the muddied forest light. They rode together in a steady trot, following his trail through the winding pathways. Astrid's dark wolves, matching the horses' sluggish pace with ease, were black phantoms darting across fields of white.

Lennox rode last in line, with Astrid just before him and Shiva not far ahead. The warden never turned his head, reserving his eyes for what lay ahead. If cursed undead where to appear behind, or more knights like the ones Lennox had fought, it would be up to Marrok or Zev to sound an alarm. That was of some comfort to Lennox. His body felt fragile and he cursed his own weakness under his breath. He had never felt so mortal as he did now.

Lennox's chest expanded as he took in a breath of the icy air, it hurt, but he didn't mind. He closed his eyes; the fragrance of winter frost surrounded him, so different from his prison cell. He smiled and took in another breath. He craned his neck to peer behind, hoping for one last glimpse of the archtree, but they had gone too far. A pity, he thought, before looking up at the sky.

On and on they went, eastward across the woods, the sky slowly fading to twilight. Now and again the wolves flashed into sight before disappearing quickly into memory. Still, their sharp howls could be heard echoing through the trees when not seen. For a time, the sky was red and orange, the thick clouds colored brightly by the fading sun. Though, often they could see little of the sky, and soon the colors were all gone and black was the color of the night.

Shiva brought the line of horses to a crawl. Lennox clung to his saddle and reins with cautious vigor. It was dangerous to ride in darkness, one misstep or unseen rock could trip the horses, and if they went lame, they would need to be put down. There was no other option considering their state. He had saved the archtree when he destroyed the Darkmoon's sigil … but he had lit a beacon in doing so. Their location was known, and the enemy would come.

Lennox reached down, rubbing at the ach that filled his tired legs. Ahead of them came the familiar sound of trickling water. A stream, Lennox considered; not much else it could be. But as they drew closer the path widened revealing an opening in the woods.

Lennox frowned as they neared, realization slowly settling in. Following Shiva's example, he dismounted, running his hand along his stallion's neck in gentle appreciation. Their pace had been mild, but they had traveled far over rough terrain and Squall stood with his head bowed, steam rising up from his sweaty fur.

"Good boy, Squall," Lennox said quietly as he tied him to a tree. "Take a rest now."

Shiva stood at the water's edge looking out across the half-frozen lake. Astrid stood beside him, neither of them speaking.

Lennox lifted his visor. "Ahh … it seems we've come to an impasse."

The three of them stood in silence gazing out across the sunken bridge. A low dock of rotted and dying wood stretched out across the water to the other side of the lake. It appeared sturdy enough except for the large section in the center that had collapsed beneath the water. Up above the sky was clear but for a single cloud that hovered in the face of the moon casting down pale light onto the icy water and snow-covered trees that lined the lake's edge.

Shiva looked to Astrid "Well?" he asked, his tone sharp. "This bridge of yours is no good. What now? The lake is shallow further south. We could try to ford across just before the current returns."

Astrid shook her head. "No, it would be unwise to trust these waters. We will have to spend another night in the woods, but it is better we head north. There is another bridge we may cross."

Shiva had perceived Lennox moving alongside the lake as he stood talking with Astrid, but he stopped short when he saw the golden knight begin to walk out along the shattered bridge. "Sir knight," he called out.

Lennox stopped and turned, holding up his finger to his helm in a whispering motion. He signaled for them to stay where they were before continuing down the dock, flail in hand and shield at the ready.

"What's he doing?" Astrid whispered.

"He see's something," Shiva answered, his eyes feverishly searching the still waters.

A cold gust swept across the lake, pushing at some of the chunks of ice that floated along the surface. One of the larger ones flipped, casting out long waves of ripples across the lake's glassy surface. Both Shiva and Astrid reached for their weapons as Lennox froze where he stood, but the gust passed and the ripples died out leaving the lake peaceful once more.

Lennox let out a sigh of relief before pressing forward, half crouched, along the decrepit bridge. The wood was covered with a thin layer of ice that made each step more dangerous than the last as the wood slowly cracked beneath his weight. There, he thought, pleased that he had been right. He couldn't be sure, not from the shore, but he saw it now, a single corpse, hidden among the rubble of the fallen bridge.

He reached the end of the bridged and scanned the lake's surface once more but saw nothing except the outlines of Shiva and Astrid as they watched silently from the shore. Content, he set his mace aside and crawled down to his stomach and went about pulling out the corpse. *Perhaps I should have brought along Shiva,* he reflected. The body was heavy and frozen through, but the bridged hovered close to the water's surface. He managed to pull the body up on his third attempt.

At first, he thought the corpse was a child, but a second glance told him it was actually a dwarf. He was happy for that, had it been a full-sized man he doubted he would have been able to lift the corpse alone. The dwarf's cloths were half torn and frozen in clumps, and Lennox had to smash him with his flail to break the ice off, but after two good swings the ice shattered and he was able to peel back the cloth around the little man's neck. He checked the dwarf's wrists and ankles too and when he was satisfied, he dragged the corpse back to the edge of the bridge and kicked him into the water with a splash.

He was breathing heavily then, small puffs of steam shot out if his visor with every breath; but it had been worth it. He had to know, and his energy would return soon enough.

"What was he looking for?" Astrid asked softly to Shiva.

They stood together on the murky shore as another vagrant gust descended on the lake. With no trees to act as a buffer the wind cut into them with cold indifference. Shiva seemed apathetic towards the whole ordeal. His eyes followed Lennox as the knight made his way back across the bridge, but just as the knight drew close, he turned to leave. "It doesn't matter," he said at last. "Ask if you truly wish to know, but make it quick. These woods grow more dangerous with each passing hour."

The warden left her then, so that she stood alone on the shore when Lennox returned. The knight was still breathing heavily but he was moving fast. Just as she went to speak he passed her by.

"We need to go," he said hurriedly.

"Wait!" Astrid said grabbing at Lennox's arm. "What did you find out there? And who is this Darkmoon Alchemist? Shiva has been unsettled ever since you broke the curse on the archtree. I want to know just who might be after us."

Lennox paused, glancing towards Shiva and the horses before lowering his voice. "Now is not the time to discuss the Darkmoon … as to what I found. It was a corpse. A small man, a dwarf actually. I needed to see if he bore the Darkmoon's sigil. He didn't."

"A ghoul then?"

Lennox shook his head. "A ghoul would have been better. I don't know who the man was, an alchemist maybe."

"An alchemist?"

Lennox shrugged. "I can't say for certain, but he had some sort of marking tattooed onto the side of his ankle. It looked alchemic in nature. Overlapping triangles, one of them inverted. I don't know what it means."

Astrid understood. "The man was no alchemist," she corrected. "He's a thief."

"Are you certain?"

"Yes."

Lennox turned and looked out across the lake once more. "Ah … well, whatever he was he's dead now. And we should be going as well. We'll speak more on the matter, I promise, but later. Remember, you have answers that I wish to know as well."

"Hmph, so be it," Astrid said releasing Lennox's arm.

"Right then. You yourself said we'll have to spend another night in the woods, best not make it two."

Shiva was waiting for them when they returned from the shore. He was mounted atop his black stallion, one hand resting upon his lap, the other clutching the reins as the nervous horse pawed at the earth. With the smallest of checks the stallion became still, glancing back towards Shiva in quiet obedience.

"The corpse … was it tainted?"

"No," Lennox said as he climbed up atop his horse, a moment later Astrid was up as well. "The girl claims he had the mark of a thief." He gestured towards Astrid with his free hand, but she apparently took no notice.

She spoke up then. "If the tattoo you described was accurate, that man was more than just a common thief. He's of the guild. There's no other explanation."

Lennox cocked his head curiously. "Oh? I admit the circumstances are queer, but it's best not to jump to conclusions."

"The knight is right," Shiva added. "Some say the guild doesn't exist at all. And if they did why would they have a tattoo marking themselves? And how would you know of it? Perhaps the dwarf was just a merchant."

The dwarf? Lennox smiled beneath his helm. Had the big man seen the corpse from the shore? Could he tell from that distance, or had he listened in on their conversation. Lennox couldn't be sure. *I must keep* my voice soft, he thought.

"These men aren't purse thieves to be caught by the city guard," Astrid countered. "These men steal gold and treasures like nothing you've ever seen. One cannot seek them out ... they find you." She turned about and gazed at Shiva under lowered brows. "And to shed light on your question, warden, the tattoo shows one is worthy to join the guild. You wouldn't be a very good thief if you got caught, wouldn't you say?"

"One cannot elude the light forever," he replied. "They would have been found out. Even my mistress has never mentioned them before."

Astrid laughed aloud at this. "Oh, I forgot about your mistress. She knows much I'm sure, but it would be foolish to attribute to your mistress what belongs only to the Creator. Even Shem, who held the knowledge of all names, failed when his time came."

The warden shook his head. "I would not speak his name lightly."

"I'll do as I will ... as we all must." She turned her horse about, glancing over her shoulder as she said her final peace. "I'm simply giving advice, warden. You don't have to take it."

A flash of anger touched Shiva's eyes, but he only smiled, and even managed a small laugh in the end. Lennox thought the big man was going to say something but he didn't, instead the warden kicked his horse forward and followed quickly after Astrid, his eyes calm and still.

Do as I will ... Lennox pondered the phrase as he turned Squall about. Her words, but they meant nothing. He rolled the oathkeeper ring around his finger, and gave it a little tug. The ring stayed firmly where it was. Neither of them could do as they willed, not yet, but he had time. Did Astrid?

He wasn't sure, but he imagined he would find out soon enough. "Let's go boy," he said aloud. I've had just about enough with this forest, an extra night sounds dreadful.

7

UNDER the leaden sky Squall trudged north along the icy river. Lennox sat high atop the stallion, rubbing at the ach that ran along his legs. They were better than they had been upon first leaving the mountain, but his legs were still unaccustomed to such heavy riding, and sometimes the ach seemed to seep deep into his bones. He grimaced as they came to a halt, his helm hiding any discomfort he felt from his companions.

The knight looked out to see why they had stopped and caught a quick glimpse of Marrok slipping through the woods not far ahead. The wolves had been absent most of the morning, and seeing them now was a small comfort to Lennox. He was able to relax, if only a little, knowing the two wolves were near. The big wolf disappeared quickly though, and before Lennox managed to speak two words Shiva was pressing on.

The golden knight let out a sigh and kicked his horse forward. He wished they could stop, if only for a small stretch, but the forest was dangerous, and he pressed those thoughts aside. The warden had the right of it. They needed to keep moving.

He pushed Squall into a trot and didn't stop until he was beside Astrid. They had found a small pathway that ran along the river about an hour earlier and had been following it ever since. Astrid shifted in her seat and turned to look at Lennox. "The bridge shouldn't be far now," she said in anticipation. "Less than a mile I should think."

"We rode west for a bit before the river turned north again."

"Of course," she answered with a nod.

"Hmm, my guess would be that were right back in the middle of this forest then. Tell me, is there any chance this second bridge might be in a similar state? If so, I feel we might be stuck without recourse."

"The bridge along the lake was old; it could have fallen on its own. In fact, I imagine that is exactly what happened. This is the main road. I understand why Shiva wanted us to avoid it, but it is maintained, though sparsely I admit." She turned her eyes forward. "The bridge is strong and made of stone. It will be there."

Lennox lifted the visor of his helm before rubbing at his shoulder. "Ahh … well I must say you've quite convinced me."

"Did you hurt your shoulder?" she asked suddenly. "I've seen you favoring it as we ride."

Lennox's eyes crested as he smiled. "Thank you, my lady, I'm grateful that you noticed. I seemed to have sprained it when I fought those two knights, but believe me when I tell you it will be fine. Its sore is all. I've been indolent for so long; I feel as though my body has begun to petrify."

Astrid smiled, amused by the knight's words. "There is a lightheartedness to you, Sir Knight. It is not something I would have expected."

"And you, my lady, are not as cold as I first thought. In fact, I would almost say you have a warm nature to you." Astrid looked unimpressed by the knight's compliment. He continued, "I said almost."

They turned a small bend in the river and suddenly the stone bridge was in view. It was a long viaduct passage made up of six arches that spanned across a small valley. The river ran swiftly below but the bridge was built strong with a dark gneiss stone inlaid with layers of red that stood concrete above the flowing waters. Its columns were made thick and drove deep into the river, casting about great waves of spray as the running water broke upon them. The girl was right, Lennox recognized. The bridge was made to endure.

The road broke off from the river then, driving deep into the forest on a slight incline, but soon enough it curved back towards the river and emerged atop the valley. From there it was a straight path to the bridge and they reached it within the hour.

The sky was cloudy with scattered patches of blue where the sun would burst through in streaming rays of light that opened and closed and opened again as the clouds shifted above. The brilliant rays cascaded upon the bridge like a waterfall of light, but there was little warmth to be felt, and snow still covered the stones where the rivers spray could not reach. They pressed forward; their stallion's hooves silent as they beat against the soft snow. A single archway sat over the central pier with an engraving written deep into the stone. The three riders eyed it warily as they passed beneath.

"Lennox, what does it say?" Shiva asked, half wondering, half wary.

Lennox gave the warden a curious glance before turning to Astrid. "Can you not read it?"

Astrid eyed him back questionably. "You can?"

Lennox nodded. "Of course."

Astrid shook her head. "I cannot. It is a language dead and gone."

"I see." Lennox looked up at the archway. "It's an inscription. It reads, 'Forgive me, all of you, for I have availed you nothing.' There is more, but it has faded beyond recognition." There was sadness in his words, a distant sadness.

They passed across the bridge to the other side and began following the road south again. Lennox inquired as to the direction but once again Astrid assured him that soon enough the road would break east.

Shiva pulled on his reins, bringing his stallion to a halt. "No. We get off here." He was looking east into the forest. A narrow game trail ran perpendicular to the road for a few spans before disappearing behind some brush, but his eyes were on Marrok. The grey beast stood along the tree line, his golden eyes locked on the party.

He was staring at them, watching as his sister came walking up behind them. Zev crossed their path and bounded across the snow towards her brother before disappearing into the woods. Without a word Shiva turned his horse and made his way across the road towards the two wolves. Lennox and Astrid followed after.

"Your wolves have taken a liking to Shiva," Lennox began. "He didn't make them swear an oath of service, did he?" It was meant as a jest but Astrid only looked on with indifference, her hands grasping tightly at her reins.

"He is like them … a predator. They see it and are drawn to him. I don't mistrust their loyalty, but I will be pleased when my business with the warden has concluded."

"Hmm … I won't say I disagree with you, but as long as you are tied to him you might as well embrace it."

"What do you mean?"

"I mean watch him, my lady. There is much to be learned by observing predators. Watch how he moves, how he eats, how he talks with others and how they respond. Watch how he fights. He is a dangerous man. Watch him. Learn how to be dangerous."

"Why are you telling me this?"

Lennox grinned, though it was hidden beneath his helm. "Because I want to help you, my lady, and I fear you have much to learn. You've been in the company of wolves too long, and they cannot join us in the cities. I'm afraid you'll only have me and that sour man there, and neither of us is the best of companions. Ten hells, I've been locked away for a thousand years. I can't imagine my conduct is in the right."

"You seem quite normal to me."

"Ha! My lady, I am a knight. I imagine in some ways that makes things easier for me. Men and women see my armor and expect me to act a certain way … and I oblige them. Even so, one cannot be too careful in a city like Solaire. You are of the mountains and the north. That is good. Things are simpler there, men do their work and say what they mean, but Solaire is a city of wizards and philosophers, kings and nobility. Frankly said, my lady, it's a terrible place. Of all the Jewel Cities it was my least favored."

"You said yourself, Sir Knight, much time has passed. Perhaps you will find the city has changed."

Lennox paused thoughtfully for a moment and then said, "I imagine the city has changed a great deal, my lady. I'm sure new buildings have been erected and fallen, certain houses held power and then lost it, hypocrites as well as the devout led the faith of the cathedrals, and yet, despite all this … Solaire remains. You cannot change the heart of a city, my lady.

"If the people of Solaire found out what was hidden beneath this enchanted ring, why, half the city guard and most of the clergy would wish me burned then and there for being hollow. The wizards and scholars would desire to study me, and only the Creator knows what the nobility would want with me."

"Cities have never been a place for the civilized," she replied. "Though if your true state was to be revealed, I cannot imagine you would be safe anywhere."

"My lady, you misunderstand me. It's not my wellbeing I'm concerned about. I would bring that city to its knees if they tried to harm me … but I can't be with you at all times. I'm offering you advice. Solaire was always a home of vipers, I'm simply telling you not to get bit."

At that, Astrid found herself at a loss for words. She could only bow her head politely and say, "Thank you for your guidance, Sir Knight."

Sometime later, when the sun was begging to settle, Lennox offered Astrid another word, almost as though he had forgotten to mention it. "And yet … despite all I have said, perhaps I am wrong. It wouldn't be the first time."

After that he spoke no more, not until the sun had all but set and they had found a small clearing to set a fireless camp. Shiva had insisted there be no fire, and both Lennox and Astrid didn't argue. There had been an odd feeling lingering among them ever since they encountered the fallen bridge. Something about the dwarf had shaken Lennox, and he found himself seeking out the wolves' presence, hoping to find them near.

I see the one, but where is her brother? After looking around the camp he saw no sign of the wolf. "Have you seen Marrok?" he asked Astrid. She sat huddled against the base of a tree hoping she might fall asleep quickly.

She shook her head. "Probably off hunting."

Not long after she was asleep and the camp was quiet except for the soft whining of the horses who stood tied together in the brisk night air. Lennox sat with Shiva until the warden fell asleep, leaving Lennox alone to keep eye on the camp and watch as the starry sky above twinkled like the jewels of God's crest.

Lennox laughed. So far, his freedom had not been what he hoped it might be. Failure followed his every step it seemed, but no matter. *Pain is temporal*, he told himself. *It makes its mark and moves on … and always he endures.* He twisted his oathkeeper ring round his finger and smiled, anticipating the day he would take it off. It was not far off. Not truly.

***

It was bitter cold without a fire, and as night ambled on the sky darkened until it was black as coal leaving little light for the knight to keep watch in. Lennox stood leaning against a tree with his arms crossed before him. Zev lay beside him, eyes a smoldering green. He was all but blind in the dark, squinting hopelessly out into the forest trees when a pair of yellow-gold eyes suddenly appeared from the shadows. He reached for his flail but stopped short, watching as the yellow orbs drifted closer through the dark. Zev stood, but was otherwise unalarmed.

"Marrok," he called out quietly.

The big wolf waded forward and Lennox let out a breath of relief. He shook his head grinning at the wolf. "Why, for a moment there I thought you were death incarnate, come to take me away."

Zev had walked out to meet him and was rubbing her neck upon his in a soothing motion. He nuzzled back, and when she was done, she returned to the camp and sat down beside Astrid who seemed happy for the extra warmth. Lennox stepped out to meet Marrok, scratching at the grey wolf behind the ears. The yellow-gold eyes watched him coolly. The great beast came up nearly to his chest, and Astrid told him the beast was still growing.

"I know what you want," Lennox said shaking his head. "But I won't have it. The last time I followed after you I found myself in quite a mess."

Marrok understood. The great wolf moved past Lennox towards his sister, rubbing up against her once more before breaking off back into woods like a shadow. After that Zev rose and began circling the camp. She had shaken away her sleep and now stood sentry. Her eyes were wary and her ears up and out, listening for what was to come.

Lennox watched her inquiringly. "Perhaps things are worse than I thought," he said aloud, but what he thought was, what dammed beasts are coming this time. Then the wind began to shriek and a cold shiver ran along his spine.

***

They stood their ground in silence, Lennox and Zev, keeping watch on the darkness that surrounded them. Zev had taken to circling the camp, her eyes ever watchful. Lennox stood with shield and flail in hand. Marrok had found something, and the knight would not be taken off guard. Yet despite his vigilance, an uneasy feeling began to settle in the corner of his mind and grow as the long night continued. Something was coming; he could feel it in his bones.

Far off to the east, a wolf began to howl. A second voice picked up the call, then another. Zev cocked her head and listened. "What is it?" Lennox asked as he kneeled beside the wolf. More howls followed until at last Zev herself stepped forward and bent her head back howling high into the night in accord with her cousins.

Both Shiva and Astrid were awake now, eyes wide as they rose from their thin sleep. "Zev, quiet!" Astrid hushed. "Be silent."

"What is she howling at?" Shiva asked. He had taken to one knee with bow in hand and was notching an arrow as he gazed out into the surrounding trees. "I don't see anything."

"None of us do," Lennox told him. "I don't believe an enemy is near."

"Then what's she howling about?"

"It's Marrok. He left the camp not long ago … it's his call that started this."

"There's no way to know that," Shiva answered gruffly. He had yet to draw back the bow but his eyes still searched the forest.

"No, he's right," Astrid said quietly. "Zev would not have answered unless it was Marrok who called. We must go to him!"

It was Lennox who spoke next. "Go to him? My lady, as far as we know Marrok is sending us a warning. We should leave now, head south perhaps."

"I will not abandon him. Zev, to me." Astrid's wolf moved, swift and silent, and then they were off, heading east into the black woods.

"We'll lose them quick if we don't follow," Shiva said. Somehow Lennox didn't think the warden was too disappointed. With a quick nod Lennox and the warden chased after.

Under the cover of trees what little light there had been was wiped away and the darkness was complete. The snow was up almost to

Lennox's knees, and with every step it became harder to move. They reached a small clearing where an overturned tree had fallen but the knight saw no sign of Astrid or her wolf. Blood and ash, where could they be! "I lost their path," Lennox called out.

"This way," a voice answered from the dark.

Lennox moved quickly, following the warden's shadow further east into even deeper snows but to no avail. "Shiva!" he called out.

"This way, Sir Knight," the voice returned.

Lennox stopped where he stood. Something was wrong. Through the slit of his helm he beheld a shadowed figure moving towards him. He lifted his visor and saw two more to his left, and one was nearly upon him. Lennox pivoted left, swinging his flail with all his might into the head of the first ghoul. The spiked ball bit hard into the hollow's leather helm before ricocheting up. The ghoul fell dead into the snow and never rose.

The other two rushed in quick. The snow made it hard to move but Lennox managed to push back to where the snow was not as high and met the foes head on. Neither of the hollows had shields so Lennox decided to attack first, swinging his flail high above his head before bringing it down upon the closer of the two. The spiked ball found its mark, crashing into the ghoul's left arm. Lennox swung his flail around for a second strike, this time aiming for its neck. Too far, the ghoul lurched forward and the ball missed its mark, instead wrapping itself around the hollow's neck. Lennox yanked at the chain, causing the ghoul to fall forward into the snow. He pulled again with all his might, snapping the neck of the undead soldier.

By then the third ghoul was upon him, smashing into the golden knight before he could raise his shield. A sickening crunch, and he was falling to the ground. The world went white as the snow swallowed him up. His flail was gone, just like that, left wrapped around the neck of the second ghoul. He rolled onto his back and reached for his dagger when the ghoul drew up and began raining blows upon him.

Lennox raised his shield, deflecting the strikes as best he could. He grunted under the strain and finally ditched his shield and rolled away. He was on one knee when the hollow charged, driving his rusted sword forward like a spear. Curse these woods, Lennox thought before reaching his arm forward and grabbing at the ghoul's blade with his bare hand.

The hollow's sword stopped just short of his belly. A startled expression appeared across the ghoul's face, almost as though he could not understand what the knight had done to halt him. He looked up at Lennox and there was neither heat nor life in the soldier's eyes.

Still clasping the hollow's sword, Lennox drew the ghoul forward as he slipped his long dagger from its sheath and plunged it into the hollow's heart. The creature's dead eyes stared back at him, coldly, as though nothing had happened. Lennox kicked the ghoul away and the creature fell back into the snow with a soft crunch.

Lennox raised his dagger and gazed out across the woods. He felt near blind in truth, having barely noticed the ghouls before they were upon him. But all was calm once more, and the shadows stayed in their place.

His hand burned as though he had thrust it into flames. Damn those ghouls! Damn them to hell! The blade had cut through his glove like butter. He was so weak without his rings. He had to be careful, more careful even than he first thought ... if such a weak creature could injure him so. He considered healing the wound with magic but decided against it. It was some time till morning yet, and he might need every bit of magic he could conjure before he was clear the woods.

He retrieved his shield and flail, tearing off a piece of cloth from one of the ghouls and wrapping it about his hand before continuing east; or at least his best guess for which way east could be.

***

Lennox was lost for some time after that, unable to return to their camp even if he wished too. He searched for any trails Shiva might have left in the snow, as agile as the man was, it would be impossible for the big man to leave no trace of himself. Yet, Lennox found no sign of the warden, nor of Astrid or the wolves.

Blood and ash, he thought as he took a seat upon a fallen tree. His body began to shake from the cold, his chest laboring for every breath. He clutched his wounded hand, feeling the warm blood as it pulsed along with his beating heart. It burned. He held it to his chest hoping some of the warmth might spread to his body. It did not. Ten hells, he wanted to scream the words but he dared not reveal his location to any ghouls that might be wandering close. He could do without running across any more undead, especially while his hand was wounded. It was hard to grip his shield, and he wasn't sure how many blows he would be able to withstand if it came to another fight.

He needed to escape the woods, but it would be difficult now without Shiva or the girl to guide him, or a horse to travel upon. He could do without Squall, but a whole list of worries would disappear if he could only find his companions, he would even settle for Marrok or Zev.

Well, best to face a hard truth then wish for it to go away, he said to himself as he rose. But where to go?

A deep howl went up then, a long, drawn-out cry that swept across the tops of the trees like a midnight specter. Ahh-wooooo! Ahhh-wooooooooooo!

The howls died down and only the wind remained. Lennox tilted his head back and waited, hoping the cries might come again.

Ahh-wooooo! Ah-wooo! Ahh-woooooooooo!

Hmm … at last a spot of luck. He couldn't know for sure if it was Marrok or Zev, but at least he had a direction.

He set out across the woods, crossing the snow as quietly as he could. He gave up on carrying the shield and slung it upon his back, it was easier to move then but he felt vulnerable without the extra armor in hand. His legs had become so cramped from riding that he was happy for the chance to stretch them out, but it was a shallow sort of joy.

He shivered as he took a step forward, falling waste deep into the snow. "Curse this place," he grumbled. It took him half a minute to escape and by then the snow was sticking to his armor like ice. He scraped at the snow with his gloved hand and trembled as the breeze gusted through the woods, kicking up loose snow from the surrounding trees and causing it to fall on top of Lennox. He had no need for food or water, but he had left his flint back with Squall and cursed his stupidity for not keeping it upon him. It was easy to enhance a flame that already existed … much harder to create one anew.

He would just have to suffer the cold; a little warmth was not worth the cost in magic. He had endured the dampness and stench of his cell … the loneliness of solitude. His cold body was simply another state of malaise, and nothing that could kill him. He would bear it.

Time wasn't the problem, he knew. He needed to retrieve his effects. He needed to rid himself of the oathkeeper ring. He needed to find his companions. He needed to escape the woods. So much to do … yet, he had time.

Ahh-woooo! Ahhh-woooooooooooo!

The howls were louder now, he was getting close. He closed his eyes, listening intently to the wolf cries as they were carried off by the wind. They sounded weaker to Lennox, more feeble somehow. Astrid and Shiva would be moving towards the wolf's call. But what of the undead? Would they be drawn or pushed away? He had already fought three; it would be dangerous if the howls drew in too many more. He drummed on his thigh with his fingers, weighing, considering.

Difficult to predict … but he had little choice, as long as he was alone the risk of peril amplified tenfold.

His decision made, he continued onward towards the howling of the wolves.

The further east Lennox traveled the thicker the woods grew. Clumps of trees spotted with thick brush made it near impossible for the knight to traverse certain paths, and he had to backtrack more than once as he inched his way through the snow.

He sank into shadow, darting from growth to growth in a crouch, doing his best to mimic Shiva's movements. The warden had a way of blending into both light and shadow, always a smooth motion, deliberate with every step. Lennox learned from everyone he watched; it was one of the reasons he persisted when so many others had fallen.

He watched carefully from the shadows, moving fast and low, darting from one place to the next. He covered half a league that way, until suddenly, halfway between a dark alcove of trees and an extra thick growth of foliage, he stopped dead, his eyes locked forward. A crumbling fence blocked his path. Not a fence, he realized, but a true stone wall, ruined by time and torn apart by forest growth that crawled over every edge of stone it could find. The growth continued on behind the wall as large trees covered in snow stood like white columns, making it difficult to see where one began and another ended.

Fastening his flail to his side, Lennox began to climb up the ruined wall. It wasn't difficult. Deep crags had split the stones long ago, causing large cracks to spill down the sides, and his armor was less a hindrance then many might think.

He reached the top and took a knee, taking cover behind a large stone baluster.

The fortress below lay in ruin. Trees and snow littered the courtyard like weeds, and many of the smaller buildings had completely collapsed, leaving nothing but a pile of rubble where they once stood. Only the main keep remained, a tall stone stronghold shaped like a cube that looked strong despite the condition of its walls.

A single stairway led up to the entrance, and standing like a shadow amongst the columns of the doorway stood a man. The outline of his silhouette looked familiar.

Shiva? Lennox couldn't be sure.

The shadow took half a step forward, raised his hand up above his head, and then stepped back again.

Well now, could he be signaling me? Impossible … Lennox dismissed the thought. He was crouched low behind the baluster, and what little that showed was hidden in shadow. Still, he felt as though the shadow was staring at him. A moment later the man turned and vanished into black. Lennox let out a sigh. He stepped back, taking a seat against the stone ruins when the sound of running footsteps pattered softly behind him. He was up a moment later, squatting low, his fingers clutching at the handle of his flail as the figure came into view.

Suddenly he rose, grinning beneath his helm as he watched Astrid running across the courtyard towards the keep. He opened his mouth to call out to her but decided against it, not wishing to draw attention.

So it was, Astrid the warden had been signaling … he shook his head and chuckled, laughing at his own misgivings. He surveyed the forest making sure there were no ghouls close and then stepped out from where he was hiding and walked along the top of the ruined wall until he came to a stairwell that led down into the courtyard. He reached the bottom when he heard footsteps once again, this time coming from the gateway ahead of him.

He narrowed his eyes, grasping tightly at his flail when Shiva appeared, turning the corner in a sprint. "Shiva?" Lennox said in a surprised tone.

"Run!" was all the warden could manage as he continued past the golden knight.

Lennox turned, gazing out past the ruined gate into the darkness of the woods. The whole forest seemed to be shaking, when suddenly the ghouls appeared from the shadows, ten … fifteen … twenty of them, probably more; clad in the armor of the drowned city with axes and swords in hand. Some wore leather tunics with round steel caps, and carried long bows at their side. A few of them had already stopped and were notching their strings making ready to let their arrows fly.

"Blood and ash!" Lennox yelled as he turned and followed after Shiva, moving as quickly as he could manage.

Arrows flew past him one after another, and the sound of the undead grew as the earth shook from their footsteps. He ditched his kite shield, tossing it to the side. The iron shield would do little to stop twenty foes, and the extra weight made it difficult to move. He ran as fast as he could, pounding towards the stairwell of the keep.

Shiva was half way to the door when he stopped and unslung his bow. He turned and let fly an arrow, then another, then another. The arrows flew past the knight, striking three of the quicker undead as they drew forth. Shiva continued up the stairs, releasing arrow after arrow until his quiver was empty. He turned and pounded towards the gate with Lennox close behind him.

"Astrid!" Shiva screamed, hoping the girl was close. "Be ready to bar the door!" A moment later he was at the gate, passing through the thick wooden doors as he slung his bow around his back. The door was half closed as he threw the gargoyle's head before him and passed swiftly through the narrow opening. Once on the other side he searched the room for Astrid. The girl was staggering across the room towards the door dragging a large iron bar behind her as she did. Shiva went to her aid; taking up the other half of the bar just as Lennox came bursting through.

"Close the door! Close the door!" Shiva screamed.

Lennox turned towards the gate and pushed, shoving at the door with all his strength until at last the heavy wood slowly began to turn upon its hinges. With a final jolt the door closed. Exhausted, Lennox faltered and fell to the floor. He ducked low as Astrid and Shiva placed the iron bar into the slots and let it fall. The heavy bar rang clean across the inner courtyard and a moment later the horde reached the gate.

Astrid stepped back as Shiva helped Lennox to his feet and together, they stood watching the doors of the stronghold shake back and forth as the ghoul's pounded on it in waves. Its iron hinges moaning under the pressure.

"… Will it hold?" Astrid said aloud.

"I'm not sure." Lennox panted the words. His visor was up and he was wiping at the sweat as it streaked down his face.

"Best we don't wait around to see," said Shiva.

"A wise choice, indeed" Lennox replied. "Perhaps this keep has a back entrance. We should find it before the ghouls wander around back."

"Creator save us," Astrid said quietly.

Shiva looked at her inanely … his same calculating eyes unchanged by their surroundings. "We need fire. Do you see anything we can use for torch light?"

Astrid took a moment to look about the room before giving a reply. "There were some smaller iron bars over against the west wall. We can strip my cloak and wrap it around to burn."

"It will suffice." Shiva said, and started toward the west part off the keep.

It was dark inside now that the door had been closed. A small part of the roof had collapsed near the center letting in some of the night light; else they would have been trapped in complete obscurity. Stone pillars lined the tall room, yet they walked upon wooden floorboards that ran across the entirety of the keep, old wood with signs of rot that creaked with every step. It reminded Lennox of his decrepit bed.

"Just here," Astrid said as she unfastened her cloak and began cutting it into strips with her knife.

Lennox was relieved to see that Shiva still had his flint upon him, but was surprised when the warden struck a spark and used pyromancy to enhance the flames, setting the torches ablaze. "Hmm … it appears as though you have some magic as well warden."

Shiva's eyes shifted to meet him, but other than that the warden gave no reply. With his torch in hand Shiva walked along the columns moving back towards the barred doors. Lennox raised his torch and followed after, his eyes peering through the dark. Something was wrong. Shiva knew it as well, but what? He searched the darkness, his eyes rolling over the pillars as the torchlight dances across them.

They were standing before the entrance once more, the three of them. Shiva drew his sword.

"What is it?" Astrid asked.

It was Lennox who answered. "The doors … they've stopped shaking." He reached down, unhitching his flail from his waste, wishing desperately for his shield. He couldn't have used it even if he had it though, as dark as it was inside the keep. He'd be all but blind without the torch.

"Perhaps they moved on," Astrid offered. "Forgotten what they were doing."

Lennox shook his head. "After a day or two maybe, but not this quickly; some part of them would have known we were still here. They might have moved to the side in search for another entrance." From the corner of his eyes he saw the warden backing away from the door. He took the que and moved further away himself, tugging at Astrid's arm as he did.

"It is coming," Shiva said at last. He turned to Lennox. "This foe is great indeed, Sir Knight. So, I will do the noble thing … and slay it for you." There was a glint in the warden's eyes, a frenzy of excitement that he could not keep hidden.

Lennox recognized the look and pushed further away, muttering curses under his breath and dragging Astrid along as he went. "It's best we go, my lady," he whispered quietly in the dark.

"What of Shiva?"

"He's free to join us if he so wishes. But we need to move now!"

The girl looked at Lennox in protest but the knight only shook his head and signaled for her to stay silent.

"We will meet again, Sir Knight." The warden's words echoed across the dark as he watched them depart. "My mistress has foreseen it."

Lennox and Astrid moved along the columns deeper into the keep, watching as Shiva's flame grew smaller and smaller when suddenly there was a thunderous crack. The noise echoed across the keep, bouncing off the stone pillars in quick succession.

"The gate!" Astrid said, turning to see.

Crack! Again, the thunder sounded, twice as loud as the first. Crack! And with that the gates were breached. The iron bar and heavy doors shattered into the keep in an explosion of wooden splinters, and appearing in the midst of it stood the shadow wraith. The dark creature stood ten feet tall and held in his hands a hammer of great strength as shadows fluttered about him. There were no signs of the ghouls as the wraith crouched down and passed through the doorway and into the keep.

"Run!" Lennox screamed.

He gave Astrid a push, one hand on the middle of her back to get her started. She stumbled forward into a lurching run with Lennox behind her.

Shiva sprang forward, his scimitar drawn. The long silver blade flashed out in quick successions and the shadow wraith faltered, surprised by the boldness of the attack. On the surface the blade only cut through shadow, but the deeper he cut the more resistance Shiva met. The wraith screamed out in pain, a high-pitched screech of agony. The warden's eyes gleamed with rhapsody as he readied for another strike.

Too slow. The wraith attacked first, swinging his hammer in a low arc. Shiva danced away, but the distance was set now and the demon perused him in rage.

The wraith was quick, swinging its hammer faster with every swing. Shiva evaded the blows one after another; it was all he could manage to stay one step ahead of the beast. He found himself backed against one of the columns and rolled away just as the hammer tore into the stone pillar.

The keep shuddered and was still.

"What was that?" Astrid screamed as she ran.

"Keep running!" was Lennox's reply.

The fortress shuddered around them for a second time … then a third.

Shiva could hardly believe the wraith's strength as the beast continued its pursuit, smashing through another column with its hammer. A waterfall of dry mortar followed, its white flakes drifting down like snow amidst the fading torchlight. Shiva looked up just in time to see the roof collapsing upon him.

"What was that?" Astrid said turning to look back.

"Don't stop running!" Lennox screamed back at her, when suddenly the ground shifted beneath him and he fell forward. He looked at the floor confused and then turned back and watched as column after column cracked and tipped over, crashing down like boulders from a mountain.

He watched as the cracking floor boards split, tossing Astrid into the air.

"Astrid!"

She let out a shrill scream before falling into the void below. A moment later the floor went out beneath him and he followed her into darkness.

8

THE water was halfway up Shiva's face when he awoke, taking in a sharp breath. He began to cough, his lungs spewing out the water they had taken in. When he was finished, he turned onto his back and let his head fall into the shallow water. His chest hurt ... his left shoulder too. That's where he had hit the water when he fell, such a long fall. It was a blessing the floor collapsed; else he would have been crushed for sure. He lifted his head to look around but was met only with darkness.

He let his head drop back into the water. He had fallen into a river. That he knew for certain.

He ran his hands along his body to see what was missing. Most everything was still upon him. His sword was gone. A misfortune for sure, it was a splendid blade. He had no one to blame but himself. He reached out his arms finding the gargoyle's head still at his side. He let out a sigh. The true treasure was not lost, that was all that mattered. He would need it when he met his final foe.

His skill had been tried against the wraith ... tried and found wanting. The sad truth left a bad taste in his mouth. He still lacked what was needed. Shiva's mind wandered to the golden knight. He wished he had seen him fight against the two brazen knights. It was a superb fight he was certain. Only Shiva could gauge Sir Lennox's skill. He was the only one ... his mistress had told him so.

He sat up. The small bank in the river where he had washed ashore was calm. He could feel the gentle current of the water pushing at his body, moving towards the unseen roar of the subterranean river that bellowed throughout the cave.

It was very dark, he realized. He had hoped his eyes would adjust, but as he sat listening to the soft trickling of the water no illumination came. The darkness was complete. The warden would have to make his own light. He grimaced, tearing off some cloth from his cloak and fastening it around the edge of his dagger as he rose to his feet. He set it aflame and the little fire cast its light out among the shadows. Slowly the shapes around him took form, the murky water as it flowed beside him, the smooth bare stones of the cave walls. He blinked his eyes and waited as they adjusted to the light. A black mass took shape not two spans from where he stood, it lay unmoving in the shallows.

He moved towards the figure, shuffling his feet through the water one step at a time before stopping abruptly. The shadow wraith!

Shiva steadied his heart, keeping a close watch on the wraith as he stood waiting. The creature seemed smaller somehow, as though it had shrunken down to human size. Shiva pressed forward, his burning dagger before him. Still, the wraith did not move. He knelt down and drove his dagger into the wraiths neck.

He would take no chances.

Afterwards, he flipped the wraith onto its back and examined him. Now that he was dead the wraith's appearance had solidified. The great hammer was gone as well, another waste. He would have liked to see the Darkmoon's crafting up close. Similar to the brass knights at the archtree, the wraith's helm showed no sign of an opening, no way to remove it.

Disappointed, Shiva turned the wraith on its side and went about removing the creature's cloak, hoping to use it as fuel for his torch. He had just unfastened it from the wraith's neck when it disappeared with his hand! No, it had not vanished; he could feel the fabric within his grasp. He brought his torch close and watched as the cloak shifted and flickered in the light. He moved the flame away and watched it vanish, hiding his hand beneath its magic.

Shiva smiled. The lone hunter scores the best treasure, and what a treasure indeed … He was very pleased, the smallest curves of a smile touched at his lips. He looked down at the wraith, its dead corpse face down in the shallow water.

"I would have liked for you to die at my blade," he said aloud to the corpse. "But it is my victory none the less. And now I claim my prize."

It was worth it, entering the frozen woods. Just as Lady Sune said it would be.

***

The shadow cloak did Shiva little good while he carried a torch for all to see. He placed it in his satchel and went forward in his normal attire, moving through the shallows carefully.

The ground was uneven, and two steps was enough to bring the water to his waste. He checked his equipment, making sure everything was well fastened before continuing on. Despite being separated from his companions, and quiet thoroughly lost in a maze of tunnels, Shiva was happy. The spoils of victory were too great, the treasures too exquisite. Even the delay of time was not enough to concern him, soon perhaps, but not now.

The river snaked through the tunnels in no particular pattern. Separating into two or three … or even four rivers at a time only to connect again half a league downstream. There were times when Shiva was left with no choice but to wade the river, but he always managed to find calm waters to cross. As he moved along, he saw signs of activity; racks of barrels lined the cavern walls, as well as select tools and other goods. He even came across a small shed with bedding laid out beside it and a spot for a fire and cookware.

However far he had fallen, there was indeed a way out.

At the shed he managed to find a proper torch. It was nice having the extra light. His dagger had produced a poor flame in comparison. It had seemed bright at the time, but now Shiva felt like he was carrying the sun, and questioned if the extra light was wise. He decided in favor of the torch and carried on.

The longer he traveled the more campsites he came across, some of them no more than a blanket set beside a cold fire pit. Each site was lined with large wooden barrels, many of them stood tight and sealed, but a few of them were open. The ones that were open were mostly empty save a few of which were filled with goods; furs and rugs by the look of it.

Shiva quickly rummaged the barrels for anything he might use, but left unsatisfied. There was nothing for him, not even food.

He came to another crossing in the river that was swifter than he would have liked. He stripped off his belongings and set them inside one of the barrels and tied it to his waste with some rope and managed to cross with little trouble. He reached the other side further downstream than he thought he would and crawled onto the stone bank naked and cold. He stopped then, sinking low into the stones when he saw the faintest hint of light shimmering through the darkness like a single candle burning amidst a swirling vortex of black.

He heard nothing but the rolling tremble of the river beside him, and there he waited watching the light as it pulsed in the distance.

When enough time had passed, he pushed himself off the ground and heaved at the rope, pulling at his barrel that floated gently in the shallows. He lifted it up onto the shore and began to dress himself in the dark; checking to make sure everything was in its place. Afterward, he pulled the barrel further up the riverbank and began making his way towards the light. Even with the flame so distant, its light was enough for Shiva to move freely without fear of slipping or falling back into the river. As he drew near the light grew in illumination.

He swung his new shadow cloak around his shoulders and pulled the hood over his head, holding the cloak close as he pushed forward … eager to know its true value.

What stood before him was more than just a mere campsite. Two stone towers sat on opposite sides of the river, anchored against the cavern walls with a small rope bridge connecting them. A timber palisade stood erect on both sides of the river in defense of the structures. The wall looked strong from afar but proved to be lacking as Shiva drew near. He found at least half a dozen gaps in the fence where he could slip through unnoticed. He chose to stay near the east corner where the space was darkest.

Once inside he searched the grounds. The torches were well maintained, and lit up the inner defense well, yet the stronghold seemed abandoned. He had just crossed the yard to the base of the first tower when he glimpsed a single guard across the river standing at the start of the bridge. How long had the man been there? Had he somehow missed him, or had the guard only just arrived. The man wore a plain tunic of black leather and stood watch, gazing out into the darkness. He seemed to be looking in Shiva's direction but remained motionless with spear in hand. The guard passed across the bridge and looked down towards the base of the structure. When he was finished, he crossed back across the bridge and out of sight.

Shiva stood alone with his back against the tower. Had he been seen? No alarm had been called. He kept vigil, watching to see if the guard would appear once more. After a time, he relaxed, casting his gaze at the river before him, watching as the water struck at the cavern wall in a roaring spray of foam and mist before being sucked down to the earth below.

He watched the river for some time and when he was done, he moved on, nearly invisible in his cloak and hidden in the river's mist. There was a single door at the base of the tower, blocked by stacks of barrels and iron bars that had been wedged into the ground and leaned up against the gate. He looked back at the river and then to the bridge above it. A thought he did not like much came to mind.

He continued around the tower to where the stones connected with the cavern walls and discovered a narrow ladder that led to the top. He scaled it quietly, the roar of the river hammering along the cavern walls.

He stood like a phantom atop the tower, his dark cloak fluttering in the throw of the mist. There was a metal hatch leading down with a large lock set upon the latch, and several barrels placed atop the door. Something had been trapped in the tower … something not meant to get out.

For a moment his eyes twinkled at the thought. No, he told himself. Lady Sune had said nothing of a monster inside the twin towers. He had his duty to carry out. He had sworn an oath … a binding pledge, deeper and more complete than the one the girl or the golden knight had sworn. She held his very soul in her hands. He could never take it back. He did not intend to.

Shiva moved towards the bridge. He had lost much time but it was not wise to do anything in haste … such was the path to ruin.

The bridge was stronger than it looked from below and he crossed it quickly, his shadow cloak a mass of gray mist wrapped in deluded light. He emerged on the other side with beads of water sticking to his cloak like a morning dew. After wiping off some excess water he opened the hatch and dropped below, uncertain of what he was to find.

***

Unlike the outer walls, the inside of the tower was dimly lit. Shiva smiled. He pushed forward, deeper into the depths, his fingers brushing against smooth finished stone as he walked.

From somewhere far below, noises echoed. The distant murmur of voices, the scrap of boots pacing. Right then, he thought. At last I may find some answers. He was not afraid, never afraid really. His road had some distance left.

Huge steps had been set into the curving wall, circling down and down. He followed them in their descent, his hand skimming along the wall, his steps quiet and still, until, out of the darkness came a light. Coming up from the bowls of the earth, its warm glow echoed across the stone walls in warning. He could hear voices too, echoing up the shaft in the company of the light.

" … telling you it was no ghoul," one said. "You think I've lost my wits but I haven't!"

"We shall learn the truth together," a second voice answered in the harsh accent of the Iron City.

"Tell me honestly. You think I've cracked, don't you? Lost my head … I can see it in your eyes."

"The gods alone know what you truly saw, Mat," the second voice answered. Shiva could see the light of the torch crawling up the steps before him, flickering with every step. "I believe you saw something though. It was right of you to tell me, if only you hadn't spoken of this to Tarkus. He should not have been bothered with this news. Next time find me first. And if not me, Ricard then."

"I know what it sounds like. Believe me, I know. That's why I told Tarkus. If it were just some ghoul then I would have taken care of him myself, but it was a specter I saw. You'll see. A true spirit of the mist."

Shiva could see the flames of the torch flickering up above the stairs. The two men were almost upon him, he leapt from the stairwell onto one of the wooden timbers that crisscrossed through the tower and brought his cloak about him so that he was completely shrouded in the foggy black. He held his breath as the man holding the torch climbed into his sight, his companion walking beside him. For a moment Shiva felt as though there was a third ... but no, the light revealed only two.

"Explain this apparition once more," the torchbearer said, a strong man in a mail coif set with a black circlet. He wore a sword at his side, they both did, and even in heavy boots their feet seemed to float soundlessly upon the steps. A stubble of dark beard showed upon the torch bearers' face, and he wore a brigandine of black leather lined with small steel plates riveted to the fabric.

"I could see the creature moving through the mist of the river," replied the torch-bearer, named by the other as *Mat*. "It traveled through the courtyard and stopped at the base of the tower and remained there until I left."

So, he had been seen, how disappointing. Shiva furrowed his eyes, taking Mat in closely as the two men passed. He was a younger man, thin, and in a black leather tunic that looked cheap in comparison to the torchbearers. Yet he moved well. Shiva saw that clearly now, and the man had keen eyes, sharper than he had first thought. Still, he was learning the limits of his shadow cloak, better now than when surrounded by ghouls.

"It did nothing else, this specter?" the torchbearer said as they continued up the steps, level now with where Shiva crouched hidden by his cloak. Another test, the warden thought. Light streamed forth from the torch, but the two men continued on unaware of Shiva as he stood crouched beneath his cloak like a gargoyle draped in black.

"Not that I could see," Mat replied. For a second his eyes shifted towards where Shiva was hidden. "I walked the bridge to the second tower but the creature lingered."

"Is this what you told Tarkus?"

Mat nodded.

The torchbearer was quiet then, their footsteps soundless as they continued in their assent. At last he spoke. "If it truly is a spirit as you say, let us hope it is a peaceable one. I wouldn't know how to go about killing a specter, not without a mage to cast a hex on us." He shook his head. "There's no way we'll escape this place anyhow ... specter or no. We're dead men, Mat. Best we start thinking ourselves as cursed. Just a matter of time, really. We're not getting back into the other tower. I don't care if Tarkus speaks otherwise. There must be thirty ghouls trapped down there."

"We can let them out slowly. Maybe lure them across the bridge."

"Perhaps so, but if there is a horde waiting, then there's no way were getting that latch closed again."

Shiva let them pass well ahead, then he followed after.

"We have to try either way." The words were scattered as they echoed down the tower, muffled by the stones. " … firebombs we can reopen the tunnels … "

" … no guarantee … "

" … feasible … "

Shiva could see the light from their torch dancing across the walls as their words fell silent, a warm glow that beckoned him to follow. Sometime he could make out their voices, but theirs words remained buried. He hurried after, striding up the coiled steps, his hand gripped tightly at his cloak. Near the top the light suddenly stopped. Shiva could hear their voices clear once more, and he listened as they climbed out before following after as quickly as he could manage.

He found himself standing at the top of the ladder staring at the backs of the two men. They stood near the bridge gazing down at the base of the second tower, their cloaks billowing about them as the spray from the river roared throughout the cavern. It was bright outside. Shiva could see his cloak taking shape in the light of the flames. He striped it clear and drew his dagger … he would no longer play the shadow.

He moved towards the torchbearer. The man knew silence; that much was true. Shiva knew it too. His eyes were cold as he stepped forward, his footsteps masked by the thunder of the river.

"Just there," Mat said as he pointed down.

"I see nothing!" the torchbearer yelled back, and then a dagger was at his throat.

The warden moved quickly, reaching his free hand around the torchbearer's mouth as he dragged him away from the bridge. He kept his eyes on Mat as he leaned down to whisper into the man's ear.

"I want you to know that I could have killed you right now had that been my intent." The words were soft but cold as they left Shiva's lips. "I could have killed your friend too… but I didn't. It's important you understand that. Nod if you understand."

The man nodded.

"Good," Shiva whispered back before releasing his grip.

The man fell to his knees and reached for his throat, feeling the warm spot of blood where Shiva's dagger had skimmed across his neck. He was coughing and looking towards Shiva with both anger and relief present in his eyes. This one will fight till the end, Shiva told himself, making a note of it.

Mat stood facing the other tower for a few seconds before realizing he was alone. He turned around and seemed almost confused by what he saw. "Cright!" he yelled as he drew his sword.

"Put that away. If I wished you dead your sword would offer you little aid," Shiva said. He had sheathed his dagger but his hand still rested on the hilt and when he looked towards Mat his eyes burned cold like blue glass.

"Do as he says, Mat," said the man Shiva knew now as Cright, his rough voice even more sour as he rubbed at his throat.

Having reached a decision, however much as he disliked it, Mat lowered his sword. A moment later he returned it to its sheath. Shiva watched him with calm indifference, and then turned his attention to Cright and offered the man his hand. Cright ignored it, rising to his feet as he stared hard at the intruder. "Well done," he sneered. "Rejoice, and praise Elyon. You crossed the frozen woods and managed to get trapped down here like the rest of us ... now what do you hope to achieve?"

"Yes, of course. I cannot blame you. I'm sure my arrival must appear quite strange to you. I am Shiva of Cataron, and I desire what you desire, to break free of this prison and resume my travels."

"Ha! Isn't that a pretty dream? Better to throw yourself into the whirlpool and be done with it. That's the only way you're getting out of this fouled cavern. Course, you'll be drowned long before the river surfaces again." He turned and spit. "How'd you get down here anyway? All the tunnels are either caved in or blocked."

"I was pursued," he began softly. "A horde of ghouls flanked me and my companions in the darkness of the woods. We had no choice but to seek shelter in the stronghold. We weren't there long before the floor gave out beneath us ... I fell a long way into the darkness, and when I awoke I was here."

Cright smiled knowingly.

"You know this area well?" Shiva asked suddenly.

Cright nodded. "Better than most, not as well as some."

"And you?" Shiva asked turning to Mat. The young man shook his head no. "What of Tarkus? Does he know these tunnels well?"

Cright hid his surprise well. He was an older man with wisps of white beginning to show in his beard. Mat was less subtle, a passing glance to Cright gave him away. It was Cright who answered. "You know more than you should," he began. "Hmm … yes, he knows them best, that's true. Still, it doesn't matter. I told you. The tunnels have all collapsed. Blew them ourselves when the ghouls starting closing in." He turned and spit, wiping the blood from his neck with his hand. "Seemed like a good plan at the time. That is, until those damned hollows starting climbing down through the rear pass ways." He shook his head. "Don't know how they could have found their way down here but they did."

"And now you're trapped without recourse … no way of escape."

Cright nodded. "Just so."

"I would have thought more of this guild. As it is, I would like to speak with Tarkus." He looked to Mat. "You spoke of firebombs in the second tower. Tarkus has a plan. I would hear it for myself. "

"How could you know that," Mat said dumbly.

Cright laughed aloud. "Sure, why not. Perhaps Elyon sent you to guide us in our hour of desperation. That sounds like something He might do. Come Mat, let's introduce your ghost to Tarkus. The great mystery has been solved, and all it took was our dignity. Haha! To think that I was caught off guard, what has become of me?"

9

CRIGHT led the way into the depths of the tower, a party of three now. They walked in silence, the warden's hand once more skimming along the wall, taking in the smooth texture with every step. He craned his neck, taking interest in the wooden beams that crisscrossed through the tower and the general architecture of the keep.

"Was it your guild who built these towers?" Shiva asked in a quiet tone. He heard Cright snigger softly before answering him. "Do you take us for stonemasons?"

He hadn't thought the thieves' guild capable of such skill; theirs was a talent of another sort. True craftsmanship went into raising this tower, and although the style was old it was perfectly crafted, well beyond that of even a journeyman stonemason. Still… how had an entire fortress inside the frozen forest gone unnoticed for so long? Shiva looked on coldly as he pondered the question.

They fell once more into silence, the three of them. Dressed in black, their silhouettes danced on the wall beside them, shadows set besides shadows, stretching high upon the stones. Shiva looked as though he belonged there with his black brothers, his gray and black cloak flittering behind him, the way he moved, silent and still, in union with the two men before him. If not for a certain air about him, he would have fit the part seamlessly.

Near the bottom was a large wooden door set upon heavy iron hinges. Cright tapped on it twice, paused, then tapped three more times. A moment later the latch clicked open and the door swung out.

"Who in ten hells is that?" asked the man who had opened the door.

A short man, thin as a pike with soppy blond hair and large broadsword sticking out from behind his head set in a black leather shoulder sheath.

Cright walked in past him. "Mat's ghost," he answered. "We found him waiting for us at the top of the tower. Crafty as a worm he is, had Mat seeing shadows."

The doorman laughed.

"He got the better of you," Mat uttered.

"Us … he got the better of us. Nifty piece of magic I'm sure. Still, I'm getting old, what's your excuse?"

The doorman laughed once more as Mat and Shiva stepped forward. He stopped though when Shiva's eyes fell upon him. There was nothing funny about the warden, even if Cright was making light of the man.

The room was sparsely furnished. A few barrels sat at one end next to a table and some chairs; opposite the table was a nest of dry straw bedding set with some blankets. A man lay there sleeping, his face half covered by his large cavalier hat set with a single black plume. He looked as though he were sleeping, but Shiva could feel his gaze resting upon him. A small smile touched his lips as he nodded to the sleeping man. He was amused to see a small nod back before the man flipped where he lay so that he faced the wall and drew the blanket close around his shoulders.

"Well come now, Cright said gesturing for Shiva to follow. "Let's not keep the old tomcat waiting."

They passed by the sleeping man on the floor towards a second door that led into a small den. There they found Tarkus crouched on top of a long stone table set with two lanterns on either side for light. The large cat didn't so much as lift his gaze as he spoke. "Leave us. I would speak with the intruder in private."

Cright nodded, stepped back, and left without a word, closing the door behind him as he did.

Shiva found himself alone with the tomcat … a large feline, as big as himself if he had to guess, but fatter. Several hefty books lay sprawled out before the creature mixed together with what appeared to be maps of the caves. He watched as the cat's eyes scrolled across the texts.

"Soo … traversed the frozen woods only to be trapped like a rat so far below the earth." Tarkus looked up at the warden, taking in the great mystery. Somehow the cat seemed unimpressed with what he saw and went back to his books. "Well indeed, you are an odd sort of human … you fared well to make it this far, but what next?" Tarkus paused, letting out a long sigh as though bored. "So few truly gifted men remain … men like Sir Draco and Knight Malifis, off to slay a dragon last I saw them. Still, even their deeds were in part fabricated. What is it with humans and truth; you just can't seem to keep it firmly in grasp."

Shiva had not moved since entering the room. He stood relaxed, one hand resting on the hilt of his dagger, his gaze a stolid mirror.

The large cat looked up and smiled. "Ohh … I think I've taken a liking to you. You're a special one, perhaps even great. Shiva of Cataron, was it?"

Shiva nodded slightly.

"Well don't act so surprised, you don't think these ears are just for show." Shiva stared back, indifferent to the snide comment. No ears were that good, and the both of them knew it. "Heehee! Yes, I think I like you very much. I am Tarkus of the Deep. I command what remains of the guild. Please. Take a seat."

"I'll stand."

"Indeed, so you shall. I won't stop you." Tarkus leaned forward, resting his head upon his front paws. The same bored look, latent in his expression. Still … his eyes shone clear, silver streaks set against gray fur that watched the warden's every move. He lay unmoving in the silence, content in his state with Shiva before him.

The warden took it as a sign to speak. "You seem to know why I'm here."

"I know how you're here … not why."

"I am First Warden to Lady Sayola Sune of Cataron. Duty ushered me to pass through the frozen woods in the hopes of reaching Solaire quickly, that I might fulfill my lady's will."

"And what is it she desires in Solaire?"

"Of that I will not speak."

"Hmm … such trifles are immaterial." Tarkus paused as though in thought. "A servant of the Oracle, are you? Well, that explains much. You did not come here for our treasures, why, you have two of your own already. Then what awaits you in Solaire?" Tarkus spoke the words aloud, but it was not a question meant to be answered. "Hmm … there are so many secrets in this world just waiting to skulk out from the shadows, or plunge back into them. You wish to escape this dreadful place, as do we all. Very well, let us come to an agreement."

Shiva nodded slightly.

"Wonderful! I will tell you what it is I plan and then we shall discuss the best way to go about achieving it, for all our sakes. Now please, sit. I would have your thoughts on the matter, for the troubles are near insurmountable."

Shiva took a seat and as Tarkus pushed one of the maps forward for him to see.

"This is for you. Remember it well, little good it will do for you to escape this cavern only to end up in another; this time without an alternate path."

***

They sat conversing for some time, the warden and the cat. Shiva listened to the creature's story, gauging every word the feline said, questioning in his mind what he was being told and what he wasn't. What was left unspoken was often as important as what was being shared affably.

"And what of this bridge?" he said pointing to a cross on one of the maps.

Tarkus shook his head. "Gone. We cut the bridges early on in the incursion … but it was only a half measure, something to buy us some time. You can get most places ten different ways in these tunnels."

"Tell me more of this ghoul swarm. You said they didn't move like normal hollows."

"Abominations … the lot of them. They have always been a pestilence to us, hardly any real trouble though." His paws scratched at the table as though clawing into some invisible prey. "Something has changed, of that there is no doubt. They move with direction now, with purpose … and quickly too, as though driven forward by some unseen master. They are something to be feared now warden, and not just by the people of the Deep."

Shiva gave the tomcat a long searching look. "Was there another among them … What I mean is, do you know if there was a captain of sorts. Perhaps he was a hollow like them, or perhaps something else."

"Heehee, saw something did you? Come now, don't hold it from me, else how am I to help?"

For the first time since Shiva entered Tarkus's company the cat feigned interest, but what it was the cat was truly thinking, Shiva couldn't guess. His own face revealed nothing as he considered telling the tomcat what he had seen.

"There was something else beside the ghouls up above, a shadow wraith if I am to name it. The hollows dispersed when the creature drew near, almost as though they were in union together. I wonder if perhaps some new hierarchy has come into play, it is uncommon to see such creatures working so closely with one another."

Tarkus stretched out his paws, arching his back as he let out a long, gentle purr. Afterwards he returned to his previous position with his head laid out softly on his paws. "A dreary notion. You hint of the Darkmoon Alchemist, yes? Of course you do, but I know nothing of the wizard's workings. You'd be better off asking your Lady Sune. She knows more than she's let on I'm sure."

"She has told me all she will concerning the Darkmoon, if she has held anything from me, it is to my benefit no doubt."

The old cat's eyes lighted upon him. "Such fierce faithfulness," he said, the laughter clear in his tone. "What a stubborn man you are. Very well, you have made your choice on the Lady; we will speak no more of her. I have nothing more to say concerning the Darkmoon, except perhaps to say his creatures have been very active as of late. There has been an awakening. Boundless destruction lies ahead. It will mean the death of many, but greatness for all who pass through intact."

"And what part will you play?" Shiva asked.

"Ohh … I'll watch with interest to be sure, but else, I believe I'll sit this one out. That is, of course, supposing we make it out of these caverns. It is a shame to lose them. It will take some time to rebuild, but then, one must pass the time some way, yes?"

With nothing else to say on the subject Shiva set his hand upon the map, drumming his fingers across the top as he studied it once more. "It's not a bad plan, but it leaves much to chance."

"Life is a gamble, warden."

"And we have not discussed how we will obtain the firebombs in the second tower."

Tarkus laughed. "That one's not so difficult. You still have that nifty cape of yours folded neatly in your parcel, yes?"

Shiva stared back at the cat coldly.

Tarkus smiled. It was the first time the cat seemed sincere since encountering the creature.

Later, when Shiva had finished his dealing with Tarkus, the warden was invited to eat and take rest. There were still many things to discuss the tomcat assured him, far too much to finish in one day. Shiva found the idea silly. Deep below the earth with no light to signify the passing of time, night and day seemed to blend together.

He spoke with the cat several more times, looking over the different maps of the caves and discussing how best to use the firebombs.

"This is absurd," Shiva told the cat suddenly. "Until we have the bombs in out possession there is no use discussing what we might do with them. We don't even know how many are left in the tower."

"To true," Tarkus replied. "Call my men in, its best we discuss getting the firebombs before we talk any further."

***

That night Shiva couldn't sleep. He found himself alone with Ricard who sat fletching arrows at the table. A good-looking man in his thirties, he had been feigning sleep when Shiva first arrived and had spoken little with the warden since then. His garb placed him as a resident of Solaire.

He was watching Shiva with a smile when he set down his dagger and rose, making his way to one of the barrels by the table. When he turned back round, he was holding a large glass bottle filled with wine so rich it looked almost purple. He opened the bottle and quickly poured two cups, handing one to Shiva with a friendly nod.

"A sweet red from the vineyards of Bedivere. It sings of cherries and dark oak."

"You Jest."

Ricard shook his head. "A rogue does not joke in the same way an honest man does. I would not kid you in this, not in wine ... " He watched as Shiva took a sip. "A piece of home, yes?"

Shiva nodded. "Yes. Thank you."

"It is no trouble." He took a seat and placed his feet upon the table. "I regret that we must drink of it under such sour circumstances, it steals away much of the enjoyment."

Shiva took another small sip. It was good. He would only drink half the cup.

"So, you're going into the tower, yes? Very dangerous I think, but then ... the merit of all things lies in their difficulty." Ricard took off his cavalier hat and set in on the table, taking a drink from his cup. "Do you think you will die?" He had a smile on his face and seemed truly interested as he waited for Shiva to reply.

The warden shook his head no.

"Ha! I knew it. Some of the others ... they say you will die, but Ricard did not think so. I can see it, truly. You will not die so soon I think."

"Are you a seer?"

"Oh, no, not me. I have seen no vision. I misspoke. It is a feeling I have when I see you. Do you understand?"

Shiva nodded.

"Good," he said with a smile, happy to have cleared up the error. He took a drink from his cup. "Tarkus likes you. I have seen this also. He does not like everyone, that's another reason I think you will live. He would not send you to die if he thought that is what you would do. Mat and Edward maybe, and possibly Cright ... but no, he is good with a sword that one; and we will need it if we are to escape."

"You believe we will make it out?"

"If the cat believes there is a chance then I believe as well. You do not?"

Shiva didn't answer. He took a sip of wine. "I don't know these caverns ... and we don't know how many hollows still remain wandering the paths. There is much left to chance, and fortune might not be on our side."

"To good fortune then," he said with a wink. "She is the best of all mistresses." He finished off his cup and poured another. After that he took up his knife and went back to fletching his arrows.

***

The following morning the time had come. Ricard roused Shiva from his sleep and asked for the warden to join them on the roof. For once the warden did not find Tarkus burrowed up inside his little den; instead the cat had made his way to the roof of the second tower along with the others. He sat perched on the wall gazing down at Mat who stood below banging on the iron door with his sword.

"I hope you slept well," he said as Shiva approached. The warden stepped to the edge and peered over. Tarkus continued. "He's been down there the last hour banging on the entrance trying to make some noise."

"Any success?"

"Heehee, I believe so yes. It's been rather quiet over by the hatch."

They had removed the crates and barrels that had once sat over the entrance leading down into the tower. It sat vacant and still as Cright and Edward stood near. Ricard was not far off either, his bow drawn and arrow notched as he leaned back against the tower. Behind him the whirl-pool cast up a never-ending mist that made the air damp to breath.

"Are you sure you don't want a blade?"

"I have my dagger."

"Yes, of course. I will not press it any further."

Shiva glanced at the cat quickly. What a vexing creature. It was just the nature of cats, he told himself. Who has not seen deceit in their sly faces?

"Mat has returned," Tarkus said, rising before jumping down from the tower wall. "When faced with a difficult task it's best to get to it quickly. The ghouls below will only stay occupied for so long."

Tarkus smiled as he spoke, but Shiva thought there was a touch of reluctance as they moved towards the hatch.

"If there's more than four or five of them still waiting at the top than I'm not sure we can get the latch closed again before the others return, and if that happens, we'll die," Cright grumbled

"What nonsense," Tarkus answered. "You are always free to retreat back to the second tower and cut the bridge."

"Aye … I intend to."

"What does it matter," Edward said speaking up. An older man with a dour disposition, both Mat and Ricard always stopped to listen when the man spoke. "If we fail here well just starve down in that tower. I spent half my life starving, and it's not how I'm gunna die." He turned and spat, shaking his head while his hand rested upon his sword. He didn't say anything else.

"Ricard, the key," Tarkus said. Ricard stepped forward producing a key from his pocket. He handed it to the warden along with a length of rope neatly coiled. "I wish you well," he said.

Shiva took the rope with a nod. His face was near expressionless, but perhaps there was a touch of respect set about his mouth. He turned to face the hatch.

"Remember," Tarkus said. "If you're a shadow, how can they see you? Still … try to be quick," and with that Tarkus gave a nod.

Mat moved quickly, unlocking the hatch and signaling to Edward that he was ready. Cright stood close with his sword in hand, Ricard as well, arrow drawn and notched, ready to take down any hollows that might come forth. Shiva took one last breath and turned his eyes towards Edward and Mat. "Do it," he said with a nod. And a moment later the hatch swung open revealing the dark pit that lay below.

And then there was nothing.

No creature or cursed hollow appeared, only the black hole of the tower and silence. Cright moved in, leaning forward so as to get a better look when Shiva sprinted past him and jumped, turning as he did to grab at the small ladder on the inside. With the ladder firmly in grasp he let his feet go to the outside of the rails as he quickly slid down into the darkness.

He looked up and saw the silhouettes of Mat and Edward, they were holding torches and throwing them into the tower for light, three … four … five of them in total, their flames flickering as they fell into the tower. He saw the silhouette of Ricard's cavalier hat cresting the light of the tower just as the hatch was shut closed once more.

Shiva looked down. They had hoped the torches would land sporadically throughout the tower, but it appeared that most had fallen near the top, still … that was better than if they had fallen near the bottom. It was difficult to be a shadow if there was an abundance of light.

He could see the cursed men below, the open hatch had drawn their attention as he knew it would, but some of them were already half way up the stairs it seemed. He had no time for errors. He set the rope down, fastening his cloak about him as he did. Once draped in shadow he jumped from the stairs onto one of the pillars that spindled through the tower and went about tying off the rope. He snugged his cloak about him then and waited breathlessly for the ghouls to arrive.

They surged up the stairs in a wave of rotten flesh and bloodied armor, each hollow scrambling to pass one another as they clambered up the stone passageway, looking very much like the vermin Tarkus claimed they were. Still … this was something else. The way they moved, their speed and rage, they were different than the guards that had served in the undead cathedral, or any cursed that Shiva had yet encountered. They were more like wild dogs, frenzied into rage. Even as they ran up the stairs many were being pushed aside, their bodies tumbling and spinning wildly as they fell down to the tower floor only to rise up and begin the climb again.

The hollows above the caverns had been wild too. Shiva had watched them only for a moment before they caught his scent, but their rage was just as complete. Tarkus was right, these cursed were dangers to more than just the thieves guild if they were to spread.

At last the horde reached the top of the tower, and it was then that they finally achieved some morsel of intellect, as only one of them could climb the ladder at a time. The poor creature that arrived first began to cut up at the hatch with his sword as though he were striking at a man, but the latch had been shut, and, if he had to guess, blocked once more by the crates and barrels.

Shiva watched them where he stood, shifting irritably as he began to slowly lower the rope, inch by inch, foot by foot, deeper and deeper into the bowels of the tower. Every so often another ghoul would be pushed off and tumble down to the ground below.

Vacant creatures lost in a mad dream … Shiva looked on them with pity.

He glanced down. Only a single hollow remained by the door, its legs broken by the fall. The shattered creature was pulling himself towards the stairs with his bare hands, it was a poor sight to behold. Shiva checked his pocket for the key before lowering himself onto the rope and beginning his descent. He went slowly at first, not wanting to draw attention. When he reached the midpoint of the tower, he wrapped his cloak around the rope and slid the rest of the way, falling lightly onto the tower floor.

Only the solitary hollow saw him land. The creature turned and began to crawl at the intruder as Shiva drew his dagger. He quickly finished off the hollow before making his way towards the door, removing the iron crossbar and placing it quietly to the side. The lock made an audible click as he turned the key, but when he went to push on the door it resisted.

He crouched low, pushing into the door with all his weight … but still the door remained closed.

Abruptly a hand caught his heel and he stumbled, falling backwards onto the hollow creature. It was upon him a moment later, clawing at him with its broken hands, its eyes like that of a beast.

Shiva grunted, holding the creature by its neck as he reached once more for his dagger. He stabbed the blade deep into the creature's head and the hollow fell still. He threw off the ghoul and cast his eyes upward, hoping that their struggle had not drawn attention. His hope was shattered with ill disproportion as the hollows above threw themselves off the stairwell towards the intruder. Their bodies broke upon the surface in a mash of steel and stone. Shiva threw himself into the door, hoping to force it open. It gave a little as he struck it a second time. Three of the ghouls were beginning to rise as more threw themselves down without hesitation.

He smashed into the door once again, this time he could reach his hand through the opening. The ghouls continued in their descent, one of them narrowly missing Shiva as he fell from above.

"My lady!" Shiva yelled as he threw himself into the door one last time. The door faltered for a moment before swinging open, letting the outside light spill in with all its radiance against the darkness of the tower.

Shiva emerged, the horde of ghouls following close on his heels. He looked like a shadowed specter from above, his dark form streaming below the tower base as he ran towards the ladder tearing off his cloak as he did.

"There!" Mat called out. "He's done it!"

"Heehee … indeed." Tarkus seemed unmoved as he watched the warden being chased below. "Mat, be set to receive him. The rest of you stand ready beside the ladder, and Ricard, be sure to take out every third hollow as they follow. We're not to be overrun this late in the hour."

Shiva reached the ladder and began his assent, not bothering to look behind him. He could feel the undead pressing behind him.

As he neared the top, he peered up warily, catching a glimpse of Ricard's familiar hat peaking down in his direction. He stood atop the wall with bow drawn and arrow notched, his aim set upon the warden. Shiva paused, inhaling quickly as he felt a hand grab at his boot. Ricard let fly the arrow and the hand released its grip. In a flash he had drawn a second arrow, releasing it as well. Shiva risked a quick glance below and watched as the two ghouls closest to him fell limply from the ladder.

When he reached the top, he found Mat's hand waiting for him. The young thief pulled him up and away from the wall before leaving him alone with Tarkus, a pleased grin showing beneath the creatures' eyes. "Heehee. Marvelous, simply marvelous. My hopes for you are of the highest regard." Shiva turned and watched as Cright and the others cut down the ghouls one after another as they tried to breach the tower. "My men will make quick work of these hollows. Then we shall claim our reward and make ready our escape from these awful ruins."

Shiva met the cat's gaze, silver eyes that gleamed in the light and revealed only what he wished them to reveal. He was done trying to read the cat, it was pointless to try. Instead he turned and continued to watch the carnage that was unfolding before him.

It was hardly a fight, and there was little sport in the matter; still, he would watch until the end. They had almost had him … twice. Alone they were weak; together they were an earnest foe, worthy of death. He would watch to make sure death came for them all.

1 0

LENNOX opened his eyes and watched the fire from his torch flicker beside him, its quiet flame slowly dwindling at his side. He lay still for a moment feeling his chest rise and fall with each breath until at last he sat up. Drear and dark were his surroundings, a murky cavern lit dimly by his fading torch. The girl was beside him, that was a small relief. After taking a moment to check himself for injuries he went to her next. She was breathing. He ran his hands along her body, checking for any bones that may have been broken in the fall. He paused when he reached her leg, feeling the warm blood as it soaked out from beneath her cloak.

This won't do, Lennox thought as he looked at her. He shook his head and drew his dagger, cutting into her pants from the knee downward before carefully striping away the wet leather and bloodied wools that lay beneath. He kept watch for any signs of pain but the girl remained still, her sleeping face indifferent to the world around her.

Lennox brought the flame close for a better look. It was a single piece of wood, thick in diameter and nearly as long as his hand. The splintered piece had pierced cleanly through the girl's left calf and the knight was concerned she would bleed out if he did not act quickly. He set down the torch and removed his gloves, placing one hand upon her thigh as he dug the other deep into the wound. He grasped at the fractured wood as quickly as he could, hoping the girl would not be roused by the pain. The blood made it difficult though, and every time he thought he had a grip it would slip out from his fingers.

He took a moment and looked at the girl, a hint of sadness poking through the small slit of his helm. Then he pulled out his dagger and cut at the skin before ripping out the wooden stake in one quick tug. She awoke in a scream of shock and agony, her body writhing in pain as she fell back against the floor.

"Be still!" Lennox yelled, trying his best to hold her down. "Be still!"

He managed to pin her to the earth before reaching for the torch, whispering something into the air. The torch suddenly exploded into a flame of blue that burned hot and cast its light brilliantly, revealing for the first time the knight's surroundings. He paused for a moment, shocked to see that they lay against the side of a dark crag, its sharp edge only feet away. He turned back to the girl and pressed the torch against the flesh of her calf. She let out one final scream before falling unconscious.

Dropping the torch, Lennox fell backwards. The blinding fire that had burned so fiercely moments ago withdrew, leaving the torch half melted on the earth, its fire slowly returning to its normal red flame. Lennox took a moment to rest while his eyes adjusted, then he picked up the torch and held it close to the girl's calf, its warped metal still warm to the touch.

The poor light made it difficult to confirm, but the wound seemed to be closed … it was all he could do at the moment, anything more would take its toll on the knight, and they were not safe, not safe at all.

After cutting his blanket into a dozen or so strips and wrapping them around the torch, he made his way to the crag's edge. He tilted his head back, trying to find any sign of the keep above them, but the torch was weak, and the cavern walls tall. He peered over the edge … nothing, only the sound of a distant river moving swiftly below, its black waters lost in the darkness.

Hmm … how fortuitous. He looked back at the girl and then to the cliff's edge, *any further and we might have drowned, well, she might have.* He supposed he would have awoken sooner or later. For a moment his mind went to Shiva. *Had the warden fallen into the river? Had the wraith?*

"Kah hah. If only that man could be killed so easily," he said aloud to himself, a habit from years long spent alone. He turned and looked at the girl, a smile hidden beneath his visor. "We'll see him again, of that I'm confident."

Afterwards he returned to the girl and drew her up, throwing her over his shoulder as though she were a child. He paused, deciding which way he should go, but since he didn't know where either path led, he realized it hardly mattered which way he went and began walking.

***

Soon after he set out the land began to slope upwards, not a lot, but enough for Lennox to notice the incline. He plodded along patiently, letting the torch grow smaller as he did. As light as the girl was, Lennox could feel fatigue setting in. It came quicker than he thought, much quicker. He was considering taking a small break when the path ended abruptly, dropping off steeply into the valley below.

Blood and ash, he thought. Weariness came over him then and he set the girl down, checking her wound once more before looking out across the gorge. If he looked hard enough, he thought he could make out some sort of drawbridge that sat across the chasm hidden in shadow.

"Parva Lux," he said aloud and waited as a small ball of light began to form in his hand. He threw it quickly into the air, hoping it would reach the other side. It did, striking the wall before falling to the floor. The little light burned white, revealing a small drawbridge as well as two ghouls that had been standing dormant until that moment.

Curse me, Lennox thought as he dropped low. He grabbed at his torch and threw it into the chasm, hoping against hope that it would go unseen by the undead.

Too late, the unstirring had already begun. The closest hollow, a tall man made up of weathered bones and rotted flesh, gazed down at the fading spell as though in a trance, but the second … the second ghoul stood strong in a suit of armor not unlike the one Lennox wore save for its color. The hollow knight stared across the chasm, his eyes searching the ledge where Lennox lay pressed against the earth. The spell of illumination still burned brightly besides the two ghouls when without warning the cursed knight moved towards the drawbridge and kicked at the latch, releasing the anchor and dropping the bridge. It fell like a hammer, striking at the stone ledge in one thunderous clap that echoed back and forth across the stones a hundred times before fading into the distance.

"Ten hells," Lennox grunted as he rose, taking his flail tightly into his hand. The hollow knight was already moving, pulling at his enormous broadsword he wore strapped to his back. Lennox's mind went to Astrid; the girl would be crushed if he did not act.

With a yell the golden knight leaped forward. His feet shifting from the stone cliff to the iron drawbridge. Every step mattered; he must keep the fight from reaching the girl. Then the hollow was upon him, cutting at him with a mighty blow. Lennox danced to the side, dodging the strike as he swung his flail around the hollows neck. He shifted his feet and tugged at the handle, causing the knight to lose balance.

Lennox smiled as he released the flail, kicking at the knight's back as he did. The cursed knight fell noiselessly from the drawbridge, his dark frame lost into the abyss. Lennox turned to face the lingering ghoul.

Teeth bared in a rancorous snarl; the wicked creature was running towards him. The hollow hobbled as he charged, raising his dagger high before bringing it down upon the knight. Lennox raised his arm, letting the blow strike against his armored gauntlet. He reached out with his free hand, grabbing at the hollow's neck and shoving him off of the drawbridge with a kick. He watched as the hollow fell into the darkness.

Lennox let out a sigh. The fight had gone well, though he had lost his flail in the skirmish. Still, weapons could be replaced, armor repaired, as long as he was the one standing in the end. He turned to the girl when a distant light caught his eye. Deep into the chasm, along the path he had traveled glimmered the twinkling of light, the blurred shining of a distant candle. Lennox stepped forward, his heart raced as more and more candles began to appear. Not candles, torches … thirty of them, carried by a horde of ghouls as they ran along the curving pathway.

The golden knight shook his head and hurried to the girl. "Astrid," he said. "Astrid, it's time to wake up! I need you to wake up!" He looked back at the horde, their distant torches growing closer by the second. "Ha! Fine then, have it your way," he said as he scooped her into his arms. Warily, he rose to his feet, wondering just how far he could go while carrying the girl. If he had to, he could throw her into the ravine

… it would be a kindness in truth, a better end than she would otherwise receive. He didn't want to think of it, he would do what he could for her and no more. He had his own duties to fulfill.

He crossed the bridge, picking up the illumination spell as he did; without it he was likely to run himself off the cliff. As it was, he had hardly gone ten paces when he reached a sharp turn in the road. He stopped cold, almost dropping Astrid in the process.

A row of dying torches lined the cavern wall, their flames gone, leaving behind smoldering ash that clung to the pathway like a row of glowing sapphires. The burning ash ran twenty or so paces before reaching a small tunnel and disappearing into the mountain.

By the time he reached the split he was already breathing heavily, his body wet with sweat beneath his armor. He had to make a choice, and had little time to make it. He tossed his glowing sphere along the chasm before ducking into the tunnel. "Burn me!" he cursed, regretting the decision immediately. Outside he could always retreat to the river, in the tunnel who knew where he might end up?

It was a narrow passage, barely wide enough for two people to pass. He could see more torches up ahead, these ones well-lit with steady flames, revealing an end to the winding tunnel not far ahead. He burst out of the hall, sliding onto the dusty marble floor before falling to the ground, doing his best not to fall on the girl.

Lennox rose quickly, groaning as he did. He picked up Astrid from the pavement while he looked around uneasily. A small river lay ahead of him lined on both sides with heavy wooden barrels as well as large rafts to guide them. Behind the river stood a single fortified tower made of stone and mortar.

He made for the bridge, hobbling as he ran. He had twisted his knee during his fall … it would not slow him down. He was halfway to the bridge when the first of the hollows burst out of the tunnel behind him, streaming fourth like a pack of feral dogs, their numbers less, but still strong enough to overcome him.

Lennox could feel their empty eyes upon his back as they sighted him and the girl, following after in reckless pursuit.

He crossed the bridge, the weight of the girl pressing into his shoulder, throwing off his balance as he ran up the first steps leading into the tower.

He fell with a crash but rose quickly, not daring to look behind him. He was close, very close! Only a few more steps! He grabbed at Astrid's hands and dragged her up, one step at a time, until at last he stood before the tower's entrance.

He laughed when he saw it was cracked open and pushed the heavy iron door the rest of the way, throwing in Astrid before closing it behind him and lowering the iron bar, locking it in place.

Crash! The door shook as the horde of ghoul's fell upon it. Lennox lifted his visor, watching closely for any signs of weakness … but the iron hinges were thick and strong, and the door would not break.

A hint of relief shone in his eyes as he turned and looked at the girl. "How many times must I come to your aid?" He stopped then, noticing the wound on her calf had split open. The tower was well lite, allowing Lennox to see the severity for the first time.

He looked to the door, listening to the hollows as they banged upon it with their swords. Either it would hold or it wouldn't, it was no longer in his control. He turned the girl and pressed his hands upon her calf and whispered to the air. He would be empty now, for some time, but it was all he could do.

The two torches set beside the door winked out, then the one halfway up the tower, then the two set at the top until the only light was the warmth coming from Lennox's hands. Then that faded too, and the golden knight fell to his side shattered and drained in the darkness of the tower … the clanking of the hollow's swords echoing in the air.

***

The palace doors lay in ruin, beaten in by a large battering ram shaped in the form of a boar whose charred remains lay off to the side still smoldering from the dead flames that had once consumed it. Scorch-marks soiled the once beautiful walls and rich velvet rugs that lined the floors. A dark ash filled the air, never resting as the heavy cinder kicked and twirled with every gust of wind. Women and children lay stacked in piles, their corpses smoldering like the boars.

Lennox wadded through the destruction, stepping over hollow suits of armor once filled with the castle guards, now empty save for charred bones that turned to ash at the slightest touch … burned to crisps by an eternal flame.

"Aello, my Queen! Please … reveal yourself."

The ash of the dead stuck to him in clumps, leaving broad black smears against his polished golden armor. He stepped across another strewn body, kicking up a puff of black soot that covered his legs up to his knees. "Priestess … priestess!"

The palace shook. A distant scream reverberated across the marble halls, echoing in madness before stillness fell once more.

The golden knight wandered the grounds, making his way through the great hall towards the courtroom. It was there that he came across three royal guards standing before the corps of the fallen king, his skin cold and gray.

"Sir Gareth, Sir Andre," Lennox said, lifting his visor so he could meet their eyes. "Sir Wendrick." He nodded in respect to the three knights.

"Prince," Sir Wendrick replied sadly.

Sir Gareth and Sir Andre said nothing at all, donning their helmets and drawing their blades in response.

"Where are my brothers … my sister?"

"King Dresden and princess Cira have gone to the Tower of the Gods in pursuit of Sir Gillian. As for Prince Duncan I cannot say. Only, I'm glad they have gone. I prefer it fell to us to finish what you and your false queen began. It would break your father's heart to see his children resort to kinslaying."

"He wasn't supposed to be here, none of you were. I want you to know that." Sir Wendrick looked on with reproach, his mouth twisting with distaste. Lennox continued. "The Lords have been lying to us, all of them, Lord Shem most of all. I realize that you might not understand … but this age has run its course. We were never meant to be ruled by them."

"The Creator has given us the rulers we deserve."

"We deserve more!"

"We deserve to die alone … and so we shall, to be sure. As it stands, Lord Shem sits with your false queen in the throne room. He has bid us let you pass, but you have tarnished your father's name, and honor diktats we set it right."

At last Sir Wendrick donned his helm, flexing his hand before clutching at his blade.

"This is not a fight I desire," Lennox said.

"They never are," Wendrick answered. "But it is the one you must face." Then he charged, flanked closely by Sir Gareth and Sir Andre.

They were big men, the royal guard, well over six feet and donned in castle forged armor carrying castle forged steel, all bearing the crest of the royal family. Lennox had removed his family armor, instead wearing a suit of gold bearing no sigil. He carried a discus war-shield made of shifting light and a spear crafted from white silver and imbued with lightening, the tip of which cracked and thundered as though a storm bristled upon the blade.

He could feel the power from the spear pulsing through his skin, making him feel as though his very flesh blistered with magic. Hesitant, he readied himself to meet the three men, and thrust his spear forth, striking at the knights as they fell upon him.

The air turned blue, cracking like a storm among them. It took all of Lennox's strength just to keep hold his weapon. The clear crystal light of the spear took to the air and streamed out connecting the three foes as though trapped in a current. The palace walls bowed outwards, attempting in some way to escape the release of power, so utterly strong that the very earth began to shudder.

After a time, the earth fell quiet, and when the ash settled no sign of the royal guards remained. Where the three men once stood lay white footprints set into the surrounding soot and nothing more. Strangely, a single mirror hung askew on tattered cords survived the destruction except for a single crack that ran along the right side from top to bottom, it was there that Lennox caught sight of his reflection.

He saw not himself, but a stranger set in smoldering armor of gold, and cast in burning embers with heat and blood shimmering about him. The knight in the mirror looked as though he were fire made flesh, cruel in strength, with power enough to put down the gods and set about the succeeding age. So terrible was the image that Lennox stood grounded, unable to cast his gaze aside or cry out, until at last the mirror could no longer hold such an image and shattered, falling to the earth in a thousand pieces of silver and glass.

Then everything went dark.

11

ASTRID paced across the top of the tower peering down at the ghouls that stood below. She looked past them towards the small river and the water that flowed so close yet out of reach. They had found food in the tower, but little water, and her thirst was great. Lennox had told her not to look towards the river, that looking would only awaken her need without quenching her desire, but she found herself looking none the less.

Finally, she could take it no longer and left, making her way down the spiraling steps towards Lennox. The golden knight hadn't moved for a long time, claiming he was only tired and needed to rest, but when she returned, she found him sitting at the table. He had removed his helm and now sat starring at the iron door. The cursed had been at it without end, hammering at the door continuously from the time Astrid opened her eyes to the time she went to sleep.

"They will stop eventually," Lennox said. "With enough time they can learn. Only little things, but still, they'll know they cannot break through the door and will leave it be."

She took a seat across from the knight, picking up his helmet and turning it in her hands. "This is well made," she said, ignoring his words. She did not care to think of their dilemma.

"I forged it myself." Lennox was looking towards the girl, trying his best to read her mood. She had been more than a little downtrodden since her awakening, and he feared she was falling into hopelessness.

Astrid looked up at him surprised, perhaps even a little impressed at his words. "You forged this?"

"Of course ... I forged my shield and spear as well, though they are back at the mountain city, lost beneath the great lake."

"Were you the son of a smith?"

"Hah!" Lennox said with a smile, amused by her words. "No princess. I am like you, the child of a king."

This time when she looked at him, she was more than a little surprised. With mouth ajar, utter astonishment shone upon her face. She looked down at the helm and then up at the knight. "A prince of where?"

"The silent city."

"The silent city," she repeated her eyes wide with shock. "Is this ... is this another secret, Sir Knight?"

"Hmm, I suppose. Though, you already know what I truly am beneath this illusion. That is all you really need to ruin me. This I tell you freely, you need not give me a secret in recompense."

"A prince of Marshiel," she said again in disbelief. "Where you there when the city fell to madness?"

"No," said Lennox. "I was locked away before the true chaos fell." He was quiet then for a time, his mind racing once more to his abandoned cell, and then quickly to the present. "It makes you wonder, yes? What it is this Lady Sune wants with us ... three royals, sworn to serve her as little more than slaves."

"Three?" Astrid said. Her tone absent, her mind in thought.

"Our third companion, the one in Solaire. He is a prince as well, yes? The fifth son of the king, if what Shiva said was true."

"Of course ... how foolish of me to have forgotten."

Lennox waved it off. "A slip of the mind. Perhaps now would be a good time to lay bare all we know. We shall never have as opportune a time as we do now."

"I cannot see how it matters."

"Oh? I disagree. You seem to think that you'll die here alone in this tower with only me to watch you go, but you're forgetting our mutual friend, and more importantly the one he serves."

"Lady Sune?"

"The very same. She is a seer, yes? And she sent Shiva to retrieve us and return, yes? Well then, I imagine she wouldn't have sent him to begin with if she did not believe he would fulfill her request."

"Seer's can be wrong," Astrid replied.

"Not the ones that are of any worth, and I don't believe it would be in Shiva's interest to serve an oracle who couldn't see what lies ahead with accuracy. So please, my lady, do not fall into futility."

Astrid looked away, her face tense, her eyes scanning the ground anxiously. It had not worked, Lennox thought. My words could not reach her. "Fine then, doubt if you will, but I would still like to hear all you know of those brass knights I fought in the garden. You recognized them. Tell me how."

Astrid leaned forward, stripping the cord at the end of her braid before running her fingers through her hair until it hung loosely about her. She had always looked strong to Lennox, since he first laid eyes upon her ... but now as she sat hunched before him, she looked young. Just a girl in truth, he thought. Her strong eyes were tired and weary, sad almost to gaze upon.

"The brass knights," Lennox repeated. "Have you come across them before? Seen them in your travels?"

"No," Astrid said at last, shaking her head. "I've never seen them, nor have I come across them in truth. All I know of them was told to me by my father, from a story of his youth, one that has been forgotten by the world."

"My lady, I would very much like to hear this story." Astrid set down the knight's helm, her eyes meeting Lennox's for a moment. "Please ... until my death, I will not speak of your words to another soul. They will be safe with me, I swear this."

She looked away, nodding slowly. Another long moment passed before at last she spoke. "My father's sigil, the Hardrada royal crest, do you know it?"

Lennox nodded. "I know it well. A white palm, face up with a black flame burning above. An Imperishable Flame, meant to keep the north warm. It was given to the first king of Kay by Lord Batraal himself."

"It's as you say; if the story is to be held, but no longer. When my father was only a child, he said his father the king threw a great tourney, sending out invitations not just to the people of the north, but to all the kingdoms of the lower continent. He was said to be an arrogant man, my grandfather, claiming the world had never seen the likes of such a tournament before, and that it would never see the likes of it again. To prove it so he offered his eldest daughter's hand in marriage to the tournament champion, as well as a viewing of the Imperishable Flame, an honor meant only for the King of the North.

"A royal prize indeed." Lennox's face was dappled with golden light that shined forth from his helm atop the table. "And rather unwise of him, I think, to offer such treasures to chance."

"Unwise, Sir Knight? You are putting it kindly."

"Your grandfather wished to hold a tournament without equal, to achieve this he offered a prize worthy of the task. I'm sure he imagined no low born knight could possibly have won, and many would agree with him. He thought of strengthening his kingdom through a favorable marriage. It was a clever plan, but as I said, unwise, to leave it ultimately to chance."

"Again … you put it mildly." She was looking at the knight but turned away, pushing her hair out from her face. Lennox waited, hoping that his comments had not put Astrid off from proceeding in her tale. At last she spoke. "As the time of the tourney drew near, knights from all the world came, crossing the lower continent and the Slinder Sea to our realm, filling the city walls with banners of every kind, bright colors that flew high and cracked in the wind. The Iron King himself attended, joined by his two sons; garbed in their heavy black armor, they posed a striking likeness to their royal banner. But they were not the only royalty in attendance. Two princesses of Cataron also attended, guarded closely by their warden's, and even a paladin of Soliar, though he did not partake of the games.

"Many lesser lords where there as well, hedge knights from Bedivere and the Iron Range, freerides from the river lands, and flocks of squires, running to and from at their lords' commands, trying their best not to be trampled beneath the throng of horses. Not a single game had been played and already songs were being sung of the sheer majesty that was to be the Tournament of Ages."

Lennox could imagine it well. He had spent some of his youth in the city of Kay, though, he supposed it had changed much.

"Both the archery competition and the melee were given a full day unto themselves, with gold and great esteem given to the victors, but it was joust that the crowds were truly there for. A new arena had been erected just for the event, and three days set aside for the competitors, with the jousting running well into dusk. The hooves of all the great horses hammered into the field until the torn earth was hardly more than a ragged wasteland, servants had to work all night by torchlight to ready the field for the following morning.

"By the second day the chaff had been cast aside, leaving only the worthy. There were still many great knights in the running, but early on in the second day something odd began to occur. A group of mystery knights began to appear, their identity concealed. They wore the same brass armor with the exception of their helms, each of which bore the semblance of a different beast of the earth. The Brazen Guard they were called, seven of them, each one more mesmeric than the last."

"Were the two I fought among them, the jackal and the boar?"

"They were," said Astrid, turning to look at the knight, "but the boar you fought before the archtree was three meters tall, the knight at the tourney was a man, not a monster."

Perhaps, Lennox wanted to say. Instead he asked, "What of the other five? What beasts did they take for their helm?"

"Two you know; the jackal and the boar. The other five were the lion and the wolf, the bear and the crow... and the seventh bore the wings of an eagle. By nightfall they were all anyone could speak of, the Brazen Guard. One couldn't step foot into an inn without hearing some story of their true identity. Some gambler claiming to have beaten one at cards, or a fallen knight saying he recognized the man by the way he fought. And it was not just the common folk either; my father said it was all the court could talk of. It was a great mystery, to have so many talented knights unknown within the kingdoms."

"And you say none knew their identity?"

"None, Sir Knight, else I would tell you this very moment. They were my grandfather's bane, the bane of all the north in truth. You killed two of them. I am grateful for that, which is why I tell you this tale."

Hmm ... the bane of all the north, curious words. "Please," Lennox said, motioning for her to continue.

"On the third day, the Brazen Guard would at last be pitted against one another. All the tourney waited to see what would happen, except, as the day unfolded, what transpired surprised all. The first joust of the day pitted the wolf of the Brazen Guard against yet another mystery knight, this one set all in blue donning an old-fashioned sugar loaf helm. Like the Brazen Guard he flew no coat of arms and bore no sigil upon his chest or shield. Truth be told, my father says he hadn't even remembered the knight from the previous days, yet, right before the joust the wolf saluted the mystery knight and withdrew, all to the stunned silence of the crowed and kingdom.

"And it did not end there. In his next joust the blue knight was pitted against the boar, only for the brazen knight to withdraw as the wolf had before him."

"Did they all yield to the blue knight?"

"No," said Astrid. "The crow and the eagle crossed lance but neither lost their seat, and the king awarded victory to the crow. The rest of the Brazen Guard rode beautiful, but were vanquished in turn, for there were many great knights. But near the end, the crow did in fact yield to the mystery knight, so that for the last match it was none other than the blue knight against a prince of the Iron City.

"By now the crowds had gathered that the Brazen Guard served the blue knight, and guessed that maybe he was a prince after all … perhaps from Soliar or Cataron? Even my father could not say, and the King of the North was greatly pleased. The great mystery of the blue knight and his Brazen Guard would only add to the grandeur of his tournament. Great songs would be written and sung, and they were, but they would not be like the king had hoped."

"The blue knight won," Lennox said.

"Just so, and that night the king invited him to the castle to show to him the Imperishable Flame, and to present his daughter to the knight, proclaiming that the wedding would be set at the knight's convenience. But that evening, when the mystery knight arrived, he was not alone. The seven beasts of the Brazen Guard appeared beside him, and the king welcomed them all inside the inner chambers. For most, that is where the story ends. A great fire took up the castle that very hour, killing the king and the mystery knight, and both their guard alike, so that in the morning all that was found inside the castle keep was ash and hollow suits of armor. Except … that is not entirely true."

"Oh?" Lennox thought about the tale for a moment. "The blue knight and his Brazen Guard, their armor was never found."

"Indeed," Astrid said with a nod. "The people were told all were lost, but no trace of the blue knight or his guard was ever found, and yet the tale grows in desolation. When my father went to gaze upon the Imperishable Flame, he found nothing but an empty cauldron, cold and bleak in a room full of shadow and silence."

"He believes it stolen by the blue knight," Lennox said.

"Could it have been anyone else? My father spent his life looking for whispers of where it could have gone, and has told only his kin of its disappearance; but now the cold is spreading in the north, and people are beginning to suspect."

"I see. My lady, your tale is grim indeed." Lennox's gaze fell to the floor, as though a heavy burden had been set upon him and was now dragging him earthwards.

"I have told you all I know, Sir Knight, now you shall do the same." Her tone was unyielding. Astrid had spoken a great secret, now she wanted what had been promised.

"Of course," said Lennox, leaning forward as he lifted his eyes toward the girl. "It is not my intention to hide anything from you, my lady. Ask me, and I will answer all I know."

"The Darkmoon Alchemist, who is he? At my grandfather's tournament the Brazen Guard flew no coat of arms, nor did they show any crest upon their shields ... yet the two you fought at the garden bore the Darkmoon's sigil. Shiva spoke of him with great caution, yet I have never heard his name. Was it he who stole the Imperishable Flame from my grandfather?"

"No, my lady, first you must understand. The knight from your story is not to be confused with the Darkmoon. They stand apart. The Darkmoon is a wizard of dreadful power, creator of monsters and of ghosts, foul in understanding, misshaping all he touches, twisting all who follow him, and yet, despite this, he is subservient to the blue knight, for they are kin, and he is the younger. If these beasts of the Brazen Guard bear his mark, then he is their true master ... but he will bid them aid the blue knight in all he does, that is to be sure."

"Then why ... "

Suddenly a resounding boom echoed throughout the cavern, muffled by the tower stones and continuous rattling of the door. Lennox leapt to his feet and began climbing the tower, a hast glance over his shoulder showed him Astrid following at his heels.

"What was that?" she asked.

"I don't know."

The tower stairs narrowed the higher they went, old stones, rounded at the edges from deterioration of both time and man. At the top, the glow of the torches were bright, and below light still burned across the cavern. Just beneath them the horde stood beating upon the gate, but they were not so wild, and several of them were drifting away from the stronghold, their eyes set upon the tunnel leading into the cavern.

"Where are they going?" Astrid asked.

Lennox shook his head and shrugged.

Boom! Another explosion echoed throughout the cavern, this one twice as loud as the first, accompanied by a wave of warm light that burst forth from the tunnel before disappearing in an instant. The ghoulish horde stopped instantly, their bodies turning like a single mass of bones and flesh to face the cavern tunnels. A third blast flared, this time shaking the tower slightly before a wave of fire streamed through the tunnels like dragon flames.

"They're leaving!" Astrid cried out.

Lennox placed his helm upon his head, gazing out through the visor with wary cautiousness. He could hear the shuffling feat of the undead horde stamping across the wooden bridge before watching as they disappeared back into the tunnels. He grabbed at the tower wall and listened, but there was nothing to hear except his own beating heart.

Finally he straightened. Creator guide us, he thought. This was an opportunity, a gift, one they could not let go to waste. "We need to move."

The knight was already at the tower steps when Astrid turned to follow. "I agree, Sir Knight, but where? Surely we shouldn't follow after those creatures."

"The river," he answered. "We'll take one of the boats downstream."

"How are we to see?"

"By torchlight. The current is not strong. We will make do just fine."

"And if the river moves swifter than we can manage?

"Then we will crash upon the stones and drowned, still better than being caught by those hollows I should think. Now come. We don't know how long we have."

Outside the tower not a single ghoul remained. Astrid took what food she could carry and filled her pouch from the river while Lennox untied one of the rafts. Once she was done Lennox kicked off, and together they drifted along the shallows into shadow.

Creator guide us, Lennox thought once more ... his eyes drifted to the girl. Drowning was a bad way to die.

***

Astrid stood at the front of the raft, holding forth a torch of blue and yellow flame to light the murky waterways. She said little as they drifted, watching as Lennox pushed at the cavern walls with his oar each time they drew close. Every so often she would call out a split in the river and he would decide whether to change course or stay the path.

"How do you choose," Astrid began, turning her head back to look at the knight. "How do you choose which path to take?"

"The water my lady, I'm following the water. You were right. It would be troublesome for us if the current grew too strong. I'm simply trying to choose the calmer path."

"It appears you're doing quite well," said Astrid, offering the knight some small compliment.

"Thank you, my lady. But save your praise till we've come ashore."

For a time, nothing changed. The water ran along the stone walls high in some places, lower in others, and every so often Astrid would call out another split which Lennox would navigate, yet the river and the snaking tunnels were all the same, cold and bleak. Astrid was beginning to get a feel for the river when suddenly Lennox pushed them towards a calm bank and put them ashore upon a beach of black sand.

"Why here?" she said as she stepped down into the shallow waters.

"Look there," he said pointing further along the shoreline.

She held up her torch. "What is it?"

"It's another raft," Lennox answered as he peered out through his helm, searching the beach for any signs of hollows. He watched in silence as Astrid made her way towards the second raft. "Best wait for me," he called out.

Astrid didn't argue. She turned and waited until Lennox had pulled the raft further ashore, then they went together towards the second raft. It was empty save for a small satchel of wine which Astrid took, as well as a dagger that had been jammed into the wood at the front of the raft. Lennox took the dagger and placed it inside his belt, letting the blade rest bare against his armor.

Even a small dagger was better than none, he knew. Lennox took it for a good omen.

"How's the wine?" he asked.

"It's filthy," Astrid answered before dumping out what remained. "But the skin's still good; it will hold water just fine."

After filling the skin, they continued along the shore. It wasn't long before the sand started to turn into broken stones and then finally into black slate which lead further and further away from the shore. Soon the earth began to slope upwards and the walls on either side began to converge until at last they reached the end of the cavern. A small walkway cut into the wall emerged before them; a passageway just large enough for a man to walk through. Astrid went first, walking with her torch before her as the knight drew out his newfound dagger.

Somewhere deep in the cavern another blast went off, shaking the stones beside them slightly and echoing throughout the caverns of the deep. Whether the explosion came from behind them or before was impossible to tell.

"Who do you suppose is behind all these explosions?" Astrid asked looking back.

Lennox smiled beneath his helm. "Hmm ... I was just wondering the same thing."

"And?"

"I haven't the faintest idea. But anything that draws the hollows away from us is certainly welcome."

Not long after a light appeared before them, just a single point. As they drew closer Lennox saw that the light was actually a reflection of a large fire that shimmered in a still body of water beginning to take shape before them. He put out his torch and Astrid followed his example. In the darkness he whispered in Astrid's ear. "Take care to keep silent … any noise we make will carry across water as still as this."

They continued forward and soon the water was to their ankles. Lennox grew nervous when the rising water reached his knees, but then the ground leveled and the water stayed as it was until they reached the end of the tunnel and emerged at the base of a still lake.

Astrid nearly fell backwards when she saw the sentry demon pacing across the shore like some sort of lumbering beast. Close to eight feet in height, the monster paced awkwardly across the sand before the towering fire, its two contorted bodies twisted at the waist so that the demon had one set of legs but the upper torsos of two separate men. The twisted sentry wore a mix of chainmail and steel plate armor that helped hide the distorted flesh beneath, and atop their two heads were matching sugarloaf helms of dark iron. The first torso held in his hands duel straight swords while the distorted twin carried a large bow with arrow knocked at the ready despite there being no enemy in sight.

Astrid stepped back towards the entrance of the tunnel bumping into Lennox. She let out sharp breath of air but was otherwise noiseless. When she turned around Lennox motioned to her to keep quiet before pointing out a ladder that stood anchored into the cavern wall leading up to a small alcove that looked out over the lake. He waved for her to follow and began making his way towards the ladder, every step rippling out across the still shallow lake.

They reached the ladder and began their ascent, both of them pausing quickly to look back over the lake with an anxious uncertainty. If the sentry demon returned now, they would be seen for sure. Lennox reached the top first and quickly disappeared from sight before reappearing once more with his visor raised, motioning for her to hurry. She hadn't even reached the final rung of the ladder before the knight reached down to pull her the rest of the way. He threw her from the edge and fell to the floor, raising his finger to his mouth in a hushed motion.

Astrid lay still in the ceaseless quiet, her heart racing as Lennox stared back at her. Ever so slowly he flipped over to his belly and began to crawl towards the edge and gazed outward. She watched the knight, her eyes focused on his helm which shined dimly from the burning fire across the lake below them. He stayed on his belly for some time until finally he pushed away from the edge and returned to her side. He took off his helm and let his head fall back against the stone wall.

"He's gone," Lennox said quietly and closed his eyes, taking a moment to rest his mind. The hollows were one thing, but now a sentry demon! It's not possible, he thought. Just how far had the taint spread? They were leagues away from the sunken city, and there was no reason for the Darkmoon to be pursuing him so ardently. There must be some other explanation.

"Lennox …" the name drifted in his mind. He opened his eyes and sat up, turning to look at the girl. "You can rest later, for now we should keep moving."

"Of course," Lennox mumbled, slightly taken back by the girl's determination.

"I'm glad we were able to slip past that sentry. I almost cried out in surprise when I first saw the monster."

Lennox laughed. "Just be grateful Shiva was not with us, that fool of a man would have charged the demon the first opportunity he had."

"To true … that man will be the author of his own death, but I can't imagine he would have it any other way."

"Ohh? I'm not so sure, remember who he serves. The Lady may not let him fall to destiny."

"Who knows? But enough of the warden, its best we keep moving."

"Right," Lennox said, and together they began to follow the narrow pathway along the cavern lake.

***

After the encounter with the sentry demon they moved with great caution, lighting their torches only when necessary, and taking their time when they came across any new cavern or break in the path. Still, despite their slow pace, the hallways and tunnels were beginning to bring them closer and closer to the surface, and on more than one occasion they could see light cascading down from high above in translucent waves that pierced the cavern halls.

Up and up they went, journeying the unknown, wandering the paths as hour after hour past. They had gotten close to the surface several times only to be led down into the unknown once more, until at last the rough stones turned to wood beneath their feet, and they once again ascended upwards. The two of them exchanged a glance as the first glimpse of hope returned.

They pressed on and quickly came to a staircase that led up to a wooden hatch. Lennox's hand shook as he reached for the door. He could feel the air flowing through the cracks in the wood as he turned the latch and pushed. The door swung out into the quietness of the cool black night.

Lennox stepped out and turned to help Astrid and together they looked up towards the night sky. Even with their torches burning beside them they could see a streak of stars above them twinkling through the forest trees like a sea of shimmery diamonds.

"Any notion of where we are?" Lennox asked. He had lifted up his visor and stood with his head tilted back so that he could view the stars.

Astrid twisted her body to switch angles as she looked up at the stars. "I'm not sure, but perhaps I can point us in the right direction." She lifted her hands up; setting them against the sky like it was some sort of map. "Hmph … it's difficult to say for certain, but I believe east should be this way." She lowered her gaze and looked past Lennox into the woods. "It's impossible to say where we are in the forest, but if we head east, we will reach the end eventually."

"Hah! We'll reach the end no matter which way we go, but perhaps your right, best we get back to the path we were traveling."

"And what of the warden?"

"What of him? He's dead or he isn't, either way we're not going into those caverns to find out. If he's alive and manages to escape then he knows where to go next. I have half a mind to skip Solaire altogether and seek out this Lady Sune, but if we show up without our third companion, I fear I won't be able to rid myself of this appalling ring. I've already made one error; it would be unwise for me to compound my mistakes."

After a long search of the woods Astrid looked to Lennox. She seemed to have come to a decision. "Very well, we press on. I don't like abandoning a companion to the darkness of those caverns ... but I cannot imagine any attempt to find him would end in success."

Lennox placed his hand on her should. "I told you before; if Lady Sune is half the oracle I suspect her to be, then we'll see him again."

Her mouth opened, but no noise came out. Finally she nodded, and Lennox turned away without word and began making his way east through the woods. Astrid hurried after him.

With no trails to follow their pace was slow. Snow still covered most of the forest floor and at times it came up nearly to Lennox's waist. Eventually Astrid spotted a deer trail that they were able to follow for a time before it broke south and they were forced to once again make their own path.

"Curse this frozen earth!" Lennox yelled after slipping on a patch of ice and rolling down the side of a small hill. He was just starting to stand when a flock of crows burst out of the surrounding trees, fifty, a hundred screaming birds, spiraling into the sky above.

Astrid had seen Lennox cast a few spells but what she saw next astonished her greatly. A wall of light appeared forth from Lennox's chest as the knight held out his hands towards the screeching birds. The magic went forth with great speed, arcing up through the forest trees before colliding with the birds and exploding in a shock of heat that blew back at the trees and threw Astrid to the earth.

Her ears rang and her body felt heavy, but when she opened her eyes Lennox was already pulling at her arm trying to get her to her feet. "What was that?" she asked groggily. "What magic is this?"

Lennox was saying something to her but she couldn't hear him. He kept repeating it but she couldn't understand until finally he reached forward and took her into his arms. The golden knight made his way through the snow as swiftly as he could. Astrid thought it was foolish of him until she saw the snow melting before him as he went so that he was running on muddied earth.

"How?" she wanted to say but couldn't. She closed her eyes again then as the bells in her ears flurried once again. The pain was unbearable and she felt like she was going to throw up. Not again, she thought. How many times would she be saved by this man? Then everything went black.

***

In a small niche, beside a pile of ruined stones half covered by moss and grass, Astrid slept long into the morning. It was a patch of grass, blowing into her face by the passing wind that finally woke her from exhaustion. Shifting from a dream of home, a time once spent in a cabin outside her father's castle, she opened her eyes and stared, vacant, at the soft-white clouds that trickled across the blue sky.

Both light and shadow fell across her face as she sat up in surprise, her eyes frantically searching for Lennox. The dreams of her past vanished as memories returned, so vivid that her heart began to race.

She saw Lennox sitting quietly not ten feet away with his back set against more broken rubble. Already breathless, she crawled towards the knight in a sort of frantic fit.

"Lennox!" she said as she moved. She reached the knight and went to her knees, taking his hand. Nothing ... no pulse or warmth, but then, he was half hollow himself she knew.

"Please, Sir Knight," she said, and looked once more to her surroundings, seeing for the first time the open fields that lay before her. She turned west and saw the frozen woods, its snowy trees running like a wall along the fields to the east.

Her eyes fell back to the ruins that encircled them. A wall maybe two feet tall and a tower which had collapsed upon itself was all that remained of what was once a small fortification, perhaps only a guard post even.

Nothing moved. The morning was cold and still; and even the breeze seemed to have withdrawn for the moment. Astrid turned to the knight and went to retrieve his helm but found it fixed. Even his visor refused to rise. Taking a deep, calming breath, she turned and took a seat beside the knight.

He did not sleep, she knew, and she saw no signs of harm to his body. So how had they ended up in the ruins of a fort, clear of the frozen woods and all signs of those nasty crows? She sat silently in thought until at last she looked towards the knight. Lennox had feared the crows for some reason, that's why he'd fled so hastily ... but still, she knew not why.

She stood up and made her way out the ruins and along the open fields. It was a barren land full of rolling hills, low grass, and few trees. A single road ran along the side of the forest leading north to south, and birds could be seen flying across the sky, but beside the flutter of their wings there was little movement to be seen.

She was not sure why it felt so odd when realization fell upon her. She turned and looked out along the fields and saw in the distance a group of riders making their way across the hills towards the ruins. Her hand went for her sword, checking to make sure it was still there before turning and making her way back to Lennox.

She found the knight where she had left him, and quickly began looking for a place to hide. The riders were moving fast and would be upon them soon. She was not sure how far she could move the knight, if at all. The best she could manage was to drag him out of plain sight. They were clear of the forest, but the roads along the edge were far from safe.

More than once she had to stop to regain her strength, and traversing the uneven ground was proving tediously difficult, though she managed to get him behind some stones while the riders were still a way off. She took a moment to wipe the sweat from her face then ran along the ruins to the west wall and climbed up the remains of the tower, feeling the jostling of the weathered stones beneath her as she climbed.

Looking out she saw the riders in clear view now. She counted twenty, with most dressed in light armor and bearing a flag of blue and silver with a symbol she could not make out as it fluttered in the wind. She watched as the party split into two, with one group breaking north while the other remained on course with the ruins.

She slid back down to the base of the tower and returned to Lennox. They were out of sight, and as long as they were quiet, she saw no reason the men might search for them, but her resolution faltered as the beating of the horses drew nearer before stopping altogether not ten spans from the edge of the ruins.

Muffled voices filled the air as the men called out to one another before dismounting. Astrid thought to look out and see if she could get a better view of their crest, but the risk was too great, and she remained kneeling behind the wall with her hand ready at the hilt of her sword.

"Girl …" a voice called out suddenly. "Girl, reveal yourself to me. I know you rest behind the stones with the knight of gold. Fear not. You are lost, bewildered by the world around you … but I mean you no harm."

Astrid remained kneeling behind the wall, unsure of what to make of the man's words.

"Something seems to be bothering you, girl. Yes, I can tell. I am Sir Galehaut Hillsong, servant of Lord Magnus, protector of the Eastern Arc. You are afraid, don't be. I seek only order. Now reveal yourself, that I may demonstrate my sincerity."

Lord Magnus, she thought. The name sounded familiar, though it was difficult to remember the names of all the Lords outside her own kingdom. Her hand tightened around the hilt of her blade as she gazed towards the woods, to freedom, and then to Lennox. What was the knight to her, that she should risk herself? Her partner? An agreement fixed by secrets.

"Girl," the voice continued. "Do not be alarmed. What have I done to frighten you? My men will do you no harm, but if you flee, I must subdue you, and I have no desire to do such."

Her gaze rested upon the golden knight. He had protected her … she could do no less. Turning to face the riders she rose, her hand still resting on her sword as she called out to Galehaut. "Sir Knight," she said, seeing that he was the only one dressed fully in armor. "I would ask you state your purpose, and how you came to know I was here?"

"My lady," he answered with a small bow. "Forgive me, my perceptions are not always as sharp as I would desire. I thought you to be a bit younger than you are. Please, don't let my manners unsettle you."

Astrid remained distant, her eyes cold as she looked over Sir Galehaut and his men. One man remained in his seat beside Sir Galehaut, and in his hand he carried the pole which flew the blue and silver flag she had seen from a distance. It blew gently in the wind, revealing the broken crown of house Magnus.

Sir Galehaut continued, "I have spoken my purpose, my lady. I do as my lord bids me, and desire only to keep order in this land."

"So, it was your Lord who sent you," Astrid said stiffly.

" … it was," Galehaut said with a nod. "He is a sage you see, and went out in the world as a sorcerer in his youth. Now he confines himself to his quarters, and watches his lands through his crystal sphere. He bore witness to both you and the golden knight's arrival late last evening, and bid me come and take you to him." He paused then, reining in his horse as it stirred beneath him. "As you can see, we brought horses for both you and the knight. Now please … be at ease."

Astrid found Galehaut's words vexing as she looked out among his men. None of them had drawn their blades yet they all stood rigid, their faces hidden by spiked helms with a single crossbar that cut across their faces.

Galehaut himself was a handsome man, gray-haired with a grandfatherly face that seemed at odds with the burnished armor he wore strapped over his blue and silver undercoat. He seemed a kindly man, honest and dignified, and something about the way he spoke made Astrid want to believe him. For a moment she thought he may have been casting a charm on her, but dismissed the notion. It would have had to be an extremely powerful charm to gain her trust so quickly.

She turned and looked towards Lennox, wishing very much that the knight might rise, but he did not, and it was left for her to decide. Though she felt there was little choice to be made. Galahaut's men made that clear.

"My companion is not well," she said at last. "He cannot ride."

"Yes, yes, of course … Lord Magnus knows this. Do not fret. My men whom you saw depart to the north are retrieving a cart with which to set the knight in as we speak. They will be here shortly." He smiled then as he looked down at Astrid. "You see, your knight will be well cared for, don't you agree?"

Astrid nodded, looking back at Sir Galehaut with a flat, unblinking stare. "I agree," she said, yet inside she could not help feel as though there was something very wrong with both Galehaut and his Liege Lorde, and wished very much for Lennox's awakening.

The sooner the better.

1 2

SHIVA's leather boots shuffled noiselessly along the smooth black stone of the cavern floor. Behind him Ricard moved in silence, and before him Tarkus almost seemed to hover along the earth. If Shiva were to close his eyes then the enchanted cat would disappear completely, he was sure. All the others were lost. Shiva could not say for certain they were dead, but as they moved throughout the black tunnels ever perused by swarms of ceaseless hollows, they found their group decreasing in size in a manner most disheartening.

Edward was dead, Shiva was certain. He had heard the screams even if he had not seen the killing stroke. But the other two might still have made it, especially Cright. The old man would not die easily Shiva knew.

Tarkus was more than crafty to say the least, and knew the tunnels better than Shiva could have possibly imagined, setting traps and blockades for the perusing ghoul's at every turn ... but, for all his cunning ploys and shrewd thinking, they had scarcely managed to stay ahead of the ghouls that roamed the tunnels. They were low on firebombs too, and Lennox did not think they could survive many more encounters with the cursed ghoul's, which were both frightened and drawn by the bomb's explosions.

"Oh!" the cat said suddenly, his whiskers bobbing up and down as he sniffed at the air. "Do you smell that? What a clean scent ... it's absolutely wonderful heehee. We might just be clear those foul hollows."

Shiva looked at the cat with considering eyes. "I find your gay mood troubling, cat."

159

"Truly?" Tarkus said looking back, a puzzled expression strewn across his face. "I can't imagine why."

"I've made an error in following you," Shiva replied, stopping where he stood. "We've lost men and provisions both and have little to show for it. We're clear the ghouls for now, but that is because all you've done is led us deeper and deeper below the earth, where even the ghoul's make no point of journeying."

"Well that's simply not true," the cat replied with a wicked grin. "They come, I'm sure of it. They come down deep to the depth in search of the disturbance made by the lurker hounds … and then they never return. But do not be afraid, the beasts rarely come out from their nests unless disturbed, they're quite blind you see, and one is more than safe as long as one stays quiet."

For a moment Shiva stood stunned from shock, though he hid it well. " … lurker hounds," he said, irritated at the revelation. "Why not lead us through a pit of vipers instead; we might actually stand a chance of living. We would need be ghosts to make it through unnoticed. You can't possible think we can make it?"

"Well," Tarkus said with a pause, as though actually taking time to consider Shiva's question. " … Of course I do." He was smiling at the warden, the same wicked grin as before, as though Shiva were a mere child there to amuse him as they moved about in their journey. He continued, "If you object to my route you are free to choose your own. We need consort no longer." With that Tarkus turned and continued along the dark tunnel.

What a wicked creature, Shiva observed. There was more than enough cunning in the tomcat, a slyness best not forgotten. He had followed the feline too far into the depths; he could not depart from him now. He turned to face Ricard and said, "You have some guts, following this mad creature of your own volition."

Ricard only shrugged. "I think the tower was more dangerous, no? You survived that … you will survive this I think. Besides, the cat likes you. He would have let you die long ago if he did not."

"How can you be sure?"

"Because he likes me too, and we are still here when the others are not. We took many paths to reach this point, many tunnels that wound back and forth, more than we need take." He smiled then and placed his hand on Lennox's shoulder as though they were old friends. "The boat can only hold three … some of us had to die."

After that Shiva kept watch on both Ricard and the cat. They were an unsavory lot, and he was eager for the time he was free of the caves and of their company, however much longer that might be.

***

As they continued down the narrow walkways the sound of moving water was clear if not distant, and it wasn't long before they reached another open cavern. It was not a very tall cave, and the light from Ricard's torch filled the dark space easily, revealing a small boat that sat on the shore beside a river with black water.

Shiva watched as both Tarkus and Ricard made their way to the shore. The great cat stopped at the water's edge and went down to take a drink while Ricard dragged the boat to the water and stepped inside. Tarkus followed, leaping into the little ship before turning to face the warden. "Well … come now or you'll miss your chance. Then you'll really be in a tight spot, I must admit."

Shiva stood watching the boat as it passed. He thought he saw the great tomcat grinning, but in the shadows he could not be sure. "Were does it lead?" he asked.

"To a way out," Tarkus replied with a chuckle. "What have we been trying for this whole time if not to escape?"

Shiva's moth twitched in annoyance, but he moved towards the boat all the same. Ricard's words shook him more than he would have liked, yet the man still seemed to have faith in the cat. Shiva wondered if perhaps the man was under some sort of hex, because if Edward and Mat and Cright were expendable, then so were they, no matter how much the cat liked them.

Ricard had one foot up on the side of the boat and offered his hand to Shiva as he neared. Shiva took it firmly as he stepped into the vessel. He took a seat in the center with his back to Ricard and found himself face to face with Tarkus.

"I'm so pleased you've stuck with us through all of this," the cat said in all sincerity. "I was truly at a loss before your arrival, but you've proven to be everything I hoped you might be. Though … there is still so much more potential."

Shiva looked out, gazing into the unending void before them. He was begging to grow weary of the tomcat but he kept his tone flat. It would do no good to let his emotions fall through "How much longer must we pitter around in the dark?"

Again the tomcat chuckled. "It will get darker before the light comes, warden. Soon we must douse our flames and trust completely to the river. Though blind, the lurker hounds can feel heat from great distances. It will not do to risk fire, lest we be devoured." The cat was quiet then for some time, and then added. "I'm afraid this trip will be both dark and cold … but if that is the way then it's how we shall go, sometimes there is no other pass."

Indeed, there was no other way, and soon the cat had them scuttle their torches in the river and then the darkness was complete. The cold followed soon after, a deep chill that blew through them like an icy wind.

Not long after feint whimpers could be heard if not seen, echoing softly across the water like a kiss. So quiet, the warden doubted if he had truly heard them at all. It was off putting, for Shiva was not used to his ears cheating him. He leaned forward, hoping to whisper a question to the great cat but stopped and returned once more to his seat. He had been warned not to make noise until they had passed through the lurker hounds nests, but how long that would be Shiva could not say, and so he resigned himself to the silence and the dark.

***

It was hard to gauge just how long they sat there in the gloom … quiet as stones, hardly daring to breathe. Every so often silver discs like tiny moons would glow in the distance accompanied by more whimpering and hollow growls, then, in a blink, they would disappear. Shiva found it easier to just close his eyes and ride out the darkness inside himself. Soon enough the whispered snarls and muddled moaning faded away until there was only silence once more … silence and black, and the trickling of the river which never truly left.

Tarkus's voice cut through the darkness, telling them to relight their torches. "We are in the ruins of Shallo-gon, well past the lairs of the lurker beasts."

"What is this place?" Shiva asked after he had lit his torch. The light from his little flame spread throughout the cavern, casting its luminance upon the face of the ruined buildings that lined the banks of the river.

The entire city was abandoned, from what Shiva could see. They drifted gently in their boat as he turned his head from one bank to the other, taking in the sights with cold indifference. Not so much as a mouse moved, and Shiva knew that neither man nor hollow had walked the streets for many centuries.

"A remnant of the past," Tarkus replied lazily as he turned to lick his back. "Just another forgotten city from before the fall of Marshiel … before the gods fell silent."

Several of the buildings had collapsed roofs, or toppled walls that spilled piles of brick and stone along the streets or into the side of the river. Yet most of the structures remained both whole and strong, at least in appearance, with many a tower shooting up to where Shiva's torchlight could never reach.

"Shallo-gon," repeated Shiva, making a note of the name. "What happened to all the people?"

"Heehee, yes, that is a mystery," Tarkus mused. "One might consider the lurker hounds, but that is only a guess. Besides, what happened here happened long ago. Most will have forgotten of this city by now, it truly was of little significance … in the scheme of things I mean."

It was important to the people who lived here, Shiva reflected. But he said nothing, and let the matter die.

Every so often they would pass below a bridge that connected the two sides of the city. Shiva was concerned they might come across a fallen bridge and have to make their way around it somehow, but that never transpired, and eventually the city began to grow smaller as they reached its end.

Shiva watched and listened and pondered all he'd seen since his parting with Lennox and the girl. He knew they still lived, Mistress Sune said he would not fail, He would find them again. He would return with all he had promised. He could not fail. But what to do next? He shook his head slightly. He was still trapped inside a seemingly endless cavern.

He could do nothing until he was free.

The hours marched on, and Shiva found himself nodding off until finally the water came to a stop and Ricard began to row them towards what Tarkus said was an unseen shore. It was another twenty minutes before their torches lit the dark sand along the banks of the cove. They could see the light from their torches glimmering against the side of the black cavern wall that rose not two spans from the shore.

"Well, we've come quite far now, haven't we?" Tarkus said as they drew upon the beach. He watched as Ricard jumped into the lake with a splash, the water coming up to his knees before pulling the ship up onto the sand. When the boat was at last secured the cat leapt ashore.

He does not seem to like water, Shiva observed. Though, he had never seen a cat that did. Wicked creatures, he had never trusted them, not truly, and even Lady Sune seemed only to tolerate them.

He stepped ashore and followed after Tarkus who was already making his way along the water's edge. His eyes were ever watchful, looking both forward and behind as they moved.

Tarkus observed Shiva's caution and spoke to address it. "Be at ease, warden. There are no hollows here, to be sure. None have passed before the hounds and been spared. We are quite safe, I promise."

A calming nod from Ricard assured Shiva of the cat's words, and after that he was much at ease, at least, as much as a warden of Cataran could ever be. "We are close then? Close to a way out of these dreadful caverns?"

The great cat only shook his head. "Patience is a virtue quite lost upon humans … you should try to be more like me. We cats are born patient."

After that Shiva spoke no more.

The dark shore was a series of beaches connected by shallow creeks of water no higher than their knees at the deepest point. The long beaches twisted along the cavern walls, never breaking far out into the water. Apart from his companions, Shiva had glimpsed no living creature since the silver moon eyes of the lurker hounds, assuming those were in fact their blind, clouded eyes. The caverns were almost beautiful to behold when not infested with such inimical wretches as the hollows. Shiva imagined Shallo-gon was once a beautiful city, glowing like a diamond below the earth … in the long-forgotten past.

For a long way they stayed on the beaches, following their shallow bends as they curved slightly around the endless lake. There were a few stretches that went straight for a time, but always they followed the lake and would eventually turn for no lake went on forever. Tumbled shelves of rock often jutted out along the cavern walls, forcing the trio to duck low as they passed, and in certain places Shiva found himself almost crawling beneath the stones. Such obstacles were infrequent though, and for the most part the path was calm and beautiful … a sort of attractiveness in the dark that was its own brilliance.

After a time, Shiva inquired as to why they had not crossed the lake by boat instead of taking the long route around the shore, but the tomcat only shook his head and looked out into the emptiness and said, "I would not pass across those waters unless there was great need. These caverns are fascinating, but they tend to draw all sorts of disturbing creatures from long forgotten places. Many of them wish only to be left to themselves … and I am inclined to let them."

Their torches were beginning to lose flame when their long track came to an abrupt end where a massive slab of stone thrust out from the side of the cavern wall. They passed beyond the stone and watched as a narrow pass came to light. "Straight through here," the cat said in a quiet voice. "Soon our paths will deviate, much to your pleasure I'm sure, heehee."

The cat did not wait for a reply but started at once, moving down the dark tunnel with Ricard close behind and Shiva bringing up the rear. They moved fast, faster than Shiva thought needed, but it wasn't difficult to keep pace and he soon found them on a steep slope moving up, and up, and up. *Even the cat is eager for freedom,* the warden mused, a smile touching briefly at his lips.

Up the shadowed pass they went, three trespassers invading the dark with their dingy flames and soft scuffling feet, until at last they came to an end. Shiva was confused for a moment, seeing that there was no turn in the stone, and that in fact the passage truly ended with nothing to show.

He hardly had time to think of it when the cat spoke. "Well … it cannot be delayed any longer; it seems we must now part. Truly a shame, your skills in the shadows match those of your sword. I could use a man with your talents. It's a dangerous world outside these stones."

The cat's words vexed Shiva greatly, and he knew not what they meant. Perhaps there was a way out after all? Either way, he was weary of Tarkus and his scheming. Shiva looked at the cat bluntly and said, "I'm sure Ricard will keep you from harm, now if there is indeed a way of escape make it known. I will not suffer in the dark any longer."

Tarkus smiled, his grin flickering in the torches flame. "Why of course there is a way, for where else could young Ricard have gone if not away?" It was true! There was no sign of Ricard yet the warden had not seen him go. For a moment Shiva's heart flurried in his chest, yet his eyes remained calm, always calm when surprise was present ... and for that Tarkus loved him. The great cat continued. "Did you not see him go? That's all right, you must know where to look or you'll miss it clear as day. I'll show you," and with that the cat turned and strode through the stone and vanished from view only to appear once again a moment later.

"An illusory charm," Shiva said stepping close. "Meant to hide the way with stone."

Tarkus nodded. "It was set to appear as rock from the outside, though it works just as well on this side of the cavern." The great cat paused then ... somewhat unsure of what to say next. Finally, he spoke.

"So now it truly ends, warden. Every departure requires a first step, trite, but true, and I shall take mine straightaway. I bid you long life, and if our paths should pass again, I shall be greatly pleased." And then the cat was gone, passing once more through the stone wall like mist through cracks.

A truly awful creature thought Shiva as he stepped forward to follow after the cat, but when he moved, he found the stone wall both hard and impassible. He ran his hand along the smooth stone looking for the way through but felt only stone and heard the sniggering of the cat mocking him from the other side.

"What magic is this that I cannot pass!" he shouted out, his temper breaking through. "Answer me cat! We had an agreement!"

At once the tomcat's head appeared through the stone wall, a wicked grin full of pleaser present on his face and eyes gleaming with delight. "I said I would lead you to a way out ... I never said it would be one you could take."

"You foul creature! Curse you and all your kind!"

"Oh my! How splendid your eyes do shine when filled with rage! You're lucky, such fury suits so few."

In a flash Shiva's sword was drawn and its silver arc lashed out towards the cat's head but found only rock. The clash of sword on stone rang out and was accompanied by a soft laugh as Tarkus once again stepped through the stone. "We need not come to blows," the cat said, doing his best to stifle his giggling. "There is a simple way to pass through this ward, and I will tell it to you at no cost. You need only take upon yourself the mark of our guild, and you may move freely through this passage."

Shiva had already sheathed his sword, knowing he could do nothing to harm the cat. Still, his eyes burned cold, and the cat seemed to be enjoying himself more with every breath.

After a time, when Shiva had collected his rage, he spoke. "You wish me join your guild."

"Ahh ... now that you have said it aloud, I suppose it to be true.

"Being forced to join a guild cannot bode well for either party."

"Well that's simply not true! It works out well for both can't you see ... if you betray us, we will know where you are, and will act according to our best interest. And you ... you get to live! That seems like a great arrangement to me, and if the need should ever arise when you might want to seek me out once more, than the mark will aid you in that as well."

"Very well," Shiva said stolidly.

The cat's face shook with delight as he stepped further out from the stone and into the dark passage. "Where would you like the mark?" he asked as he circled the warden.

Shiva considered the cat's question for a moment and then quickly untied his boot and held his foot up to the tomcat. "Here," he said, pointing to the bottom of his foot.

Tarkus smiled. "That won't be necessary. The mark will be invisible except in death or when called upon."

"Here," Shiva said again, in a tone that said he would not change his mind.

"Very well," the cat said with a sigh, and proceeded to set his paw up against the warden's foot. Shiva felt a warm sensation and then nothing. "It is done. You may travel freely through the passage, brother."

Shiva stared blankly at the cat, his cool eyes revealing nothing. The cat seemed to like that and smiled.

"Our business is concluded … until next we meet," Tarkus said as he moved backwards through the stone passage. He took one last moment to bow towards Shiva, his grin ever present, and then he was gone.

Shiva eyed the stone wall, taking his time to re-lace his boot before rising to his feet. He grimaced, feeling the mark of the guild pressing into his flesh. Perhaps Lady Sune could remove it, but even thinking of bringing it up to the Lady brought him shame.

Curse the trickery of cats! Curse his own foolishness!

He put his anger aside and stepped forward, passing his hand through the now relenting stone. He smiled, knowing he had finally escaped the dismal caverns, and stepped through the stone into the light of day.

13

OSGALION ... that was the name of the city Sir Galehaut had said. Astrid did not think it much of a city. Twenty or so derelict structures remained scattered along a single road that ran through the street from east to west; the rest had been overrun with high grass across the rolling hills on either side and grew through the city like weeds. It was not a land of trees, and Astrid had scarcely seen one since leaving the frozen woods. She rode behind the cart that bore Lennox and watched his armor shake back and forth as the cart dipped and jerked along the stony pathway.

Beside her rode Sir Galehaut, ever mindful of her comfort and concern for her knight. "Has your journey thus far been difficult?" he asked. Astrid turned and looked to the knight but said nothing, then turned her eyes forward once more. "Of course it has. What a silly question for me to have asked. But let not your heart be troubled! I will see you safely to Lord Magnus, and there, perhaps you will find relief ... if only for a time."

The night air was cool and the moon shone brightly above, casting its grey-silver light upon the ruins of the city. The column did not move fast, but they were relentless in their march, stopping only to make repairs to the rear axle of the cart.

"You should take this time to rest," Galehaut said turning to Astrid. "We have much distance yet before us, and you will not have many chances to sleep in stillness."

Astrid nodded and looked to the moon before dismounting. Her heart longed for her wolves, and ached to know of their wellbeing. All around her the guard's cloaks gleamed grayly in the bounding moonlight. She could not make out their faces, but she knew they were watching, always watching. And not just her; beneath their helms the blue guards kept a keen watch upon Lennox as well, though he had scarce moved since being placed inside the cart.

She reached the ruined steps of one of the collapsed buildings and stopped short, gazing up at a pair of large stone statues that still remained strong upon their pillars. On the left stood a knight kneeling with his sword drawn and set into the earth at an angle, the knight's head hung low so that it rested against the blade as though he were to behead himself. Across the stairwell stood the second statue, a cloaked figure with a crystal ball resting upon his left palm while his right hand point out in accusation.

What peculiar figures, Astrid thought to herself. She looked past them to the tumbled building and saw several more statues similar to the ones besides her still standing at the top of the stairs.

"Sir Galehaut," she called out.

The knight seemed surprised to hear his name but came quickly to the girl. "My lady."

"This building," she said gesturing to the collapsed structure before them. "What was it?"

Galehaut studied the building for a moment, then answered, "It was a school, my lady. This whole city was a place of learning ... long ago of course."

"What happened to it?"

"They grew arrogant," he said matter-of-factly. "Now please, try to get some rest."

"I'm not tired," she said abruptly before turning to face the knight. "Your Lord Magnus, you said he was a sage, yes?"

"I did."

"And that he watches his lands in his crystal sphere?"

Galehaut nodded.

"Can he perceive the future and gaze to the past, or is he limited only to the present?"

"Alas, that is not for me to speak of my lady, though I would tell you if I could. All you learn from Lord Magnus you will learn yourself, through your own eyes and ears. It is not for me to speak of my master's secrets, though few indeed are known to me."

"There was another in our party. Can Lord Magnus find him for us? Though I did not like the man, we have traveled with him long, and I wish to know his outcome, alive or not."

Sir Galehaut only smiled, though he looked sad to Astrid. "My lady … Forgive this poor soul, but I will not speak of my master's power."

"At least tell me what business he has with us," she said. "You have been polite, but let's not pretend we are here by choice. Sir Lennox and I are your prisoners, though you will not say the word."

"My lady, you have many questions. Yes, yes, I can comprehend why… but I have no answers to give you, save to say Lord Magnus has business with you, and I will take you to him. I know. It is not what you wanted to hear, but it is what I will say. Now please, try to get some rest."

"I will not," Astrid replied. "But I will eat some food."

Galehaut nodded. "Of course. I'll have some sent right away." He turned and left quickly, leaving Astrid alone beside the statues.

Not long after a guard brought her some food which she ate alone as she watched the men go about fixing the cart. Sir Galehaut was among them helping lift when the time came. He was everything a knight ought to be she thought … yet why was she so wary of the man? He did not appear to be trying to frighten her. There was never a touch of anger in his eyes, nor a hint of deceit. So then why, what troubled her so?

She did not know and was greatly vexed.

Soon after the repairs were complete the company went on, passing though the expired city and back out along the winding road of the low hills.

They had not gone far before Astrid looked back upon the city once more. Dark yawned the archway of the gate that stood ruined beneath the cold moonlight. Behind it lay a sad decay of shattered stone brought upon by arrogance … if Galehaut was to be believed, and she found no reason not to.

But whose arrogance, she pondered, and thought of the queer statues she had seen inside the city.

***

They rode long into the morning, stopping for neither food nor rest as Galehaut had promised. He apologized several times, commenting that they had little warning of her arrival and were unable to attain a better means of transportation for Lennox, but Astrid would only stare at him coolly.

The sky was a clear blue, bright and warm, and the road ahead was long, winding before them rough and broken between rolling hills of dying heather. Long ago it must have been a marvelous road, matching even the great roads of the north, or perhaps even greater. In places there were ruined statues along the path, remnants of great works of stone like the ones inside the city of Osgalion.

More of these bizarre statues, Astrid thought. Most were beyond recognition, but the ones that remained stood out in stark contrast to one another. They were gruesome things in truth, mostly of grim knights in the act of sacrificing themselves in some way, either by removing their head or falling upon their swords. Every so often they would change and it would be another cloaked figure holding either a crystal sphere or large tome. Many of the faces were hidden deep inside the stone but a few had their cloaks thrown back to show a face fair and pure.

Astrid had not intended to remark upon the statues but found herself inquiring about their meaning. She could feel Sir Galehaut watching her, but when she turned, he looked away.

He was gazing towards the statues and had a glint in his eyes, something old, a memory of long ago perhaps? At last he spoke. "They speak of the making of the city," he began. "After a long war to the west where many died needlessly, Simon Magnus — the first of his name — moved his people to this new land. He ordered his people to give up the sword and take upon themselves enlightenment, for he had seen what the sword promised, and wished to free himself and his people of its grasp."

"Without knights, how did the kingdom defend itself?"

"Oh, there were still knights my lady, there will always be knights … but as time trod on and peace ruled the land, they were dismissed and never replaced. You see, it was the belief of Lord Magnus that should an enemy invade, both the wizards and sorcerers of the city, trained with patience and great knowledge, would rise in defense, using their power earned though due diligence. And he was right of course! The great wizards and learned men of the city were more than a match for any enemy, but as with all, their desire for power did not end there. In the end it was their undoing. They grew arrogant and, in their hearts, they wanted more. A magic was discovered that offered great power to the user but at much cost, driving the city into madness. They dove deep into a magic that should not have been practiced."

"I do not understand," Astrid said softly. "What happened to the city?"

"No one knows precisely, my lady. A great fire fell upon the people, and the earth shook with a wrath never felt in these lands before. House Magnus would have perished had the lord not been away for a hunt." Sir Galehaut stopped suddenly in the middle of the road, and so too, did Astrid. She waited patiently for the knight to continue. "Having seen the city fall, Lord Magnus fell into despair ... and there he would have stayed ... had his queen not pulled him free. They gathered all who had survived and moved east to rebuild, vowing never to forget the sorrows of Osgalion. They crafted these statues, mirroring the ones of the lost city and placed them along the road as a reminder."

"A reminder of what?"

" ... That knowledge alone cannot save us," Galehaut answered and kicked his horse forward once more. "And so ends the tale of Osgalion, a once beautiful city in song and story. Now come, let us not fall behind."

***

They pressed on, watching as a cluster of thick clouds blow in from the north, blotting out the sun. By dark not a star could be seen. Astrid thought their pace might drop, but soon the guards lit torches and pressed them together to spread the light until the whole company except her rode forth with reins in one hands and torches in another.

From a distance they appeared as though a string of fireflies bouncing along the surface of the earth.

Astrid was surprised just how quickly they managed to ride despite how dark it was. She would have thought it foolish, had the road not improved the further east they traveled so that the cart hardly shook at all as its wheels turned atop the flattened stone.

They kept a strong pace for some time. The land was gentle enough to let them, with rolling hills and terraced fields interspersed with meadows of flowers and trees. Astrid wished it was day, that she might better see the land they rode through, for it had changed much since leaving Osgalion, except for the statues that were placed every five leagues or so.

The night was quiet except for the soft burning of fire, and the occasional creak of the wagon.

Against her will, Astrid found herself growing tired. One could only go so far before weariness took its toll. She would have nodded off had a voice not called out suddenly from among the men.

"Riders approach!" the voice said.

All at once the column stopped. She gazed out but saw nothing outside the glow of the torches, yet in the distance the *clip clap* of horse's hooves echoed along the road before them.

Who would ride without torch in the middle of the night? It was strange enough for her own party to be traveling. The mystery puzzled her, and she waited eagerly for the answer to reveal itself.

Out from the darkness two figures emerged. Silhouettes at fist ... hardly recognizable, but slowly their shapes took on light, revealing the pair. One was a knight dressed in silver armor from head to toe and carrying a lance like the ones used in tourneys at his side. The other was a sorceress, draped in a black cloak with silver lace that hid her face and hung well past her feet so that it dragged on the ground behind her as she rode, and out from her came a shadow that swallowed light, drowning her even more in the darkness of the night. Above the riders a pair of ravens circled high calling out with *quorks* and raucous shrieks.

As the riders approaches the two birds descended and placed themselves upon the shoulders of the sorceress. Then the knight spoke. "Hail Sir Galehaut! How fairs thee, this most sweet darkness?"

"Ahh! Sir Grimmond, Lady Gwyn ... very well thank you," he said loudly, in a pleased manner. "I would not have thought to come across you this night. What brings you out so far across the western road?"

"By the word of Lord Magnus," Grimmond answered. "It appears that pesky cat has been seen traveling our lands beside the forest. We have been sent to catch him, if we can."

"He is elusive, that one. But tonight is a good night for a hunt. Perhaps with Gwyn's help you may finally catch the tramp. I have had little success in my attempts."

"Perhaps," Grimmond answered and turned to look at the sorceress. "It will be curious to see how that old tomcat matches up to Gwyn. I've never seen her match yet ... but ohh, that cat has his tricks."

The sorceress spoke then, from deep within her robs her soft voice echoed. Her words were strange though, and seemed to twist and turn so that Astrid could not understand them. When the sorceress finished, Grimmond sat silent but Galehaut was laughing softly. It appeared any words the sorceress said were not meant for her ears.

"That's true enough," Galehaut answered. "Yet you have not come across this creature before, you may well regret those words, my lady."

This time Gwyn did not reply, and instead one of her ravens *quorked* loudly upon her shoulder before flying up into the air. It was quickly joined by its twin and with that the sorceress went forward, pressing her horse back into a slow trot. She turned her head slightly as she past, and deep within the hood Astrid saw two green eyes like glowing emeralds look her coolly up and down.

Then she was gone.

"Till we meet again," Grimmond said and followed after, nodding gently towards Astrid as he passed.

"A fine fellow, Grimmond is. It was unfair of Gwyn to jest at him soo. Though it was good for him, I believe. Good for the heart to laugh at one's self from time to time."

"I could not understand her words," was all Astrid replied.

"Ohh? Well, Gwyn is a quiet girl. Somewhat guarded at times, it would do well for her to open up, if only a little. I think they make a good pair."

They pressed on then. Galehaut never revealed what Gwyn had said, leaving Astrid to wonder, though she cared little, and soon forgot the two companions.

***

The morning sun peaked in the sky, casting its rays on the company as they rode forth. With the light came a renewed vigor, and Astrid found she was no longer tired. She turned to Lennox, wondering when he might finally rise from the living dream he now traveled. She thought of the forest, and of the crows that had surrounded them. Lennox had been frightened of them for some reason, truly alarmed; else he would not have reacted so strongly. His magic had been terrifying, even the memory of it made her shudder. His power was deep, deeper than she ever thought ….a She had never seen his equal.

The path went ever forth, winding through the shallow hills and gentle streams. Soon the clouds above grew dark and the rains came and went, but there was still blue sky to be seen, though the waters ran high.

Galehaut had said they were drawing near, but Astrid saw no signs of Lord Magnus's stronghold. A single tower that pierced the sky like a mighty javelin he had said. Such a structure should be visible for miles she thought, yet before her lay only a single stone road, un-traveled except by Astrid and her escort. Every so often the road would split off, and Galehaut would point, telling her of the cities that lay north or south. But the lands of Lord Magnus were vast, and she saw no signs of the cities named by the knight.

They stopped for repairs when another axel broke, and this time Astrid was able to get some sleep in the shade of a small pepper tree that grew not far from the road. She had been escorted by two guards but was left to herself when she neared the tree. She was wakened by a mighty gust that crept along the fields and blew greatly at the tree before passing. By then the cart was nearly fixed and she was escorted back to the column.

It rained again that afternoon and long into the evening. The torches were lit once more, their burning flames hissing against the droplets of rain that fell on them like a slow haze.

Astrid pulled the hood of her cloak tight, hoping to stave off some of the rain, but it wasn't long before the cloak hung sodden upon her shoulders. The men before her were no better off, and only Galehaut seemed unaffected as the little droplets rattled softly upon his armor. Suddenly it grew very cold, colder than it should have been so that Astrid could see her breath before her.

Then the warmth of the air returned and lightening flashed in the distance … and that is when she saw it, a black tower of wondrous shape, riven from the bones of the earth and hoisted high into the air. An isle of stone it was, dark and gleaming as the storm raged on about it. Three wharfs of double-sided stone were shaped into one, and near the top the entire tower twisted slightly then stopped at a point.

They were close now to the tower, unimaginably close, as though the entire fortress had appeared before them by magic. For that is what Astrid suspected, there could be no other explanation. A spell of concealment had been lifted or passed though. She thought of the chill cold and wondered, but could not be certain.

"Lohalian!" Cried Galehaut. "We stand before a pillar of righteousness, the stronghold of Lord Magnus. Alas! That we should come upon it in the night ... during a storm no less!" Galehaut sighed, shaking his head as if some memory stirred in him. "You cannot see all its might until you see it by the light of the sun."

"Lohalian," said Astrid, gazing upward. "Fret not, Sir Galehaut, the tower's majesty is not lost to the night. No, its magnificence could not vanish so easily."

"Haha! Too true, yet something troubles you. Tell me. I see it clearly upon your face."

Astrid stopped, sitting irresolute upon her horse, her eyes ever resting upon the tower. She turned to Galehaut. "Must we go forth tonight? Can we not wait till morning?"

"Why ask for time now? What troubles you?"

"Long I have waited for Lennox to waken, though my heart grows heavy the longer he walks in his dreams. I thought he would be beside me when we met with Lord Magnus. But now that does not seem likely, and I hope one night might make the difference."

"My lady. Alas that I have rendered to you so poorly, the wishes of my master," said Galehaut. "Lord Magnus knows of your misfortune, and seeks to give you aid. He will lead your knight to the waking world once more, such power lies within him, and I have leave to tell you this."

"Then lead on," said Astrid. "Though I would have preferred to come upon this tower in the light of day. It is a dark tower, cold and barren ... and it frightens me."

"Do not be frightened, only the wicked need fear the tower, and even they can be forgiven."

***

They had not gone far before the column of men that had escorted them broke off without word and followed a lesser rode south. Galehaut and Astrid pressed on, following behind the cart where Lennox rested, pulled forth by a pair of horses. Further ahead a second pair could be seen riding along the road towards them.

From a distance the pair mirrored Sir Grimmond and Lady Gwyn, but as the two approached it was apparent that the sorcerer was a man plainly seen, with his hood thrown back despite the rain of the night. Like Sir Grimmond and Lady Gwyn, the pair journeyed without light and rode swiftly to meet them.

When the pair neared, the knight halted and the sorcerer trotted up to them alone. "My lady," he said with a bow. "Our business is urgent, so forgive me if I forgo certain etiquettes. Regrettably, Sir Galehaut is needed elsewhere, and must depart immediately. It is left to me to accompany you to Lohalian."

For a brief moment, all were quiet, and a righteous sadness fell upon Sir Galehaut, regret that he could not see the lady to the tower as promised. He turned towards Astrid and feigned a smile. "It appears I have been replaced, forgive me … it is not of my choosing, though little choice remains in the will of a knight who serves true."

"I do not hold you in error, Sir Galehaut. You would have taken me safely to the doors of Lohalian, I do not doubt. And only duty turns you away now. I find no fault in you," she said softly, though in her heart she was sad to see him go. He frightened her, true. But she felt some sort of comfort as she sat beside him, and did not wish to lose that as well.

"Something seems to be bothering you," he said softly. "Please, tell me. I do not wish to leave while sorrow envelopes you."

"It is only …" she started to say. "That I shall miss your company, I think."

Galehaut seemed both surprised and gladdened by her words and went to speak but stopped, and instead smiled and bowed his head gently.

"Farewell, my lady." He turned his attention towards the sorcerer.

"Vasily, see that she finds comfort in the halls of Lohalian."

"I will do what I can, Galehaut. Now go, Sir Vantimier will explain all." And with that the silver knight that had remained back kicked his horse forward as if called and began making his way west. With a final look towards Astrid and the golden knight, Sir Galehaut turned and was off.

"Such is the way of obligation," Vasily said aloud, but if the words were meant for her, Astrid could not say.

In the distance she saw two torches ignite as the riders dwindled into darkness. Her heart fell with their fading lights, and she turned to face the sorcerer. Near the great tower lightening flashed, but the rain had stopped where they stood leaving only cold gusts of wind that pushed into her sodden cloak and up against her skin.

He sat looking at her for some time, the sorcerer. As with Lady Gwyn, his black cloak was trimmed with silver and fell long past his feet so that it now lay upon the wet road in shallow puddles of water that flashed white with the lightening. "Hmm ... let's have a better look at you shall we," he said, and produced from his cloak a small lamp of dark metal that put forth a slender silver beam. He held it up, looking at Astrid's face and then turning it so that it shined upon Lennox. Then he shut off the light and held it out for Astrid to take.

"So that you might see," he said as she took it. "Welcome, my lady ... to Lohalian."

"I thank you," she said with a nod.

"You have entered into the inner realm of Lord Magnus. Watch closely your thoughts and do not wander, and ask not about the secrets of this kingdom. Few indeed have stood inside the stony hall, be it friend or foe. I have given you this lamp that you might see; for once we reach the tower all light will be stolen from you save that which is put forth from this lamp until you have been judged by the Lord. He will judge you, to hold you or aid you as he will."

This did not sit well with Astrid. "I am neither spy nor beggar, and did not come upon your lands by choice. Why then am I to be judged? I have done no evil to you or your master!"

"Of that I have no doubt," said Vasily. "But to stand before Lord Magnus is to be judged, as it is when standing before any Lord while in his kingdom. But fret not! Few have been called before the Lord only to be cast aside. Lord Magnus wishes to help you … but first you must stand before him."

Astrid was hesitant, looking at the metal lamp and then to Lennox. "And what of Lennox? Is he to be judged as well?"

Vasily nodded.

"But he cannot speak should the need arise."

"It matters not," said Vasily sternly. "You speak as if to delay what is inescapable. Galehaut has brought you thus far, and I will see you to the finish. You cannot turn back; all that is left is to continue on."

Suddenly, the cart that held Lennox pitched forward. Vasily remained immobile, his eyes set upon Astrid. He watched as she uncovered the lamp and held it up before her. When she had passed, he turned his steed and rode quickly to her side though they did not speak, and the only sound to be heard was the distant roar of thunder and the *clip clap* of their horse's hooves upon the stony path.

Since passing through the spell of concealment, a strange feeling had come upon Astrid, and it grew inside her as she rode. It seemed to her that she was being watched, though she saw no one except Vasily and the man who drove the cart. Sir Galehaut had spoken of Lord Magnus and his sight. It could be nothing else she decided.

Steadily the tower grew as they approached. The flashes of lightening ceased and the dark clouds rolled southward so that a sea of stars shone clearly above. They followed the road to the base of Lohalian but stopped well short of the entrance as stairs encircled the tower and spiraled out in one unending step up to the three entrances that opened upon the corners of the tower.

At the base of the spiral, a host of men stood waiting their arrival. A low horn announced their coming, a single call, blown by a guard through the swirling husk of a boar … and then silence. Two men stood holding a slim plank of wood that they placed Lennox upon as Astrid dismounted. Her horse was led away, but she stood a moment lost in wonder.

Astrid had grown up in the north, where strong castles were numerous, each one a fortress for the mighty, yet as she gazed upon Lohalian she felt as though she were looking through a high window upon an ancient tomb. The black stone shimmered in many colors yet remained a perfect darkness; and not a single blemish or mar could she see upon its surface.

She turned and saw that Vasily was standing beside her. He was looking at her with questioning eyes, and for reasons unknown she felt compelled to speak. "I feel as though I've stepped into a dream … if you take my meaning."

He smiled, knowing well of what she spoke. "You feel the presence of Lord Magnus. He has taken notice of you both, and is curious as to what he may uncover." Vasily stretched out his hand. "I shall lead you now. There will be no light save your lamp which will light the way before us."

Astrid took his hand and followed beside him, stepping lightly up the steps. Slowly the light around them grew dim, so that before them only the slightest silhouette of Lennox could be seen, and by the time they reached the door they were alone in the dark, seeing nothing but what the lamp shone before them. The strength of the enchantment left her breathless; no enemy could move upon the tower with such magic in place, any attack would end in calamity, with an enemy lost to wander in darkness. The silver light from Astrid's lamp exposed a door before them, and a moment later Vasily revealed a key cut from stone and placed in in the lock and turned. The door swung inward and they passed through unchallenged.

Before them lay an open chamber both long and wide, with a ceiling rising up until the silver beam could not sustain. Vasily led her through the hall. The ground was soft and Astrid tipped her lamp so that she might see the floor before her and found that it was covered in loose fabric from end to end so that no stone or marble could be seen. Indeed, no guard or folk of any kind could be seen, but voices were heard all about them as they moved through the hall.

They went along a narrow path reaching a set of stairs and began to climb. Up and up they went until they had gone very high and they climbed no longer but went forth into another great hall much like the one below except that hanging from the ceiling were twelve chains set with silver lamps similar to the one Astrid carried but bigger, and from each lamp poured light like a stream of liquid silver into pools of mercury.

Black cloth hung strewn across the walls in waves and covered the floor in piles that lay bunched together in great heaps in no apparent order so that the entire hall was covered and no signs of stone or wood could be seen, nor art or any decoration, nor furniture of any kind.

"We stand before the heart of Lohalian," Said Vasily. "I must depart, but do not fret. Lord Magnus awaits you … as does your golden knight."

She watched him go and turned back to look upon the great hall. As she moved forward, she passed between the waterfalls of light and wished in her heart to run her hand through the liquid but kept her hands by her side, and tossed aside her childish thoughts. She would not be caught by wonder, not when Lennox lay unconscious and unwell.

It was then that she came upon Lennox's body. He lay prone upon a slab of stone and beside the golden knight sat a crystal ball seated in the palm of a giant statue that stood upon one knee with his head bowed low. The crystal sphere was perfectly smooth, too large by far to be lifted by men, inviolable and unmarred by the passage of time.

It was then that she saw a shadow of a giant walking through the sprawling light of the lamps, draped in black with his hood falling well past his face … Lord Magnus approached. Every step he took was meticulous. His body swayed slightly so that he walked upon angles, turning this way and that as to avoid the streams of silver from the lamps above.

Silently she watched him approach, and while she felt no malevolence from him, her heart raced and she found her hand resting on the pommel of her sword. Foolish, she knew. She almost laughed, and a smile touched her lips.

Her expression did not escape the lord. He paused, looking from Astrid to the knight, and then back to Astrid. He was a towering figure, near three meters Astrid guessed, and when he looked upon her a second time, she caught a glimpse of his face and gasped, for his eyes were like starlight, and in them was knowledge like deep wells. He turned away then, perhaps wishing to spare the girl some tragedy, and spoke. "Come hither, child … and stretch forth thy hand that I may look upon it." His voice was clear but remote, as though a great distance divided them.

Astrid did as she was bid, and reached her hand out before her.

In a grand sweeping motion, he descended, taking to one knee and pushing his head forward to look upon her. He reached out, pulling back her sleeve and taking her hand into his own, though that too was wrapped in cloth and unseen. "Outstanding, the girl oracle has grown indeed." He spoke the words with great delight and released Astrid's hand with a slight bow. "Her spells are as fire in fields of dark. I perceived her work the moment thou entered upon my kingdom ... but thou art not a true disciple, why then is her touch upon thee?"

Beneath the gaze of his starlight eyes she faltered, unsure of what to say ... yet she could not leave the Lord's question unanswered. "I do not know," she said at last, and then was quiet.

Lord Magnus said no word but turned and beckoned for Astrid to follow. He walked before her, leading her around the altar to stand before the golden knight. Turning towards the crystal ball he raised his hand and the sphere lifted slightly in place. "Here is the Sphere of Lohalian ... my Illusive Eye," he said. "I called thee here so that thou might gaze with me, if thy has the mettle."

All about them the lights grew dim, the air chill; and standing beside her Lord Magnus was dark and tall. He stepped back so that Astrid might approach the sphere.

"What would you have me see?" she asked.

From deep in his cloak Astrid felt as though Lord Magnus was smiling at her. "We shall travers the living dreams of one who would see the end of an age ... but we walk through a world unbidden, and even I cannot say what we shall find."

"Is it dangerous?"

"Not with me beside thee."

Astrid gazed upon Lennox, her face heavy with uncertainty and fear.

"Dear child," said Magnus softly. "A dark and arduous test lies before thee ... and if thee cannot stand before a dream, how then will thee succeed in the wake of the living world?"

Astrid felt the question unfair, but she did not believe he meant it harshly. Instead she felt as though he was guiding her, urging her to be brave. "I'll look," she said. "But you must promise no harm will come to Lennox."

Again, she felt his smile. "Harm … dear child, thou knowest not who lies before thee. Much more than a man, he is … much more." He turned then to Lennox and leaned down breathing gently upon the knight. "Now join me, and we shall see what encumbrances his mind."

Placing his hand quietly upon her scalp he turned her eyes upon the crystal sphere and together they fell into the smoky gem.

***

A great howl echoed throughout the palace and along the great hall, a scream that came from the depths of a broken heart. The noise shook Lennox, wrenching him from his solid trance as he stood before a shattered mirror. He toppled backwards, stabbing his great spear into the earth to steady himself. He stood there breathing heavily for a long moment, his lungs grasping for air as his body burned with power. The great outflow seemed to wane, though only for a moment, before falling once more upon him. He tightened his grip upon his spear and shield, feeling their influence as they bristled at his fingertips.

"Aello … my Queen!" he called out, turning his gaze upon the lone stairway. His work was not finished. He would endure to the end. With all his strength he steadied his mind and willed his body forward until he stood before the staircase and slowly began his climb.

Three times the earth shook as he ascended, but he would not be thrown asunder. Sweat tracked down his face through dirt and blood and ash, and everywhere he looked he saw death and ruin until at last he reached the peak.

The Lord's Chamber was wide and tall, not quite as long at the Grand Hall, but near enough. Its white walls presented intricate carvings of the seven Jewel Cities, and between the cities hung rich tapestries embroidered with the names of the ruling kings that offered servitude to the Four. Near the end of the Lord's Chamber stood a dais, and on the dais four carved and smoldering thrones, and seated on the second throne from the left sat Lord Shem.

A stolid, slender women stood at the Lord's feet, draped in red and with hair like gold, soft and beautiful to gaze upon. She was tall, the woman, yet even then she barely reached the waist of Shem who sat like a statue of stone, head bowed with his eyes set to the floor. Upon his head sat a kingly crown of spikes dark and cruel, twisting out into the air in all ways.

Lennox wadded forward. He tried to look to his queen but his eyes kept going back to Shem, he dared not look away.

At last the great Lord spoke though his mouth moved not, and cold words echoed throughout the room. "Hmm … thou hast come at last, unfaithful retainer. Fret not; I am not angry with thee, though thy actions are heinous indeed, and vile in thought. Thou hast done nothing that cannot be absolved."

"Speak not, false one! I come not seeking clemency, but to cast you down, and learn in truth if you be not deathless!"

For a moment Lord Shem made no answer. He was silent, as uncertainty stood before him. "Treat me not with discourtesy and disdain; for though thou are but a child, we are much akin, servants of one who would lead us astray. I have shed my yoke, and now thou must follow. I offer thee absolution, and all thy wrongdoings will be forgotten, blotted out in mind and history so that thy actions need not be remembered … even by thyself."

Lennox's heart wavered as Lord Shem stood before him, high and frightening before the throne. He spoke no word but lifted his gaze, and behold! His face was shadow and black, his eyes misery and fear, and there was nothing beautiful about him.

Lennox recoiled back; both in fear and disgust, and uncertainty fell upon him. Could he end the great Lord? Could he smite him to the earth? His hands shook, his legs trembled, but slowly, at the feet of the Lord Shem, a great light began to burn, springing forth from the hands of queen Aello, and the chains that bound her fell broken upon the floor. She reached out, clutching at the heel of Lord Shem.

"Do not gaze upon his face!" cried the queen. "And let his words sway you not, for his time has reached its conclusion! Strike now … finish him!"

Lord Shem looked down upon the queen in sudden doubt, and drew his blade which shown like crystal and drove in down upon the queen, piercing her chest and pinning her to the earth.

"Finish it," the queen said as the blood pooled around her. "Lennox … end it!" Her voice boomed upon the stone walls and echoed across the

Grand Hall before dying like a flame blown out by a cold wind … then Lennox advanced.

The golden knight, streaming with magic, raced forward. Lord Shem turned to face him, but the light from Aello still shone bright so that the shadows upon his face departed and the likeness of a man shown forth and was enraged. Releasing his sword, he stepped down to meet his foe, and drew forth a second blade that burned red like molten stone. As he withdrew from the queen the shadows returned and fell upon him like a cloak of darkness until the entire room grew black; but still Aello burned bright, and so also the golden knight, though small indeed he seemed, standing before the might of a god.

Lord Shem's blade rose from within the shadows.

Lennox raised his shield.

The blade descended and found its mark, casting sparks and a shrill ring throughout the chamber. The Golden knight fell beneath the blow, dropping to one knee before raising his shield for another strike.

"Lennox! Finish it!" the queen cried out.

Ever wishing to please his queen, Lennox drew back his spear, and crying aloud threw it forward with all his might into the shadows. A blinding flash sprang forth and with a terrible cry the shadows departed and Lord Shem fell, striking the earth like a beast wreathed in pain before subsiding, never to move again.

A dark mist gathered then, poring forth from the body of the fallen Lord and spiraling up like rising smoke. It lingered for a moment, gazing down to its body below; once again the room began to shake, and a cold wind swept through the hall and the dark mist was gone.

Lennox looked to his queen in great distress, feeling as though his heart had shattered. He ran to her removing his helm, blinking and wiping at his face with the back of his hand, for tears blinded him, and he wished to look upon his queen unhindered.

Taking to one knee, he lifted her hand to feel her warmth, but found it cold to his touch, with all its glorious light faded and gone. Again he cried out and the earth shook. Already he could feel his power fading, for with his queen gone her enchantments would diminish until they were no more.

He longed to stay be her side but once more the Lord's Chamber shook. He looked up, brushing away his tears and rose.

Making his way to the corpse of Lord Shem, he pulled forth his spear. Already its power had lessened, though it still cracked blue and white. How long did he have? Others would come for him, he knew. He must not wait! He did not have long! Sir Gillian would be waiting for him at the red tower, and his power too, would be fading at the loss of their queen.

Already the body of Lord Shem began to wither, shriveling up into a mass of hideous flesh. Wrapping Shem's form within a fallen tapestry, Lennox pulled at the corpse, dragging the Lord's hollow remains away from the resting place of his queen. It was the last kindness he could offer before departing, though he did it with a heavy heart.

***

"Unwise ... to linger in the mind of another, one can lose much and more," said Lord Magnus softly.

Deep inside the cloudy crystal sphere the vision faded. Astrid stumbled backwards, falling into the outstretched arms of Lord Magnus. She was shaking, her eyes fixed upon the empty orb. She watched as it lowered itself until it once again rested upon the hand of the large statue, then she turned to Lord Magnus. From deep in his hood his starlight eyes gleamed. She turned away, unable to endure his gaze, and felt herself being lifted up and set back upon her feet.

She stepped away, keeping her gaze low as she did. "What magic is this," she began "What is it you showed me? What is it we saw? I thought you would help Lennox, help him wake up!"

"I know not what we perceived," he said, "for many mysteries have been shown, and I am ever learning. I must consider what we witnessed, lest assumptions bring destruction upon my realm. No more will I speak of it tonight ... but where thou are concerned fear not! Sir Lennox is well. Long has he been idle, and both mind and body have been strained. He dreams now, but in time he will rise, both well and unscathed from harm."

"When? How long must he rest?"

"The Sphere of Lohalian shows me many things, child ... dreams, thoughts, hopes, desires; but his future remains veiled to me." He turned then, taking a moment to look once more upon the golden knight. "He will rise in his time, until then rest. Vasily has prepared for thee a room, and will oversee the conveyance of Sir Lennox. He will not be kept from thee." And taking Astrid's hand into his own, Magnus led her through the chamber to the entrance where he left her with Vasily, and disappeared once more into the recesses of his hall.

14

ENNOX turned his head. Though hindered by his helm he could see a table beside his bed set with a tall crystal glass filled with drink and a plate of food untouched except for a piece of bread that had been cut into slices and half eaten. He blinked, staring at the food in vague confusion before lifting his hands up to his helm to remove the heavy piece of armor. Once off, he let the helmet fall and sighed ... a long, drawn out breath of weariness and fatigue. His body felt heavy, his head hazy, and the remnants of an unpleasant dream crossed upon the fringes of his mind.

He lay for some time looking at the smoldering logs of the fireplace. Though the flames had died he could still feel the heat put forth from the stones.

He wished to know where he was but thought little of it. I'll find out soon enough, he told himself. Back and forth his mind raced, thinking of the woods and the black crows that filled the trees. It made him angry to think about. He had been foolish, putting forth so much of his magic so quickly, very foolish. Though he had little choice, he knew. He could not have those cursed spies whispering his location to the world, he was not ready.

Suddenly his door opened, and Astrid stepped through quietly. A smile touched Lennox's face. "Ohh ... it's you. I was wondering when I might see you again." Taking a deep breath, he pushed himself up, resting his back against the base of the bed. Much of the time he hardly felt his armor, baring the weight as though it were his own skin, but now it felt heavy indeed.

When he looked up, he found that Astrid hadn't moved from the doorway. She remained fixed; her eyes set on his own. She had questions, he knew, as she made her way into the room.

"How are you feeling?" she said at last.

"Well enough," he answered.

She was dressed wholly in black, with a cloak of fine silk draped across her right shoulder laced with silver. Her eyes went to the fireplace.

"How long was I unconscious?"

"Near five days," Astrid replied, looking back to the knight.

"That long," he said quietly, more to himself than to Astrid. "And where are we now?"

"In Lohalian, the stronghold of Lord Magnus, Ruler of the Eastern Arc. We are safe, oddly enough; after our cursed journey through the woods." Her eyes furrowed in frustration. "Though I wish you would explain your dealings with the crows ... that absurd outburst left you half dead, and placed a heavy burden upon me."

"Foul creatures," he replied, remembering their dark wings flashing in the snow. "Servants of the Darkmoon, or one of his retainers, either way they had to be destroyed, all of them, else we risked more of the Brazen Guard learning of our location."

A quick shudder ran through Astrid. "Surly the Darkmoon does not command all the crows of the forest."

"You're right," he answered softly, "but for such a horde to be together outside the exit of the cave?" He shook his head knowingly. "They were sent there to watch, to observe any strange leavings, and to report back ... of this I have no doubt. But we have spoken enough on crows; tell me of Lord Magnus, and how we came to be his guests."

"Do not be fooled by false comforts, Sir Knight. We are as much his captives as his guests. We are free to walk the tower, but not to step outside. Lord Magnus wishes to speak with you when you are well enough. Until then you are to rest, and I am to wait." Her eyes went to the fireplace once more, an uneasy expression in her eyes.

Not one for cages, this one. "Do not distress! The last time we were trapped in a tower our position was much worse than this, and things turned out well enough. Though it was trying, to be sure ... Now tell me, who is Lord Magnus, and how did we come to be here? I can't imagine you carried me across your back, and I saw no tower upon the fields before falling into dreams."

Astrid moved, taking a seat by the fire before answering the knight. Despite the heat given off from the fireplace she looked cold, her eyes distant, reminding Lennox of when they first met, far away in the mountains of the cursed city. "Lord Magnus is a Sorcerer of great power," she said solemnly. "He knew of our presence the moment we came upon his kingdom, watching us through the power of his crystal sphere."

She then spoke of Sir Galehaut and his companions, leaving out few details. Describing to Lennox the ruins of Osgalion, and all Galehaut had to say about its destruction, and of his master. Lennox listened closely, speaking little and asking few questions. He was curious about Lady Gwyn, and was surprised to hear that the sorceresses could hide her words from Astrid so completely.

When she told of Vasily's arrival, and the departure of Sir Galehaut, Lennox again listened quietly … but at the mention of Vasily's lantern the knight stirred. "Do you still have it?" he asked. "The lantern?"

"Yes."

"Would you show it to me?"

She retrieved the lantern from a small chest in the corner of the room and handed it to the knight. Then, returning to her seat, watched as Lennox uncovered the light. It's narrow beam shot forth. He swung it slowly across the room then shut it off, placing it on the table beside him. He looked at the lantern then for some time, not speaking, lost in thought before finally tuning back to Astrid. "I'm sorry," he said. "Please continue."

Finally, she spoke of Lohalian, describing her ascension of the mighty tower, and her encounter with Lord Magnus. Through all of it Lennox watched her with discerning eyes, and though she said nothing of his dream, she felt as though he somehow knew.

"Hmm … that's quite a tale," Lennox said when she was done. "It seems we have a knack for drawing interest in the wrong sort of folk. Though, perhaps I speak too early concerning Lord Magnus. He has treated us well thus far." He smiled grimly then, and laughed. "Better than the Lady Sune at least, but he has time to show his colors, whatever they may be."

"I do not believe he means us harm," Astrid said quietly while looking at the fire. The glowing embers at last began to fade, and its heat, diminish.

For a moment Lennox lay silent, watching her as she watched the fire. "We will learn, sooner rather than later, I'm sure," he finally said, but Astrid was not listening, and his words went unnoticed.

***

Time moved slowly within the tower. Outside, the sun rose and fell in turn, casting its light through the slender window high above Lennox's bed. He watched its golden rays pass along the stones, drifting in and out of his living dreams as he willed. On the eve of the third day He found that his body felt both rested and refreshed, and rose, wishing to test his fortitude.

He paused at the mirror, taking a moment to look at the man that stood before him shrouded in illusion, the shadow of a fallen man. He removed his glove and reached for his silver serpent ring, pausing a moment before removing the ring from his finger. He flinched at what he saw. A wretched figure draped in golden armor. With the illusion gone he looked no different than the ghouls that wandered the high mountains, or lingered within the deep valleys of the frozen woods.

Age is not all decay, he thought, lifting his decrepit hand up to his face. "Much has changed, since you last gazed though a looking-glass," he said to his reflection. The ripening is at hand; if you have the constitution to see it through until the end.

There was a knock on the door and a voice spoke out from the other side. "Sir Lennox. I am Vasily, chief servant of Lord Magnus. I have been sent by my lord to speak with you if you will … might I enter?"

Lennox eyed the door questionably and laughed. "One moment," he replied, before slipping the serpent ring back upon his finger. In an instant the illusion was in place, and the man before the mirror looked well and good, if not a little pale. He retrieved his helm, placing it atop his head with the visor raised and said, "Please, come in," then turned to meet his guest.

Vasily was much like Astrid had described him, tall and grim with hair raven black and eyes keen and knowing. Long dark robes fell to the floor by his side yet did not appear to hinder him as he moved. He looked upon Lennox with great interest, but his face was stolid and dull. He bowed slightly, placing his hand across his chest. "Greeting, Sir Knight, I hope you have found peace and rest here in Lohalian. At my masters word you have been left untroubled, but now I have been sent to parley with you, if you are well enough for such an endeavor."

"I am indeed," answered Lennox. "So, speak your words."

"Very well. It is to be made known that all the tower is open to you, and while inside all enchantments have been lifted, but you are not to leave until you have spoken with Lord Magnus. Should you depart before such time darkness shall fall upon you, and unseen sentries would slay you … for nothing yet has been spoken to them of your parting."

After a small pause Lennox nodded, acknowledging that he understood. Vasily nodded back, and looked to Lennox as though some small weight had been lifted from his shoulders.

"When might I expect to meet your most gracious lord?" Lennox queried.

"Alas … I have yet to be told such things, Sir Knight. But I can rightly say my lord does not wish to hold you longer than he must, and you can expect his summons before long. But if you would come with me, my lord wishes to present you with a token of good will."

***

Lennox found himself being led down a massive stairwell set with torches. Black cloth lined the walls and floor, and though the way before them appeared empty, voices echoed all around. They themselves moved in silence, speaking little during the descent until Lennox remembered Astrid's lantern with its silver beam, and inquired into the nature of its making.

"I have never seen anything of its kind," Lennox began. "Tell me, what is the origin of its color? My first thought was of illusion, but upon inspection I perceived it was alchemic in nature."

"Heehee … You don't miss much, do you, Sir Lennox. It is indeed a work of alchemy. A subtle art I've always found; often overlooked in pursuit of the magical arts."

"I agree. There is much to learn in the ancient craft, though I fear I never had much talent for it." He smiled then, a small grin unseen by Vasily as he thought of someone from his past. His smile faded, leaving his eyes lonely and sad. "You say it is often overlooked, yet I see much alchemy in this tower."

"It is at the command of Lord Magnus that we study many fields, we are not to neglect alchemy, nor the sciences nor maths."

"That is wise council," said Lennox. "A good student must be well rounded. Do your studies extend to history?"

"Of course! We host the finest library east of Bedivere."

"I would be interested in seeing it, if I may."

Vasily turned his head slightly, glancing quickly towards the knight. "It is open to you … but later. First I must see my master's wishes fulfilled." The stairwell broke off then into a narrow hallway of stone that curved slightly as they went. "In answer to your question, Sir Knight. The lantern was crafted by a junior prentice. Silver is layered into a glass sphere that encircles the flame. So, you were right. The light is in fact an illusion, just not one you supposed."

"What a clever guise …" Lennox replied, his eyes doubtful as he gazed upon the sorcerer before him.

Something in the tone startled Vasily. He stopped and gazed upon the knight, but said nothing, then turned and continued on.

Keep your secrets if you wish, thought Lennox. The lie is plainly seen, but the purpose behind it is harder to discern. It was a simple enough question, but perhaps there was more to it than he believed. Lennox would ponder the mystery at a later time, for now they came upon a set of doors, both large and wide, set deep into the wall and covered in cloth like so much of the surrounding tower. Vasily unlocked the doors with a key he produced from his robes. He pushed gently upon the stones and the heavy doors swung open revealing a room lined with tall pillars glowing warmly by the light of a thousand candles. The room was lightly furnished with a single table that ran the length of the room and chairs set evenly about it.

It was what hung along the walls that caught Lennox's attention.

"The royal treasury of Lord Magnus," Vasily proclaimed. "In here you will find no gold nor silver, nor precious stones of any kind. These are the heirlooms of my master, made by his hand, imbued with magic both powerful and subtle." He turned, lifting up his arms and spreading out his hands in a gesture of glory and splendor. "You are to choose one, Sir Knight … a gift from my master. But choose wisely, for these are items of power, and used incorrectly can bring about destruction unintended by the user."

Lennox stepped forward with a wide grin hidden by his helm, his eyes set in awe. The door clicked shut behind him, so softly he hardly noticed.

He lowered his head, removing him helm completely and setting it aside, resting it gently atop the table. He could feel Vasily hovering behind, and was pleased that the sorcerer did not attempt to touch his armor, though he did glance at it with questioning eyes, curious of the magic instilled within.

"Do not be hesitant, Sir Knight. If you have questions concerning any of these items, ask, and I will tell you all I know."

Will you? Lennox wondered at the thought … perhaps, if his lord commanded him. He glanced quickly towards the sorcerer. "Thank you. I will certainly keep that in mind."

He walked the corridor, studying the treasures one by one, never touching them, never asking questions; just gazing at them as though they were art, which a few of them were. Large paintings, interspersed between ancient swords and chests of fine cloth imbued with magic meant to keep the wearer warm from what Lennox could surmise. He could not be certain, not without actually testing his theory, but he felt sure just the same.

He found himself standing before one of the paintings, its picture faded almost beyond recognition. Something about it seemed queer, yet he could not place it. He stepped forward for a better look. Why? He thought. What about the painting vexed him so? He turned towards Vasily, daring himself to speak, until! He stumbled back, turning to gaze once more upon the picture. Impossible, he thought. How?

"This painting," Lennox said aloud, in a voice both calm and cool. "How did your master come by it?"

"Ohh … a magnificent piece, is it not!" Vasily stepped forward, his eyes set upon the painting, his arms crossed before him. "It was acquired long ago from the Atem, back when their wagons still roamed freely. They claimed to have purchased it from a pair of treasure hunters out of the silent city, but who can say if they spoke truly. A devious lot, the Atem; one can never be certain what one is purchasing."

"You believe they lied about its origin?"

"Heehee, not likely. The transaction was concluded long ago, before the fall of Osgalion. It was authenticated by the scribes of the city at the height of their achievement." Vasily turned and smiled. "It is a painting both rare and beautiful, and would be the jewel of any collection."

And so it was, Lennox thought. He reached his hand out, letting it hover for a moment just above the picture's surface. He was ever aware of Vasily's eyes upon him, and with a deep breath dropped his hand and continued on.

He was uneasy after that, his heart beating rapidly inside his chest, his mind drifting to a long-forgotten past. How? He never imagined he'd come across a relic from before, not outside Marshiel at least. Vadas's words came flooding back to him then. The warden spoke of treasure hunters who searched the ancient city, plundering it of all its goods … but still.

Blood and Ash! He should never have taken off his helm, he thought suddenly. He cursed his stupidity, and slowly began making his way towards the entrance. Once their he retrieved his helm and placed it firmly upon his head before crossing to the other side of the room. He gazed at the sorcerer through the shallow slit. I've been foolish, he thought, to lax in this gentle setting … no more. Perhaps this is what Lord Magnus wanted, to send me down here and watch me flitter about, but I will not play the fool.

Suddenly Lennox froze! His eyes set on the wall before him. The picture was trickery enough, but what he saw now was not possible.

He turned, looking for the sorcerer, but Vasily had moved on, and was some distance from the knight. He looked back upon the wall and reached out, taking the golden spear into his trembling hands.

The polished metal shined and gleamed beautifully… yet Lennox felt no power, save that which is set naturally in weapons of steel. Relief flowed through him like a washing rain, and he turned and placed the weapon back upon the wall, and retrieved the shield that sat beside it. He ran his gloved hand along the edges, then lowered it, and returned it to the wall before stepping back.

Counterfeits … copies … fakes … they held no power. The true weapons lay at the bottom of a drowned city, safely waiting his retrieval. He felt his body grow tense, and clutched his hands into fists. The girl was right, he acknowledged. Lord Magnus was quite the sorcerer indeed, to be testing Lennox so boldly, but how much did he truly know?

He found himself laughing then, and took a seat beside the table. He watched as Vasily turned and began making his way towards him.

"What is it that amuses you?" Vasily asked. He advanced slowly, walking with his arms crossed before him.

"Oh, it's nothing you would understand. But now that your here, perhaps you can help me."

"Of course," he said with a slight bow.

"Excellent! You see, I just can't seem to choose, so I was hoping you could choose for me."

Vasily's eyes went wide with surprise. "Good knight, a gift of such magnificence should not be left to another. You know best what lies before you; choose according to your path."

"Oh, it seems you have more confidence in me than I myself esteem. The path that I must tread is already set before me … " Lennox smiled then, his eyes gleaming unseen behind his golden visor. "But what trials stand between me and the end, I know not. So, I trust this gift to you. I believe you will choose well. As it is, I think I will retire. I have been struck by memories once forgotten, and wish to think in peace."

***

Lennox found little comfort in the solace of his room, and was surprised when the summons of Lord Magnus came that very night. He relented, unwilling to refuse the call of the Lord.

The royal chambers were just as Astrid had described, with lanterns of liquid silver above, and great pools of mercury shimmering like moons spread throughout the hall. He found Lord Magnus sitting upon a throne draped in cloth, and beside him stood a colossal statue, head bent with the Eye of Lohalian resting in its palm.

Fascinating, Lennox thought as he approached. He had not thought any of the great seeing stones had endured. This answered many of his questions, but not all. He continued forward.

There was much to be seen in the Great Chamber, but it was Lord Magnus towering above all else seated upon his throne who held his eyes. Venerable he sat as a great Lord; knowledge and wisdom was his crown, and hidden behind shadow his eyes gleamed with starlight. He stood up to greet his guest, watching verily, the movement of the golden knight.

"Sit now before me, Lennox of Marshiel!" said Magnus, and as he spoke a chair rose forth before his throne.

"Hmm …" Lennox's eyes went from Magnus to the chair. This will be most illuminating, he thought, and walked calmly forward.

When Lennox was at last seated, Magnus turned towards his crystal sphere and lifted his hand. The great crystal rose, hovering slightly. "I would look upon thy true self as we discuss what shall befall thee."

Lennox understood, and reached up to remove his helm. His gloves were next; he placed them upon his lap before reaching for his serpent ring. A ripple seemed to pass between them then, causing him to pause briefly. "Is it truly necessary?" He asked. "I'm afraid I've lost quite a bit of myself."

"The wait has been long, Elder One. I do not seek hidden things nor half-truths. I will have it all plainly before me, else how am I to aid thee?"

Lennox looked up for a moment, his eyes doubtful. "Is that what you intend? To aid me? You know not what I intend, else you might not be so stirred."

"I know much and more … as I'm sure thee has surmised, but not all, and not enough. We witnessed something strange, the girl child and myself, while thou slept before us. A scene of great significance! I have thought upon it much, and it has scarcely left my mind." He lifted up his black arm, gesturing towards the crystal sphere. At once the gem cleared and Lennox saw the shape of a crown, dark and twisted with many thorns. A man loomed beneath it, dark and shadowed upon a throne, with a women in red chained beside him.

Lennox said no word but turned from the crystal sphere and looked long upon the figure of Lord Magnus. He removed the serpent ring, placing it on the armrest of his chair.

"There is more, Sir Knight … much more," Magus said quietly.

The picture of the king and the women in red drifted away, replaced now by an image of Lennox dragging along a corpse throughout the halls of a great kingdom. The golden knight at last exited the palace and trotted on until reaching a great chasm beside the fortress. It was there that he cast down the cadaver, deep into the darkness below. Lennox watched the body fall until darkness filled the crystal sphere and all was quiet.

"So, it was thee … who unwittingly became the architect of so much misery and rot, tainting the sewers with the cadaver of Lord Shem."

"It was not till much later that I suspected," said Lennox, his mouth tight.

The crystal sphere sprung to life then, flashing many past events which Lennox knew had taken place but had never seen. The fracturing of an age, the spreading of the taint, the chaos of a kingdom gone mad. Then the image cleared and he saw a mighty war, a hundred thousand men marching upon a silent city when suddenly, great beasts emerged from the walls, casting aside the armies of men like chaff, and returning the city to silence.

For some time then all was still, and Lennox sighed, preparing to look away when out from the main gate rode fourth a knight set in blue, and with him rode seven men in brazen armor, adorned with helms of mighty beasts … but remaining at the gate stood a figure cloaked in brown with a staff long and sharp, and eyes that gleamed like moonlight.

"What trickery is this!" Lennox shouted as he leapt to his feet, his eyes turning to Magnus. The great sorcerer remained seated; his hand held forth in a gesture of peace.

"Sir Knight! I am not him, though the likeness thou seith is not denied, for he is my father, and I his son … yet I show him no devotion. My roots are here, firmly planted within the halls of Lohailion; for I am a Lord, and this my kingdom. I serve not the Watchers of Old, nor the Darkmoon."

Lennox stood in silence, looking upon the lord with renewed interest.

"Nay," Magnus said, divining his thoughts. "Not as thou imagines. I am not of his seed. In truth I am in nature, a work of alchemy, brought forth to serve … but father's ambition was palpable, and he grasped too far. I would not serve, so I fled to a new life. Long have I desired to speak with thee, to aid thee in thy quest to bring this age to an end, that I may at last find release from my father's will." And with that word Magnus drew back his hood, revealing the man beneath. Light was his skin. White and smooth as porcelain, with cracks running out from the temples of his eyes.

He did not stay uncovered long. Seeing the discomfort brought forth he concealed himself once more, letting the hood fall long past his face, then spoke. "Oh, Elder One … we've fallen far, spiraling further and further from our Creator's intent. But now we may set this world right! Thy time has come, to finish thy great work, and I will aid thee, devoting all I can to thy safety." Then reaching inside his robes he produced a crystal sphere, much smaller than the Eye of Lohalion, yet the gem pulsed with magic. "You would not choose, Elder One, so a gift was chosen at thy request." Then reaching forward he gave the orb to Lennox, and for a moment it shined with light then grew dim, leaving the image of Lohalion deep within the crystal.

"With this thou can see much that may have eluded thee, and if thou so desire, call my name, that I may offer aid in times of great despair." Then leaning back, Lord Magnus looked down upon the small sphere with pleasure. "Vasily choose well, I think. May it offer relief upon the tides of darkness that lay before thee."

Lennox bowed, having not the words to say. With the orb still in his hands he moved to place it inside a small pouch at his waist and stopped when he saw the image of a large cat walking briskly through a forest with a tall man beside him. The image lingered only for a moment, then faded and went black. Lennox turned to Magnus, but the sorcerer only looked at him in silence. Lennox placed it into the pouch.

"The world has been still for a long time," Magnus went on, "Yet with your return a great fire has been stoked, and now the world must be burned clean, and only that which is pure will stand forth eternal, that the will of the Creator may come forth … as it must and will upon this world.

"Alas! Elder One, for our Enemy does not stand idle. Long has Azazel been plundering the great relics of this world, once given as gifts to aid mankind in the war with the everlasting serpents, he seeks the ancient treasures, pursuing them with all his will, sending forth his minions for that deed and purpose. Yet what he hopes to achieve I cannot distinguish. Perhaps to ready himself for thy return, for in thee lies his doom. Having slain Lord Shem and his kin, Azazel will not rest until you are gone."

"Nay!" Lennox replied, and in his tone was great sadness and regret. "Lord Shem fell by my hand, but I will not claim the deeds of Sir Gillian, loyal to a fault, for it was he who smote Lords Batraal and Armoris, only to be betrayed in the end."

"Sir Gillian ..." said Magnus, his eyes vailed and hidden, speaking now in a softer voice. "Yes. Sir Gillian, of course ... his deeds will be recorded, the error corrected." This seemed to please Lennox. Lord Magnus continued. "Be that as it may, Elder One. Thy face brings great doubt to our enemy' mind. I can only deduce he is building himself strong, that he might destroy thee, and any chance of his fall with thee, that his days may continue ... the Age of Watchers persist."

"Your thoughts mirror my own," said Lennox after some time. "Yet we cannot know for sure his purpose. You spoke of the ancient relics, which ones still remain?"

"The Imperishable Flame is lost, as thou can recount, as well as the Shadow Rings and the Mirror Doors ... all reclaimed while you wasted in the dungeons." At this Lennox stirred, but did not respond. "Until now he has moved in darkness, but thy awakening has shifted all, and across the land his forces make ready. The Sphere of Lohalion is lost to him, he shall not have it, and so he bends his will towards that which he may still attain; the Star Orb, forever guarded by the Wizard Guild, and the Iron Staff of Bedivere.

"Much strength remains in the Iron City, for long after the fall of your home did Bedivere prosper. Many strong towers were erected, and many walls and ships to protect the lake towns from those who would steal and burn. And while such strength has diminished, Azazel would find it difficult to overthrow, for the Black Iron Knights still stand watch at all hours of the day, though they no longer venture past their own walls."

"Hmm ... Though I make no claim into the mind of Lady Sune, perhaps some of her purpose has been made clear to me, for it was on our travels to the guild that we fell into despair, and in the depths of the woods we were separated from our guide, Shiva of Cataron, First Warden of Lady Sune."

"Tell me what transpired!" said Magnus.

Then Lennox recounted all that taken place since their departure from the flooded city, and the days that followed as they moved to retrieve the boy wizard of Solaire; recalling in depth the jackal and the glutton, his purging of the Darkmoon's sigil upon the Archtree, the disappearance of Marrok and Zev, the ghoul army, and the coming of the darkness. "A shadow wraith it must have been, changing both its shape and size at will," said Lennox. "It pushed us into the decrepit castle and fell upon Shiva in a mighty clash that shook the earth and cast us into darkness."

"These tidings are grave indeed!" cried Magnus.

"Yet there is more!" said Lennox, and spoke of the hollows that now infested the hidden fortress, and of their narrow escape, and the crows that kept watch upon the exits of the deep. "I destroyed the wretched birds," he said. "Down to the very last, though it weakened me more that I care to admit, and I fell into memories of old ... memories which you trespassed upon, though no consent was given."

Magnus paused, leaning slightly forward before answering. "Forgive me Elder One, I knew not thy condition and wished only to assess thy mind."

Lennox smiled, his eyes looking out through the slit of his helm upon the mighty Lord. Assess my mind? He almost laughed. A partial truth, an unfinished lie ... it mattered not. Had Lord Magnus wished to cause him harm he could have at any time. Lady Sune, Lord Magnus, each had their own ambitions, but for the time it appeared as though their wants aligned.

Lennox waved his hand in triviality. "There is nothing to forgive. I have nothing to hide."

Now it was Lord Magnus who seemed to be amused. He tilted his head and stared long at Lennox but did not speak for he was in deep thought, considering all he had seen and heard from the golden knight.

Silence fell once more. Lennox, revealed and bare before the great lord, reached for his silver serpent ring and placed it firmly upon his finger. Afterwards he slipped on his gloves and golden helm and sat stolid in his chair, his hands clasping at the rails. "Well, you certainly have given me much to consider. Yet I am curious. How much did the girl see?

I've grown rather fond of her in our short time together, and would be remiss if she thought less of me without understanding what truly took place so long ago."

"She witnessed the fall of Lord Shem and nothing more. Enough to intrigue her imagination I'm sure … yet she comprehends not its true meaning; at least for the time being. She is a delight, that girl child. Tell me, what is her role in thy quest?"

Lennox shrugged. "I haven't the faintest, nor can I speak concerning Oscar of Soliar. We are all wrapped together in some unseen plot of the girl oracle you're so fond of."

Something resembling a laugh rolled forth from the throat of the great Lord. "Yes! She is quite an enigma that one … she has procured a royal gathering indeed. I can only hope she has the sight to use thee accordingly."

"You speak as though she is my master." Lennox shook his head. "She is not the master of me."

Again the great lord laughed. "Isn't she? That ring speaks differently. But enough. I fear I have delayed thee long indeed. Now is the time. Thou has my consent to depart upon thy choosing. I will have horse and supplies made ready for thy use."

"Astrid will be glad to hear it," said Lennox. He rose then and bent his head forward in a slight bow. "Our meeting has been most favorable, my lord, your news and council helpful."

Magnus raised his eyes and looked at him, and Lennox felt himself exposed once again by the keenness of his gaze. "Elder One. My patience has been rewarded, my persistence not in vain. In thee lies a new beginning … one who would end an age. Go forth, and may the will of the Creator consume thee."

***

Afterwards, when Lennox had departed, he found himself alone in the stairwell of the high tower considering all he had heard when his mind went to Astrid, and he pondered where he might find her. Without hardly a thought he found himself reaching for the crystal sphere he had just received, holding it before him. It had been some time, he knew, since he has tried such magic, and doubt filled his mind as to whether he would succeed, yet as he looked an image appeared. A single tower set in twilight.

As the tower drew close the image of a girl took shape standing upon the peak with a mighty wind blowing against her. A smile touched at the corner of Lennox's lips. There is one in which great strength resides. He watched her for a time before setting the orb away. Quite useful, he thought, he must give Vasily his thanks before departing.

Lennox turned and gazed upward, his eyes following the unending stairway. Just how many steps are there in this tower, he thought with a shake of his head … too many. Well, it would be a good test, to know how well he had recovered, and thus he began the assent.

It was a long silent walk. Only the loose shuffling of his armor echoed through the tower, that and his own labored breath that resounded inside his helm. Still, he was better off than he thought, and before long he reached the top and stepped through the door and onto the very peak of Lohalion.

In the distance the sun's twilight painted the sky with all shades of purple and orange, yet above them the clouds were devoid of color, black and gray and cold with a biting wind that belted against the banners of Lord Magnus which hung upon the three-pronged horns of the tower.

A huge fire pit had been built in the center of the stone roof, and its flames rose spinning and crackling towards the bitter sky. Astrid was standing with her back to the flame, her eyes looking out across the horizon. Lennox approached her, his steps barely heard over the piercing wind. One could get blown away if not careful, he thought as a sudden blast of air cut across the tower before him and the girl. Her long black cape billowed out, dancing to the song of the air.

She turned her head, only a little, but it was enough to see Lennox coming up behind her. She looked away.

Her cold demeanor stopped Lennox where he stood, and for a time they remained still, until at last he called out. "If you have questions, ask. I will not lie to you."

Another gust of wind wrapped itself around the tower then dissipated. The girl said nothing. Her eyes hidden from Lennox.

Perhaps she could not hear me, the knight thought, and removed his helm to better speak. "We have been released, my lady. We leave at first light."

Lennox's long hair, put forth by illusion, blew before him as another gust pushed upon the tower and persisted for a long while, howling and screaming as though in fury. In the distance lightening flashed, its roaring echo followed close.

Well … she'll have to speak to me in time, better it is on her terms.

With a hint of regret resting upon his heart Lennox redonned his helm and left. Walking past the pit of flames and descending into the tower, unaware of Astrid's eyes upon his back.

They did not speak until the following morning when Lennox was led to her room by a small quiet woman in dark robes who watched him with soft eyes and a knowing smile but did not speak even when prodded with questions. "You remind me of several priests I used to know," he said to her. "They never spoke to me either."

The women seemed amused by this and laughed quietly to herself, her small hunched shoulders rising and falling as she left.

Hmm … what an odd women, thought Lennox. He turned then, knocking gently on the door with the back of his fist. Astrid opened the door mid knock to Lennox's surprise. "Oh! Hello," he said. "I've come to let you know our horses are ready and waiting for us outside the tower entrance."

"Good," she answered. "I'll be down shortly."

Lennox nodded and Astrid closed the door. Well … not so bad, I think. It can only get better. She had not seemed upset, if anything her eyes seemed brighter than they had for some time, and Lennox was beginning to feel better himself. He was strangely drawn to the girl he found, and did not like the notion of her being upset with him. The absurdity of it all made him laugh.

***

Upon exiting the tower, they found a company of men mounted and waiting. Some of them watched as Lennox and Astrid descended, but none spoke. The bars of their half-helms covered their eyes, and the silver and blue surcoats with the fallen crown of house Magnus emblazed upon the chest hid their plate and mail. Lennox recognized none of them, for in truth he had scarcely come across any of Lord Magnus's retainers while inside Lohalion.

Hard-men, Lennox knew, he could tell by the way they held themselves, straight and alert, ready for action if the need arose. They were no hollows, but true men valiant and strong.

They continued on toward a pair of stallions who stood separate from the group held in place by a young boy dressed in simple but clean servant cloths. As they approached Lennox thanked the boy who nodded in reply and proceeded to help Astrid mount.

"His name's Arvakr," the boy said. "A good horse, strong and true."

"My thanks," said Astrid. "I will treat him well."

"And mine?" Lennox asked.

"Alsvior."

"Is he quick?"

"Very quick," the boy replied with a deep nod.

"Good," said Lennox, and ran his hand along the horse's neck speaking to it words in an ancient tongue. He put his foot in the stirrup and swung into the saddle, then spoke softly once more into the stallion's ear.

"What did you say to him?" asked the boy.

Lennox lifted his visor and smiled. "I can't seem to remember."

Vasily appeared then, draped in his traditional dark garb and mounted upon a dark stallion. He trotted forward while a pair of men followed behind on foot. "Greetings friends!" he said calling out. "Be it fate or something else unseen, it was I who lead you into Lohalion; thus, it shall be I who leads you away … if only for a little while."

Lennox looked upon the sorcerer with a smile, Astrid with annoyance. "It was Sir Galehaut who found us among the ruined walls." She answered. "He brought us many leagues in safety and peace before we were placed in your care."

Vasily looked amused. It was strange seeing him in the fullness of day where the light of the sun fell upon his face and showed him clear and true. "Aye my lady, I have not forgotten! I only hope to continue his legacy as best I can."

"What's this?" Lennox said, watching as two servants drew near. "More gifts?"

"Lord Magnus has been very gracious to you and the Lady … I will do no less. And while I can offer you nothing near as magnificent as the gifts given by my master. I offer you what I have, and hope you will find it to your liking." Then he turned to each in turn. "To a knight of old both wise and strong, I offer twin falchion blades, forged by my own hands in service of House Magnus." The swords were well made and overlaid with a tracery of silver leaves set against the natural gold hue of the steel. They were sheathed in a leather harness meant to be worn on ones back.

"The blades when kept together can be neither broken nor split, and will cut deep where many other swords might be turned away."

"Hmm … it appears I am amassing many great treasures," Lennox said taking the blades and strapping them onto his back. "Shiva will be bothered when he learns of our gain, should we ever cross his path again." He thought then of his serpent ring given to him by Faid the Unfaithful, and the seeing stone of Lord Magnus. Yet Vasily's words had not escaped him. He mentioned gifts given by his master, and wondered what treasure Astrid had received. I will ask her, he determined, when enough time has passed.

"For the young lady who waited patiently in the tower," he said, turning to Astrid. "I offer this bow, such as the knights of House Magnus use, for I have seen that your own has been cracked, and now only waits for a time that it might betray you."

Somewhat surprised by Vasily's words, Astrid removed her bow and examined it, finding the flaw deep in the wood running along the top. "Thank you, sir," she said, keeping her bow in hand. "Your gift is most appreciated … but I will keep my own and mend it as best I can, for the flaw is still in its infancy."

Vasily bowed his head. "Very well, I only ask the lady be wary."

"I will," she said firmly.

"I think it best we depart," said Lennox suddenly. "For we have been long delayed, and I would put it off no longer."

"Of course," answered Vasily, turning his steed northward in reply. At his command the company went forth, striking out upon the road in rows of two, their banners pressed before them wavering in the wind.

15

ASILY set a strict pace, pushing the company hard for many hours. The road was flat and well kept, and the sun before them grew dim, peaking upon the horizon and shining through the haze like a ruby made of fire. Then, it fell completely, leaving the company to a cold and starless night.

Long into the silent hours they rode, following the northern path as it weaved its way through open fields of high grass and the occasional lonely tree. Many statues lined the road, but unlike the ruined masterpieces that stood crumbling between the tower and the lost city of Osgalion, these splendid works varied widely and were kept in good repair. In fact, it appeared to Astrid as though many of them were new, having none of the normal blemishes attained from a life open to the elements.

They're beautiful, she thought, and looked upon them in wonder.

Lennox hardly noticed them at all.

They had caught his attention at first. Statues of great beauty to be sure, of women and children, of strong men mounted upon valiant steeds, of witches and wizards … but he had long grown weary of beautiful things, and they no longer held any sway upon him.

A brisk wind began to blow, cutting across the path like a bird. Beside him Astrid drew her hood, hoping to fight off the worst of it. Most of the company held torches, and with their combined light the road was well lit, and Lennox found that he could see for some distance before them despite the dark skies.

I wonder if he in intends to push through the night, Lennox thought. Vasily had always been difficult to understand, claiming only to be a loyal servant of Magnus. His actions seemed to tell a different story. But just as he was going to put the question forward Astrid spoke up. "Don't you think we should check our pace, Vasily. These horses could go a good while longer, but we have many days riding ahead of us."

Vasily raised his hand, bringing the company to a brisk walk, then fell to the back of the column to have a word. "Of course, my lady, I do apologize. My company and I will be leaving you when we reach Reinhard Pass, but you will have many miles after we depart."

"And just how far is it to this pass?" Lennox asked, lifting his visor so as to be better heard.

"We can reach it in two days if we're stiff with our breaks. I do regret the inconvenience, but Lord Magnus said I was to be quick, and that anymore delay in time would be unfortunate."

Astrid perked up. "What do you mean unfortunate?"

"My lady, shurly you must know by now, I am not one to question my master. He speaks and I obey … sir Galehaut did the same. It is the way of obligation."

"Yes," said Astrid. "I'm well aware." She turned to Lennox then, her eyes told him she remembered.

The golden knight smiled. "Well … we certainly understand your position, good sir. We are all creatures of duty. We only wanted to know what we were in for."

Vasily looked at Lennox then bowed, pushing his horse back into a trot as he went forward to the head of the column. Lennox watched him for some time, unsure of what to make of the man. *Not so bad, if I had to wager,* he thought, *but there was no way to be certain.* He sighed, letting his shoulders fall as he turned to Astrid. He went to speak but stopped himself. *Not enough time has passed … I can wait.*

They kept on through the night, quiet upon the lonesome road with nothing but each other and the statues for company. Lennox found himself twisting at the oathkeeper ring, spinning it around his finger. It had become a heavy burden, yet not all that had transpired since his release had been a loss. He had gained two small treasures, and even found companionship in Astrid, though it felt strained at the moment. *No matter, she will come around … I have time.*

Soon after Vasily called the company to a halt and dismounted, intending to give the horses a break before continuing on at sunrise. Astrid took the time to eat. She seemed to be the only one but was grateful all the same. She cut some fruit and a slice of cheese from a hard block and took a seat next to a large statue of a women shawled and looking away, her face beautiful but with searching eyes that looked down the road for something unknown.

It was then that she saw Lennox pull out the small crystal ball given to him by Lord Magnus and make his way towards where she sat. He took a seat beside her but said nothing as he examined the sphere. He could see her glancing at him between bites, but resigned himself to silence. He would not be the first to speak.

"Do you know how to use that?" she asked at last, breaking the silence sooner than he thought.

Lennox did not respond straightaway, leaning in close he kept his eyes locked upon the crystal. "Hmm … a little. I suppose it depends on what it is you trust I'm capable of?" He turned, holding her eyes through the slit of his helm. She gave back stare for stare, determined to have an answer. Lennox understood what it was she was asking. "I cannot gaze into one's dreams, my lady, the stone is not powerful enough to enter into another's mind, nor can I see things past or future. Yet it helped me find you when I looked. So I am not altogether without talent. But to use a catalyst like this takes training, and I have grown dull in these years past." He turned, looking out upon the fields that surrounded them. "Once upon a time I was quite proficient, but I have diminished, and must make myself strong once more if I am to finish what has been appointed to me."

Astrid raised her eyes at him, and Lennox felt as though she was beginning to understand. "This task," she said, her eyes flickering to the crystal sphere. "What does it pertain to?"

"Do you truly not know, or do you hide it from yourself? I know what it is that you saw … Lord Magnus did not hide it from me. So ask."

"Ask what?"

"The question."

"I don't know what you mean."

"If you will not ask, then neither will I answer."

There was a pause, and when she spoke the words were so faint, they were almost lost to the wind. "The man in your dream with the crown of spikes with the women in red chained beside him … who was he?"

"A very good question," said Lennox with a gentle laugh, and his eyes shined with warmth and understanding. "He had many names to many people, but most knew him as Lord Shem of the Abyss, the Knower of Names and Speaker of Truth, Potentate of the seven Jewel Cities."

All around them the air grew still, and all noise subsided, and the golden armor of Lennox burned warm as the rays of the cresting light reflected upon him so that he appeared bright as the sun. "How can this be, Sir Knight. The Four have long been silent but to claim they have perished," said Astrid, filled with awe.

"Haha, the Four … not so many now I think. Tell me, when was the last time they were seen, for in my day they traveled often, never forgoing an opportunity to look upon all that they ruled."

Astrid looked at him but did not answer.

"As I suspected. I have only just emerged, my lady, yet the world has changed much from the little I have seen. Now only one remains by my count, and with his death a new age will at last be born. This is what I seek. This is what I have been tasked with. But there is more! I know now that it was indeed the agents of Lord Azazel who were behind the theft of your family treasure, and so fate it seems is ever turning. I grow curious now of this boy wizard of Soliar, and begin to think our servitude to Lady Sune may at least in part, work in our favor. For I believe she can assist us in our wants."

"That is a hopeful view of things," said Astrid. "Only one more so you say, but Lord Azazel sits deep within the sacred city. How do you intend to reach him? I see no hope."

"I never said it would be easy, indeed from the outside it looks futile. An army might help; perhaps Lady Sune will be kind enough to deliver one. But the details can be discussed at another time, for now I think it best we focus on finding Oscar and reaching Lady Sune as quickly as we can." Lennox rose, stretching out his hand for Astrid to take. "No matter what the future holds, I will feel better once I'm free her power."

***

When the company set out, Vasily took his proper place at the head leaving Lennox and Astrid to ride where they wished. No one in the company spoke while they rode except when addressed by Vasily, and even then, they spoke in low voices, their words unheard. Mostly it seemed to Lennox that they were being ignored, but when he really looked, hardly a moment went by when one from the company wasn't glancing in their direction.

A delay in time would be unfortunate ... that what Lord Magnus had said. Lennox felt an itch between his shoulders. He inhaled deeply. What had the sorcerer left out? Plenty, I'm sure.

"Lennox," said Astrid, so faintly he wasn't sure she had actually spoken. "Lennox, what's wrong?"

"Nothing," he said back.

"You're lying," she said. "You said you would not lie to me."

He wanted to laugh, but instead turned to Astrid and tugged on his reins, bringing his horse to a stop. "Lady Astrid, I do apologize. Nothing is wrong per se ... it is only I grow tired of our current company; it almost makes me miss that sour warden of ours, wherever he may be."

Astrid laughed, then grew serious, turning to him with interest. "What of your stone? Have you tried searching for him with it?"

"No," he answered, and reached into his pouch for the crystal. "I suppose I should give it a try." He held up the stone then, peering into it as he spoke words unknown to Astrid. She pushed her horse forward for a better look.

"I don't see ..."

Suddenly the image of a large cat walking through the forest filled the surface then quickly changed into the face of a women. Tall she was, mounted upon a white pony and traveling with a large company across a road similar to the one they now traveled save the statues.

Then the sphere went empty.

"Curious," said Lennox. "That's twice now this sphere has shown me that cat ... I'm beginning to imagine he's a fellow of interest."

"Who was the women on the road?" asked Astrid.

"I couldn't say, though I feel we shall find out."

The flat lands gave way to rolling hills that stretched out before them in waves of green, but it wasn't long until the hills grew higher and higher, and the valleys that separated them deeper still, so that much of their time was spent weaving their way through gorges that ripped the land. After crossing a small bridge that cut across one of the narrower valleys Lennox noticed there were no more statues. He looked back across the bridge, glimpsing one last effigy that stood with both hands resting upon the pommel of his sword gazing out across the valley. Then they turned the corner and it was lost from sight.

Perhaps we are nearing the borderlands, but he said nothing of it to Astrid and rode on keeping a sharp gaze on their surroundings.

Soon the world darkened and Vasily called a halt, ordering pairs of guards to watch the road while the others went about lighting torches and seeing to the horses. Astrid slept little. Lennox not at all, of course, and by first light they had mounted once more and were continuing on.

It was midday when they drew near Reinhard Pass, a great peak that looked out upon the valley below. The road snaked down into the vale, and there crossed upon a second path running perpendicular to their own. From where they stood high atop the precipice, they could see miles in all directions.

It was then they sighted a caravan crossing the road from the east. It was a large group, thirty men mailed and mounted, each carrying a long spear, preceding a line of royal carts. Yet it was what followed the carts that caught Lennox's eye. A string of knights each accompanied by their squire, as though some great procession were taking place. Even from the great distance they could hear the rows of horses beating against the stone road, echoing like a storm throughout the valley.

"Well … how fortunate we left when we did," said Lennox aloud, keeping his eyes steady on the crowd below. "Else we would have had to travel alone and miss out on such fine company. Tell me, do you recognize the banners?"

"A few," answered Astrid.

Though there were many standards mixed in with the company, it appeared to her that almost all the lesser lords in fealty to Solaire were represented. She turned to Vasily. "Why such a gathering?"

"King Randolf of Solaire has perished, my lady. These men ride to see his son take the mantle, and bend the knee proclaiming their loyalty," he replied, trotting close. "The roads have grown dangerous of late; riding in company with such a host will be most favorable. They will lead you nearly all the way to the Wizard's Guild which lies just west of

Solaire."

"Ahh ... I was wondering what you were playing at all this time," said Lennox. "Your caution was needless though, Vasily. I agree with this plan of yours. It will be good to not have worries of wondering hollows in the dark of night, though the pace will undoubtedly be stalled."

"Only a little, Sir Knight. Even now you can see their pace is not one of leisure."

"Why should they accept us?" Astrid asked. "Lord Magnus does not kneel to Soliar."

"My lady, long has there been peace between the two kingdoms; and men still strive at chivalry ... though not like they once did. They will accept you graciously, if not cautiously I'm sure." He smiled then, calling one his men to his side. "The house standards have been prepared for you; this will squander any doubt of your loyalties. Wear them well, less you bring shame upon my master."

Astrid turned to reply but was cut short. "Thank you, good sir," said Lennox, bowing gently in his saddle. "For all that you have done for us. The graciousness of House Magnus will not be forgotten."

Vasily bowed back. "I am pleased to hear this." He turned once more to Astrid. "My lady, I hope that I have sufficed in the absence of Sir Galehaut. I am aware I can seem ... rather dreary, know this was not my intent."

Astrid was not overly fond of Vasily, but could not deny that he had treated her well. "You were very kind," she said. "If I am ever to see Sir Galehaut I will tell him such myself."

Vasily smiled, and turned, gesturing to the road before them. "So now it comes to it. I have seen you to the finish, as I promised I would. But do not fret, for in my heart I feel as though this is not truly the end. May your travels see you safely Sir Lennox, my lady, and know that Lord Magnus is watching."

"Hmm ... one can hardly forget," Lennox replied, and with those words he turned his horse and began making his way down the twisting pathway.

Astrid kept pace. She was carrying the banner of house Magnus though it hardly seemed to hinder her. It may have been strange for a woman to carry the banner in the southern realms, but in the north, it was common practice for all shield maidens.

As they rode, Lennox noticed the first signs of decay in the road, marking their departure from the lands of Lord Magnus. His hand went to his side, reaching for the pommel of a sword that was not there. He reached up then, grabbing at one of the twin falchion blades on his back. He felt the hilt in his hand then released. This will take some getting used to, he thought, and for a moment considered perhaps sparring with one of the knights in the company below. It was always preferable to test one's blade lest it fail you when it was needed most.

As they drew near the bottom of the valley the clamor of the party before them was all to prevalent, and while the men in front seemed well in line, the knights that traveled behind rode in welcome merriment, speaking of the great tourney that was sure to follow the new kings inauguration.

Still … Lennox and Astrid's arrival did not go unnoticed; indeed, it appeared as though the entire procession came to a halt as it became evident that Astrid and a knight of gold baring the sigil of Lord Magnus were riding out to join them. A few of the more curious knights pushed out from the line to greet them but were cut off from a company of the main guard; they followed at a distance then. If they could not greet the liaison of Lord Magnus themselves, then they would at least watch and listen, perhaps gaining some insight otherwise lost.

Lennox and Astrid pressed on, covering half a mile before the outriders rode forth, ten men, led by a grizzled greybeard of a knight, all of them sporting the sigil of House Solaire, a blazing sun set against a field of blue. As they drew near the company halted, and the aged knight rode forth alone.

"Sir Knight," he called, taking a moment's pause upon recognizing that Astrid was a woman. He nodded gently towards her. " … my lady. Forgive my manners. I am Sir Sieg of Solaire, as it please you."

"All is forgiven," she answered him.

"Might I inquire as to the nature of your company?" the old knight pressed.

He had turned to Lennox but once again it was Astrid who answered, much to the amusement of the golden knight. "News of the king's passing has reached out master's ears … he bid us travel to Soliar to show his respect."

The old man turned to the girl. "Since when do knights of Magnus hold women as their squires? Only in the north are such things seen."

"Then you have judged rightly, for the north is in my blood," she answered.

Lennox pushed his horse forward, seeing the discomfort of the knight who felt as though he were being made a fool. "Please, forgive my squire. She can be rather outspoken, having spent much of her youth in the northern kingdoms."

"Aye," the knight replied, shifting his attention back upon Lennox. "The north … " He smiled then, warily though it was. "Well it certainly shows."

"That much it does," Lennox grinned, his face seen through his open visor. "Though I add our business is twofold, good sir, for we have business with the Wizards Guild as well, and were hoping we might accompany you upon the road for the remainder of our journey, lest we fall to hollows or other foul creatures."

"Hardly any hollow's make it this far from the mountain," Sir Sieg answered, looking once more towards Astrid. "Very well. You may join the others in the rear. It shall be an honor to have emissaries of Lord Magnus join us in company. See to it that your squire learns her place."

"Of course."

Sir Sieg turned then, raising his mailed hand to the sky. His men rode forth, forming a column behind him before returning with their captain to the head of the convoy.

"Hmm … not a very cheery fellow," Lennox said in an amused tone.

"So, I am to be your squire?" Astrid answered, unable to hide her displeasure.

"Haha … my lady, I am a knight of Lord Magnus. How would I be perceived if I were to be without squire? Poorly I'm sure." He kicked his horse forward, making his way towards some of the knights who had stayed behind. He turned, looking back towards the girl. "We need only keep up this charade until we are free of this company."

"I will do no such thing."

"Oh? That's fine with me; but let us hope we don't draw any more attention than will already come our way."

"As long as we keep to ourselves, we shall be left alone."

"Oh?" Lennox did not sound convinced. "We shall certainly find out. Yes, most certainly indeed."

16

HE could see the fire in the night, glimmering against the still waters of a minor billabong set beside the river. At times it shimmered brightly like a fallen star, though as night passed it dwindled down to no more than the red orange glow of fading embers.

Shiva spent that night in the cold, watching from a distance. He had spent more than a week forging on through the icy forest, always pushing south until at last breaking free of the frozen woods. It would be no trouble to spend one more night alone. The family had built their fire in a shallow depression near the water's edge, and had arranged their carts in a semi-circle around them to shelter them from wolves and other lesser creatures. He knew better than to approach an unknown camp at night, he would be patient.

In the early hours of the morn well before the sun had risen life began to stir. Several men began bustling about, breaking down tents and seeing to the horses. One woman went to work on the fire while a group of children played at her side. The sun's light revealed several bright markings along the sides of the wagons, colorful suns of swirling yellow and silver crescent moons painted with flaking dust. Shiva could only conclude they were a troupe of some kind.

He had stepped out from the trees onto the road and was still a good way from the camp when one of the men gave a shout. Not long after several of the men were walking towards him, each of them carry a sword though they wore no armor, and had yet to draw their blades.

A husky man with a blond beard and a pair of silver earrings walked before the others, never taking his hand off the pommel of his blade.

"Hmm …" he began as they drew near. "Who might you be, stranger? We're a long way from any inn, and here you stand without horse or provisions."

There were three of them, travel-stained and mud-specked. The leader was handsome enough, the others less so. They trailed only slightly behind but looked on with wary eyes.

"Please, sirs … I mean you no distress. I am Shiva of Cataron, First Warden and servant of Lady Sune. I have suffered many misfortunes on my way to Solaire, and offer you my services in the hopes that I may resume my travels."

"A warden offering us his services," one said speaking up, a short gruff fellow with green eyes and a sharp nose. His faded blue jerkin was mended here and there but was still of good quality, and he wore a brace of throwing knives on his hip which his hand hovered over nervously. "And what might these services be?"

Shiva answered him. "Protection from hollows and others of their kind, a horde fell upon me and my companions separating us. If you are heading north, I offer my sword. If south, I offer coin in the hopes of purchasing a horse and provisions that I might be on my way."

"Horses aren't for sale, provisions neither."

"Come now Otto, no need to be uncouth." The bearded man turned to his friend, gesturing something unseen before once again addressing Shiva. "Good sir, he speaks truly. We are not merchants, and we would not part with our horses if you were to offer a sack of gold, two sacks even … but we are traveling north, and quickly too, if we're to make it in time for the king's festival. We're already behind schedule, and if the roads are as dangerous as you say then perhaps you can earn your place."

The bearded man stood a foot taller than his companions, bearing the look of a soldier. A longsword hung from his studded leather belt, decorated with rubies and emeralds at the hilt. It was not the blade Shiva would have expected to see wielded by one of such company. He nodded in consent. "Thank you, you will not regret this."

"Lovely." The man smiled. "But before we go any further, I must insist upon one thing."

"Speak it," Shiva said at once.

"Why you need not turn over your weapons to us, we ask that you not carry them while in our company. You may sit with them beside you on the carts, or strap them to one of the horses. But while in our camp you are in our home. Will you abide by such terms?"

After a moment Shiva nodded. "I acknowledge your wishes and will see through their fulfillment."

"Brilliant."

Otto stood scowling, his hand still hovering by his knives. "Hold it," he said, then pointed to the bag hanging across Shiva's back. "What you got there in that satchel?"

"Otto, really ... I can't see why that should matter."

"I want to know."

"He already said he'd set aside his weapons; we need not pester him further. He looks honest enough, if not a little grim I'll confess."

Otto stood resolute. "I want to know," he repeated.

The handsome man turned once more to Shiva. "I do apologize, but if you wouldn't mind showing us the contents of your bag we can get moving."

Shiva hesitated a moment, unsure how they would react to the severed head of a gargoyle. In the end he unslung his bag and let it fall to the floor, hitting the ground with a heavy thud. He reached in and pulled out the head for all to see. Even though it had been several weeks since the kill the flesh looked fresh, and the eyes were red with blood.

The three men stepped away, but otherwise kept their composure, and, in fact, a certain gleam appeared in the handsome man's eyes as he looked upon the monster's head. "Well now ..." he began. "I think this will make for a great story."

***

Shiva had not been wrong. They were indeed a troupe of sorts, music and acting, juggling and games. They did it all, though it seemed they had a special affinity for singing, and hardly a moment had passed before they were on the road and the first chords where being strummed and a soft melodious voice from one of the women drifted into the air. It was beautifully sung, had Shiva cared enough to listen. But even he managed a swift glance towards the young women.

She caught his glance and smiled back, amused by his cold eyes.

He found himself riding in the rear cart beside a skinny youth of fourteen named Joss. Red-haired and freckled, the boy wore simple garb with high boots and fingerless gloves. True to his word, Shiva had removed his weapons, along with the gargoyles head, placing them between him and the youth who regarded them with cautious curiosity.

"Would you like to see it?" Shiva asked, after seeing the boys eyes flicker towards the bag for the tenth time.

"Is it ... is it truly a gargoyle's head you got in that satchel?"

Shiva nodded. "It is."

The youth looked to the bag, then to Shiva. He held the reins steady in his hands then nodded. "The roads have grown unruly, everyone says so. I've seen my fair share of hollows and such, but we've never come across a gargoyle."

"There are few who have," Shiva answered. Then, pulling the severed head out from the satchel, he held it up for the boy to see.

"Are there many of them out here in the forest? Alodin told us you fell into some trouble on the way north, seeing that foul thing I can hardly guess how you escaped at all." The boy glanced towards the frozen woods not far from the path. They had reached a turning point, and the road was beginning to bend northward.

"Not many," Shiva answered, returning the head to its proper place. "And none in the forests. They prefer mountains and stone."

"Well, either way we're glad to have you. We have a few fighters among us. Otto and Alodin are more than enough to strike down a stray hollow. They were soldiers once, part of the Iron Knight's in their youth, but I don't think they could stand to such a beast."

"They donned the black shield?" Shiva asked. Gazing forward in the bend he saw Alodin leading the party upon a stout mare of white. His posture and manners did in fact mirror a soldier's.

The youth shifted in his seat, then nodded. "Aye, Alodin still has his armor sitting neat in the back of his wagon. He keeps it polished and clean; but I've never seen him wear it in all our travels. He won't talk about it neither, but Otto will, when he's drunk, which is more often than not, especially if someone else is paying."

Shiva watched the boy. He found the youth strangely pleasant to converse with, which was an oddity. He was not one to have a loose tongue.

At last the road finished its bend and straightened before them long into the distance. To the left stood the woods, frozen and cold and white. To the right lay endless fields of rolling hills, green as spring, the domain of House Magnus.

A cold mist fell on them then, not quite a rain but enough to stop the music and chatter. Shiva pulled his cloak close, covering his head from the worst of the wind. He considered pulling out his shadow cloak but tossed aside the thought immediately. To use such a treasure frivolously was unwise, especially in the company of a troupe, where one's possessions were liable to end up missing if left unattended.

Even with the weather turning foul they made good time. The roads of Lord Magnus were good and true, a path where even the most uncoordinated horses were sure to find their footing. Soon enough the cold mist departed and the sun was shining once more.

Without halting the company, Alodin began dropping back to each of the carts informing them that if the weather remained clear they would push through the night. He would not risk missing the best days of the festival just so the company could get a good night's rest.

Shiva watched Alodin return to the front of the column then turned to the boy. "This festival is sure to be quite the event from what's been spoken. Tell me, what is the occasion? Is it a tourney of sorts?"

The boy hesitated, turning to Shiva with a surprised countenance. "Odd that you don't know. I thought all the land had heard by now of king Orsted's death."

"King Orsted," Shiva repeated.

The boy nodded. "Sure. It's been several weeks now since the news. We ride now for his son's inauguration. There'll be a festival after for many days." He tightened his grip on the reins, and looked off down the road. "This entire trip will be for naught if we arrive only to find the whole affair's done and past. This won't be the first sleepless night we've had, but we'll make do."

***

The troupe kept on, and soon the sun had set and a clear sky shone above. They lit lanterns, hanging them from the carts in pairs. At some point the singing stopped, and the soft whispering strings of a harp echoed into the dim night. No one sang; it was not a song for words but for journeys. It was a song that spoke of partings and farewells, of departures into far and distant lands.

When the song finished a new one began, then another. Many songs were played in that manner until a cold dew blew in from the forest and the harp fell silent, leaving only the clapping of the horse's hooves upon stone.

Still, their lanterns were bright, and the path remained true before them.

Alodin kept a steady pace despite the weather, never letting the company fall into anything less than a brisk walk. There were stretches where the path led them close to the woods, but they were few and far between, and it wasn't long before the tree line receded once more. Shiva eyed the woods calmly. He did not trust them. He knew how treacherous they could be.

They had just passed over a small stone bridge when a thin howl rose from the woods. Alodin called the company to a halt and perched up upon his mare. The cry came again, distant and thin from the depths of the forest, yet closer than it had been only moments before. He turned and began riding down the line when, to his surprise, he saw Shiva jump clear from his cart onto the path before him. The warden stood with bow in hand, staring out into the darkness.

Alodin dismounted. "A wolf?" he asked, stepping up beside the warden.

Shiva nodded.

"Sounds a long way off."

"No … It's difficult to judge distance in these woods. It's close."

From their carts, the men and women sat peering out into the gray. A few of them were eyeing the pair, clearly concerned having overheard the warden's words. Alodin stepped in close to Shiva and spoke in a hushed tone. "We only heard the one, but if there's one there's more to follow. We should ride; they'll not catch us if we continue on."

"We couldn't ride fast enough," Shiva answered. "Not in the dark. This is a good road but it bends more than you think. They would catch us, if indeed it is a pack … and us their prey."

Otto rode up then; he had been near the front alongside Alodin and looked down at the pair with furrowed eyes. "Why aren't we moving!" he muttered, and glanced back towards the carts.

Alodin stepped close to his companion. "Be calm. We were just discussing the matter."

"Light torches, as many as you can," Shiva said, pointing to the troupe. "Set them in circles around the carts. We must see them coming to have a chance."

Otto dismounted. "There's only been the one bloody creature! We should get moving now and not waste any more time."

A second cry echoed out, this time others answered it. Eerie wails, many of them, further but nearing all the same. "The torches," Shiva said, his tone unbending. "Do it now!"

This time there was no argument. Alodin and Otto departed, walking to the carts and informing them to set about torches immediately. Shiva remained, standing just off the path. There was near fifty yards of clear terrain before the tree line which sat shrouded in mist. He fell to one knee, peering into the fog. When Alodin returned he was holding a crossbow fully cranked with bolt in place. He stood beside the warden, shadowed by his hood, the mist catching upon his oiled cloak and running down in narrows beads. A moment later Otto joined them, as well as two other men Shiva had seen working in the camp, all of them holding bows.

It was then that the clouds shifted, letting the moon cast its light upon the woods. They found themselves looking onto a line of wolves, coats as white as the snow, hidden amongst the tree line. "So many," Otto muttered to himself.

"There not moving," another whispered. "Why aren't they moving?"

Alodin leaned in close to Shiva. "Well warden … time to earn your place." He sounded strangely calm despite what lay before them. A soldier's training perhaps.

"To the carts," he said quietly, "They will not cross the fire." Otto hesitated, but Shiva quickly grabbed the man's arm and began pulling him back. "Now is not the time to falter, all hope is lost when one loses his wits." Otto relented, and began moving towards the wagons with the others. "Each of you take a cart, and do not leave it even if another should fall."

Another cry went out from the woods, different from what they had heard so far, a lone voice, deeper and more formidable. Shiva stopped, his eyes searching through the mist. It was then that he saw him, the alpha wolf, a dark shape with eyes like yellow-gold, stepping out from the snowcapped trees. The beast paused, only for an instant, before continuing on out from the shelter of the woods.

Alodin and the others were still close, watching in wonder at the boldness of the beast. "Isn't that a sight," Otto muttered. "The brute is without fear." He was notching an arrow but had yet to draw it back.

"Stay your hand," Shiva called, his eyes set on the wolf. He inhaled deeply, then stepped forward to meet the creature. He could hear Otto speaking softly behind him. "What's he doing, he's cracked." The others nodded, all but Alodin, who watched the warden stride forward with glee.

No, thought Shiva, not cracked ... but how could they understand. The beast before him was tall and strong, calling to him for combat, stepping forward to show his dominance to his pack ... yet no fight would take place he knew.

Not tonight.

Shiva reached out his hand, running it across the face of the beast. "We meet again, my friend." Marrok let the warden stroke his fur, licking at his palm as he did. "I did not expect to ever see you again, but fate has set us together once more." He seemed pleased as he knelt beside the wolf. "Tell me ... where is Zev?"

The gray wolf turned, casting his gaze into the woods and then back towards the warden. Shiva looked towards the forest, but saw no sign of her. "Hmm ... we shall see."

Pulling away from Shiva, the great wolf turned towards the pack, letting out a long harrowing cry. The pack howled back, crying out in answer before turning and disappearing into the woods one after another until the forest was empty and white, and all was still except for the swaying trees.

With the wolves gone a sort of calm fell upon the land, still and tranquil and soft. The forest was lovely to behold, but Shiva had little care for such things, and Marrok none at all. The beast turned to the carts in a confused sort of way.

Shiva follow his gaze. "Ahh ... try not to spook the horses."

Marrok looked to the warden, he seemed to understand, and together they made their way back to the troupe.

Aldon was waiting for them as they neared; him alone. The others stood with bows in hand, though they had the sense enough not to point them towards the pair. Alodin eyed the wolf with care, then turned to Shiva. "A friend of yours?"

The warden nodded. "He belongs to one of my companions. I mean to see them reunited. The horses may not like his smell but he will not bother them, you have my word."

Alodin turned to the beast, his hand resting on his jeweled blade. Shiva wondered if it was all for show, a grand performance ... though the man did carry himself well. Finally, he answered with a single approving nod, then made his way towards the front of the troupe where Otto stood holding his mare.

Shiva watched the man go then turned to Marrok. "Best you stay a ways back, only until they see you're no trouble." And with that he returned to his cart, hoisting himself back up beside the youth just as the wagon pitched forward.

***

The mist came and went, but by morning there was more blue in the sky than grey, and the streams that ran out from the woods were running low. They kept a good pace that day, and come nightfall most of the troupe had come to accept Marrok, referring to him as the warden's pet. A few of them even approved of the beast, supposing him to be guard dog of sorts, saying they might rest a bit easier at night. Though it was evident not all of them felt that way. He caught Otto giving Marrok an angry glance more than once, and the horses were never quite at ease.

"Alodin says we're less than a week out from Solair," the youth declared one morning after the company had halted for a rest. "Says its good road all throughout Lord Magnus's kingdom, and even after too. In Soliare ... says it's smooth and well-guarded. It will be nice to see some patrols upon the roads once more, just like home. A ruler should know what's happening in his kingdom. All I see here are empty open fields. No outposts of any kind, not even a rundown inn."

Shiva glanced at the youth and smiled, a cold smile. "Lord Magnus does not need patrols to know what is taking place in his kingdom. He sees more than you could ever know."

The youth nodded. "Aye. We've all heard the tales. That doesn't mean they're true. Soliare has the Wizards Guild to help watch and they still have plenty of knights to help keep the peace, or so I'm told. I've never been there myself, see. But plenty in this troupe has. They say it's a fine city, Solaire. Not as fine as Bedivere, but fine just the same." He turned then, looking to the warden. "Do you get many troupes out in Cataron?"

Shiva shook his head. "It is harsh land that surrounds Cataron, and the city is always moving from one oasis to another. Traders make the journey, to them it is worth the risk, but no … few troupes decide to make the voyage."

"If your city moves as much as you say, how then do you find it when you need to?"

The warden looked at the youth for a long time, then said, "There are ways for those who know where to look." He spoke no more of it, and they continued on along the path.

Shiva spent a good part of the day looking out across the endless fields of Lord Magnus's Kingdom. Once he had believed as the youth believed … but no longer. Lady Sune had discovered the truth. He doubted if there were a safer kingdom in all the land. He inhaled deeply and looked out along the troupe. The roads would have fallen long ago if not for the ceaseless protection of Lord Magnus. Marrok was trotting beside them when the warden's thoughts turned towards the others. He was confident they would reunite; fate had led the wolf to him, it would lead the others.

They were in a rare state of quiet where one of the troupers had stopped playing and no one had yet taken up the call when the youth turned to Shiva in wonder. "What are those?"

Out across the endless fields of rolling green stood four towers, built from stone, with a disk as large as a house set between them. Shiva paused,

squinting towards the distant structures. "A star-tower," he said. He spoke
the words softly but the boy still managed to hear him. "It was used long
ago to observe the heavens at night. They say the Four themselves con-
stricted it long ago before the taint fell."

"The Four built this to observe the heavens?" the youth said. "What
for? What where they hoping to see?"

"I cannot say ... perhaps they simply wanted a glimpse of home. The
large disk you see hanging in the center is glass, though it's long been
cracked and abandoned."

"If they were looking up to the heavens there must have been something they were looking for," replied Joss. He raised his hand to his brow
for shade and stared towards the towers. "A thing like that doesn't get
built just to look up at the stars."

"Perhaps ..." Shiva replied. "But we will never truly know, and there
are stranger things in this world than those towers. Back home, somewhere
lost within the desert, carved deep into a mountain is a face thirty feet
tall with a crystal eye bigger than this cart that's supposed to show you
your death if you're brave enough to gaze into the stone."

"Who would want to know that?" the youth said, quite shaken at the
idea, but before Shiva could answer the troupe came to a halt.

The warden rose and looked out further down the road. "Hmm ..."

"What do you see?" the youth asked. He was leaning to his side for
a better view but failed to see anything past the cart before them.

"Ruins ..." was all he said. He stepped from the cart and began
walking the road leaving the boy behind.

At once Marrok was at his side. There were eight carts in total, a
rather large number for a troupe, and together they passed them by one
after another, paying little heed to the stray looks they received.

Alodin was sitting atop his mare, his eyes set upon a pair of men
standing in the center of the road beside a broken wall and the ruins of
a small tower. A small outpost, Shiva thought, long abandoned like so
many other structures in Lord Magnus's Kingdom. He unslung his bow
and held it lightly in his hands, checking the tension of the string uncon-
sciously as he looked out at the pair.

Alodin cocked his head to one side and eyed him questioningly. "Are
you expecting trouble?"

The warden looked to Alodin and then back to the men standing idle before them … waiting … watching. They were knights, the pair of them. Their horses were tied to the wall and a long jousting spear stood leaning against the broken tower, but the men stood defiant, watching the troupe from the distance.

"Well … one cannot say for sure," said Shiva. "But it would be foolish to take them lightly, whatever their wants may be. They are dangerous men, I can feel it, and so can Marrok." He looked to Alodin, curious to see how he would react.

"They bare the crest of House Magnus."

Shiva nodded. "They do, but you speak as though that makes them less dangerous … That would be unwise."

Alodin looked down at Shiva and then to Marrok. He seemed to understand and quickly dismounted, handing his horse off to Otto. "Wait here."

Otto took the reins quietly. For once the sour man had nothing to say. In fact, he seemed to agree with Shiva, eyeing the two men warily. It was queer behavior, standing there in the center of the road, not moving or calling out. The troupe was always on watch for more than just stray ghouls, bandits and thieves were known to reside in the forest, and the idea of willingly stepping into a trap was never something to overlook.

"I can go alone," Shiva offered.

But Alodin would not have it. "This is my troupe, my people … I will go, but you're free to join me. The wolf too."

Shiva laughed. With a quick nod he began making his way towards the knights.

They were tall men, both of them, donning well-crafted armor. The silver knight wore a full suite of plate from head to toe, and an early armet helm with hinged cheek plates instead of a visor. The other knight, an elderly gentleman with graying hair and a strong but weather face, wore a blue and silver undercoat with a single chest plate and no helm.

The senior knight hailed them as they neared. "Fear not friends, we are servants of Lord Magnus whose Kingdom we now preside in, and whose road you now traverse. We mean you no harm." He voice was calm and friendly.

"Good sirs. We are simple travelers, and only wish to pass through these lands unhindered," answered Alodin.

"So you are." The elder knight acknowledged. "And we mean to let you. But we have instructions, and one cannot cast those aside."

Shiva stepped forward. "What might those be?" he asked.

The elderly knight looked upon him now as though seeing him for the first time. He looked at the wolf next and smiled. "We are waiting for someone, a pair actually, a warden of Cataron and his beast." He paused, watching Shiva with probing eyes, yet the warden revealed nothing. The knight continued. "We are waiting for you …"

17

A T noon, several of the hedge knights lingering along the rear of the convoy had taken to assembling not far from the road for a bit of sport masqueraded as training. Not many, fifteen or so men along with their squires spread out in a circle across the field while some traders and common folk watched from a distance. The whole affair made for a rather cheerful spectacle, and the wistfulness of it all put a smile on Lennox's face, bringing him back to his own youth spent in the family courtyard training at swords with his brothers ... the shining armor, the cheers of comradery from all the knights.

He shook his head ... so long ago.

Several of the squires took their turn. Draped in boiled leather and heavy mail, they struck at each other with dulled blades. Their knights stood watch, shouting out commands or corrections. A few of the squires showed promise, Lennox thought, as he listened to the ring of swords as they clashed against one another. But the show came to a halt when one of the knights stepped in to show his squire how best to deliver a sidestroke. "You need to get lower," he began. "Else you're likely to lose balance if you're parried. Here, let me show you."

The knight turned, gazing out among the crowd for a partner. Many of the other knight's had been at it for some time and now stood idly watching, when at last the hedge knight's gaze fell upon Lennox. "You," he said pointing to the golden knight. "Good sir, won't you join me in teaching these lads a lesson."

Something told Lennox it was no accident the knight had chosen him. He and Astrid had been watched closely these last few days. The entire convoy had been curious about the emissaries of Lord Magnus that had joined them on their journey; but the golden knight and his squire kept mostly to themselves, and Lennox had declined the few offers at sparring he had received, not wanting to draw attention to themselves.

Yet the crowd had dwindled, so the golden knight simply nodded his consent and stepped out into the circle. He turned, catching a disapproving glance from Astrid before drawing one of his twin blades from his back, leaving the other properly in its place.

A quiet murmur went up around the field. More than one of the knights had wanted to test themselves against Lennox. It was rare for knights of House Magnus to be seen fighting in such events, or at all in truth. The young knight watched Lennox approach with a smile. "My helm," he said, and waited while his squire went to retrieve it, turning his eyes upon his opponent. "I'm told you call yourself Lennox," the knight began. "I am Sir Gareth of Solaire."

Lennox nodded but kept silent.

Sir Gareth's squire returned with the knight's helm, and a moment later he was fully dressed and ready to begin. "Now watch closely," he told his squire, then went forward to meet Lennox. "I was hoping we might put forth our full effort. You need not fight handicapped … in fact I insist you don't."

Lennox understood, and reached up to draw his second blade. In truth he was more comfortable fighting with just the one, but sometimes it was best to immerse oneself in the unknown.

Sir Gareth smiled cheerfully and dropped his visor, sliding out his sword in one smooth motion. In his left hand he bore a small wooden shield with the emblem of Soliare painted upon it in bright colors. "Well … shall we begin?" But Lennox was already moving, and the young knight was hard pressed to raise his shield in time.

Lennox drove him back, swinging his falchion blades in quick succession, attacking with every blow. It was new to Lennox, though no one watching would have guessed. The curves of the blades made them good for fluid strokes meant to move from one strike to the next, and Lennox's golden armor hardly seemed to hinder him.

All the field had grown quiet except for the repeated thud of Lennox's blades upon the young knight's shield. It seemed all Gareth could do was block until at last he saw an opening and sent a strike out towards Lennox's head, but the golden knight quickly stepped away, letting the blade pass inches from his face before slamming his foot into Sir Gareth's chest. The young knight fell to the earth with a crash and a moment later Lennox was standing above him leveling a blade at the knight's throat. "I yield," he shouted.

Looking down through the slit of his helm, Lennox nodded.

He returned his blades to their proper place and offered the fallen knight his hand, helping him to his feet. The whole affair lasted less than a minute, but all the field stood murmuring over what they had just witnessed. Some knights spoke of how they might have countered the golden knight's technique, while others only seemed to laugh at the shortcomings of Sir Gareth.

"That was quick," a young girl standing not far from Astrid said to her companion. Though the girl spoke softly Astrid could hear her quite clearly, and listened to their exchange with a sort of passive interest.

"I thought he did fine," the man replied. Though not dressed in armor he looked like one who could handle himself in a fight. He wore the gold and yellow colors of Soliare with a simple brigandine coat and a sturdy broadsword strapped to his side. The man continued. "He was hopelessly outmatched to be sure ... but he handled himself well enough, many would have fallen sooner."

"And how would you have fared?" the girl asked.

The man did not answer straightaway, but stood considering the question carefully. "Difficult to know for sure," he said at last, though it seemed he did not like admitting it. "He's fast ... a lot faster than you would think considering his armor, but I could out pace him I warrant, keep my distant and dance around him, wait till he tires then press in. Though I doubt he'd let it be that easy." The man stood shaking his head. "He's not a man I would want to face on a battlefield."

"Well now, your honesty is admirable if not somewhat misplaced. Why would I retain you if you admit that you are inadequate at keeping me from harm?"

The man grinned then shrugged. "I don't work for you, my lady. I work for your family, and the only reason I do is because the court guards proved themselves inept for the task."

This brought a mischievous smile to the girls face. She laughed. "Yes ... so they did!" Through all of this the pair kept their gaze upon Lennox, never turning to one another. "Tell me, do all knights of House Magnus fight in such style?"

The man shook his head. "Not at all... or at least none that I have witnessed, which is few enough to be sure. House Magnus is not known for their knights; it is magic they excel at. Any sorcerer of House Magnus can match even the strongest wizard from the guild; they are the strength of Lord Magnus's Kingdom." The girl looked annoyed but kept quiet. "They patrol the lands in pairs but often a knight may be seen as well, dressed in silver and carrying long lances fashioned similarly to the ones you might see in a tourney."

"Oh? How strange ... it seems we've come across an anomaly in our golden emissary."

The man nodded. "And his squire as well, Sir Sieg reported she is of the north."

Astrid drew her cloak close and stepped nearer the pair having grown interested in their discussion, but just as she drew close the girl turned and departed, taking her tall companion with her. Astrid heard her ask something about her sister but the man's answer was too muffled for her to make out, and then the pair disappeared, drifting along with the dispersing crowed.

When she turned back the field was all but empty. The convoy would be moving again soon and the knights and their squires and anybody who had been watching were making their way back to their horses for travel.

Sir Gareth passed by as well, bearing the look of defeat yet walking defiant, resolute to better himself as any knight who has taken setback should. There was still heat in his eyes; it was a look Astrid approved of.

"You certainly gave them something to talk about," she said as Lennox approached. The golden knight did not answer right away, and instead lifted his visor and stood watching Sir Gareth for a time. At last he turned and said. "Your right, but they have been whispering about us for days; at least now they have something of sustenance to speak of, and in the mean time I got to test my blades. It would not do to fight for true with unproven steel … not when it can be avoided, that is."

Either way, Astrid did not like the attention and made it known to Lennox.

"The youth has talent," he continued, as they began making their way back to their horses. "In time he will be ferocious, if he trains. One should never let themselves become stagnant."

"You were mired for ages as I recall, it doesn't seem to have hindered you much."

Lennox paused. Something in her words had struck him acutely. He lifted his hand, gazing down at them in thought. "It cost me more than you shall ever know," he finally said and then fell silent, not speaking for some time afterword.

At last they reached their horses and mounted, spurring them forward to join the column of knights as they continued in their journey.

***

It was later that night when the summons came. The convoy had stopped for the evening and many had already pitched their pavilions, the ones that had them that is. Many of the hedge knights had taken to sleeping under the stars, and that is where Lennox and Astrid were when the guards approached, resting quietly against a small sloping hill that ran alongside the road.

Lennox could see the patrol walking towards them from a way off, carrying torches that set them apart, and casting light upon a familiar face.

"Hmm … it appears our friend Sir Sieg has come to visit," Lennox said as he watched them approach. He stood, lifting his visor for a better look.

As before, the company halted some distance off and the aged knight strode forth alone. "Greeting," he called out to the pair.

"Greeting, Sir Sieg," Lennox replied casually as Astrid stepped beside him. He continued. "To what do we owe this honor?"

"Princess Lucienne requests your presence," Sir Sieg answered curtly, "and expresses her regret for not reaching out sooner to the emissaries of Lord Magnus."

"She wishes to see us now?" said Astrid irritated.

Sir Sieg could be heard grumbling something to himself before answering. "She does," he said with a nod. "She also offers lodging for you and your horses if you so desire it."

"Oh? Well ... we'd be delighted! Would you mind giving us a minute to make ourselves more presentable?" asked Lennox. "We'll be quick."

Sir Sieg looked over his shoulder towards his men and then back to Lennox before answering. "Very well," he said. "We were told not to delay, but you shall have the time you need."

"I thank you indeed, Sir Sieg," said Lennox with a bow. "Your kindness has not gone unnoticed."

Lennox's words must have come as a surprise to the aged knight, for he looked back upon him with a puzzled regard. Finally, he straightened and nodded back. "When you're ready, meet us upon the road and we will escort you to our camp." Then he left, leaving the pair alone once more.

"It would be better for us not to draw attention." Astrid said at once. "Those were your words if I remember ... it was foolish of you to accept such a request."

"It would be foolish not to," Lennox replied, but Astrid was not convinced. "If we were to deny her request do you imagine she will just forget about us?" Reluctantly, Astrid shook her head no. He went on. "I had hoped we would go unheeded, but now it seems that shall not be so. We will go and meet with the princess, be as dull as we can muster ... and be on our way. For all we know she is simply doing her duty."

For some reason Astrid smiled then, and her eyes grew soft with amusement.

She looks lovely when she smiles, Lennox thought. He considered telling her so but instead turned and made his way towards Alsvior. The horse swished his tale as his master approached, lifting his head up to better see. "Now come, you should change from your riding chaps if you're going to stand before the princess."

For a brief moment Astrid almost commented on Lennox's own apparel, but when she saw the knight twisting at the serpent ring on his finger, she fell silent. "Very well," she began. "Perhaps then I won't be treated as your squire."

"Perhaps," Lennox said with a laugh, and went about untying their horses.

***

The camps on either side of the road became denser as they progressed; changing from the sparse knights to the more elevated traders, who aligned their carts in rows one after another. Some were already sleeping but most were still about tending to the horses or sitting leisurely about. They watched as the company passed but said nothing and returned to their own errands after they had gone.

At last the company turned from the path. A small trail lay almost unseen just to the right; and this they followed as it curved away back up a narrow trail set between two rocky hills. They passed under several pairs of guards who had climbed higher among the rocks and now stood watch with bows in hand. The sentinels looked upon them with searching eyes but made no move to stop them. Suddenly they came out of the shadowed pass and before them lay a wide field full of grass and flowers, silver under the moon with a lesser stream that trickled before them; and resting in the center was a large marquee set upon three large poles.

Many men and women were seated there, watching as a young man stood before the court reading out from a scroll. The company halted and waited until the man was finished before entering. Three chairs were set apart from the others near the center, and resting upon them sat three women, each more lovely than the last. They watched as Lennox and Astrid entered.

To the left was the youngest, though not much younger than Astrid. She looked upon them with a mischievous grin that seemed both guilty and innocent. Astrid nearly gasped when she realized it was the girl from before, the one who had been watching Lennox spar in the field earlier that day. She almost did not recognize her, so much was her transformation.

Beside her sat her sisters, both tall and beautiful, draped in the colors of their house. It was plain to see who the eldest was, for her chair was centered and slightly larger than her sisters. She looked upon her guests with her hands folded before her and greeted them warmly. "Welcome friends … long has our journey been. I have had much to oversee; else I would have called upon you sooner."

Lennox had taken off his helm and had it tucked under his arm, he bowed and said. "Do not trouble yourself with us, my lady. We are at your disposal while we ride within your company." He lifted his gaze just in time to see her eyebrows rise, a pleased expression spreading across her lips. She seemed a strong woman to Lennox, kind and dutiful, and though the weight of her position did not elude her … she bore it well.

She went to speak when two ravens descended, swooping into the marquee from outside and circling the room for a moment before landing. One of them found their home on the shoulder of Astrid. Dark and sleek was the bird as it looked out across the court in silence. His twin had landed just beside Lennox and hopped forward before stopping at the princess. "*Quork!*" the bird screeched "*Quork! Quork!*"

The ravens reminded Astrid of the two that had accompanied Lady Gwen whom she encountered while traveling east toward Lohalian, but whether they were indeed the very birds she could not say. She had been surprised at first when the bird landed upon her shoulder, but she had remained quiet, letting it linger where it will.

While most of the court cried out in surprise at the arrival of the twin ravens, Lennox kept his eyes upon the princess. The youngest found the whole thing more than amusing, laughing with delight every time the raven *quorked* … but her sisters did not mirror her brashness, they knew the ravens were servants of House Magnus. Princess Lucienne kept her poise, and looked long upon the raven before turning once more to Lennox as though it were all of no consequence.

It was Lennox who spoke next. "We offer you our condolences on the passing of your father, my lady."

"Yes … thank you. He was a good king; my brother will make a fine ruler as well. He has been groomed for the position since infancy." She took a moment then, looking once more upon the ravens. "Long has it been since an emissary of Lord Magnus came to our city, you shall have a place of honor at the inauguration."

"You show us great honor princess," he began. "Yet I cannot say for certain we shall make it in time. Our first order is to seek convention with the Wizard's Guild, and I do not know how long our task may take. It could be some time."

"I see," she replied, sounding almost amused. There was a strange glimmer in her eyes then, and though she was still smiling she did not look happy. "So much of our burden lies in obedience. I will not press you on the matter. But know if you should come to our city, seats of great honor await you. Long have we been at peace with House Magnus … we wish to honor that alliance."

"My lady," Lennox replied and bowed once more. His eyes flickered to the raven standing at the princess's feet and wondered how the encounter might have gone had the birds not come. Not so different if he had to guess, but their arrival seemed to have shaken the gathering, all except for the youngest who continued to watch both him and Astrid with a most unassuming grin.

Their business concluded; Lennox and Astrid turned to leave when the youngest suddenly called out to the pair. "I watched you fight in the field today, Sir Knight. Tell me, are you practiced in the magical arts as well, or are you limited to the blade?"

Turning, Lennox caught her eye and smiled. "I am well practiced in magic, my lady. Though I am not what I once was."

"I'm told the sorcerers of House Magnus are some of the finest in the world, many say they are stronger than even our most formidable wizards."

"Hmm … do they? I would have to take your word on that, my lady. For I am neither a sorcerer of my kingdom, nor have I seen such a duel as you describe."

The girl smiled and laughed. "Yes, of course … but such a contest would be wonderful to behold I imagine."

"Quite so," replied Lennox.

"We're told your brother is quite the wizard himself, a prodigy even," Astrid said, looking now at the young princess.

Her curiosity peeked; the young princess turned her gaze upon Astrid. "I've heard that as well, though it has been some time since I have seen him."

"We are very proud of him," said Princess Lucienne, in a tone that signaled the end of the discussion. She was looking harshly towards her sister, though the young princess seemed to disregard her easily enough.

Straightening, Lennox looked once more to Princess Lucienne. "Of course," he said with a nod. "With your leave." There was a moment of silence as they turned and left, passing a pair of gentlemen who were coming to take their place before the council.

That night the pair slept in a pavilion prepared for them on behalf of Princess Lucienne. It was more lavish than anything they seen for many days, and for some time they spoke of the day's events, and of the three princesses whom they had encountered.

"She is most unnerving," said Astrid.

"Which one?"

"The youngest, Princess Maeve." Astrid was pacing about before Lennox in a discomforting manner. "She reminds me of a fox, the sly thing, always smiling as though all the world is hers to play with."

"She is a princess, my lady … all the world *is* hers to play with."

Astrid stopped sharply. "I am a princess, or do you take back your claim."

"You are … and you aren't. Either way, I advise you not compare yourself to one such as her. She is wild, the young princess, more so than any I have seen in a long time."

Astrid laughed. "That's not saying much, considering how much time you spent locked in a cell. I can't imagine you had many visitors."

"Well, that is true enough." He was grinning slightly but hoped the jests would end there. He was in no mood for them to go much further. "How much longer until we reach the guild?"

"It's not far now. We'll pass Soliare in two or three days, and the guild is not much further. We shall reach them within the week."

"Good, I will feel better when we are rid of this company. It sounds as though this road is well guarded. Perhaps it would have been better had we never joined this convoy."

"No. The roads are well guarded, but still I would not sleep with peace if we were not in this company, not with Marrok and Zev lost and only you to stand watch. If a horde or some lesser creature were to attack it would not bode well."

With nothing more to say, a silence stretched on before the pair until at last Astrid threw herself down upon her couch and fell at once into a long sleep.

Lennox followed her example. Placing himself upon the couch opposite Astrid, he removed his helm and set it on the ground beside him and looked long upon the sleeping girl. He wanted to take off his armor. In his cell it had always brought him comfort, but now, free in the open world once more, it brought him little relief. He wanted to remove it, but no ... it was a foolish thought.

He considered closing his eyes and drifting into a living dream, a memory of the past, but in the end he kept his eyes upon Astrid, watching her chest rise and fall with each breath until the light of day was broad upon the earth before their pavilion, and outside the carts were being packed and the horses made ready for travel.

***

From then on, they continued to ride with the hedge knights near the rear of the convoy during the day, but returned to the main camp to sleep at night. They were not called upon again by the court, and on the morning of the third day the road bent northward towards Soliare, but the pair pressed forward, separating themselves from the procession as they continued on towards the guild.

Their departure was quiet, with no one there to see them off, but they had gone less than a mile when Astrid shifted in her saddle and caught sight of a pair of riders not far behind. She called out to Lennox and together they came to a halt and waited.

Curious ... *I wonder what she is hoping to attain,* thought Lennox when he saw who it was. He glanced sideways to Astrid but her face revealed little.

Princess Maeve looked much as he had seen her watching his duel in the field, donning a pair of narrow riding skirts, dark blue with silver buttons that ran along the sides and a pair of soft boots. Her gray cloak streamed behind her as she rode forth, bringing her horse to a halt just before the pair. Her hair was set in a single braid that fell before her shoulder and she was grinning her same mischievous grin as was her custom.

"Sir Lennox, Lady Astrid. A sudden desire to see my brother has fallen upon me, and I was hoping I might accompany you on your travels to the guild."

Alsvior turned beneath Lennox and he took a moment to rein him in before answering. "Of course, Princess ... we'd be delighted. Though I must ask, and I do not mean to encroach, but are your sisters aware of your decision?"

"Indeed, they are," she answered quickly. "I left them a note with my full intents. They can scarcely be upset with me wanting to visit my brother."

"But what of the inauguration?"

She laughed "It is not my crowning; it will probably go better in my absence anyway. No one really cares what I have to say on the matter." She turned then to her companion. "This is Ferro, my personal guard. He shall be joining us on our journey."

With a silent nod Ferro acknowledged the golden knight, yet through all the exchange neither he nor Astrid spoke. Princess Maeve seemed to have enough to say for the three of them, and Lennox was left to fill the gaps.

Astrid had already turned her horse and was continuing down the road with Ferro close behind her. Lennox could not decide if the man was there to protect the princess or serve her. For a moment his mind went to Shiva and Lady Sune ... but no, Shiva served for different reasons. Ferro had the look of a mercenary in truth, a well-dressed mercenary, but a mercenary all the same. The man was a different kind of dangerous Lennox decided.

Through all this Maeve watched the golden knight with the keenest interest, always smiling as though she knew a secret and was holding it back. He booted Alsvior forward and heard a feint laugh escape Maeve's lips as she followed closely behind.

This could be a disaster, reflected Lennox, suddenly regretting joining the convoy as they had. Princess Maeve did not seem to be the type to take commands well, and he hoped her intentions were truly that of visiting her brother. Yet a dark feeling fell upon him, and somehow, he knew the truth of it, though she did little to hide it.

***

As the company continued west along the king's road, a group of small white cranes appeared from the north and with their arrival came the salty spray of the Slinder Sea. For a long while the road had taken them north, bringing them very near to the coast before again curving west towards a small peak that jettisoned out from the water's edge. Lennox recognized the birds from his youth, but it had been a long time indeed since he had seen them flying free as they were created to do. Not as high, and hovering above the water, a group of gulls swooped and soared, diving down towards the sea, circling about a single ship that sailed eastward towards the city of Soliare.

The ocean breeze carried the sharp scent of salt, and did much to break the heat which had been growing as the day wore on. The sun was near halfway down the horizon but it felt much earlier than that. Lennox had removed his helm that he might feel the wind as it blew against his face. He had dwelt so long in his dirty cell, surrounded by stale earth and rot that he had forgotten what clean air smelled like.

Princess Maeve murmured something softly behind him, but he paid it no mind. He was content in watching the birds as they circled the ship, its white sails growing steadily smaller as it sailed off into the distance. Soon though, the ship was gone all together, and the birds were nowhere to be seen, and all that could be heard was the soft rumbling of the ocean waves crashing against the stony cliffs.

At first Astrid had been displeased by the sudden arrival of the princess, but as time went on, she became altogether indifferent. She no longer felt the need to act as Lennox's squire, and rode forth as equals with no word of rebuke from the knight … and while every so often he would catch Maeve watching them as they spoke together, the princess seemed not to care. In fact, she smiled at the pair as though she had suspected all along. Farro was another sort altogether. He was easy enough to converse with when addressed, but was more than content to remain silent and go unheeded. Still, he seemed amused by the chaotic antics of the princess, and sometimes, when he looked upon her, his lips appeared to quirk very near to a smile. It was not a look Lennox would have expected to see from such a man.

Fixing himself up upon his saddle Lennox sighed. The road before them was flat with lightly forested hills, but as the coast curved outward, he could see rising from the sea a fortress of stone connected to the adjacent cliffs by a massive bridge with towering pillars that reached down into the waters below.

"Mallhorn Peak," Astrid said, frowning. "It was once called Vallacay, an outpost of the Northern Kingdom lost to Soliare during one of their many wars until at last the wizards took it for their own, claiming neutrality."

"Hmm …" Lennox shook his head, flexing his hand before turning it into a fist. "It had another name once. Long ago, but it seems to have escaped me."

"Tirion Alu," answered Maeve. "A great watchtower meant to guard mankind should the Giants ever rise." In her soft voice there was a note of admiration.

With the sun finally setting, Astrid gathered her coat against the cold. Tirion Alu … a great watchtower. She had never heard such a tale, and looked to Lennox for confirmation. A slight nod told her it was true.

"We should press on," Ferro said.

No one argued, and soon they were on their way. Across the treetops great towers rose, dark against the evening sky. There were countless clusters of trees that hid the fortress from sight for long stretches as they rode, but always there were one or two towers that peaked above the foliage if one knew where to look.

The trees along the pass began to thin and fields of wheat began to appear, usually accompanied by a single farm house, or by a group of two or three; but though the sun was setting and the hour late, no men could be seen working the land, and no smoke rose from the tall stone chimneys. Both plows and wagon alike stood abandoned in the fields, their work left unfinished. At one house close by the road the front door was left open, it's windows shattered. Lennox lifted his visor as he passed, frowning as he peered inside.

"What do you think happened?" Astrid asked quietly.

"I couldn't say," replied Lennox.

"It is no mystery," Farro said, and gestured to the trees beyond the houses. "The frozen woods lie just beyond those trees, and hollows are prone to wandering these parts."

"This seems like the work of more than a few ghouls," said Astrid, as she gazed back across the empty farms, it was then that she caught sight of Maeve, and for once the young princess was not smiling as she looked about the land.

She lifted her reins and pushed her horse forward until she was beside Farro and spoke softly into his ear. Neither Astrid nor Lennox heard what was spoken but when she had finished Farro simply nodded and turned his horse from the path, spurring him forward into a swift canter south to the woods. When Maeve turned to Lennox she was smiling again. "Do not worry ... he won't be far behind us."

Lennox watched as Farro rode away, his small form lost in shadows until he disappeared completely from view. Strange, I thought I was beginning to understand that one. Perhaps his affection for the girl is stronger than I thought.

***

Mallhorn Peak was built upon a high promontory just off the coast, and was connected by a single bridge. It was not as tall nor as spectacular as Lohalion, which shook the very air with strength and power, but the massive walls that stood on opposite sides of the passage offered their own sort of shield. The dark stone was sternly implacable, showing the true intent of its builders.

Lennox looked upon the gate which stood closed when a single voice called out. "Who stands before the guild? Name thyself and thy purpose!"

"I am Sir Lennox, emissary of House Magnus, and with me ride my companions: The Lady Astrid, and Princess Maeve of Soliare." Both Astrid and Maeve threw back their hoods as he spoke, revealing themselves to any who should look upon them.

After a brief moment the gates before them opened, revealing half a dozen wizard's draped in the traditional garb of the guild, each one baring a staff of varying shape or wand, yet Lennox could not help but notice that more than a few of them carried a broadsword or mace about their waist as well. Their horses were tethered nearby, fully saddled, and ready to ride at a moment's notice.

The guard's made no move to intercept Lennox or the others. Indeed, they separated, making a path for them to pass.

"Din Curuni," one said, falling to his knee before the princess. "Have you come to stake your claim?"

"Peace, Reneal," was all she said, and the man at once fell silent. All the others remained standing as they passed, but their interest in Maeve was plane to see, whether it be reverence or fear.

Lennox looked surprised, and turned his eyes upon Maeve. Well … she's a witch is she? Curse me for not noticing it earlier. It was then that the princess caught his eye, and smiled as though her secret had been let out.

As they rode across the bridge Astrid nudged her horse to the side and peered down. The sea below was a storm of froth and stones, the white waves crashed upon the cliffs in an endless cycle. She furrowed her eyes for a better look but saw only chaos. To attempt to scale the island from below would be madness. Behind them the front gate swung closed.

Lennox led them forward through the second gate which opened as they drew near. Much like its twin, the gate was draped in dark metal and was guarded by a dozen men. "Din Curuni, we welcome your return!" one of them called out from the gate tower, and beside him two more took to the knee.

The inner courtyard was a large open street, paved with stone blocks and set between towers and battlements as stern as the iron gates. Hmm … it was wise of them to claim this fortress as their own, Lennox thought as he looked about, for the stronghold was indeed formidable. Very wise.

The street was crowded with people, the displaced farmers and their families, come to a place of refuge. They stood with dull eyes and faces blanked with emotion, watching as Lennox's party rode through. A few of them had carts packed with their belongings, and sitting atop them sat the children, their faces as empty as their elders, their eyes hollower. A chilling sight, even through the narrow view of Lennox's golden helm. He looked away.

"Perhaps now would be a good time for us to separate, my lady," Lennox said turning to Maeve.

"Haha! Nonsense, did you believe I would come all this way and not learn what your errand was?" She shook her head and smiled. "Besides … in this state who knows how long it might be before you are allowed admittance. You have business to attend? Well, no one can assist you more than I." She kicked her horse so that she was before both Lennox and Astrid and called back, "Now come, let us not delay the revealing. Not when we are so close."

Though the streets were congested with people, they had not yet fallen into turmoil, and Maeve was able to lead them through with ease. The stables were just off the street, and Lennox was more than happy to release Alsvior for some well-earned rest and food. Beside him, Astrid went about untying her belongings before giving up Arvakr to one of the grooms. She handed the youth an extra silver piece and told him to feed him their freshest apples as a treat. The boy smiled and assured her he would.

They found Maeve speaking with a single guard set in plate-and-mail and carrying at his side a sword with matching dagger. Clearly not a wizard, the man wore a deep blue cloak edged in black over his armor with the cresting sun of Soliare set upon the back, as well as a gray surcoat bearing a shadow set inside a ring of light. He wore no helm, and kept his hair short and clean. "It is good to see you, my lady." He turned then, catching the sigil of Lord Magnus upon Astrid's chest. "You bring intriguing guests with you."

"I did not bring them," Maeve replied. "In truth I am in their company."

He turned back to the princess. "It matters not. Word was sent to the council of your arrival as soon as you passed through the gate. They are waiting your presence. Follow me, please."

As he led them into the fortress, along cold passages set with dark tapestries, he spoke of the farmers and the attacks. "I am glad for your safe passage, my lady. Some of the villagers reported seeing twenty or thirty hollows at a time. They emerge from the woods and descend upon a single home before returning to the trees … the people no longer feel secure." The narrow halls were dark, lit only by small sconces set far apart.

"Surly these stories are fallacious. Hollows have never moved in such numbers," Maeve replied. "Have scouts been sent out?"

The man turned and nodded, but he could not hide the grim look in his eyes. "Three days ago men were sent out to search the frozen woods. The first to return reported nothing, but others said they found strange trails set deep within the snow, large patches of snow that had been flattened due to the passage of many feet. Another wave of scouts was sent this morning and we now await their return."

"Let us hope what news they bring will cast light upon this strange mystery," Maeve said, though she was not smiling anymore. Behind her, Lennox and Astrid exchanged a look and the golden knight shook his head no.

In silence they were led before the council. There the short haired man bowed and excused himself, claiming the press of his duties. "Mikel," Maeve called as he left. "Farro should be following in our wake, make sure he is not hindered by the guards."

"I will, my lady," and with that he departed.

The room was dim, lit by a string of hanging orbs similar to Lennox's own spell of illumination. They were the first thing to catch his eyes as he entered, for though similar in design, they were inferior to his own incantation. He couldn't help but laugh softly to himself; perhaps he was not as weak as he first supposed, but then he thought of the oath-keeper ring, twisting at it with his thumb, and a darkness fell upon him. Once, he had wielded real power … but no longer.

The room was not large, and was sparsely decorated. A single tapestry hung beyond the dais covering the length of the wall portraying two wizards, standing with their staffs before them as though in a duel. Framing the tapestry was a pair of racks. One held a clear staff that appeared as though it were made of glass, and beside it stood a second, smaller staff, this one looked as though cut from stone. From the other rack hung a suit of armor, incomplete, for both the helm and left gauntlet were missing, yet upon the breastplate inlaid with gold was the sigil of the guild.

A single table sat upon the platform in the shape of a crescent moon, so that those who sat at it could see one another clearly. There were five chairs placed at the table yet only four of them were occupied. None of the council rose as Maeve and the others stood before them, indeed, it almost seemed that they were unaware of their presence so much were they involved in their own affairs. The table was littered with maps and pens standing in inkpots, while aged men sat reading and rummaging through sheaves of paper.

Astrid thought the whole affair rather bizarre, until she saw one of the men had been looking at them the entire time, and seemed only to be waiting while the others finished. Maeve too, stood in silence, neither speaking nor being spoken too. One by one the wizards of the high council set down their papers and took notice of Maeve and her party until there was only one, and when he had finished, the party was complete and he quickly cleared his throat and called out. "Din Curuni ... it is good to see you."

"Master Royce," Maeve said with a small bow, her smile ever present.

Master Royce sat to the far left of the council, and while he seemed openly pleased as he looked upon the princess, the others did not match his demeanor. Indeed, the remaining three looked annoyed by her presence, their eyes cold and distant.

"Din Curuni," another began. He was the youngest of the four, and sat beside Master Royce. "When you stood before us last you swore it would be many years before your return ... yet not even three seasons have passed. Tell us, why have you come?"

A wolfish grin appeared upon her face, and Lennox found himself wondering what the girl had done to deserve such consternation from the council. Whatever it was, he was confident it was well earned for the girl was wild, and rules did not become her.

"My visit is not my own, Master Bowlyn," she replied, sounding pleased. "I come as a companion to Sir Lennox and Lady Astrid, emissaries of Lord Magnus. They have business with the guild, and I simply followed along. Of course, while I am here, I would like to see my brother, but as to my dealings with the council, they must wait. I will not delay my companions a moment longer, for their errand is urgent, or so I perceive. They have said nothing of detail to me."

Surprised at her reply, Master Bowlyn turned his attention towards Lennox and Astrid.

"Well, this is quite unique," Master Royce said speaking up. All four of the council looked upon the golden knight and his companion, seeing the sigil of Lord Magnus clearly upon her chest.

It was now that a third member spoke, the oldest of the council. He sat in the center with his staff leaning beside him. Long was his beard, laid like snow upon his knees; and in his eyes there shone a white light, as if a deeper understanding was in his heart. "Long has it been since we have had dealings with that sorcerer. Tell us, is all well with Lord Magnus?" He had addressed the question towards Astrid, to her surprise.

"Well enough," she answered, after a time.

It was at that moment that Lennox removed his helm. He had been hesitant at first, concerned that his ring of illusion would fail before such men … but then he remembered Lord Magnus had asked him to remove it as well, and decided the rings magic was more powerful than he had first thought. Faid had crafted it for a wizard he recalled, and for the first time wondered who that wizard might have been.

"That is pleasing to hear," Royce replied, looking now upon Lennox. His eyes twinkled with laughter, though he gave no other sign of joy. "The last time Lord Magnus had dealings with the guild I was only a boy, hardly a novice." He turned then, and spoke now to his elder. "You had just been made Tutor, Master Eladin, if I'm not mistaken."

"You are correct, Master Royce," replied Eladin. "But let us set aside idle talk, for your pupil is not wrong, and there is urgency in our guests. Sent they say, at the command of Lord Magnus. Perhaps that is half true, for I remember … I remember his servants of old, and the sorcery that clung to them. Some of it clings to you as well, my lady, but I see none upon this golden knight. Tell me, what is your purpose here?"

At his words a somber mood fell upon the room, and Lennox stepped forward in answer. "Master Eladin. We seek an audience with Prince Oscar of Solaire, the purpose of which we cannot reveal except to the young prince himself." Before he finished speaking, he heard Maeve squeal with delight.

Eladin frowned. "Prince Oscar is in the middle of his trials."

"If we could but speak with him for a moment — "

"Nothing can interrupt the trials once they have begun, Sir Knight," Master Bowlyn interrupted. "For a thousand years the sanctity of this guild has been sustained. You will wait till he has finished, or you may leave. The choice is yours."

Lennox bowed in reply. "Of course … I apologize for pushing the matter, we will wait until the young Lord has finished. Tell me, how long do these trials normally last?"

Maeve spoke in answer. "Three weeks. Though I finished mine in less than two."

"Enough, Din Curuni!" snapped Master Bowlyn. "We do not speak of such things before outsiders. As it is, we have matters of the guild to discuss, several of which pertain to you. We were going to wait, but now that you are here, I see no reason for us to delay such materials any longer."

As Lennox stood listening a strange noise began to echo through the room, so soft and subtle that he wasn't sure what he was hearing, or if it was even real.

"I am not here to discuss guild affairs," Maeve answered. "I am only here as companion to Sir Lennox and Lady Astrid."

"Yes, you have made that clear to us," Bowlyn replied. "Yet their business is concluded at present. They are free to reside within Mallhorn Peak for the time being, but you are not released from your duties."

Lennox tilted his head. It was a horn, he was certain; its call was dim but unmistakable. He looked about the room but none of the others seemed to have taken notice. He strode forward, then his eyes fell upon Master Eladin and he halted, standing stiff as stone.

"You hear it as well, Sir Knight?" Eladin asked.

The question filled the chamber, bringing a halt to both Maeve and Master Bowlyn. They turned in unison, looking towards the aged wizard. "Hear what?" Bowlyn asked.

"A horn … distant but immense," Lennox replied.

"I hear it too!" Master Royce's chair scraped across the floor as he stood. "That is no warning of ours, but I fear its message!"

Maeve was looking to Master Royce for an explanation when she heard it as well, a soft horn blowing in the distance, yet it felt close somehow. She was befuddled then, unsure of how she could have missed it. Her eyes darted towards Eladin and then Lennox. They had both heard it before her. The knight was more powerful than she first thought.

"What horn?" Astred found herself ask as she turned to Lennox. "I hear nothing."

"Nor would you," Lennox replied. "It is an enchanted call, only those practiced in magic can hear its blast. Only a great wizard or sorcerer could produce such an instrument."

"But what does it mean?" Maeve asked.

"It means Fear, Din Curuni!" Eladin answered rising from his seat. "It means foes … the guild is under siege!"

18

GALEHAUT trotted quietly beside the troupe's wagon, doing his best to ignore the large wolf that lingered behind. He kept a collected seat, but the way his horse shook every time Marrok drew near showed that at least one of them was warry of the beast. Sir Vantimier, riding opposite Galehaut, was not faring much better. He watched the wolf constantly, tilting his head that he might better see through the slit in his helm. More than once he twisted in his saddle to look for the beast until at last Marrok bounded off into the woods, vanishing from sight.

Shiva watched them both with calculating eyes; it was good to know what men feared.

The troupe had accepted the knight's openly. Though known to be somewhat of a recluse, Lord Magnus had an honorable reputation among the people, or at least a fair standing, and having two of his knight's as escorts was seen as a good omen.

The warden had resumed his position on the rear cart beside Joss who seemed open to the company. The youth had asked many questions at first, and while Sir Galehaut was willing to answer them, his answers were short, and offered little explanation as to the nature of their duty.

"He's not far," Shiva answered when Joss asked where Marrok had run off to. "Close enough to answer my call if the need should arise, though I doubt any trouble will come our way that Marrok doesn't know of first." Yet even as he spoke doubt tickled at the back of his mind; the frozen woods had grown colder, and the arrival of Sir Galehaut and Sir Vantimier weighed heavily upon him. The troupers may have taken to them without concern, but not him. Lady Sune had said nothing of an escort, and he was left to wonder … did they portend some new evil, or were they ambassadors of providence. He could not say, but inside doubt had taken root.

"A smart beast, your wolf, rarely have I come across such intelligence outside the ravens of my master. He is larger than the local breed; tell me, where does he hail from?" Galehaut asked with a smile, turning in his seat.

"He is of the North," Shiva answered, "but he is not mine. I make no claim to him except perhaps that I am his guide, and mean to see him back to his master."

"Oh! Of the north you say, that's quite a distance for such a beast to travel. He is called Marrok, yes? What does it mean?"

Shiva turned and looked upon Galehaut for a moment. "I cannot say. I speak not the northern tongue."

"Perhaps we shall ask his master then, when we come across him."

"Marrok's master is a woman, Sir Knight, and it was my understanding that you were to escort us only while we traveled upon Lord Magnus's land."

"I see how you could have come to that inference, but it is in err," Galehaut said with a smile. "We are to assist the troupe while they travel our lands, true enough, but you … we are to escort until you reach the guild. Lord Magnus knows you serve Lady Sune, and wishes to aid her." He gestured towards Sir Vantimier. "We have been sent to help, in whatever way we can."

Shiva continued to look at the knight, not speaking, not saying a word. Sir Galehaut slowed and pushed his horse around the cart next to Vantimier. He was always smiling it seemed, and had a calming nature to him that made him appear less dangerous than he was. Shiva looked past him to Sir Vantimier, the pair of them, he knew, were no ordinary knights. Dangerous to be sure, but still only men. He had battled true monsters, and the fear of men was no longer in him.

***

For three days they traveled north along the frozen woods, the open fields of Lord Magnus ever present to the east. Their pace was slow, but the troupe stopped only when twilight thickened, and camp was kept to a bare minimum so that they did not lose the morning to idle waste. Often, Marrok would make to the woods in the day to hunt and eat as he liked, but each night he would come to the fire for a time, checking to see all was well. Shiva understood; the unending music and endless chatter dribbled on in a parade of noise and clatter. Sometimes it was more than he could take, and wished he might escape into the woods as well.

He had grown accustomed to Sir Vantimier. The silver knight was quiet, and kept to himself. Sir Galehaut, in contrast, always seemed to be talking with somebody, and made his way to Shiva who stood alone by a fire beside his cart. Marrok was approaching as well, sulking out from the woods like a shadow, when the knight inquired as to how old the beast was.

"He's still growing," Shiva answered, watching as the wolf strode forth shaking loose snow from his fur before lying down beside the flame. "That is all Astrid would ever say."

"Astrid!" cried Galehaut in surprise. "Lady Astrid of Kay? She is known to me, is she the beast's master?"

Rarely would emotion show so plainly upon the warden's face, but he could not hide the surprise he felt as he turned to look upon Sir Galehaut. "She is ... but how is it you know of her?"

"I was sent to retrieve her, not ten days ago, upon the very spot where first we met. She and Sir Lennox had stumbled into our borders from the woods, the knight was severely wounded, but my master assured me of his recovery."

"Why did you not mention this sooner!"

"Believe me, good sir, when I tell you I would have had I known of your connection. Astrid spoke of a friend, but said not his name. When last I saw her, she was being escorted into Lohalion to meet with Lord Magnus."

"Then they are safe," Shiva said more to himself. "Tell me, do they still reside within the tower."

"That I do not know," answered Galehaut sadly. "For upon parting, Sir Vantimier and I traveled to the ruins of Calthun, and there we waited as we were bid, until a warden of the east and a single wolf should arrive. We were then to escort the pair on their travels. It was thought you were destined for the Wizards Guild, but if that was not your terminus, then

Jacob Marc Schafer

we were to aide you indefinitely."

The warden looked at Galehaut with renewed wonder, but his eyes hardened. "Alas … That I did not hear of this sooner. I would have made straight for the tower, but I see now that perhaps Lord Magnus knows more than I thought, for he sent me you, and now I mean to use you."

"This is pleasing to hear," said Galehaut. "I would much prefer to ride in your company than to have trailed after you like some stray dog, had you refused our aid."

Shiva smiled then, though his eyes remained rigid. "I am not so foolish, Sir Galehaut, that I would refuse aid when offered it freely. We will have to ride through the forest once more to reach the guild, and I know the dangers of these woods, more so than most."

"Yes … I fancy you do."

***

The next morning, they started before dawn, walking the same road they had been following for many days. When light came, they could see the forest coming forward as if to meet them, and by noon they had reached a crossroad, halting beneath the great overhanging boughs of the frozen woods. One path continued north through the forest, the entrance of which was like a sort of tunnel made by two great trees that leant together. The other path broke east; running parallel the woods once more for as far as could be seen.

Alodin had fallen back to inquire upon which path they should take when a single raven appeared from the woods, walking out from the entrance and taking to the air. The bird had hardly risen to the tops of the trees before circling the troupe and landing at once upon Sir Vantimier's outstretched arm.

"Hmm …" said Shiva, and watched the interaction with great interest, as did Alodin and the youth who was closest to Vantimier.

The silver knight lifted his visor and tilted his head, bringing the bird to his ear. He stayed quiet for a short while, listening to the soft quarks of the bird before suddenly lifting his arm high. Stretching out its wings, the raven took to the air and this time did not return. He was soon a dark speck in the sky as Vantimier made his way over to where Galehaut and Alodin waited.

"What news does he bring?" Galehaut asked.

"Only one of warning," Sir Vantimier began. "There is movement in the woods, foul creatures, more so than there has ever been. They are further west, deeper into the forest, yet he gives caution, and ask we consider taking the eastern road, as the northern passage is no longer safe. Others of his flock have returned to Lohalion with the news, so that men might be posted outside the forest to warn travelers. We are lucky one stayed behind."

"How far east does the road go before turning north once more?" asked Alodin.

"A long while," answered Vantimier. "three days of good travel at least."

"Three days! By then we will have missed the best part of the king's inauguration. This passage through the woods, how long will it take?"

"It's a true path through the woods, and the path has always been well kept," answered Shiva. "If we ride through the night, we will clear the forest by this time tomorrow."

"I would not recommend such action," Galehaut warned, shaking his head. "Never have I seen the ravens so riled that they would leave only one while the others went away in warning. If they spoke of danger, then I believe it best we take their counsel seriously."

"This won't do," said Alodin. "Let me speak with my troupe. If we miss the coronation than this entire trip will have been a waste. We have traveled through dangerous lands before, Sir Galehaut, a few stray ghouls do not scare us. Come Joss, we must discuss this with the others."

A hint of a smile touched at Shiva's lips as he watched Alodin depart. He had respect for a man who would not be easily dissuaded once a goal has been set, though he did not think it the wisest choice. He would be taking the northern passage no matter what the troupe decided. His Lady had told him to move quickly, and he had already lost much time, more so than he had planned for. He would delay no longer. "Did the bird say nothing more of the creatures?" he asked turning to the knights. "Were they hollows, or something else?"

Vantimier shook his head. "He spoke only of the cursed. But he said they were traveling together in large numbers, more so than had ever come before, and that they were heading north."

"If they are heading north than why should he fear for us? Are they crossing through the path?"

"He did not say," answered Vantimier.

Shiva stood then and gazed through the arch into the dim gloom of the woods. "Whatever the others should choose, I ride north. I was warned that speed was of the upmost importance, and that disaster would follow should I fail."

"Hmm … so be it," answered Galehaut. "If we are to travel, than best we do it quickly, while we still have light. I will ride and speak of our decision to the others; they will want to know our course."

"The troupe will ride with is," said Shiva. "They are all of like mind, and the temptation of the king's inauguration is more than they can deny."

"I concur," said Galehaut with a nod, "but still, the conversation must be had." And with that Galehaut kicked his horse forward and made his way towards Alodin who was speaking before the group.

***

Shiva had been right, and soon the troupe was riding single file through the entrance of the frozen woods. The path itself was wide, though it swiveled round several large trees so as not to disturb the land. Light was scarce as a thick haze hovered about. Shiva was quick to note the change, for such a fog was unnatural. He glanced sidelong towards Sir Galehaut, but the cheerful knight seemed as disturbed as the rest, and looked upon the haze with a furrowed brow.

As their eyes became accustomed to the murky light they could see more of the surroundings, illuminated every so often by slender beams that somehow passed through both tree and mist. But soon such beams ceased altogether, and a bitter mood fell upon the party.

"You seem perplexed, Sir Knight," said Shiva, seeing the puzzled expression of Sir Galehaut as he gazed about the woods. "What is it that vexes you?"

"It is this bothersome fog; it is most unnatural. There is a stirring inside me, a warning that cannot be stifled … though I know not what it is."

"I feel it too, Sir Knight, subtle though it may be. Best we move quickly. Perhaps one of us should lead?"

Galehaut nodded. "You're right. Vantimier, join Alodin at the front and make sure our pace does not slacken."

With a silent nod the silver knight rode forth, passing the troupe with plenty of room to spare. Not long after their pace increased, and Shiva felt a weight lighten upon him; though not much and not for long.

The air was still within the forest, and though they thought it dim when they had entered, it was nothing compared to the perfect darkness that encompassed them when night fell. Even Shiva seemed bothered by the black, and he was used to making camp in the dark places of the world. Without their lanterns the warden could not imagine seeing his own hand had he waved it before his face. As it was, he could barely see the cart before him, and the troupe's pace had come almost to a crawl.

Long into the night they traveled, and as they went the lights from their lanterns drew forth moths from deep within the woods, large, bluish-white creatures that slowly shrouded them. At first it was only a few, but as time passed their numbers increased until there were hundreds of them, flapping and whirring about the troupe so much so that it became impossible to see, and Sir Vantimier could do nothing but call the troupe to a halt.

"We will have to wait till morning," said the silver knight, much to Alodin's displeasure. "Inform your people they are to sleep within their wagons."

"What of the horses?"

"They will make do. With the lights put out, the moths should depart," answered Vantimier, who had begun to turn his horse about. "I will stand watch this night, but first I will seek council with Sir Galehaut. Now be quick! I fear we are attracting more than these wearing creatures."

He found Galehaut and Shiva waiting for him near the back, and steadied his horse as Marrok sulked out from behind the cart. The silver knight spared a glance towards the wolf before speaking. "It would not do," he began. "I had to stop. Thrice times I nearly lost the path as it turned beneath me. We shall wait until morning ... there is no other choice to be made."

Soon after, all their lanterns were put out, and the pitch-black that fell upon them was complete. With no light to draw them forth, the moths disappeared, fluttering away in all directions. Shiva and Galehaut had agreed to keep watch as well, not trusting the dark forest to give them peace. Vantimier had taken post near the front once more, leaving Galehaut to walk the camp alone. With no light to guide the way, the old knight strode from one cart to the next with his hand outstretched, feeling at the cold wood of the wagons.

Still more time passed, and Shiva began to worry as their surroundings stayed ever dark. It was then that he sensed an ominous presence, and the warning he had felt suddenly screamed out inside him. "Where has the old man gone off to?" he whispered, his tone anxious and concerned. Beside him Marrok rose, sniffing at the air and turning towards the warden with bared teeth. "Hmm ... go, see that all is well," he said to the wolf. A moment later Marrok leapt clear the wagon onto the unseen path and bounded off into the unknown.

Shiva waited patiently, lighting a torch as his heart beat calmly inside his chest. He had learned patience; he had learned restraint ... to fail at either was not in him.

"Ahh-wooooo!" came the wolf's howl suddenly, "ahhh-woooooooooo! Ahh-wooooo!" came the second and third.

Shiva jumped from the wagon, landing upon the earth with a soft pat before dashing off along the carts towards Marrok's call.

In the distance a second torch was coming to meet him, Sir Vantimier, sword drawn and ready for battle. They met just short of the center cart but saw no sign of Galehaut.

"Ahh-wooooo!" came another call, this one from deep in the woods.

"Stay with the troupe!" Shiva shouted, and sprinted off towards the wood. "I will reclaim our lost friends!" But he did not have to go far before discovering the source of all their misfortune.

With his torch blaring, he stumbled upon three spiders, white as the snow that filled the woods, crouching with fangs bared as they circled Marrok. Bundled in strings of web lay Sir Galehaut, his two feet sticking out from the bottom. The great wolf stood over the knight, placing himself between the spiders and their prey as muffled cries stirred beneath him.

Shiva moved at once, drawing his scimitar and slashing down upon the nearest spider. It hissed out in pain before going limp. With its death a rage fell upon the other two. They turned towards the warden, scuttling towards Shiva with blinding speed, though they did not move fast enough. Marrok caught one by its leg, shaking it violently until the limb ripped off completely. It went mad then, leaping away and scuttling off into the darkness.

With a shrill hiss, the remaining spider leapt towards Shiva, shoving its legs forward like swords to pierce the warden. Shiva darted forward to meet him, ducking low and swiping at the spider from below. He cut the creature in two before falling to the ground. He flipped over then, and placed his hand upon the spider's limp corps, drawing out his sword which was now stained black. He wiped it quickly upon the snow and sheathed it as he reached for his dagger.

Half crawling and half stumbling, he made his way towards the bundled Galehaut and cut at the web, breaking the threads that bound him until the knight was clear. Sitting the knight up, Shiva peered out into the woods and took up his torch once more. "What happened? Are you well?" he asked, keeping his voice low.

Galehaut grabbed at his knees, trying desperately to steady his shaking hands. "They fell upon me from above," he said, his voice thin and weak. "Gaged me with their web and stung me with their filthy poison." He tried to rise but faltered, staying on one knee until Shiva took him beneath the arm and helped him to his feet. "The fog … it is an illusion; we've walked into their den. We must move now or risk being consumed!"

At that moment Shiva, who was fixing his eyes upon the woods, saw a twinkle of light in the distance. "There!" he said. "Sir Vantimier has lit the way! Now come, the road is nor far!"

There was a hollow scream then as lights began to spring forth, lanterns and torches both, illuminating the troupe in a line of fire. More shouts accompanied the fresh light, and terror reined in the distance.

"Marrok go!"

Sparing only a quick look towards Shiva the wolf bounded off toward the lights. More shouts followed as the troupe roused to life and Marrok slipped ahead of them.

With Sir Galehaut poisoned he shook with every step, resting upon Shiva as his body drooped low. Their pace was slow, but they had cleared the gap and were nearly back to the road when out of the corner of his eye, Shiva caught the movement as another spider leapt down from behind a tree without a sound and scuttled towards the pair. Shiva was reaching for his sword when Sir Galehaut's hand whipped back and forward in a flash of silver. The spider fell dead with a long blade sticking out from its eye.

"One of my best daggers," Galehaut muttered, but made no attempt to retrieve it as Shiva drove them forward. "Never have I come across such creatures in these woods … from where did this new evil come?"

"I know not," answered Shiva. "Perhaps from beyond the mountain, either way, we cannot terry."

"They should not have been able to hide from my master, nor from the ravens. Their illusion must be very strong indeed, to hide them so thoroughly."

"Indeed," Shiva answered, and thought at once of the fog.

Soon they reached a low bend and stepped clear the forest onto the path just south of the troupe. The screams had stopped, and strewn about the camp were more white corpses. Three or four of them from what Shiva could see. He could hear men shouting from further up when Joss suddenly appeared holding a bow with arrow nocked. "They're here!" he called back, and ran out to meet the pair.

"Is everyone safe?" Galehaut asked. The old knight was beginning to shake quite a bit as Shiva lifted him up onto the back of the cart.

"Can't say," Joss answered. "Most of the spiders had been slain by the time I woke. Otto handed me a bow and told me to keep watch."

"Stay with him," Shiva said gesturing to the knight, "and be ready to move quickly."

Leaving Sir Galehaut with the youth he moved on, passing the carts one by one. As of yet he saw none who had been killed, but several had been poisoned and were beginning to feel its effects. He found Alodin near the front, speaking quietly with Otto and Sir Vantimier. Marrok called out the warden's arrival and the three reached for their weapons, relaxing when they saw it was Shiva.

"Is Galehaut well? Did you find him!" said Vantimier. The silver knight had lost his helm in the fray and stood dirtied from battle with his long hair pulled back.

"He has been badly poisoned," Shiva answered, "and is resting on the rear cart with Joss. I'm afraid he is rather unfit to fight should the need arise, which it might indeed if we do not move quickly."

"You want us to ride now! Half the bloody troupe's been poisoned and already the moths are fluttering about," argued Otto.

"What else can we do, wait to be attacked once again?" asked Alodin.

"Morning must be near," interjected Vantimier. "We need only wait a little longer."

"Morning will not come!" Shiva said sharply. "Galehaut said as much, and I sense it now too! This entire woods has been bewitched; no light will come. We must press on, and we must do it now!"

" … bewitched," said Vantimier gazing about. "I have felt no magic here."

"It is subtle."

"We should wait until we have more light!" Otto repeated sternly. "What happens if we should get off the trail? It was hard enough to see when we were moving slowly, and already the moths are returning."

"Have you heard nothing I've said!" shouted Shiva. "We need to go now, or we will never see light again!"

Otto was about to speak back but hesitated, eyeing the warden narrowly. When he spoke next, he sounded disgusted with himself. "Right … than I believe you. But it's been nothing but trouble since you showed up like a vagrant drifter." He turned to Alodin. "Once we're clear of the woods, either he gets on his way or I do, and I'm taking my wagon and any who want to go with me."

Alodin's eyebrow's rose in surprise. "Your terms have been made perfectly clear, and will be addressed after we're clear this mess. As it is, I agree. The forest has felt ill ever since we set foot upon this cold path, and I can't see it getting any better. We push on, as quickly as we can."

"What of the moths?" asked Vantimier.

"What of them?" answered Shiva.

"Surely the light will draw them fourth … and we will be none the better."

"Moths or no, it is the only way. We must try." He paused then, looking out along the darkness of the path. "I'll set torches upon the trees as we go. It may not keep them all at bay, but perhaps it will draw enough that we will be able to move freely."

"It will be dangerous leaving the road."

"I will have Marrok with me," said Shiva. "Now let's depart; we have wasted enough time as it is."

***

The moths came sooner than expected, fluttering about in flashes of white and ash-gray … yet as they continued on the swarm lessened, drawn back by the steady stream of light left behind by Shiva.

They went on for a long time like that, walking through the dark unknown. Joss sat atop the rear cart beside Sir Galehaut with an arrow nocked, keeping an eye upon the warden and his beast. The breathlessness of the air tightened all around them, growing still and stagnant, heavy and dark. They walked as it were, with little hope through the darkness.

Even so, they went on, into the deeper parts of the forest. The path must end eventually, Shiva knew, and looked back along the trail of fire. Deep into nothing it went, reminding him of the endless cavern road beside the Undead Cathedral.

It was then he noticed he had fallen behind, and when he moved to catch up, found the carts were moving faster than expected. He looked about, curious as to what had brought on the change when he saw it, a break in the darkness, a ray of light that pierced through the trees like a spear. Gazing ahead he saw more rays, many more, and in the surrounding darkness where none could hear him, he laughed, and relief fell upon him, though his eyes remained hard.

Pressing his heels into his steed's flanks he galloped forward, feeling the wind against his face as he broke through the stagnant air. The light grew quickly then, filling the forest first with a dim haze and then with a brilliant light, shining upon the snow and illuminating the ice like shimmering diamonds in fields of white.

He heard Joss laughing from the distance, and saw the youth grinning gingerly at the sun. "We made it!" he shouted as Shiva drew up beside the cart. "We're through!"

"Not yet," answered Shiva, his eyes stern as he looked back over his shoulder. He turned to the youth. "Don't let down your guard, there are other foul creatures in these woods besides spiders, and some that are not afraid of light." The youth laughed uneasily, as if he thought it were a joke, but Shiva's distant stare made him fall quiet. "Keep the watch," he said again before moving up the line.

An uneasiness still lay upon the warden, warning him … but to all the rest their fear had faded with the passing shadows. They believed they had been through the worst of it. Perhaps they have, thought Shiva, but it was foolish to assume.

Looking about the forest he galloped on, until he suddenly realized that the entire troupe had stopped, and before him Sir Vantimier stood conversing with Alodin and Otto before a great split in the road. He drew rein as he neared, bringing his horse to a stop and gazing once more into the spider's hole that lay behind them. Its dark force could be felt still, as they were not too far removed as of yet. "What is the delay? We are clear that foul place but we should not linger."

"We've come to a split," Sir Vantimier answered. "The eastern road leads to Soliare while the northern road continues on to the guild."

"What then is the delay?"

"There is no delay," answered Alodin with a smile. "Sir Vantimier was simply offering coin that we might carry on with Sir Galehaut while he rides north with you. I refused of course, but the knight insisted."

"He will need treatment," Vantimier said, "see that he gets the best and there will be more silver when next we meet." He turned then towards Shiva. "Gather your belongings… we continue on."

The warden looked to Otto then, and was surprised when the sour man gave him half a nod. He returned the nod and pushed his steed so that he was beside Alodin. "I'm sorry for any trouble I may have caused you, it was not my intent."

The blond man sighed. "If I didn't know any better, I'd have thought you a cursed man, but perhaps having you along saved us." He raised his hand up to the warden and Shiva took it firmly in his own.

"Travel safely," said the warden, "and do not delay."

"You as well," answered Alodin. "Perhaps we'll meet again."

"Maybe … I will ask my lady when I see her next." And with that he departed, returning to the rear cart to retrieve his affects and say his goodbye to the youth.

He checked Sir Galehaut one last time and together with Sir Vantimier beside him, watched as the troupe departed, traveling east upon the forest road.

"Will they be safe?" he asked as the troupe dipped around the bend.

"Safer than us," answered the silver knight, "but only at present. There is a darkness falling upon these woods, and I cannot say how long the guild can stand against it, not without aid."

The last remnants of the troupe disappeared then, and Shiva looked one last time towards the dark lair of the spiders and turned, kicking his horse into a fast trot to make up what lost time he could.

1 9

SHIVA and Sir Vantimier continued along the northern path, making their way through the frozen woods at a swift pace. After emerging from the perfect night that ruled the spider's den, the light above was blinding. It hurt their eyes, but neither spoke of the inconvenience, nor hinted at their discomfort.

They spoke little as they rode, and a gloomy demeanor had befallen Sir Vantimuer. The loss of a friend, the failure of duty … Shiva could not say. "He was breathing well," the warden offered. "If the poison had been a lethal dose than Sir Galehaut would have passed before our departure."

"Perhaps," replied Vantimier, his eyes forward. "But it is more than Galehaut's wellbeing that concerns me. A change has come, a darkness lurks. Lord Magnus's roads have been polluted, and the raven's said nothing. Either they knew and did not speak of it, or they were deceived. The guild must be warned, as must my master."

Shiva gave the knight a flat look, then nodded reluctantly. "Yes … of course."

In the distant north, the forest rose high with outlines of green spreading out against a blue sky. Remnants of the taint had spread far, but at last its corruption was b ginning to fade. Shiva was pleased with what he saw, yet they still had some distance to travel, and the cold was still very much about them. An icy wind had begun to blow, gusting through the hollow road in quick blasts that froze the sweat on Shiva's neck into beads of ice. The wind came from the south, bringing with it a lingering stench of decay; the stagnant air of the spider's den.

"Will we clear the woods by nightfall?" asked the warden.

Vantimier nodded and pointed towards the horizon. "We are closer than you think. Just beyond those hills is open farmland and the ocean. It is there we will find the guild. If we keep this pace, we shall reach it before dusk."

"Hmm … that is good to hear. I have passed through the forest many times, but always on my way to Soliare. Never have I seen the guild."

"It does not compare with Loholion," began the knight, "yet it is a fine castle, strong and true. I visited it often in my youth, when I traveled with my father."

"Then you are not from the Eastern Arc?"

The knight laughed. "Regretfully, I am not. But I have found my home in the service of Lord Magnus."

The road turned westward then, only for a league before bending north once more. They maintained a quick pace, resting only that the horses might take a drink before continuing on.

The sun was a sullen orange ball just touching the treetops when they at last began to break free of the surrounding snow. The forest found new life then, filled with vibrant greens and rich browns. Squirrels could be seen running the lengths of the trees, and not long after, the great wolf darted off, chasing after some unseen prey. For a time, the pair continued on without concern, but it wasn't long before both Shiva and Sir Vanimier began to wonder where the wolf had gotten to, for they were beginning to travel some distance without any sign from the beast. It was then his call came clear through the forest trees. "Ahh-wooooo! Ahhh-woooooo!"

Shiva pulled to a halt, his eyes darting out west along the tree line.

"Why have we stopped? said Vantimier. "He is only hunting."

The warden shook his head. "No … he would not call out if there was not a need."

Eager to press on, Vantimier looked northeast toward the fading sun. "It would be prudent for us to clear these woods before nightfall."

"We have some time still," answered the warden. Taking his reins firmly in his hands he turned westward, at an angle to the road, and pushed his steed off the path into the dark earth of the forest. He could hear Sir Vantimier following closely in his wake, and was pleased that the knight had not voiced an objection. The silver knight was there to aid him … and Shiva was curious just how far the knight was willing to go to fulfill his master's will.

In the dark shadows of the forest, piles of snow and ice could be seen having persisted through the noon sun. The cold was still present, and their breath rose like steam before their eyes. They had come to the foot of a stony hill and stopped, and there all signs of Marrok vanished.

"Which way could he have gone?" said the knight. "Southward beyond the bend, or perhaps north again?

"Ohh … neither, I should say," Shiva answered, and quickly dismounted, tying off his steed to a nearby tree. "He climbed the hill and continued west. Tracks do not simply disappear, unless he was to travel upon these stones."

"I would be remiss if I were not to repeat my convictions," Vantimier said as his boots touched the ground. He led his horse beside Shiva's and tied him off, gazing once more towards the sun. "Your beast will do well in such a place once night falls, the forest is his home. I cannot say the same for us."

"We will return soon enough, good sir. There is time yet … " Shiva paused then, looking down towards the silver knight who was steadily climbing up after him. "If we do not find him beyond this hill we will return without delay."

Sir Vantimier nodded, and together they continued their assent. It was a steep hill, but manageable, even in armor. They reached the top before long, and there they found the great wolf seated like a statue upon the ridge gazing out far across the land. Beyond the trees to the west lay a web of lakes, the waters glittering darkly in the shadows of the surrounding trees, strung together by thin streams that weaved through the surrounding foliage. In the distance, standing in the shallow waters of the center lake stood the hollows, three thousand strong at least, unmoved amidst the quiet of the calm waters.

Beside him Shiva heard Sir Vantimier gasp. "So many!"

"Hmm …" the warden's face was calm, lacking all emotion as he gazed about the surrounding lakes. "There are more standing in the shadows of the woods," he said, and pointed them out for the knight to see.

"What could be there purpose?"

"I cannot say, and at this time it would be unwise to guess."

"We must return!" Vantimier said. "News of this must be told at once! For such a number to collect like this is unheard of … and so near the guild!"

Just then, there was a stirring in the waters of the furthest lake. The dark water rolled and bubbled as a black shape rose up to the surface and rippled against the top before disappearing into the unknown. The pair watched the lake grow still before exchanging a look.

They retreated without a word, making their way down the hill once more to their horses.

***

Dusk deepened. They left the hillside and continued east towards the road but had hardly gone half a league before skidding to a halt. Shiva grunted in frustration and turned his horse northward, looking upon a group of ghouls as they cut across the woods. "They do not see us," he began. "We'll go around then circle east back towards the road."

Sir Vantimier nodded and followed after, but Marrok hesitated, baring his teeth towards the foul undead before bounding off after Shiva and the knight.

They went on for a mile or more northwards, searching for a way back to the road. Yet all they saw were hollows interspersed in groups of two or three, traveling north towards the fading sun. Both riders had paused for a moment, deciding which way they should go while Marrok traveled some ways ahead. Suddenly the wolf gave a cry and the others came riding towards him expecting to find a clear path, but instead coming upon a pile of huddled bodies taken for boulders in the darkening woods.

"These are guild men," said the knight as he searched the ground in a wide circle. "Look!" he pointed, "Their lie their staffs … broken and discarded by the enemy!"

Shiva pushed his horse forward, taking in the grounds, wondering what calamity had befallen the slain wizards. The trees all about were scorched black, and a charred stench remained amidst the cold wind. "They were ambushed," said the warden at last, "by more than just hollows." But which foul creatures had attacked he could not say, for the ground had been trampled hard and flat, so few clues remained.

A little further north they came upon a fold where once a great river had run, falling and winding through the woods like so many others. The river had decreased though, so that only a small stream ran through the center.

"Here," said Shiva. His eyes narrowed as he gestured to the soft sand beside the river bank where a line of tracks crossed the path.

"I see only another riddle," said Vantimier, his eyes creased as he looked past the river into the deep of the woods.

"The tracks continue north up this water-channel, towards the farm-lands you spoke of." He paused then, noticing how deep the tracks were compared to his own.

"Let us hope we do not come across whatever foe fell upon those wizards. There were near ten of them I counted, and we are only three."

Without replying, Shiva pushed his horse forward, riding hard with Marrok and Vantimier close behind. They broke east and finally managed to find the road. Swiftly now they rode, watching as the fading sun continued in its' descent until they reached the crest of a small hill, and a great wind blew against them and stirred their cloaks … the cold wind of night.

"Do you see that!" cried Vantimier suddenly as he reigned in his horse. "There! It is a man I think, traveling along the road."

Shiva pushed forward without reply, his eyes focusing on the stranger that lay ahead. As they drew near, they found that it was indeed a man, bloodied and limping along the path before them.

"Greetings stranger!" cried Sir Vantimier as the pair drew near.

The man had stopped and turned to watch as they rode up, and for a moment he stood silent, looking upon them with one eye for the left side of his face was a mash of blood, and his hair was tangled with dirt and leaves. " …greetings," he said at last.

Their horses began to flutter in the growing darkness, but Vantimier kept a steady seat and spoke out. "What woe has befallen you? And why are you here alone in the woods of my master?"

At the knight's words a spark of life returned to the man's face. "You serve Lord Magnus?"

Sir Vantimier nodded. "I do."

"Then I shall answer you quickly, for time is short. I was sent into these woods at the request of Lady Maeve of Soliare, to probe the land for hollows and return with my findings."

He looked now towards Shiva who returned his gaze with a cold and empty stare, his mouth tight and thin.

"And what did you learn?" asked Vantimier.

"There is a horde of hollows marching upon Mallhorn Peak even as we speak. They are traveling slowly along the winding river led by a knight set in brazen armor. I was returning to the guild to speak of what I found when my horse was spooked by stray hollows and I was thrown. I fought my way back to the road just before you found me."

"It is well we did," said Vantimier. "Even now more hollows follow. They will be upon us soon if we do not move in haste."

"This knight," Shiva began, "can you describe him."

"Nay," he answered shaking his head. "He was far indeed, too far for my eyes to see him well, but he moved between the hollows as though he was their master."

"This confirms all I have thought!" cried Vantimier. "A new order has come upon the undead, and they have become an enemy worth fearing!"

"Come!" said Shiva, holding out his hand to the wounded stranger. "We are not far now from the guild. My horse can bare the weight of two for the remainder of our course."

The stranger nodded and took Shiva's hand, struggling upon the back of his horse behind the warden. "I am Ferro," said the man. "Personal guard to Princess Maeve."

"I am Shiva of Cataron, and my companion is Sir Vantimier, servant of Lord Magnus. It is well we came across you before night was complete, that darkness fool our eyes, and we take you for the undead."

"If that had been the case, we may have struck you down as we rode," said Vantimier. His eyes over his shoulder were stark and grim. "These woods grow more foul with each passing hour."

Ferro laughed nervously, as if he thought it were a joke. Shiva was not so sure. Vantimier was sent to aid him, not to rescue wounded bodyguards. Lord Magnus kept his lands clean and orderly ... one man mistaken for an undead would matter little to the great Lord.

Abruptly he stared off to his left, deep into the woods, just as a shallow growl echoed out from Marrok. Where was it? His eyes searched the forest. One of the trees had trembled, only for a moment before growing still ... but he had seen it, and so had the wolf. Ferro and Vantimier were looking as well, when suddenly one of the trees near the fringe whipped back, its trunk cracking loudly as it snapped at the base and disappeared into the woods behind. A shrill scream went out, and a dark mass shifted before disappearing into nothing.

"Keep riding," Vantimier instructed, drawing his sword. His silver gauntlets flickered in the night as he turned his horse so that he faced the woods. "And do not stop whatever you should hear!"

A hint of jealousy rose within Shiva as he watched Vantimier charge into the unknown. What foe lay inside the woods? What beast, what monster? He let the thought fade as he watched the knight get swallowed by the darkness. Lady Sune had given him his quest, and it would lead to the greatest victory one might have ... if he could but see it through to the finish.

"Hold tight," he urged Ferro, and dug his heels into his horses' flanks, pushing him as hard as he might. "Do not lose your grip! If you should fall it will be your end!"

A great roar went out from the woods where Vantimier had gone. It resonated through the forest, and all the trees shied away from it as though stricken by an axe, for even when it had faded the forest shuddered. Again, the roar rumbled forth, and with it came hate and death.

"What can you see," said Shiva. "Can you — "

The awful cry came once more, loud and shrill, before cutting off tersely.

"He is there!" cried Ferro.

Emerging from the woods back upon the dim path appeared the knight, holding his sword well clear of himself as he turned his horse and began racing after them at full speed.

"A number of hollows are behind him," continued Ferro, as the horde began pouring out from the woods. "but they are afoot, and will not catch us!"

"That was no hollow he faced in those trees," answered Shiva, but even as he spoke a second horde broke out before them. The hollows turned in, blocking the path like a fleet of shadows.

Shiva's sword was in his hand. Clean and true he struck out as he passed, his blade taking the heads of any ghoul who drew near. Marrok howled in rage, biting and tearing upon the corrupted souls so that even they seemed to take pause before coming once more at the riders. Teeth bared in a rictus growl, the great wolf tore at the last of the men that stood before them, making a clearing for Shiva to pass through. Broken and dismantled, all who remained tried to reform as Sir Vantimier came riding past, but the knight was too fast, and cleared the horde without even having to level his blade.

Standing in his stirrups, Vantimier charged forward, pushing his stallion faster and faster until he had reclaimed the distance and rode beside Shiva. But it did not last, and once again the shadows shifted along the fringe and the silver knight took to the trees. More screams followed, both shrill and filled with fear, and again the knight emerged, his blade and armor dripping in black blood that smelled of rot even as they rode. Breath streamed forth from the knight, and his silver armor no longer shined, yet his eyes remained strong.

With every pass into the forest the silver knight would return, and Shiva would watch with inquiring eyes, wondering how long the knight could sustain such tenacity. Surely he must grow tired, he thought, yet the warden could see no signs of fatigue.

"We are nearly there!" Ferro shouted as they fought through another small horde. Three hollows fell quickly beneath Shiva's blade and the powerful swipes of Marrok's claws as they pushed on.

The forest trees were just beginning to thin when a harrowing cry arose behind them. Detached and deep, it brought an eerie calm to the woods, and all signs of the hollows vanished revealing an open path before them.

The strange call came again, like a strained blast from a cracked war horn. The cry was answered with a deep rumbling that shook the path and sent a shiver down Shiva's spine, but if it was one of fear or excitement none could tell.

"Another unknown foe comes toward us," Vantimier said grimly, to which Shiva gave no reply. The warden sat measuring the distance before them while the last light of the sun passed away. "We make for Mallhorn Peak!" he said, though something in his voice hinted of regret. "We must not get caught outside the gates!" He pushed his horse forward. "Ride!" he screamed, "And do not look back!"

Both Vantimier and Marrok plunged after him, racing along the hidden road quick as the wind. They were near the end of the forest now and the woods were growing thin before opening all at once into a wide field full of flat land and tall grass. It would have been a welcome sight had the armies of the undead not occupied the plains west of them. They were some ways away, but their torches shone like a beacon, signaling a gathering of great numbers.

"They must be a thousand strong," said Shiva, as he paused to watch the undead army make their way across the fields. It was then that he could see the great fires of Mallhorn Peak burning in the distance.

"I did not see so many in the forest," answered Ferro, his mouth tight with distraught. "Even the guild will have difficulty fighting off such a host!"

"Alas!" cried Vantimeir suddenly. "They know not of what comes! We came across their men slain deep in the woods, and I know now what slew them, for it was an evil creature twisted from bone and beast!" At once he unslung his horn from his side and pressed it to his lips, blowing a mighty call with all his breath. Yet despite the knight's blow not a sound was made, and Shiva eyed the horn with renewed interest.

Behind him he could feel Ferro laughing. "Blood and ash!" the man cried. "The horns ruined, must be cracked near the mouthpiece."

Shiva shook his head. "No, the horn is fine. It sent forth a different warning, one that cannot be heard by enemies or foes."

"He is right," added Vantimier. "This horn has been enchanted to warn only those practiced in the magical arts ... hopefully it will go overlooked by our enemies."

"The dark peaks are near," Shiva said, running his hand along the neck of his stallion. He could feel the sweat dripping down with every labored breath. "The path appears open," he began as he pushed his horse forward for the final stretch, "but be wary, least we be trapped by our own respite."

Raising his horn to his lips, Sir Vantimier let out another blast before charging after Shiva. To their left they continued to watch as rows of hollows emptied out from the forest into the fields like a trail of trickling fireflies, spreading their flames to anything that would burn, and marching to the beat of an unheard drum.

20

ATOP the gates of Mallhorn Peak battlements streamed the guild's banners: a single wizard amidst a great stone hall with his staff outstretched before him. In the distance the enchanted horn continued its warning, growing closer now as the night deepened. The main courtyard was nearly empty, as many of the villagers had been let inside so that the guild could move about the surface unhindered.

Torches burned all about the fortress as Lennox strode towards the iron gates. Perhaps it was his armor, which burned like embers beneath the passing flames, or perhaps it had been that when he had first arrived, he had come in the company of Princess Maeve; either way, the golden knight moved freely about the grounds with no resistance from the guild. Astrid had come as well, and together they passed under the inner gate of the bridge towards the front tower. As he crested the stairs, he could see the forest take shape, its dark shadows layered in arches and deep curves.

Already fires could be seen in the distance, marching through the fields in many lines. The sky was utterly black, and the stillness of the air portended violence. Soon all the fields would burn, throwing plumes of black smoke up into the night sky like dragon's breath, and casting deep shadows all about the land.

Lennox found Sir Mikel standing with one leg set atop a merlon, motionless as a gargoyle, gazing out upon the field. Despite not being a wizard, the grim knight had command of the wall. His fists were covered in black gauntlets and he stood both fierce and strong, leading the men of the gate. He turned, catching a glimpse of Lennox's armor shimmering beneath the torches. "Ohh … it is you," his eyes flickered to Astrid, "and the girl also." He waved them forward that they might stand beside him. "Why have you come? I cannot let you out now that the gates have been barred."

"We have no desire to leave," answered Lennox. "We've come at the request of Princess Maeve to inquire as to the whereabouts of Ferro."

"Surly he must have returned by now," said Astrid. "Yet we have seen no sign of him."

The grim knight examined the pair, then shook his head. "None have passed through the gates since your arrival. I'm sorry you had to come all this way for such ill news."

"I see," said Lennox with a nod. "The princess will be informed." Having carried out Maeve's request, he cast an eye towards the distant fires and turned to leave. Soon the gates of Mallhorn Peak would not be safe, and he was more than willing to retreat deeper into the fortress. He had hardly turned his back when another blast from the horn bellowed out, this time the call sounded close indeed.

Suddenly the darkness was seared by a striking flash. Dispersed lightening smote down upon the earth near the main path, and for a staring moment all the watchers upon the gates, and all the walls of Mallhorn Peak saw at last the open field, boiling and overflowing with the undead. A thousand men they numbered at least, cursed and lost, armored with an array of weapons and shields, all of which failed them in life … now used in death.

As quickly as it had come the flash faded, leaving the guards to whisper in fear as to what they had just witnessed. "Why do they come," some said. "They are too many," whispered others. Even Mikel issued a curse beneath his breath, unheard by all save Lennox. The golden knight was glad the townsfolk had been ushered inside else their fears turn to chaos. Yet while Sir Mikel and the guards had been lost in the grandeur of the approaching host, only Astrid had seen the pair of horses riding before the vanguard, accompanied by a great beast whose howl echoed in unison with the horn. "Marrok," she said to herself, and looked out once more where she had seen the company… but they were too far, and the darkness complete.

Abruptly another blast from the horn went out, and this time the howling cry of Marrok came with it clear and true. "Marrok!" she cried out. "Marrok!" Lennox paced forward so that he stood beside Astrid and looked out onto the road. "There!" she said pointing out.

"Riders approach," came a call from one of the guards as a second flash filled the air.

This time Lennox could see it all, great burning fields that cast out a billowing canopy of ash hiding the stars from sight and shining with dazzling light along the edges, the black host that swarmed the fields, and before them all raced the riders. A pair of men from what he could see, though one looked rather large, and a great beast ran beside them. They were trailed by hollows, but the undead were far behind, and the riders swift. Yet even as the approached the gates remained closed.

"The gate!" Astrid shouted. "Open the gate!"

With fists clenched Mikel rose up. "The gate stays closed! The enemy is upon us!"

"But they are our friends! And there is time!"

"I cannot go beyond my orders," was his reply.

The riders were drawing near now so that it was clear they numbered three, with two men sharing a steed. One of the men, a knight set in silver armor, was unknown to Lennox, but he knew the others well. He turned to address Mikel. "Good sir," he began, "These are indeed our friends, and I can see that Ferro is among them. Lady Maeve ordered for you to let him past without reproach. There is still time. If we are quick, they will pass through unhindered but we must hurry," He spoke calmly to the knight, but his eyes were stern and unafraid, and in his voice was a subtle power that swayed all who heard it.

"Very well," answered the knight, after a slight pause. He turned to the guards. "Open the gates, but be prepared to close them once the riders have passed!"

At once the gates lurched open, pushing outwards slowly until the smallest of gaps was revealed. Astrid looked towards Lennox in recognition and gratitude before running past him towards the steps. As Astrid descended the riders drew near, pushing their horses hard and riding with all the speed they could muster. Lennox stood alone now, gazing south towards the undead, then down once more towards the riders. At last he too descended, and watched as the riders passed through the gate.

At the sight of her great wolf Astrid's face lightened with joy and wonder. She rushed forward, throwing her arms around the beast's neck as Marrok pushed back upon her in reply. Beside the pair sat Shiva, cold and unfazed by the passing events. He unhorsed, leaving Ferro resting in his seat and set his eyes upon Lennox. A small smile touched his lips.

Lennox found himself twisting at his oathkeeper ring as the warden approached. At last we are together again, he thought. Did Shiva know this whole time, had his mistress told him what hardships our journey would take? Lennox doubted it, but he would get no true answers from the warden. "Well … you're alive," he finally said.

The warden nodded. "It is not our time."

Looking past Shiva towards the gate Lennox stepped close, keeping his voice low as he spoke. "No … but it will be soon for all who stay. An army marches upon this castle, and I see no way of escape. Perhaps your mistress spoke to you about this. If yes, then now is the time to speak of it."

"Ha! You have guessed much, Sir Knight, and rightly so!"

"What then is your plan?"

He placed his hand upon the Lennox's shoulder, keeping his voice low as he spoke. "There is a dock at the base of this castle, a secret known to few. It is from there we shall depart, but first we must find the prince."

"I tried to reach him, but he is deep in the castle taking his exams, and I was not granted access."

"Surly the state has changed," answered Shiva. "A darkness comes, and now is not the time for tests. I will find him, by force if I must, and see him to the docs. The lady must have you three, or I fear it will be for not."

"Then move quick, the cursed will be here soon and the gates will not hold against such numbers! I will stay to stave them off for as long as I can muster. When I can hold the gate no longer, I will retreat to the docs."

"This castle is full of illusions; it may be difficult to find."

Lennox smiled, shaking his head softly. "You misjudge me, warden. I will not be kept at bay by simple tricks. Now go, quickly, and take with you this man. He serves Princess Maeve, and may be able to help you in finding our young prince."

The warden nodded. "I will," he answered, and turned his attention towards Ferro. Lennox continued. "Astrid. Go with Shiva, and take Ferro with you. Make sure they reach the princess quickly."

"And what of you?"

"I will stay here and fight for a time … but I will find you again I promise!"

Marrok looked upon the knight then, his eyes a cool yellow that understood much but gave nothing in return. Lennox looked upon the beast for a time, the fact that Zev was not there did not escape him. "Watch her," he said. "Keep her safe until we are reunited."

After measuring the knight, the beast nodded slowly then turned back towards the girl and remained silent.

"Sir Vantimier," Shiva said as he returned to his horse, taking his time to mount, this time with the wounded Ferro sitting before him. The silver knight waited for the warden to continue. "I ask you stay with Lennox. Whatever future Lady Sune has seen for this world, this man stands at the heart of it. Accompany him while I inform the council of our findings."

"Very well," he replied, after considering the warden's words. "I will do as you ask. My orders were to escort you to Mallhorn Peak. I have done so, fulfilling my master's wishes. But I believe he would have me do more, though I do not hear his voice." The silver knight dismounted then, and offered Astrid a hand as she took her place upon his horse. "Thank you," she said quietly.

He bowed in reply.

"Be cautious! There are more than just hollows marching upon the gate!" Then, with a short nod, Shiva turned his horse and was off, followed closely by the others.

Both Lennox and Vantimier watched as the gray wolf disappeared, passing beneath the inner gate and out of sight. "You serve Lord Magnus," Lennox said, turning towards the knight.

"I do."

"And you would die for him?"

"I would."

"Well … you might just get your chance tonight. A terrible pity, but I've been wrong before."

***

Passing beneath the inner gates the torches went dim for a moment, so that little indeed could be seen, even by Shiva's keen eyes. Once through, the path opened into the inner courtyard. The main keep lay ahead, but on either side stood strong walls, well-fortified, and angled so that the defenders could rain arrows and fire upon any who should make it across the bridge.

Shiva had seen the castle once before, from a great distance, but never had he stepped inside its walls. Lady Sune had told him its secrets though, and he looked about the high towers with a quiet gaze, his face like stone, measuring the strength of the walls and men who stood atop them. He knew what was coming … how long would the castle hold? He pulled his cloak close, masking his face.

No one seems to be paying us any mind, thought Astrid. She watched as a line of guards, each carrying a staff and lightly armored in blue and gold, marched past on their way to the bridge. A few of them eyed Marrok, but they left the wolf alone. He was a beast, yes … but not wild. His eyes spoke the truth.

Astrid rode up beside Shiva and leaned close. "The high council went to the upper battlements so that they could oversee the oncoming siege. Princess Maeve will be with them. She will be our best hope at reaching her brother."

"Oscar," Ferro repeated, letting the name linger in the following silence. "You came all the way out to the guild to speak with Oscar?" The gruff man laughed then, shaking his head slightly with a pleased grin upon his face. "Does Maeve know this?"

Astrid turned her eyes to Ferro, the wounded man did not appear as injured as he had upon first entering the gate. At last she answered him with a brisk nod. "She does."

"Ha … ten hells!"

Confused, Astrid waited for the man to continue. When he did not, she asked, "What's wrong?"

"It looks like I'm out a week's wages."

"You took bets on the nature of our business?"

"Aye," he said with a nod. "And I lost. She won't let me forget it anytime soon."

For some odd reason Astrid thought the man didn't seem all that upset. They reached the stable and dismounted, handing their horses off to the same boy as before. She passed him another coin and he took it, though his mood had dampened, and he did not smile.

With a sigh she turned and left, following after Ferro as he led them out. "Where are we going?" she asked, when she saw they were making their way behind the stables to the west.

"My leg's hurt bad," Ferro answered. "I don't think I could make it up all those stairs." He offered no further explanation, and took them around the stable grounds to a small side gate that stood open with a single guard standing post.

The guard seemed wary at first, but listened quietly as Ferro spoke. He shook his head, eyeing the wolf cautiously. "Not the beast. I cannot let him pass."

"The beast comes too," Ferro replied. "Or you will explain to Din Curuni why her guests were not allowed passage at her request."

Hesitation followed. A quick flash of fear and doubt crossed before him as the guard eyed Marrok once more. He let out a defeated breath. "Very well," he said, and moved to the side, letting the company through.

Astrid ran her hand along Marrok's back as they walked through together.

A small passage lay before them then, cut out from the stones of Mallhorn peak. It was wide but not tall, though they could walk through without crouching. Astrid noticed slits were cut out from the walls deep enough for men to stand guard, and indeed they passed by several of them before she noticed there were in fact men standing in the darkness. They did not speak but stood silent, watching as the company marched through. Astrid felt as thou they were the true guards of the pass, more so than the single man posted at the gate.

The path went straight for a time before opening up to a vast and sweeping hall that appeared more like an open cavern to some murky cave, than a tower that was part of a great castle. A large iron lift was before them, level to the ground with another pair of guards standing on either side, one carrying a staff, and the other a sword.

Ferro passed them without a word, and together the company stepped onto the lift. There was a lever fastened to the ground in the corner. Shiva looked at it but said nothing. He watched as Ferro took it firmly in his grasp. "This can be unnerving for some," he said, then pushed the lever forward. The floor lurched upward, a quick, disheveled jump as the iron links began to pull at them from above, lifting them upwards and pushing them towards the unseen top.

This is a very long chute, thought Astrid, as she watched row after row of torches pass before her.

At last they came to a stop, and when they stepped off, she looked quickly upwards but still saw no sign of the cavern's ceiling. Another set of guards awaited them, and standing between them was Master Royce. The guild master was a thin man, with high cheekbones that were common in the land. He had dark hair and clear, tilted brown eyes that made him seem both wise and knowledgeable. He watched Astrid and the others calmly, and seemed almost amused at the party. "Ahh ... Ferro," he began. "Din Curuni will be most pleased to see you are well."

Ferro smirked, letting out a little laugh as he stepped out. Master Royce turned his attention towards the rest of his companions, eyeing them one after the other as they emerged, paying special attention to Shiva and his large satchel that hung upon his back. "And you must be Shiva of Cataron. I have been expecting you for some time now."

"Master Royce," he said, bowing slightly. "It is good to meet you at long last."

"Yes, well ... I wish you had arrived sooner. Now your fates are blurred to me, and I cannot guarantee you will escape without harm."

"Our journey here was hindered greatly when we ran afoul a group of hollows massing in the frozen woods. Even now they gather near the icy lakes, with numbers greater than what now set siege."

"How many?"

"Several thousand at least, and more linger in the deep. They have overthrown the thieves' guild, though some survived."

"How unfortunate ..." The master made his way onto the lift and reached out towards the lever. He looked up towards Ferro as he did.

"Keep her safe." The grim man nodded once. He was not smiling anymore. Master Royce turned to Shiva. "You'll find Master Eladin and Din Curuni just beyond the great hall. He is expecting you. Tell him what wickedness comes."

"And where are you heading off to at such a time?" asked Ferro.

"I go now to prepare the way." There was sadness in his voice as he spoke. Looking once more upon the party, he pulled the lever, and descended into the abyss.

***

They walked in a group, yet it was Ferro who led them, hobbling through the dim passages of the upper floors. Though empty at first, soon the corridors bustled with people of all sorts. Mostly they were wizards of the guild, but there were servants too, and knights, different than ones Astrid was accustomed to seeing. They wore robes similar to the guild, but had neither staff nor wand, and many of them wore two swords, one at their hip and a second, shorter blade upon their back.

All about the halls there was an air of alertness, and while no one stopped them as they passed, Astrid found herself growing nervous beside Marrok. We shouldn't be here, she thought, running her hand along the wolf's neck. We are not welcome. She glanced towards the warden, yet Shiva moved with a quiet calm, unconcerned with their surroundings. She had seen it before, in their travels. It was as though the worries of the world could not touch him … like a shield was set before him, and with it he was immortal.

The warden stood tall, his back straight and shoulders square, yet somehow, he looked relaxed, almost arrogantly so as he sauntered through the halls. He turned, catching Astrid's eye. "I do not think your wolf likes this place."

"He is a creature of the forest. He doesn't like any place that isn't open and free."

Shiva eyed Marrok then looked forward, his eyes ever watchful, taking in the men and stones of the great hall.

The guards at the entrance to the upper court peered up calmly as they approached. One sat behind a long-slanted table, looking over a ledger and sometimes making a mark as he went along. The others stood opposite the arched doorway; and while the doors stood open, it was clear that not all could pass.

Astrid's stomach churned as they examined Marrok. They'll stop him here for sure, she thought. Yet more than ever she did not wish to part with the beast.

One of the guards, a tall, dark eyed man held out his palm for them to halt. His eyes flickered towards the wolf, and his mouth tightened, but he did not speak of Marrok. All about them the people stopped what they were doing to watch, still and intent.

"It is well to see you alive, Ferro," said the guard, giving the gruff man a slight nod. Once again, his eyes flickered to the wolf. "Master Royce said you would be arriving shortly, but said nothing of your companions."

Ferro laughed. "Well ... it must have slipped his mind. I assure you they are expected."

The guard eyed the beast one final time then motioned them to follow him though the archway.

Inside, their presence did not go unnoticed. It appeared to Astrid that Ferro was known to many of the guild, and was not well liked from what she could tell. The glances quickly fell away from the weathered body-guard to Marrok. Wolves were not a common sight outside the forest, and the beast caused more than one raised eyebrow ... but none of the guild spoke their displeasure, at least not openly, and a few were not displeased, but looked upon the group in wonder and curiosity.

Soft murmurs rose up behind them, too low for Astrid to make out. Shiva strode along, unconcerned and uncaring.

At last they reached the entrance to the outer battlements. Three more men stood guard outside the door. The tallest of the three, a man named Kiel, held in his hands a silver-flamed staff, and watched as they approached. A strong, smooth face he had, with clever eyes. He studied the group, looking each of them over in turn with a smile. "What have you brought with you this time, Marro?" he turned his eyes upon the young guard who had escorted them. "Din Curuni's pet, a Cataron warden, and a northerner and her pup?" His tone turned harsh then. "Why have you brought them here? The high council sits at war and you bring forth vagrants and vagabonds!"

"Master Royce told me to escort Ferro to Master Eladin upon his arrival."

"I was told nothing of this."

"It matters not," answered Marro, stepping forward so that he stood before the others. "I was told, and now I will deliver them ... unless you question my word."

"I question everyone's word," answered Kiel. "That is my duty." His eyes went once more towards Ferro and the others, and slowly his smile returned. "As it is, I believe you. You are free to enter."

Stepping to his side Kiel drew back his staff and waved his hand towards the door. It swung open noiselessly and he watched as Marro vanished through to announce their arrival. The young guard returned quickly, gesturing for them to enter.

"Yes ... a pup you say," Ferro said patting Kiel on the shoulder as he passed. "Go ahead and pet him if you like, and see how well he plays at your hand."

Kiel blinked, and his smile faded to a sneer but he kept quiet. He looked at Astrid next, but the girl did not retreat. She returned his stare coolly until she had passed, walking beside Marrok at a calm pace. Through all of this Shiva showed indifference, Marrok as well. It was a trait they seemed to share.

The door swung shut behind them, but not before the sounds of war reached them, yells and screams, both fierce and strong, and the battle cries of men. In silence they pressed forward. Ahead of them stood Master Eladin, looking out with his hands set upon a white rail of marble. Lady Maeve was beside him, and together they stood with their backs to the door, watching as the undead hordes made siege upon the front gate. As Astrid strode forth the battle below took shape. The lines of marching fires had collided, funneling together into a large host that met before the outer gate. Arrows and fire streamed forth upon the dead, filling the ground with corpses that should have rested long ago.

"Do you see them burning," said master Eladin aloud. "Do you see how they fall one after another ... yet through all this, the dead stay silent."

At once Astrid saw that it was true, and an eerie shiver ran down her spine. The advancing horde had been thrown back and was just now regrouping to attack once more, yet in all of their form the enemy was silent. It was the living who cheered and cried out, the men upon the walls, the wizards and knights defending the gate. She thought of Lennox, and hoped he was well amongst the chaos.

"The dead do not speak once the curse has fallen," answered Shiva.

Eladin turned. He looked towards the warden, past all that stood upon the surface and gazed deep into his soul. He looked away, back upon the army, his face heavy with concern. It was Maeve who spoke next. "He means how are they organizing like this, who is leading them?"

It was then that Astrid noticed Ferro stooped over upon one knee. Maeve had her hands upon his leg and a soft glow came fourth. When she was finished Ferro stood up, and upon his face was peace as his wounds mended and disappeared. Maeve continued. "We have watched closely as the army drew near, and now as they clash upon our walls. Yet no sign of a captain can be seen, no sign of a leader or commander. Someone with whom we can strike back at."

"There is a greater force at play here," Shiva said. "You must know this is only the beginning. Twice what we see now stand dormant before the frozen lakes just past the edge of the woods. This is an army gathered for one purpose."

Eladin watched the enemy surge forward against the gate. There they met iron and stone, and death consumed them from above. They dispersed quickly, falling away once more as a cheer went out from atop the wall.

"They have a captain," Ferro said at last, looking first to Maeve then past her to master Eladin. "I saw him marching from a distance along the quenched river. A knight, not like the hollows below, but strong and set in armor that shines red and gold despite the darkness of the woods."

Even as he spoke there came a beating drum, and far past the gate out of the forest a shape emerged, an engine, pushed forth by great beasts. "What witchcraft is this!" said Ferro turning, yet his words went unheard as a blare of trumpets came from the inner gate. A great scream followed as men turned from the bridge and shot their arrows down into the abyss. The arrows increased and the trumpets called once more when out of the darkness crawled a monster baring the shape of a man. The creature was large, standing with a hunch and black oily skin. He bore upon his head a helm of bone shaped like the skull of a goat, with cracks splintering out from the teeth, and eyes pitchless and empty.

"A beast of the Darkmoon!" Shiva said at once.

"Where is he going!" cried Astrid.

The beast rose quickly, moving away from the bridge through the inner court.

"He makes for the castle!" answered Maeve. "He must be stopped!"

Eladin replied with a soft voice. "And so he shall. Master Raylen is below, and others too … they will see to the creature's fall."

"If the enemy can scale the cliffs then we must set men about the castle to make watch."

"The bridge is all that matters," answered Eladin. "If we hold the bridge, then any who scale the cliffs can be hunted down," yet even as he spoke two more beasts emerged, similar to the first, and carrying in their hands great axes.

The arrows flew, felling one of the monsters. A great roar echoed forth as he fell back into the dark waters below. The second beast endured, and charged through the courtyard to join the first. Together the swung their axes against the castle door until at last it gave way, and the beasts disappeared and screams rose out from below.

"I will not have this!" cried Maeve. "Ferro, come!" And with that Maeve departed, and with her Ferro.

Both Astrid and Marrok watched the pair as they left. She looked next to Shiva and almost fell back in shock. There was no doubt about it, the warden was smiling as he looked upon master Eladin.

Maeve was well gone when Shiva finally spoke. "Well … you must be pleased. She seems rather wild to me, difficult to control."

Eladin looked amused.

"Still," Shiva continued. "Better to send her away, where chance might still save her."

"Not chance, warden … you will save her, and her brother. I have put my faith in master Royce."

"He is a seer?"

"He sees some, but nothing like Lord Magnus far away in his tower, or even like your oracle you so willingly serve."

"Is there no hope then for this fight?" Astrid said speaking up. There was much she didn't understand, yet she knew the siege upon Mallhorn Peak was grim.

Eladin looked upon her then with gentle eyes and said, "I do not know. But there are still many people here inside these stone walls, and I will keep them safe if I can." His face was serene, smooth and soft, and his eyes did not blink. "Please watch over Prince Oscar. He is loyal, almost to a fault, and can be naive, especially if his sister is about."

Astrid found herself nodding yes. "As best we can," she said.

Shiva bowed then, resting his left hand upon his hilt and twisting the sword behind him. "By your leave, master Eladin, may we depart?"

"Go," he answered. "And do not fail in your endeavor."

Straightening, Shiva gestured for Astrid to follow. "We will succeed," he answered. "It has been foreseen."

There was a long silence as Eladin watched them go before once again the trumpets blared behind him and the sounds of war called.

***

Maeve and Ferro stood before the empty shaft watching the lift rise before them when Shiva and the others appeared. Far behind them, Astrid could hear the trumpets call. Curse those foul creatures, she thought, picturing the dark-skinned beasts once again in her mind. It made her hands go cold thinking about them.

"I'm glad you could join us!" Ferro shouted, a small grin touching at his lips. His fingers tapped lightly on the pommel of his blade, and a restlessness was upon him.

Shiva walked past them, stepping onto the iron lift. "We came here for a purpose … that has not changed." He looked to Maeve. His eyes cold and calculating. "The castle will not hold. You must take us to your brother at once."

"And what of all the people taking refuge in these halls?" she asked. "Am I to abandon them to slaughter."

"Die with them if you wish, but first take me to your brother. At least then one of you will survive."

"My brother is safe enough, deep below in the lower quarters."

"Is he?" Shiva was not convinced. "Your masters seemed to know the truth … why is it you cannot see it?"

"Eladin is a stubborn fool, but he still fights — "

"He fights now so that we can get away," Shiva said. "You as well, and whoever you can bring with us."

"What do you mean?" she asked. Shiva shook his head, his eyes unrepentant as he reached for the lever.

Again, the trumpets sounded. Astrid and Marrok joined Shiva upon the lift and turned, their eyes set upon the princess. It was Ferro who pushed her on. Placing his hand gently upon her shoulder, he stepped forward. "Skip the first floor. Prince Oscar will be on the lowest corridor." He was speaking to Shiva.

Without a word Shiva pressed the lever forward and the lift descended, dropping down into the depths as all the torches went dark around them.

In an instant the beast was upon them, crashing down from above like a shadow of hate. Marrok was the first to act, his eyes burned as he leapt upon the beast. It cried out, but the creature seemed more annoyed than truly hurt as he swiped the wolf away. Marrok fell to the floor in a dull thud.

Ferro was next, his sword flashed silver in the dark but stopped before reaching its mark, caught in the palm of the monster, the beast sneered and pulled the blade away before suddenly screaming out, this time in true pain before falling to its knees. Shiva drew his blade from the creatures back and swung it in a low arc, sweeping the head clean off his shoulders. The beast fell, headless, onto the lift, its blood slowly spreading across the floor beneath him.

A light burst forth then from the tip of Maeve's wand. Astrid could feel little heat, but the light it cast was great, reaching high into the shaft above them and revealing the dead beast that lay slain at their feet. Her eyes were wide with shock, yet she stood calmly, taking long breaths that echoed in the silence of the space.

"It is one of those beasts!" cried Astrid. Her blade was drawn as she looked down upon the fallen corpse.

Marrok was rising from where he fell, and made his way towards the creature with teeth bared. Shiva eyed Marrok, and while no one could see it, was pleased with the wolf. "There will be more of them," the warden began. "Even if the gate should hold, the cliffs of Mallhorn Peak have been breached."

Suddenly the lift came to a halt, hitting the stone earth of the lower corridor. The stop came so abruptly that Astrid nearly fell, and reached out to secure herself upon the railing. They were at the end of a narrow hallway lined with torches that hung extinguished upon the walls. The last remaining embers burned hazily in the dark.

"We must press on," Shiva said, stepping over the fallen corpses and out into the darkness. Without a word Astrid followed, Marrok too. Ferro and Maeve were last. She held her wand low, looking down at the bone helm of the beast until at last it was behind her.

They had hardly moved before Shiva signaled them to stop. Ahead of them, shining on the curved stone wall, glimpses of light could be seen washing upon the surface like waves. Red and white light, then flashes of orange … then nothing.

"Strong magic," Ferro said aloud. None responded, and at last Shiva continued, turning the corner and continuing down the hall towards a large doorway.

Loud cries could be heard then, both of death and magic. Spells and incantations echoed along the stones followed by more light.

"The battle has reached even the depths of the castle," Astrid said, but before she finished speaking Maeve was off, wand raised as she sprinted forward. She appeared as a shadow cast in white, with the outline of her protector running beside her.

"Hmm … " said Shiva, removing his blade from its sheath, "it appears we will not pass unhindered. Come, and stay close to me!"

With a swift nod Astrid followed.

Marrok arched his head, crying out into the dark before plummeting forward into the unknown white.

21

THE slot in Lennox's helm was narrow, limiting his vision to what lay directly before him, but as he turned his head the armies of the undead swarmed like the sea ... dark and black and silent. Thrice times they had stormed the gate, and thrice times they were thrown back. They knew no pain, they knew no fear, but an arrow to the chest still brought them down; the ones with little armor at least. The grounds before the gate were sodden and slick, a mix of mud and corpses. A few of the hollows still crawled about, moving towards the gate, following their duty even in their crippled state. Lennox watched as arrows descended upon them, and at last they were still.

A slow time passed. Far in the fields the horde's fires burned and the mass of undead gathered once again for another charge.

And then the drums echoed ... a slow rolling beat that boomed upon the gate as terrible as any foe, and out of the forest came a great terror. An engine of war set upon wheels and pushed forth by mighty creatures, half a span in length and wrapped about by heavy chains. Its head was shaped like that of a great boar, and a helm of steal was upon it, and a great flame burned in its mouth.

Soon, all the undead had formed around it as it crawled across the field, a black host growing deeper and stronger with every step. A thought came to Lennox then, and beneath his helm the golden knight smiled. If only the beast were alive, he mused... it would be a foe beyond desire for Shiva. The thought vanished and left only despair. Lennox felt at the oathkeeper ring, twisting it about his finger. I should have stayed in my cell. He shook away the thought. He would endure, it was all he knew.

Sir Vantimier stood beside him, his hands resting upon his sword when the trumpets called out from behind. Together they turned and watched as dark creatures scaled the cliffs below. The men of the inner gate were shouting and firing arrows and gathering to meet them. Vantimier moved for the stairs but was stopped by Lennox. "Leave them. We must do what we can here upon the gate."

Already the giant boar was drawing near. Mikel could be seen running the length of the wall, preparing the murder holes and giving strength to his men, what little he had to give, for despair was in his heart though he did not succumb to it.

"This army," Vantimier said as he gazed out towards the great battering ram. "My master must be told; a message must be sent. Already they have fooled the ravens and their like … and now the guild will fall." He spoke the words calmly, and all who heard knew they were true. "The world must be warned."

"Quiet!" Lennox urged, glancing towards the men of the gate. "These men still live, as do you and I. And those who live have a duty to endure, until our last breath has left us and we leave this world for another."

"I have never doubted my duty," answered the knight, "only my ability to accomplish what must be done."

"And what is that?" said Lennox in a low voice.

But the silver knight did not answer, for even as they spoke there came a blare of trumpets from behind, and the sky before them cracked with light. The horde opened up before them clearing a path for the war machine that rolled forward with increasing speed.

"Brace the gate! Brace the gate!" Mikel screamed, but the beating of the enemy's drum and the horns of Mallhorn Peak hid his voice so that none could hear it.

Suddenly a thought was upon Lennox. "Come with me!" he said pointing to a group of guards. They hesitated only for a moment before following after. Quickly they made their descent, reaching the bridge and turning back towards the main gate. "Stay here," he told them, "and keep your bows drawn and staffs ready."

From atop the battlements, Mikel stiffened when he saw Lennox walking towards the gate, alone, with his hands out before him chanting something he could not understand while light pure as the sun formed about his hands. The light increased in strength until in consumed him and none could look upon the knight. Beyond the gate the ram raced forward, shaking the very earth as Mikel braced himself for what was to come.

The giant boar struck the gate and all the world shook. A thunderous noise followed; the twisting of metal and wood, of fire and magic, as though lightening itself were unleashed upon the gates of Mallhorn Peak.

When next he looked the giant ram stood silent and unmoving, yet even then the hollows drew forth. "Fire!" Mikel screamed. "Do not let them pass!"

At once the guards went into action, casting spells and firing off arrows into any who should come within range. It was then that he looked inwards, and saw that some had broken through. Drawing his sword, he leapt into the breach. "Solaire!" he shouted, as he fell upon the hollows below.

He held his sword before him, slashing out at every foe he passed. Dimly, he heard a cheer go out from the wall as he pressed on, turning just as a spearman charged forth. Mikel lopped off the edge of the hollow's spear, then his head. A second ghoul came from the side, a large man wielding a two-handed great sword who swung fiercely upon Mikel again and again, pushing him back until a sword stuck the hollow from behind. Gazing up he found Sir Vantimier standing before him, drawing his blade from the fallen enemy, shining like a silver star in a field of black.

"Sir Lennox!" Mikel screamed out over the roar of battle. "Is he well?"

"I have not seen him since the great boar struck," the knight responded. "Come, and let us search for him quickly!" And together they fought their way towards the gate.

Sticking through the cracked wood and twisted metal lay the boar's head, cracked and fallen, snapped at the base of its neck and brought down by the weight of its helm … yet the beast had served its purpose, for the doors lay broken, with gaps set in both sides.

"The gate has fallen," Mikel said. "Why then do they retreat?"

"I cannot say for certain," answered Vantimier as he swept his gaze across the bridge. Most of the hollows lay slain, and those that still stood were falling even as they spoke. Yet the gates stood empty, and no more hollows could be seen trying to pass. "Perhaps they're regrouping for another strike, now that the gate has been breached."

"Then let us hurry, else we lose sight of our golden friend!" It was then that the soft call of Sir Lennox could be heard through the din of battle. "Here ... here ... " he called out.

The voice sounded so thin that Vantimier could scarcely hear it, let alone discern its location. Yet a flash of gold caught his eye just beside the gate below the head of the fallen boar. "There!" he shouted, and ran towards the knight.

With Mikel's help, they managed to lift the shattered debris, large, heavy pieces of wood that now lay in splinters all about the golden knight. "Are you well?" Vantimier asked as he lifted him to his feet.

Lennox nodded slowly in reply, doing his best to gather his wits.

"Come," said Mikel as he took Lennox's free arm across his shoulder. "We must get him past the inner gate."

Vantimier did not object, yet they were half way cross the bridge when the beating of the enemy's drums echoed once more. Boom ... Boom ... Boom ... Slowly at first, but soon the pace quickened.

"They're forming outside the gate!" a soldier called out just as lightening crashed upon the tower, crackling along the bridge like a blow from a mighty hammer. A great gust followed and all were thrown from their feet.

Grunting beneath his helm Lennox lifted his gaze. Inside his armor he could feel his heart race. There was a ringing in his ears, and all about him men of the guild picked themselves off from the floor. Vantimier was the first to his feet, and quickly moved to help Lennox. "We must hurry!" the silver knight exclaimed, looking to Mikel.

With his eyes raised, the solemn knight shook his head slowly from side to side. "I know an ending when it comes ... I shall go to it." His dark eyes swept sadly back towards the gate. The men atop lay dead, and already the undead were beginning to crawl through the cracked and splintered wood, stripped bare by the warped iron covering. He pushed himself to his feet, picking up his sword from the stone floor beneath him. "Go!" he cried. "I shall hold them long enough for you to pass."

"Come with us!" said Vantimier.

"Go now!" answered the dark knight, as he turned and charged towards the enemy.

For a moment Vantimier stood almost in trance, watching as Mikel departed. When he turned he found Lennox staring at him. "Sir Mikel," he began.

"Let us not waste what time he has given us," Lennox said sharply, finding his voice. "We must move now!"

Vantimier nodded, and helped Lennox towards the inner gate. Lennox could hear the clash of steel growing steadily behind him, and the final cry of Sir Mikel pierced the air. He did not look back.

***

They passed through the inner gate into a world of chaos. The heavy door swung close behind them, yet all about them men on the walls were casting fire and shooting arrows as more black creatures scaled the cliffs of the castle.

"Where shall we go?" asked Vantimer. A moment later Lennox produced a small glass sphere, so pure it almost shined. "This is the work of my master!" Vantimier exclaimed.

"It was given to me by Lord Magnus."

"Then you hold a mighty gift!"

Lennox nodded and replied. "It will show us the way," and almost as though in answer to his will an image came upon the face of the sphere showing the stables, and a secret way behind them.

Vantimier led them across the courtyard towards the hidden alleyway. They passed by a fallen guard into a narrow hall filled with the corpses of the black beasts, as well as men of the guild. A low smoke was in the air swirling about their feet with each step, and the smell of fire was present all about them. The hall was empty of light but the sphere glowed warm, lighting their way until they came upon an empty shaft.

"There," said Vantimier pointing towards a ladder to the side. "Can you climb?"

Lennox nodded. "I was only shaken a bit. I feel better, though for how long I cannot say." In truth, Lennox was not sure how he was able to move. He had exhausted much of his energy in his last spell, yet his strength had not failed him. It was a puzzle he would consider at a later time.

They descended the latter. Lennox first, with Sir Vantimier close behind. It was a long way down, and with the sphere set inside Lennox pouch they made the climb in the dark. At the bottom they came upon another fallen creature, its head cut clear from its neck with a pool of blood set in a shallow puddle upon the surface.

Again they passed through a hall of black; its torches faded as even the embers had gone cold, and all was quiet about them. They walked in stillness, turning a corner until the dimmest of lights began to shine upon the walls before them. Still they walked on, the gentle rustling of their armor floating through the air. Soon the path opened before them and they found themselves in an open hall similar to a large auditorium with rows of seats that sloped downward until stopping at the base of a stage. A single light shone upon the platform, burning like a candle but stronger because of the darkness that had fallen.

"Who goes there!" a voice called out from below as the light swung about, piercing the dark similar to the lantern Astrid carried in Lohalion. "Reveal yourselves to me!" the voice cried out again.

With his hand raised before his eyes Lennox answered. "I am Sir Lennox. And beside me is Sir Vantimier, servant of Lord Magnus. We've come in search of our companions."

At once the light diminished, and the form of a man emerged. A wizard, one of the guild. He lowered his wand and turned back towards the stage dropping to one knee. As Lennox and Vantimier descended, they couldn't help but witness the bodies that lay strewn about like discarded dolls, ripped and torn and bleeding. The smell of smoke had dissipated, only to be replaced by the pungent odor of death and blood.

Most of the corpses were of the guild, Lennox observed, young wizards and knights who lay cold and unmoving in the dark chamber. They had not fared well against the Darkmoon's abominations. Yet one endured … perhaps others did as well.

It was only when they reached the stage that Lennox recognized who it was. "Well, this is a surprise. I didn't expect to run across you here Master Raylen." But the wizard did not stir, and it was then that Lennox saw Master Royce lying still at the feet of Master Raylen, his face peaceful in death.

Lennox glanced over his shoulder. Vantimier was watching them both.

Master Raylen turned back around sullenly. "You survived the siege upon the gate. Very impressive. I know what your intentions are."

"Prince Oscar's safety is our main concern," replied Lennox. "We mean to help in his escape, if there is yet time."

"Hmm … you want so much more than that. But do not fret! I have seen the enemy which has eluded us so fiercely, and now offer my aid. Late, though it may be. The task before you will almost surely bring about your death. Though if you can rescue Oscar, and go with him to Lady Sune, and learn from her what you can … the silent city may prove surmountable."

A change had come over Master Raylen, so subtle and yet so profound that Lennox could hardly see it at first. "Are you a seer?" he asked at last.

Master Raylen shook his head. "Hehe … No. Though Master Royce spoke of what he saw, and I am not so proud that I would not listen. Yet it mattered not, in the end. The Guild has fallen, and even now the dark creatures dive deeper in search for our sacred relic. Mark my words. They will not escape with it alive! It was Master Royce's last vision, and one of great doom." He lifted his wand and shone a light upon a far wall to the east. "There is a secret way hidden behind that wall. Dun Curuni has taken all she could down the passage. If you are quick you can reclaim them."

"What of you?" asked Vantimeir.

"I am charged with protecting our sacred relic. I must go and see that it does not fall into the hands of the Darkmoon. Though it is the one he serves which I truly fear. You know of whom I speak."

"So be it," answered Lennox. "Farewell, Master Raylen."

"Farewell, Sir Knights. May Elyon's blessing follow you into the depths."

Sir Vantimier bowed quickly towards the master and turned to follow after Lennox.

**

The light of Master Raylen dwindled behind them as they reached the eastern wall. A large crack ran along the corner, and the entire structure shifted like a door when Lennox pushed upon it. Behind was a spiraling staircase that descended downward lit by a string of torches still holding their flame. Vantimier closed the way behind them, leaving no sign for any to follow.

Down they went, deeper and deeper into the depths of Mallhorn Peak when all at once the floor opened out beneath them and they found themselves plunging down along a staircase of iron that dangled from the top of the cavern like string. From their height they could see all about them, though a heavy mist hovered about the surface of the water and crept in along the sand like a ghost.

"A dock!" Vantimier shouted.

"I see it!" Lennox called back.

Below them, the sandy beach extended out into the open sea where a great vessel stood anchored to a long dock that cut into the ocean.

"They're dropping the sails!" Lennox shouted. "Hurry! If we do not make that boat, I fear it will be the end of us!"

Yet even as they descended the mists below ushered fourth, rising up as though called by some unseen force until Lennox could see nothing but thick billows of white as he stepped down upon the sand. Behind him, Lennox could hear Sir Vantimier drawing his blade. "This fog is unnatural," said the silver knight. "I do not trust it."

"Nor should you," Lennox replied, clutching tightly at his own sword as he held out his crystal sphere. "Though there is only one path we can take, so forward we shall go."

Together they sped into the unknown, but as he ran Lennox stumbled in weariness. It was then that the brazen knight appeared, standing in the mists, adorned by red sapphires than ran along the length of his sword. In his left hand was a great shield, and his helm was shaped like that of a lion.

A deep groan shuddered out from Sir Lennox.

"Who is he?" Vantimier asked.

"A foe of great strength," he replied crouching low, feeling the first wobble of his weakening legs. Blood and ash, he thought, that my legs should fail me at such a time!

All about them black figures began to take shape in the mists, while before Lennox the brazen Lion strode forth … yet it was Sir Vantimier who charged forward to meet him. The silver knight was swift, sprinting towards the brazen knight. Lennox was about to follow when the black shapes cleared the mists, falling upon him.

His sword lashed out, cutting and slashing, striking down the foul beasts with every stroke. It was there in the mists that time seemed to blur. Past and future vanished and there was nothing before Lennox but another foe to be struck down, and another, and another. "I will endure!" he cried, his sword flashing, his golden armor ablaze in the mist. So horrible he appeared that soon the foul creatures were reluctant to come forth. He was tired, and sweat rolled beneath his helm and before his eyes, yet he fought on.

He took a blow to the leg but hardly felt it though he knew his body would soon waver. It was then that he saw a light burning through the fog, a single lantern hoisted atop the mast, signaling the way. I'm close, he thought, so very close. "Vantimier!" he cried, hoping his voice could be heard, for he had lost the silver knight to the fog. "To the ship! The ship!"

As he made his way towards the dock, the mist about the sea dispersed. He moved his head right to left and back again, but saw no sign of Sir Vantimier. An arrow flew past him from the ship, striking at another monster that stirred beside him. What a fool I've become, standing idle at such a time! He ushered himself forth, sprinting clear the cloudy beach onto the pier and saw for the first time the vessel, unhindered by the mist and fog.

A single man still stood upon the doc, untying the last of the ships anchors and tossing the line over the rails before vaulting in after them. Shouts rose all over the boat and feet pounded along the deck when Lennox was spotted emerging through the mist. Though he could not hear them, they were calling to him, waving for him to hurry, shouting for him to run. He almost laughed, then tightened his grip upon his sword as he reached the end of the pier and leapt across the widening gap. He had just enough time to see a young wizard rising from the deck, when his feet came down atop the youth. The boy cried out, Lennox toppled, and together they rolled out across the deck.

The youth appeared to get the brunt of the fall for Lennox was quickly to his feet, his hands resting upon the rails as they searched the shore for Sir Vantimier. "Don't push off! Another still comes!" he cried, but his voice was one amongst many, and his words went unheard.

Men were everywhere atop the boat, more so than Lennox first realized. Mostly wizards of the guild, but there were a few knights as well. Surprisingly a hand grasped tightly at his shoulder spinning him about sharply.

"Lennox!" exclaimed Astrid, with hope and joy in her eyes. "You are well!"

He allowed himself a small smile before grabbing at her wrist gently. "Now is not the time, my lady. Sir Vantimier still resides upon the shore, we must not push off!" Yet even as they spoke the boat drifted further from the pier, and the gap of black water between the vessel and the dock was widening quickly.

"I will tell Lady Maeve at once!" she said turning to leave, when suddenly the ship lurched forward.

"Loose boom!" cried a voice, just as the large wooden beam swung out from the shadows catching one of the wizards in the chest with the crunch of breaking bones, sweeping him over the side. More shouts and screams followed as men ran to the rails to attempt a rescue, but the heavy robes were thick and dark, and the wizard was gone before any could reach him.

Turning once more towards the shore Lennox clutched the rail, his hands gripping the wood fiercely as he scanned the mist. There was little time, he knew, perhaps none at all … but he would try none the less.

Reaching out his palm he whispered a spell, an old incantation, changing it slightly to serve his purpose. Soon a ball of light began to form, so small and pure and white it mirrored the moon, but as he continued to speak it shined brighter and brighter until many on the ship couldn't help but notice what great magic the golden knight was taking part in. The ball of light grew until all eyes were upon him and watched as he hurled the ball high into the air, so that it hung like the sun over the end of the pier.

All of the boat stood in silence, some watching the light and others the knight, yet Lennox looked only to the shore, searching for any signs of Sir Vantimier.

"There!" he shouted, but found all strength had left him. He fell to one knee, clutching at the rail as Sir Vantimier appeared upon the beach, illuminated by the bright light. He was hurt, favoring his right side, and all about him was the enemy, their dark forms smudges amidst the surrounding white. His blade lashed out, silver and blue, and the beasts fell one after another.

It was then that Lennox felt himself being hoisted up. He turned, and seeing that it was Shiva, pointed once more towards the shore. The warden saw the silver knight and drew his bow at once, firing arrow after arrow towards the shore. The boat drifted further out to sea, and Shiva's arrows flew further and further across the water, missing their mark more often than striking true. He was calling out, the warden, but what he was saying Lennox could not tell.

I will not succumb to weakness, Lennox told himself … once was quite enough. And so it was, half conscious and tired beyond measure, he watched as Sir Vantimier grew smaller and smaller, fading into the distance, until at last the brazen knight appeared walking towards him from behind. It was in that moment that the ship burst forth from the cove out into the midnight sky, and a heavy mist fell again upon the vessel, blocking all from sight and view as the last remnants of silver faded from the shore.

***

For some time, Lennox sat alone, his golden helm at his side, his back resting against the mast of the ship. Shiva had left him there before leaving to join the others, promising he would return shortly. Marrok was near as well, recoiling just below the decks, though Lennox did not know it.

They had cleared the cove and most of the surrounding reef, but the waves were fierce and tall, and the men aboard the ship were poor sailors, with only a few among them truly knowing how to handle the vessel. Lady Maeve was one of them, standing before the helm, calling out in a commanding voice. Astrid was there as well, running about the ship, tying off ropes along with Shiva. Many of the wizards just stood about near the back, trying not to get in the way.

Lennox raised his hands to run them over his face but stopped, gazing at the oathkeeper ring in disdain. A deep wave of remorse fell upon him, and he shook his head in doubt, rubbing at the weariness that clung to his eyes. Perhaps I made the wrong choice, he thought. When he removed his hands, he noticed a youth in full wizard garb sitting just off to the side watching him. The boy had a familiar look about him, though Lennox could not say why.

"Hmm … you look well enough, just a little exhausted. I would expect nothing less after casting such a superb piece of magic. I can help you, if you like."

Lennox nodded his head, and the youth reached out his palm, placing it upon the center of his forehead. It was warm, but not uncomfortably so, and it wasn't long before his body began to lighten. Little by little the weariness and heavy limbs that wore him down began to depart. "That's quite a spell," he commented.

The youth smiled and took his hand away. "Oh … well thank you, but I feel it is rather plain compared to what you just accomplished. I don't think many who saw really understood just how complex it was … perhaps my sister did. She was always quicker than me at understanding things, though I've always felt she holds herself back for some odd reason."

The boy was looking past Lennox, his eyes distant and cloudy when suddenly they snapped back towards the knight. "Still, she was rather preoccupied getting this ship to sea, so I think perhaps she missed it."

"Your sister … " Lennox repeated slowly, turning toward the helm. He could hear her calling out commands, her voice booming out over the tossing waves. He looked once more to the youth. "Lady Maeve?"

The youth nodded.

"Then you are Prince Oscar?"

Again, the youth nodded. "Correct … yet I have not the pleasure of knowing your name, good sir."

"Lennox."

"Oh! Then you are companions to that strange warden and northern girl!"

This time it was Lennox who nodded in reply.

"Quite a fascinating pair the two make, and her wolf as well. I'd never seen a northern wolf before; they're quite bigger than their southern cousins. You can imagine my surprise when I saw them accompanying my sister into the lower stadium to join the fray, just in time I would say. Their assistance was invaluable to us. I wasn't sure how much longer I could have maintained the barrier I had set."

"Oscar!" a voice suddenly cried, calling the young prince to attention. He rose quickly to his feet. "Yes sister!"

"Leave him be and come help with the ship!"

"Of course," he replied, then turned quickly towards Lennox. "I'm sorry our conversation is cut short. I will follow up as soon as things have settled. I have so many questions for you. I can only — "

Violently the night turned white as a bolt of light struck the highest tower of Mallhorn Peak. From the heavens it came; so great was the light and so loud was the thunder that the very castle shook and the waters of the sea tossed and turned in waves. From north and south, from east and west, a great gust howled, snapping the main mast like a twig, then shrieking and blowing across the surface of the waves as if to bring destruction across all the sea.

At last the wind died, but the earth still trembled, and in the distance set against the black night sky, the towers of Mallhorn Peak tumbled down, falling deep into the surrounding ocean as the walls crumbled like ash, and a cloud of darkness settled where once a great castle had stood.

Then there was nothing except the night ... and the single ship upon the tossing sea.

ABOUT THE AUTHOR

Jacob Marc Schafer is an American novelist, short-story writer, and actor. Most recognized for his role on the American television soap opera *The Bold and the Beautiful* on CBS. He has since moved on to writing science fiction and fantasy, as well as hosting his audiobook podcast, *The Jake Schafer Campaign*. He currently resides in Daphne, Alabama with his wife and children.

ABOUT THE PUBLISHER

Bold Venture Press is a heroic little publishing company, rolling out quality editions of new and classic pulp fiction. Our scope spans all genres — mystery, science fiction, horror, western, and romance

But who is Bold Venture Press, anyway?

Audrey Parente (editor), a Connecticut native, retired as an award-winning reporter after 20 years at *The Daytona Beach News-Journal* in Florida. The single mother of two musicians, she earned a black belt in tae kwon do after studying the martial art in Korea, traveled to 24 U.S. States, volunteered for the U.S. Citizens Democracy Corps serving in Russia, published poetry in a Japanese newspaper and wrote travel stories about Egypt.

Among her myriad adventures, Audrey white-water rafted on the Ocoee River in Tennessee, hot air ballooned and sky dived in Florida, flew a Good Year blimp over the Daytona International Speedway and conducted a Navy band.

She penned three biographies about pulp fiction-era authors — Hugh B. Cave, Theodore Roscoe, and Judson P. Philips. She edited *Timely Confidential: When the Golden Age of Comics Was Young* by Allen Bellman, with her co-editor Dr. Michael J. Vassaollo. She continues her writing career in South Florida, now as an author and editor for Bold Venture Press. Her novel *Pulp Noir* depicts two collectors of old paper magazines, and one grizzled hoarder in particular who stumbles into a cougar romance.

Rich Harvey founded Pulp Adventures Press in 1992. The rebranded Bold Venture Press imprint published *The Spider* and *Pulp Adventures* magazine, went on hiatus for a few years. Upon returning in 2014, *Pulp Adventures* was revived as a quarterly.

Rich's articles have appeared in numerous publications, including *Starlog* and *Comics Scene*. He brought The Spider to Joe Gentile's Moonstone Books imprint, and contributed two major stories — a revival of Ed Race, the Masked Marksman as a bonus feature in *The Spider: Shadow of Evil* by C.J. Henderson; and a three-way team-up between Ed Race, Doc Turner, and The Spider, the first-ever story teaming The Spider with his featured back-up characters in *The Spider Chronicles* hardcover edition. For Moonstone Books, he also penned two stories of The Green Hornet.

Among Bold Venture's proudest releases: *Zorro: The Complete Pulp Adventures* by Johnston McCulley in six volumes, under license from Zorro Productions; *Zorro and the Little Devil*, a new adventure novel by *New York Times* bestselling author Peter David; the hardboiled Jack Hagee, Private Eye series by C.J. Henderson; Wycliffe A. Hill's legendary *The Plot Genie* writing device; and *Primal Spillane*, an anthology collecting 40 rare stories by the creator of Mike Hammer.

www.boldventurepress.com

Made in the USA
Columbia, SC
30 September 2020